SPELLED

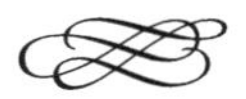

CAMILLE PETERS

SPELLED

By: Rosewood Publications

Rosewood Publications

Salt Lake City, Utah

United States of America

www.camillepeters.com

Cover Design by Karri Klawiter

To my wonderful family,
whose constant love and belief in me have helped me to live my dreams.

CHAPTER 1

The problem with baking up spells was there were so many things that could go wrong. I frowned at my rather lumpy cookies, burnt around the edges and hard as rocks when I bit into them. Ew. No way I was going to eat these. I sighed as I dropped the tray unceremoniously on the counter before squinting at the faded recipe titled "Eliminating Grief" in *Enchanted Sweets and Delights*.

My cookies looked nothing like the illustration. What had gone wrong? I'd included all of the correct ingredients. I nibbled my fingernail. Perhaps that extra spoonful of unicorn tears had tampered with the recipe, causing them to overbake and dilute the magic.

I sighed as I pulled out a clean mixing bowl, determined to keep trying until I got it right. I'd just started measuring the flour when the bell above the bakery door jingled. I gasped, slammed the book of magical recipes shut, and shoved it in a drawer. Footsteps approached the back kitchen before my brother, Ferris, appeared in the doorway. Of course the intruder was him, coming to annoy me even during my time of grief.

I rested my hand on my heart, beating wildly beneath my fingertips. "You scared me."

Without any sign of remorse, Ferris warily eyed the drawer I'd hidden the book in. Too late I realized a corner stuck out, preventing the drawer from closing all the way.

"You're baking from that book again, aren't you, Rose?"

I scowled. Years ago, Ferris had developed the annoying habit of shortening my adorable name after it'd occurred to him that being the eldest should have domineering perks to it.

"Rosie," I corrected for what must have been the millionth time in the course of our annoying life together as siblings.

"You know Mother and Father told us we're not to bake from that book."

"I'm not planning on giving away what I bake, so what's the harm?"

"It's still dangerous. Magic is too fiddly to tamper with. If you should get the recipe wrong..."

"I never get any wrong." Except for every attempt to bake a relief from my all-consuming grief...and then there'd also been that time Eileen and I had accidentally made enchanted pudding that resulted in three days of uncontrollable laughter, which a group of village children had consumed after sneaking into the kitchen to pilfer pastries. My lips twitched at the memory, even as my heart wrenched to be thinking of my missing best friend.

Ferris leaned against the counter and glanced at my rather pathetic-looking cookies. "What are these supposed to be? They wouldn't happen to be an example of your getting the recipe wrong, would they?"

I bit the inside of my lip to hold back a sigh. "If you must know, they're a spell to eliminate grief. Or rather, that's what I'm *trying* to make..." I twirled a strand of my golden hair around my finger as I frowned at this morning's disaster. I slid the book from its hiding place and flipped it open to my bookmarked recipe. "I must be doing something wrong, because no matter what treat I bake them into—whether cookies, tarts, or shortbread—they always turn out like *this*."

Ferris's disapproving look—which had been directed at the book in my arms—softened slightly. "You're still trying to bake that?"

The near constant anguish that had been gnawing at my heart all week attacked anew, squeezing my insides with tight, burning pain. I blinked back my tears. "One doesn't just get over the disappearance and likely death of her best friend."

"No one knows what's happened to her," Ferris said, his tone uncharacteristically kind. "She's only been missing for a week."

"A week where all manner of dreadful things could have transpired."

I clutched the edge of the counter as my mind raced with the horrific stories that had been occupying my thoughts ever since the night my best friend had failed to return from the enchanted Forest surrounding our village. No number of search parties had uncovered any trace of her.

"She could have become lost, and after days of wandering without food, suffered a tragic demise. Or she could have been devoured by wild beasts. Or"—I shuddered in horror —"maybe she was *murdered*. *Oh*." I buried my face in my apron.

"Where do you come up with this nonsense?" Ferris asked, his expression twisted in disgust from my recitation.

"Books, of course."

He snorted. "Of course. Just because it's in a book doesn't make it plausible."

My eyes widened at such blasphemy. "Of course it does. How is a storybook any different than a book of history?"

"One day I hope you stop living inside your head and finally join the real world." Ferris looked as if he had a multitude of other annoying retorts to that statement, but to my surprise, rather than arguing with me, he instead rested a light hand on my arm. "I know you're upset about Eileen, but this"—he jerked his head towards my recipe book—"won't bring her back."

"It'll at least help dissipate the pain."

I returned to my baking, dumping my pre-measured flour into the mixing bowl before pulling out the jar of fairy dust Mother and Father kept in their "off-limits" cupboard. I carefully measured out a teaspoon. As I did so, a tear escaped and slid down my cheek into the bowl. Hopefully, it wouldn't hurt the recipe's outcome.

"Rosie?" Ferris stepped forward to wipe away my tears with a surprisingly gentle touch. "Are you going to be alright?"

My lip quivered and I frantically wiped my eyes with the back of my hand. "Whatever fate has befallen her wasn't supposed to happen. Heroines don't die in their own fairy tales."

"Life isn't like your stories, Rosie," Ferris murmured as he wiped away another tear with his thumb. "It's best you finally realize that."

I clenched my jaw. He was wrong. Believing anything else was out of the question. No matter how tragic certain chapters seemed, ceasing to believe in happy endings was something I would never do, despite how dark this chapter currently was.

"Rosie dear, you're burning the custard."

Mother's voice tore me from my daydreaming—or in this

case, once again reliving the dark memory from last week that had changed everything. As midnight approached, Eileen's mother had rushed into the bakery during a terrible storm—dripping wet and sobbing, her expression wild and her eyes frantic—and informed us that Eileen had gone missing, having never returned from the Forest.

My constant worry knotted my gut. What had happened to her there?

"Rosie, the custard." Mother gently pushed me away from the hearth and took over stirring the custard.

I blinked dazedly. "Oh, sorry, Mother."

Not ceasing her stirring, she laid a gentle hand over mine. "Perhaps you should take a break today. Your father, Ferris, and I can manage."

Guilt swirled through me alongside relief. Unless I was trying to bake my ever-elusive grief-eliminating spell, the thought of spending an already hot afternoon over a sweltering fire was not at all appealing.

I nodded. Mother offered a tight smile as she caressed my cheek with flour-coated fingers. "Don't give up hope, dear; she's only been gone just over a week." Despite her assurances, she gnawed her lip worriedly. A week was a long time to be lost in an enchanted forest that possessed a mind of its own. "Perhaps you should read. That always cheers you up."

I'd been inhaling scores of books the last several days, mostly fairy tales, to somehow try to dispel my aching grief. Immersing myself in magic and happily-ever-afters helped me hope they still existed.

But one could only escape the real world for so long, for no matter how many times I lost myself within the pages of a book, I was eventually forced to leave. Once I did, I found myself swirling in the dark despair that came from the absence of my best friend and the unsolved mystery of what had become of her.

I suddenly couldn't remain confined in the bakery any longer, the place I'd tried time and time again to bake a way to escape my heartache. I'd just started to untie my apron when the bell above the bakery door rang, signaling the entrance of a customer.

I wandered into the front of the bakery and froze at the sight of an elderly woman wearing a patched dress and stooping over a cane. It took me a moment to recognize her as the village storyteller.

For the first time since Eileen's disappearance, a thrill rippled up my spine. A visit from the storyteller was a rare treat indeed. What a perfect way to remind me that perhaps the world wasn't as bleak as it seemed, even though the anguish riddling my heart suggested otherwise.

"Can I help you?" I asked as she hobbled over to a display of freshly baked cookies.

The storyteller paused and stared unblinkingly up at me, her clear grey eyes looking as if her mind were elsewhere. "One honey-lemon muffin," she finally said in a raspy voice.

"Certainly." I carefully wrapped one up for her, my hands shaking in excitement as I cast several sideways glances towards the storyteller, still staring off into space. What could she be seeing? The rumors wandering our village whispered that her stories were more than fantastic tales—they were predictions of the future. Was she thinking up such a story now? How thrilling would it be if I, Rosalina, were witness to one of her fantastic tales, concocted right in this very bakery?

I finished wrapping her muffin and slowly approached, not wanting to startle her from whatever revelation she was surely experiencing. It took a full minute before she stirred, blinking rapidly as she turned back to me.

"Your muffin." I held it out to her, hoping she'd share something with me before she took it. But no. She accepted her treat with a soft smile before pressing her payment into my palm.

"Thank you, dear." She suddenly squeezed my hands and stared at me, as if searching for something. I waited in anticipation, holding my breath, hoping...was she about to prophesy? Her wrinkly hand patted mine. "Don't be upset, my dear; your friend is quite safe."

The tears I'd fought against all week came gushing out. "Is she? Are you sure?"

The storyteller nodded and gave my hand another affectionate pat. "You'll see soon enough that I'm right."

She started to turn but paused, glancing over her shoulder to give me another penetrating stare, as if looking into my future once more. I waited with bated breath.

She smiled, crinkling her ancient face further. "You have quite the adventure ahead of you. Keep an eye out for your own prince." And with that, she slowly tottered out of the bakery.

I stared out the window and watched as she took one wobbly step after another until she was swallowed up by the crowd. My heart pounded as her words swirled through my mind. *Keep an eye out for your own prince.* What a fantastic statement! But what did it mean? How could I find a prince in my small village of Arador?

I was still trying to decipher it all when the door opened again and Eileen's mother, Doreen, entered the bakery, her eyes bloodshot as usual.

I stiffened. Ever since Eileen's disappearance, I'd avoided Doreen as much as possible. Witnessing the grief of a woman who'd not only lost her husband years ago but now her only child made my own torment more sharp and agonizing.

I managed to move to poke my head into the kitchen. "Mother, it's Doreen."

She immediately removed the custard from the hearth and strode over to pull Doreen into a hug. "Any news?"

"I'm not sure."

Mother yanked herself away to gape at her. "Then you've heard something?"

Doreen held up a gilded envelope, her name and mine addressed in elegant calligraphy. "I just received this by courier. It bears the royal seal."

I gasped and scampered over to see for myself. The Sortileyan emblem stared back at me in purple ink. "What does it say?"

Doreen fiddled with the edges. "I haven't opened it. I can't imagine why I'd be receiving anything from the royal family. It can't be good news."

How could she possibly delay? Already my fingers itched to tear it open. It wasn't every day that common folk received royal correspondence.

Mother seemed to be thinking the same thing. She frowned at it. "The only way to find out is to open it."

Doreen handed it to me, unable to open it herself. I carefully slid my nail beneath the seal and unfolded the creamy stationery, gilded in gold. "His Royal Highness, the Crown Prince Deidric, invites Doreen and Rosie of Arador to the palace..."

I stopped reading, my mind frozen in shock. I, Rosalina, had just received an invitation to the Sortileyan Palace? Even in my most fantastic fantasies, nothing like this had ever happened to me. The familiar excited flutters that filled me whenever I wove tales returned, and my imagination—which had lain nearly dormant this past week—began to stir awake from its grief-induced slumber as all the possible reasons behind the summons tickled my mind.

Mother took the invitation and read over it. "A royal

carriage will arrive tomorrow to escort you to the castle. Hmm, it doesn't specify a reason."

"Perhaps they have information concerning what happened to my Eileen," Doreen said.

Mother opened her mouth—likely to mention that the royal family wouldn't concern themselves with such trivial matters as consoling the mothers of missing peasants—before she closed it with a tight smile.

"Perhaps they do. Regardless, one can't ignore a royal invitation from His Highness. I just wish I understood why they're also sending for Rosie." She frowned at me.

I didn't care what they wanted me for. This was the most spectacular thing that had ever happened to me. I, Rosalina, had just been invited to the royal palace! I wrapped my arms around myself with my first true smile since Eileen's disappearance. Ah, bliss!

At this unexpected turn of events, a new hopeful possibility took center stage in my mind. "Perhaps Eileen's wanderings in the Forest led her to the palace and she's been residing there, safe and sound." Yes, that had to have been what happened. Best friends didn't die tragically in *The Story of Rosalina*, not when I was the one writing it.

I stroked my fingers reverently over the royal invitation that had triggered this spectacular plot twist in my grief-filled week. My forehead furrowed as I noticed a bulge. I peered inside to discover another note tucked away, written in a familiar hand. My stomach jolted in excitement.

"A note from Eileen!" I pulled it out, but before I had a chance to read it, Doreen pounced on it and wrenched it from my hand. She unfolded it and read rapidly.

"She's alive!" She pressed her hand to her heart, looking near a faint in her relief. "She's at the palace now. She says she has the most fantastic news to share with us, but nothing can be better than knowing she's alive and safe." Tears poured down her cheeks.

My own joy bubbled over. My dearest friend was alive. Naturally. Tragedies didn't belong in my story. How could I have ever considered any other outcome than a happy one?

"Oh Doreen, I knew you'd find her." Mother pulled her into a hug. "I'm so happy for you. When will you leave?"

"The moment the carriage arrives. I won't delay being reunited with my Eileen. I hate to ask you to spare Rosie from the bakery on such short notice, but the invitation specifically invites her to come."

"Of course Rosie can go. I feel better knowing she'll be traveling with you."

With an excited squeal, I tripped over my skirts in my frantic dash upstairs so I could immediately pack my trunk. I stopped short at the top of the stairs. The village storyteller had been correct—my best friend was safe. If she'd been right about that, she could also be right about my finding a prince. And what better place to find a prince than at a palace? Tomorrow's grand adventure couldn't come soon enough.

CHAPTER 2

Why did thrilling adventures take so long to get started? We'd been bumping along in this carriage for what seemed like hours, during which very little had happened except for slight variations in the otherwise near-constant woodland scenery.

I pressed my face against the glass and watched as the endless trees of our woodland kingdom passed by. "When will we ever arrive?"

I turned not to Doreen—who'd spent the entire duration of the drive staring unseeing out the window—but to my cousin, Gavin, who as a nobleman was my most prestigious distant relation, making him the natural choice to escort us to the palace.

"Soon," he said, his voice strained, before adding in an undertone, "but not soon enough for my liking."

I rolled my eyes. Gavin had complained about my excited jabber ever since the endless carriage ride had begun. I couldn't fathom his reasoning; filling the dull silence was better than enduring it. And naturally, I, Rosalina, would do my part to make the beginning of this soon-to-be adventure as thrilling as possible for all involved.

"Are you still stubbornly determined not to share even a tiny bit of Eileen's juicy story?" I asked him for perhaps the dozenth time. The sound of her name caught her mother's attention. Gavin sighed and leaned his head back against the seat.

"I'm not even going to humor you by repeating the same answer I've given every other time you've asked." For unfortunately, he'd proven relentlessly stubborn when it came to extracting information.

"Why ever not?" I asked. "Ignoring a lady is rather rude, Gavin."

He muttered something indiscernible under his breath before closing his eyes as if he meant to nap. Considering Doreen wasn't up for conversation, I refused to allow him that for very long; then I'd be left without a conversation partner entirely.

To keep myself occupied, I chronicled all the things I wouldn't miss about my old dull life in Arador and anticipated all the magical moments I was sure to experience during my upcoming adventure. Thus entertained, I managed to be silent for three agonizing minutes before I thought of something more to say.

I turned back to Gavin. "Have I had a chance to tell you the story about—"

His groan cut me off. "Please Rose, not another story."

"Rosie," I snapped. He, like Ferris, had a strange aversion to using the cutest version of my name.

Gavin rubbed his temples to ward off a headache, as if this entire carriage ride had been wearing. "How about another tactic to enduring this journey: silence."

"How boring," I said. "If you don't like my stories, then the least you can do is share your own rather than complain."

"Have you heard the tale about the aggravating distant cousin who talked too much? I hear that one doesn't end well."

I pursed my lips. *The Tale of the Sister Who Never Stopped Jabbering* was my own brother's favorite story. "I have it: share a juicy tale about the Dark Prince."

Certainly, he must have plenty of those. The infamous crown prince of Sortileya always had such thrilling rumors circulating about him. Considering Gavin spent a lot of time at the palace dealing with boring trade affairs, he'd surely have something thrilling to share.

Unfortunately, Gavin was proving to be the most disappointing of companions on this trip. He straightened in his seat with a sigh. "Nothing interesting, I'm afraid—unless you want to hear about his involvement in trade negotiations with the surrounding kingdoms."

I wrinkled my nose. Ew. "Come on, Gavin, can't you humor me with just one juicy tidbit about the Dark Prince? If you share one with me, I'll..." I frantically tried to come up with something that would be a worthy trade.

Gavin gave me a mischievous smirk. "You'll be quiet for the remainder of this blasted trip?"

That would most definitely *not* be happening. "How about this," I said. "I'll share the rumors I've heard and you can tell me whether or not they're true."

"Untrue," Gavin stated immediately.

I pouted. "You haven't even heard any yet."

"Don't need to," he said. "Anything coming from your imagination is far too dramatic to be real."

I sniffed. "How rude." But his bad manners wouldn't dissuade me, not when telling stories was such an excellent way to pass the time. "I shall ask you anyway." I tapped my lips thoughtfully before deciding on the most perfect one to begin with. "Did he really poison his intended, Princess Rheanna of Draceria?"

"No," Gavin said flatly. While his answer was most disappointing, at least he was humoring me...for once.

"Can he transform into a dragon?"

Gavin looked at me as if he found me utterly daft. "No."

I frowned. How unfortunate. I was certain I'd heard that he could.... "Oh wait, that's his sister, the Dragon Princess."

"Princess Seren can't transform into a dragon either." Gavin's tone was hardening, as if he found me both ridiculous and annoying. Strange.

"Does he really have a dungeon full of torture devices?"

Gavin gave me another baffled look. "Of course not."

"How do you know?" I challenged. "Have you ever gone inside the dungeon?"

"Well, no..."

"So then you wouldn't know." My overactive imagination excitedly played out a possible scenario in my mind: Eileen hadn't sent for us at all; she'd tragically perished in the woods...no, even worse, she'd been murdered by the Dark Prince, and now he wanted me next. My cousin had been hired to kidnap me to take me to my demise, where I'd be held hostage and subjected to all sorts of torture in the Dark Prince's dungeon. Coldness seeped over me. Oh, how horrid!

I refused for my story to end in tragedy. My heart hammered as I frantically searched for an escape. The door. I scooted towards it and reached for the handle, moments from attempting to wrench it open...but paused, blinking rapidly. Now was not the time to allow my imagination to run amok. I created stories for many reasons, both for attention and for much-needed entertainment in my dull life. Neither reason was valid now.

I took a deep, calming breath, and attempted to tame my

imagination. I peeked tentatively at Gavin, who was eying my progress towards the door, ready to yank me away should I actually attempt to escape the carriage.

"You're not kidnapping me as part of some dastardly plot, are you?" I asked, not really believing it but wanting to be sure.

He rolled his eyes. "Kidnapping you? Of course I'm not."

I sat back against the velvet seat with a relieved sigh. "Right. I'm not being taken to the Dark Prince's dungeon." Saying the words out loud further tethered my mischievous imagination, desperate to escape and continue the dark version of this story.

Gavin dug his fingers into his hair, as if he meant to yank it out. "Thank goodness we're arriving soon; I can't take much more of your dramatics."

Doreen pulled out of the stupor that had consumed her our entire journey. "I can hardly wait to see Eileen."

Nor could I. My anticipation for our reunion grew with every turn of the carriage wheels. I wriggled restlessly in my seat. When would we arrive so I could finally see her?

I perked up and glanced out the window just as the trees thinned and the majestic Sortileyan palace loomed into view, a vision of marble and gold accents, all glistening in the sunlight. Ornate gardens, comprised of a rainbow of flowers and manicured shrubs growing in artistic arrangements and patterns, surrounded the royal residence. It was the most majestic, beautiful structure I'd ever seen. To think that I, Rosalina, was moments away from entering a real palace. How thrilling it'd be to wander its opulent corridors in real life rather than through the pages of a book. Ah, bliss!

There wasn't a moment to lose. The moment the carriage slowed, I scrambled out before Gavin could even attempt to assist me. I hurried up the steps to the large, intricately carved wooden front doors, where I was certain the most fantastic adventure awaited me.

The moment the doors swung open, Eileen—wearing an elegant gown of navy silk with pearls woven across the bodice—pounced on her mother, who promptly burst into tears and hugged her tightly. Eventually, Eileen managed to untangle herself from Doreen to embrace me. I squeezed her close, pulling away only enough to beam at her.

"You're alive!"

She nodded, smiling brightly midst her tears. "I'm so sorry to have caused you and Mother to worry." She wrapped an arm around Doreen, who gave Eileen a snuggle in return as she buried her tear-streaked face against her hair.

"But what happened to you? We've all been thoroughly puzzled and worried sick by the mystery of your disappearance."

"I got lost in the storm and the Forest led me here, where I got caught up in a competition vying for the crown prince's hand."

A mischievous smile caressed her lips as she escorted us into the entrance hall, where a man leaned against the wall, watching the reunion with a wide grin. Ooh, he must be her true love whom she'd told me about before her disappearance; I recognized him by the portrait she'd drawn of him. What was he doing at the palace? Furthermore, what was *Eileen* still doing at the palace? I was practically bursting with curiosity.

Eileen extended her hand towards him and beamed as he laced his with hers. "Mother, Rosie, this is my fiancé, Aiden."

Fiancé! I beamed at Aiden, who smiled warmly back, instantly earning my approval. "This is the man you met in the Forest, isn't it? I *knew* he was your true love. And now you're to be married?" I pressed my hands to my heart at the sheer wonder of it. "How splendid. It's the perfect fairy-tale ending."

My heart warmed for my best friend, especially considering she'd been stubbornly resistant to love for years. How wonderful that she was finally to have her own happily ever after, as all heroines were meant to.

"I know, isn't it wonderful? I never dreamed something like this would ever happen to me, and yet here we are." Eileen laughed, her eyes bright, and allowed herself to receive another tender embrace from her mother.

"I'm so happy for you, dear." Doreen turned and smiled at Aiden. "I'm so pleased my daughter has found a man who will cherish her."

Aiden bowed, first to Doreen, then to me. "It's a pleasure to finally meet my fiancée's dear mother and her story-loving best friend. I've heard so much about both of you and am looking forward to furthering our acquaintance."

Ooh, such a proper gentleman. I gave Eileen an approving smile, which she returned, seeming on the brink of floating away in her happiness. "You must be tired from your long journey. Come, let's have tea."

Gavin excused himself, and a bowing footman opened a door to a lovely parlor that was a vision of cream carpet and rose-pastel walls. Two guards stood rigidly against the back wall, one dark-haired and handsome, one with sandy-brown hair and rather rough features. I looked at them briefly before taking in my surroundings. Eileen's fiancé was obviously a man with title and prestige to have free rein of the palace. But where was the royal family? If only I could meet them.

Aiden and Eileen sat together on the sofa with Doreen sitting on Eileen's other side, asking her daughter many eager questions. I gracefully settled into an armchair across from them and looked around in a wide-eyed daze. I,

Rosalina, was inside the *palace*, and it was far more elegant than I could have ever imagined. I ran my fingers along my seat's silky fabric. So this was what palace cushions felt like.

My wondrous inspection of every fine detail of the opulent room was interrupted by the arrival of a maid, who set a tray laden with dainty floral cups and delectable-looking tarts on the tea table before Aiden and Eileen. She curtsied. "Tea, Your Highnesses."

Aiden nodded his thanks as my heart flared in excitement. Wait...*Your Highnesses*? But that was impossible. Eileen's fiancé couldn't possibly be—"Are you the Dark Prince?" I blurted.

Eileen and her mother's whispered conversation immediately ceased as Doreen stared at Aiden—*Prince Deidric,* I hastily corrected my far-too-casual thoughts—in astonishment.

He chuckled and nodded. "Forgive me for failing to properly introduce myself. Yes, I'm Deidric, the Crown Prince of Sortileya, but I prefer to go by Aiden with my close friends and family."

Doreen immediately stood to curtsy, but I sat frozen in astonishment. Even for me, lover of stories, this revelation seemed far too fantastic. Slowly, life stirred in my limbs, allowing me to leap to my feet and spin towards Eileen.

"You're engaged to a *prince*? A real prince?"

Eileen smiled shyly. "I suppose so."

I continued to stare, frantically trying to piece together this incredible revelation. "A *prince*!" I turned my astonishment towards the man in question, who looked both entirely ordinary and utterly princely. "A *real* prince? And you never thought to tell me?"

Eileen shrugged, as if this development wasn't the most incredible thing to ever happen to a girl. "Well, I didn't know he was a prince until just a few days ago."

"Oh, Eileen, this is *wonderful*." I knelt down so I could pull her into a tight, *I'm-so-blissfully-happy-for-you* hug. While I'd always adored stories of common girls winning the hearts of handsome princes, to think such an incredible thing had happened to *my* best friend...imagine!

And if Eileen's fairy tale included such an outcome, did that mean mine could as well? After all, the storyteller had mentioned a prince....

While Eileen hugged me back, it wasn't with the proper enthusiasm she should be displaying at such a fantastic development. "Goodness, Rosie, you sure are excited."

"Why shouldn't I be?" I yanked myself away so I could gape at her. "You do know what this means, don't you? You're going to be a *princess*, and then one day *queen*!"

"Yes..." For a moment, the light dimmed in Eileen's eyes before she smiled again. "I'll get to be with Aiden, which is all I care about." She squeezed his hand, and although he squeezed hers back, concern lined his expression, Eileen's brief melancholy clearly not lost on him.

He leaned towards her ear. "Darling, are you sure you really want—"

"I'm sure," Eileen stated, and as if to reinforce her answer, she kissed his cheek.

He relaxed and turned to the maid, whom he instructed to serve our tea with a rather regal wave of his hand. I watched in fascination as his orders were immediately obeyed and I was handed a cup of royal tea. The steam rose from the cup to tickle my nose in its mouthwatering rose blossom and raspberry scent. It was certain to taste far better than any tea I'd ever had; everything was better at a palace, after all.

I took a dainty sip and was not disappointed. Delicious, just as royal tea should be. I sighed with utter contentment. Here I sat in a palace having tea with Eileen, who was thankfully safe despite all my unfounded fears of the past week. Joy filled me to see her interact with her mother and fiancé. In all the years we'd known one another, I'd never seen such light in her eyes. My smile matched hers as I imagined her future happiness.

I waited for a pause in her conversation with Doreen. "When is your wedding?"

Eileen lit up. "In two weeks. The invitations are being sent out tomorrow. I'd be honored if you'd be my bridesmaid."

I clasped my hands at the delightful thought. To think that I, Rosalina, would be part of the royal wedding of my best friend, a future princess! It was positively magical. My imagination immediately stirred as possibilities of what the grand event would be like danced across my mind. I ached to ask for more details and even to begin helping Eileen plan, but she'd turned back to her mother. But no matter. I was content to wait.

We passed a lovely tea enjoying delectable cinnamon-vanilla biscuits—which were almost as delicious as the ones we made at the bakery—and listening to Eileen recount her story about how she and Prince Aiden had met, along with the Princess Competition he'd instructed the Forest to lead her to so that she could win his hand. It was utterly romantic —all the stories I'd read about over the years come to life. If my best friend could experience such an incredible happily ever after, surely I could too.

When Eileen finished her story, I seized the opportunity to sidle closer. There was no room for me on the settee, so I opted for kneeling in front of her. Eileen greeted me with a smile and clasped my hands in hers.

"It's so good to see you again, Rosie."

"And you. I've missed you this past week and was so

worried about you. Best friends should never be apart that long."

She smiled. "You're right. We've spent nearly every day together since we were children."

All the memories from our years of friendship flittered through my mind, accompanied by a strange ache. Now that Eileen was going to be a princess, she'd move into the palace, and I'd be left behind in Arador. But at least she'd be happy. That fact would hopefully ease the loneliness I'd surely experience without her.

Prince Aiden wrapped his arm around Eileen, tugging her away from our conversation. "Shall we give your mother and Rosalina a tour, darling?"

I beamed at her nod. I, Rosalina, was about to wander the palace corridors. It was too thrilling an opportunity to delay any longer.

Prince Aiden and Eileen led the way from the parlor while Doreen and I followed, the two guards who'd stoically watched us throughout tea bringing up the rear. Eileen paused to turn towards them.

"Forgive me for failing to introduce you. These are our guards, Duncan and Alastar. Alastar kindly watched over me throughout the Princess Competition."

I curtsied to both guards, who each gave me a slight bow in return. The proper formalities concluded, I turned away, eager to see more of the palace. I stepped into the marble corridor and eagerly looked around for where to explore first. Elegant decorations ranging from paintings, tapestries, and statues filled the hallway, along with countless doors, each inviting me to peek inside to see what lay behind them. Beyond this hallway lay another also full of large doors, and then another, and another...endless possibilities, right at my fingertips. I shivered in excitement. There would be no returning to my boring life in Arador for me. Perhaps Eileen would allow me to live in the palace with her.

"Where do you want to see first?" Prince Aiden asked.

Every single book I'd ever read that contained a castle ran rampant through my mind. "The ballroom. No, the library. No, the throne room…or perhaps the secret passageways. Anywhere. *Everywhere.*" And without waiting for His Highness to select a destination, I scampered ungracefully down the hall.

Eileen giggled behind me. "There she goes." I was vaguely aware of her asking someone to keep an eye on me so she could spend time with her mother, but I was too distracted to pay attention.

I turned first one corner, then another, and quickly found myself in the elegant entrance hall lit by a glistening diamond chandelier. I gaped up at it. Oh, it was positively lovely.

My attention was quickly captured by a towering door, guarded by two rather serious-looking men in uniform. Ooh, could that be the throne room? I absolutely had to see. I hurried over. I'd no sooner reached out to graze the gold handle than their spears crossed to block me.

I gasped and leapt backwards…right into a rather firm chest. I *oof*ed. "What are you up to, Miss Rosalina?"

My breath caught. Whoever this tall, broad man I'd run into was, he knew my name. I swiveled around and came face-to-face with the serious brown-haired guard Eileen had just introduced me to. In my distraction I couldn't remember which this one was, Duncan or Alastar. It didn't matter though, not when he was being meddling.

I gaped up at him, unsure what a heroine was supposed to say to a guard who'd thwarted her attempts for adventure. Before I had a chance to find the words, he took me by the arm and led me away from the doors blocked by those rather sharp-looking spears.

My words, which had been mysteriously absent up until now, tumbled out as I tugged against his hold. "What are you doing? Unhand me this instant; I need to see what's behind that door."

"No you don't," the guard said. "His Majesty is currently entertaining many regal guests and would be quite upset if you barged in uninvited."

"The king is behind that door?" I turned and craned my neck to see. "Can't I meet him?" After all, I'd already met the prince, making an introduction with the king the next natural step.

"Are you a foreign advisor who's been invited to engage in serious political discussion?" he asked.

"I'm the future queen's best friend." Oh, I loved the sound of that.

"Close in importance, but not quite. Unfortunately, even an esteemed lady such as yourself doesn't have permission to run everywhere she desires."

"But I'm in a *palace*," I said. "It's not every day something so incredible happens to a common girl such as myself, but it's something I've dreamt of my entire life. Normally heroines in fairy tales have to do an honorable deed to an enchanted sorceress disguised as an old beggar woman before going on such a magical adventure..." I trailed off, getting all fluttery at the thought of my great fortune at finally having something exciting occur in my rather-average life.

The guard's gaze didn't leave my face during my recitation, nor did his serious expression falter...except for the brief moment when the corner of his lips *twitched*. But despite his subtle change in expression, he didn't detour from his objective of escorting me away from the room I desperately wanted to explore.

I tugged futilely on his iron grip. "Release me at once, you dastardly fiend."

He cocked a single eyebrow. "*Dastardly fiend*?"

I momentarily paused in my attempted flight. "Isn't that the most fitting description for a villain? I read it years ago and have been anxiously awaiting the day I could use it myself. *Dastardly fiend* perfectly conveys your role in my current predicament, don't you think?"

The guard gaped at me as if he'd never seen anything quite like me before. I used his temporary distraction to once more attempt to escape, but his hold was too firm for me to yank free.

"Please enlighten me," he said. "What have I done to deserve the title *dastardly fiend*?"

"You're thwarting my attempts to explore."

"And in that dramatic mind of yours, that's a capital offense?"

"It's quite close." I made another attempt to escape, one that was sadly futile. I groaned in what I hoped was the properly dramatic way for a captured heroine. "Despite my best attempts, I still find myself trapped in the villain's clutches."

The guard actually *snorted* of all things, which was strange, considering villains chortled in all the books I'd ever read. This guard was likely performing his villainous role wrong for the sole purpose of aggravating me.

"Don't *snort*," I snapped. "Villains *chortle*. If you're going to haul me off to the dungeons for the mere offense of exploring, the least you can do is play your role correctly."

"My apologies," the guard said with all grave sincerity. "I'm still in the middle of my villain lessons and haven't yet learned the fine art of the *chortle*. I shall study it at my break so I don't disappoint you in any future encounters we may have."

"Villain lessons?" I grinned. "How delightful."

"Indeed it is. One must do all they can to become *dastardly.*"

"Considering you've yet to complete your training, you're doing an aggravatingly good job."

"Natural talent, would you wager?" As he spoke, he tugged me firmly but with surprising gentleness in the direction of the parlor.

I stomped my foot. "I expect to be treated like a lady, so unhand me at once."

His lips twitched. "Unfortunately, I'm afraid I must disappoint you. You strike me as a *lady* who always has mischief up her sleeve, which means I can't have you poking around in places you shouldn't."

"You're ruining my story," I grumbled. And things had been going so well in this chapter until his cruel interference.

"Are we in a story?" While the guard's serious expression didn't even crack, amusement glistened in his eyes. Great, having fun at my expense. He played his villain part well. "If we are, it's not my intention to ruin your story; I'm merely taking this current scene in an unexpected direction."

I momentarily paused in my attempt to tug myself free. Wait, was he playing along? Or was he teasing me? "What direction are you anticipating for this scene?" I asked stiffly.

"A reunion," he said as we turned a corner to enter the corridor where Eileen and Doreen stood listening as Prince Aiden discussed the history of a painting that had captured Eileen's artistic eye.

Eileen brightened. "There you are, Rosie. I was afraid in your excitement you'd gotten lost, so we decided to wait for you and Alastar to return from your exploring so you wouldn't miss Aiden's tour."

It was impossible to get lost with *that guard* on my trail. I huffed when my new antagonist handed me over with a bow, as if he'd fetched me like a servant would bring Their Highnesses a cup of tea. I scowled at him and he merely raised his eyebrow, as if in question. The fiend.

I immediately dismissed all thoughts of the stoic guard the moment Eileen proposed showing me the palace gardens. I wouldn't allow the annoying Guard Alastar to ruin not only my first time in a palace, but my time with my dear friend. Whatever came next, it was sure to be grand.

CHAPTER 3

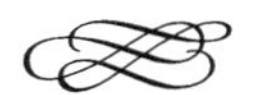

I'd never lain on a bed so soft and comfortable before—it was certainly made of actual clouds—yet sleep still stubbornly alluded me. I'd been tossing and turning for at least an hour. Every time sleep almost lured me into the magical land of dreams, the reality of my amazing situation would settle over me: *I'm spending the night in the majestic Sortileyan Palace, for my dearest friend is the future Queen of Sortileya, making me, Rosalina, practically royalty.* My toes curled in excitement. Ah, bliss!

As the first hour of sleeplessness drifted into two, I finally realized my insomniac foe had vanquished me. Who could sleep in a *palace*? Palaces were not meant to be *slept* in; they were meant to be *explored.*

I immediately scampered from bed to light a candle. The dancing flame glistened against an object decorating the mantle. I squinted through the shadows and an excited thrill rippled over me—it was a golden sphere. I reverently picked it up and turned it in my hands. I'd once read the most fantastic story about a princess who dropped a golden ball into a pond, where she discovered it possessed the power to lead her to her true love. Perhaps one day it could do the same for me.

I started to carefully place it back before changing my mind and tucking it into the pocket of my dressing gown; maybe it'd lead me somewhere special in tonight's explorations. I inched the door open to the empty marble corridor, lined with dozens of doors on either side—doors which I, Rosalina, Palace Explorer, was about to discover what lay beyond. I shuddered in anticipation.

I tiptoed past the guards standing rigidly outside the door to Eileen's guest room. I ignored their baffled expressions to see a royal guest out of bed long after midnight and pattered to the next corridor, where an entire palace lay at my disposal.

Unfortunately, this first hallway's doors were all locked, as were those in the second. I huffed in frustration as I gave a futile yank on yet another firmly bolted door before wandering down a staircase to a lower floor to try additional rooms, all of which were annoyingly also locked. I sighed. Exploring a palace by night was a lot more exciting in books. I tried to squelch this disappointment as I pattered down another staircase.

I'd no sooner jumped from the third step to the landing than I careened into a tall, firm body. I gasped and stumbled backwards, but before I could fall, the mysterious individual seized me by the waist to steady me.

"Miss Rosalina?"

My heart lurched as I raised my candle to illuminate the face of Eileen's head guard, Alastar, the very one who'd thwarted my earlier explorations. In a palace that contained hundreds of guards, why *him*?

"What are you doing here?" I snapped. "And why are you planted at the bottom of this staircase?"

He cocked a single eyebrow, his expression as stoic as

ever. "Forgive me, but I've been ordered by His Highness to thwart any attempts made by his esteemed guest to have a pleasant evening. On the off chance this royal guest came down this particular staircase after midnight, I was to remain here to knock her off her feet and under no circumstances stray from my post."

I glowered. When he put it that way, he made my accusation sound downright ridiculous, but there was no way I'd leave this interaction without the upper hand. "Are you attributing our unexpected encounter to mere chance?"

"Not mere chance," he continued, as serious as ever. "In my villainous studies, my marks in 'annoying royal guests with perfectly timed inconveniences' were rather high, a relief considering I haven't yet mastered the chortle, otherwise I'd be chortling right now on a scheme well done."

"You make up for your failed chortle by aggravating innocent heroines."

"Excellent. My professor will be pleased."

A strange thrill from our word spar rippled over me. Imagine: I, Rosalina, was engaged in a battle of wits with a royal guard in a palace in the middle of the night.

"If you weren't planted here for my annoyance, what are you really doing here?"

He studied me as if debating whether or not to divulge that information before he cocked his head. "Why don't you guess? Our brief acquaintance has already taught me that you're going to come up with something far more interesting than the truth."

Already my mind was brewing up some excellent possibilities. I tapped my lips with my forefinger. "You're a spy engaging in a secret mission against the crown; you've just left—or are going to—a romantic rendezvous; or perhaps you were sleepwalking before my careening into you woke you up, in which case your ill timing at being at the bottom of this staircase when I descended is even more incredible."

He finally reacted—the corner of his right lip twitched. "Wrong on all accounts."

"Even the romantic rendezvous?" That was the scenario I'd most hoped was the truth. "Aren't guards known for having flings with the maids?"

"Sorry to disappoint you. Unless you're the woman I'm scheduled to meet, that particular theory of yours is sadly false."

I pulled a face. Me being romantically involved with a royal guard? Such a ridiculous scenario was definitely *not* in my future. "Then why are you really here?"

He leaned against the wall. "Would you be horribly disappointed to learn I've just finished my guarding shift and am on my way to bed?"

I frowned. What a boring answer. Unless—"You're lying. In order for me to slip away for my own explorations, I had to pass by the guards stationed in front of Eileen's door, and you weren't amongst them."

"Are you always so accusing? My shift ended an hour ago."

"It shouldn't take you an hour to get from your post to your bedroom." This guard was clearly up to something, I was sure of it.

"Wandering the palace isn't a crime, Miss Rosalina, else you'll find yourself in the dungeons for the very offense of which you've just accused me."

He had me there, but I refused to be vanquished by the likes of him. "Your story still seems suspicious. What are you really up to?"

Guard Alastar gave me a searching look, as if I were a complicated puzzle, and didn't answer. Aggravating man.

"If you're not going to tell me, I'll be forced to discover the answer myself."

"Of course you will." For some reason the right corner of his lip was twitching again, and I felt the strangest urge for him to actually *smile*. I'd never met a man so sullen-looking as him.

"Would it kill you to actually smile?"

"It would, in fact, on account of a wicked curse placed upon me as an infant."

He leaned against the wall between two floor-length vases. My imagination immediately stirred. What multitude of secrets could such exquisite vases contain? Perhaps an ancient king had discovered them on a noble quest and stolen them from a dragon's lair, which meant they were enchanted. Or perhaps they held a dastardly secret, such as a stolen cursed artifact. I'd have to sneak back to investigate them later...

"What far away place has your mind gone to now?" Alastar asked.

The familiar excitement I got whenever I told a story settled over me the moment I began. "I was just thinking how those vases probably contain something extraordinary, such as a map to a hidden treasure, stolen jewels, the lost diary pages of a captive princess, or perhaps even ingredients for a mystical spell."

Not budging from his folded-arms pose, Alastar peered inside the one nearest to him. "Or a dragon's egg. Come look."

"Really?" I scampered over and peered inside, only to find it empty. I pouted. "You spoiled the story."

"Giving up the possibility that the other vase contains something fantastic so soon?"

His words eased my disappointment. "Then I won't look

in the other vase so I may forever imagine it contains something magical."

His lips twitched again. "So tell me, if your quest isn't to investigate the royal vases, what is the princess's prestigious guest really doing wandering the corridors so late?"

I nibbled my fingernail. "I obviously wanted to explore."

Alastar raised his eyebrow, the only change to his seemingly-constant grave expression. "At night?"

"When else would I explore?"

"I'm going to make a wild suggestion for *during the day*."

I narrowed my eyes. Despite his deadpan tone, a teasing glint filled his eyes; indeed, he seemed to have been teasing me since the moment we met.

"If you must know," I said heatedly, "night is the superior time to explore because everyone knows it's the best time to discover secret passageways. Besides, a certain royal guard thwarted my explorations during the day." I glared at him. His expression didn't even falter.

"Of course," he said with a solemn nod. "It's also the best time to exercise the dragons that normally guard them, give them a chance to stretch their wings."

I startled. "There are *dragons* in the palace?" That couldn't be true...could it? How splendid!

Alastar furrowed his forehead. "Are there?"

My excitement deflated. Aggravating man. No need to waste any more of my precious exploring time on the likes of him. I gave him a delicious glower and spun around to storm down the hall. Unfortunately, he quickly caught up to me with his much longer stride.

"Leaving so soon?"

I turned a random corner and then another, having no idea where I was or where I was going, but not caring. "The point of a dramatic exit is for the heroine to get away from the annoying ogre bothering her." I glared at him again, hoping he'd take the hint that the ogre in question was *him*.

He stroked his chin, as if deep in thought. "Ah, I see why it didn't work. You forgot your snappy retort in that dramatic exit of yours."

I froze. "Oh dear."

He nodded solemnly. "Indeed. Hence I'm following you in order to give you the opportunity to correct your faux pas, but before you do so, might I ask you a question first?"

I sighed. "If you must."

"Do you have any idea where you are and, more importantly, how to return to your room?"

I opened my mouth to snap out a confident lie, but no sound came out. Instead, I imagined wandering these hallways lost for weeks or even months before dying a dramatic death, by either starvation or being devoured by one of the dragons, about whose actual existence Alastar had been rather vague.

I swallowed. "No."

"I see. Then may I offer my escorting services? I'd be happy to return you to your bedroom."

A flush of heat tickled my cheeks as I lowered my gaze. "Haven't I already kept you up?"

"Not to worry; I found our interaction a pleasant diversion from sleep."

I peeked up at his face, gauging his sincerity. Although his expression hadn't changed, his eyes were lit up in a friendly way. I managed a smile as I accepted his offered arm and allowed him to lead me silently throughout the shadowy hallways.

"Are you quite familiar with the palace?" I asked.

"I've served as a guard here for many years, and before my appointment, I grew up alongside the prince, where we spent hours traipsing these corridors. I consider the palace my home."

What a wonderful story. I ached to press for more details, but considering the late hour, that desire would have to wait.

"Is there a reason for your inquiry beyond mere curiosity?" he asked.

"Curiosity played a part, but I also hoped you were familiar enough with the palace to know the way to the kitchens."

"It appears a detour is in order." He turned around to go back down the hallway until we reached a fork, where we veered left. I skipped alongside him.

"I'm so glad you know where the kitchens are. I can't stay away from them for long. Do you think Prince Aiden would grant me permission to use them?" I was bound to make lots of friends at the palace, none of whom had yet tried any of my famous treats. The thought of their delighted smiles as they savored my delicious recipes caused me to grin.

"Considering your relationship with the future crown princess, I'm sure that could be arranged," Alastar said.

My smile widened. Excellent.

As Guard Alastar led me to the kitchens, I tried my best to memorize the route, using the decorations lining the corridors as landmarks. The door to the kitchens was tucked between two still-life paintings of fruit, which would make it easy to find later. And I would, for I had plenty of baking to do.

"Is there anywhere else you'd like me to take you before retiring for the night?" he asked.

"No, thank you." As much as I yearned to see more of the palace, exhaustion began to press against my senses. My explorations would have to wait for another time, ideally taken with my best friend so I could spend time with her again.

Alastar bowed and led me back to the guest corridors. As we walked, I peeked up at him, searching his expression. What sort of treat would this stoic guard prefer? Berry tarts, perhaps? Or strawberry shortcake? Perhaps a cream-filled pastry?

His gaze shifted down to me. "Is there a reason for your staring?"

"I'm contemplating which dessert is your favorite. Everyone has one."

He stared at me a moment before returning his rigid attention back ahead to the darkened hallway. "Do I?"

"Of course you do." I nibbled my fingernail, considering. "I have it, your favorite dessert is vanilla pudding."

His lips twitched. "Not even close."

"Chocolate cake? Brownies? Custard?"

He shook his head for each guess.

I sighed. "Won't you tell me?" How could I bake him his favorite treat if I didn't know what it was?

"Perhaps it's a secret."

"A challenge. It shall be my quest to figure it out." A delighted thrill rippled over me at the thought of embarking on it.

Despite having felt I'd been wandering the palace for hours before Alastar had shown up, we quickly arrived back at the guest hallway. Alastar paused outside what I assumed was my door and bowed.

"Good evening, Miss Rosalina. Unless something dramatic happens sometime tonight, I trust I'll see you in the morning as I resume my usual role of guarding Her Highness."

With a goodnight nod, he turned and walked down the corridor. I leaned against my door and watched him until he'd disappeared around the corner, my heart beating frantically, all from a mere stroll after midnight.

~

After I somehow managed to calm my excitement from having not only explored but nearly gotten lost in a magnificent palace—imagine that!—I managed to fall asleep. I awoke early the next morning and followed the scent of bacon to the private dining room.

The first person I looked for upon entering was Guard Alastar, curious about his reception following our spontaneous midnight stroll. He stood rigidly against the wall and met my gaze with as rigid an expression as ever, making no acknowledgement that we'd been Midnight Wanderers, let alone that he even *knew* me. My jaw tightened. Stupid guard.

I took my place beside Eileen, whose own seat was scooted close to Prince Aiden's. She turned from chatting with her mother to smile in greeting. "Good morning, Rosie. How did you sleep?"

I ached to tell her of my midnight wanderings but shifted under Prince Aiden's own listening attention. What had been a grand adventure the night before now seemed utterly childish. I didn't fancy being thrown in the dungeon should I have poked in places I shouldn't have.

"I had trouble falling asleep. How can one sleep in so grand a place as this?"

Eileen used the hand not intertwined with her fiancé's to squeeze mine. "I'm not surprised. I'm sure your imagination was running wild. Frankly, I expected you to have gone exploring."

How had she known? Had someone told her? I glared at Alastar, the obvious tattler, and he finally cracked his proper-guard pose to tilt his head at me with a challenging look, as if daring me to confront him.

There seemed to be no hope for my ever keeping anything secret. "I may have done a bit of that."

"Did you?" Eileen's eyes lit up as she shared a smile with the prince. "I knew you would, especially after midnight, considering you'd find exploring at such a time an even grander adventure. You're nothing if not predictable, Rosie."

"I'm not *predictable*." I sharpened my glare at the offender, Guard Alastar. He'd tattled; I *knew* he had. I was sorely tempted not to figure out his favorite treat after all. "And I didn't get to explore much; everything was locked."

"My apologies for that," Prince Aiden said. "If you wish, you may explore to your heart's content today."

Eileen brightened. "I was planning on going over some of the wedding plans after breakfast, but we can explore immediately afterwards. First I can show you the—"

"Actually, sweetheart, we have a meeting after breakfast," Prince Aiden interrupted.

Eileen's smile faltered. "A meeting? What meeting?"

"My dignitaries want to meet their future crown princess and outline some of your duties. I told you about it last night."

"Oh." Eileen's smile vanished completely. "I see."

Prince Aiden eyed her expression with a worried one of his own. "Did you really forget?"

"No," Eileen said hastily. "I mean, perhaps I did. I'm just not used to my time no longer being my own." She sighed. "How long will it last?"

Prince Aiden frowned. "You don't want to go, do you?"

"Of course I do," Eileen said. "It's what's expected, isn't it? It's just that..." She nervously swirled her eggs around her plate. "They're not going to like me, are they?"

"Of course they will, darling." Prince Aiden rested his hand over hers. "You'll be just fine. Please don't worry."

Eileen took a steadying breath before smiling at him assuredly. "I'm sure I will."

The prince still appeared worried as he searched her

expression. "I'm sure it won't take longer than a few hours," he said. Eileen's eyes widened. Prince Aiden hastily continued, "We can plan something fun for when it's over. How about we show Rosalina the rest of the gardens?"

"Yes, that would be lovely." Eileen's answering smile was not only genuine but enthusiastic. "Would you like that, Rosie?"

"It sounds positively wonderful," I said. "Although there's something else I'm also hoping to see—can we visit the dragons?"

Prince Aiden actually *snorted* in a rather unregal manner into his juice while Gavin—who was unfortunately dining with us—predictably laughed.

"*Dragons*? Where did you get such a ridiculous notion as that, Rose?"

While I'd always *imagined* dragons existed, in truth I wasn't entirely sure whether or not they really did...until last night, when a certain guard had acted as if they were not only real, but could be found within the palace. I spent a rather unpleasant moment burning with mortification before it swelled into anger. I turned this wrath on the traitor in question.

"You told me there were dragons."

Alastar cocked an eyebrow. "Did I?"

"You most certainly did. You said dragons guard the secret passageways."

Gavin doubled over, laughing even harder, whereas Eileen and the prince turned bewildered expressions towards Alastar, whose own expression, unsurprisingly, didn't alter in the slightest.

"When did you tell Rosie something so ridiculous, Alastar?" Eileen asked.

His gaze shifted to hers. "I encountered Miss Rosalina

during her midnight wanderings, Your Highness, where she proceeded to accuse me of being a villain."

"You've just proven your villainous role now," I snapped. "You told me there were dragons, so if there aren't any, you lied."

Alastar's glance shifted back to me. "Did I?"

I slammed my hands on the table, shaking the cutlery. "Yes, you did. You knew I believed you. It was a heartless act to toy with an innocent damsel, making you nothing more than a vile villain."

He cocked his eyebrow again. I was really starting to hate that habit of his. "It appears my lessons are paying off."

It was official: I would hate this guard forever. Cheeks burning, I sank further in my seat until my nose hovered over the edge of the table before stealing a hesitant glance at the others.

Gavin, being the goofball that he was, laughed silently; Doreen was especially occupied with her food, as if pretending the recent confrontation hadn't occurred; Prince Aiden seemed thoroughly bewildered as he gave Guard Alastar a look as if he'd never seen him before. Eileen, however, smiled knowingly, a glint in her eyes.

"Now Rosie, you met up with Alastar last night and he told you there were dragons in the palace?"

I glared at him accusingly. "He did, and since that was clearly a lie, you should sack him."

"Oh Rosie, I couldn't do that. He's not only an excellent guard, but you two get along so well, which will be perfect when he comes with us on our outings."

I straightened immediately, ramming my elbow against the table in the process. "He'll *what*?"

She blinked at me a bit too innocently. "He's my guard, hence he'll accompany us in order to protect me."

I gaped at her before skewering Alastar with another glare. "How…lovely."

"Indeed it will be, Miss Rosalina," he said, as serious as ever. "If you'd like, I can walk the dragons while I attend you and Her Highness so you have a chance to see them. No worries about them eating you; they don't eat during exercise…usually."

I rolled my eyes while Prince Aiden leaned back in his seat, watching our exchange with the same strange smile as Eileen. She squeezed his hand before glancing at my untouched plate with a frown. "Aren't you hungry, Rosie?"

"I've lost my appetite." How could one eat in the presence of their antagonist? I glared daggers at Alastar. Rather than wither beneath it like he was supposed to, he merely did that lip twitch of his again. He sure liked to play his part all wrong. I'd have to remain on my guard whenever I was forced to be around him, which unfortunately would likely be quite often.

CHAPTER 4

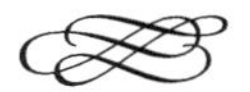

We picked our way along the leaf-strewn path that wove around the foliage of trees in the Forest. I shivered in the brisk, pine-scented morning air as I glanced over my shoulder at my foe.

"Why does *he* have to come? Your fiancé is perfectly capable of protecting us on his own."

"He's my guard," Eileen said simply. "Thus he must accompany me wherever I go, just as Guard Duncan always accompanies Aiden." The prince's guard and the attending servants had been following us just as discreetly as Guard Alastar, but unlike that of my foe, their presence wasn't unwelcome.

Her answer was the same one she'd repeatedly given my prime complaint these past three days, days which I'd enjoyed immensely, especially considering we'd experienced many marvelous things straight out of a storybook. My favorites included spending hours catching up with Eileen, being introduced to the king and Princess Seren—a meeting which had been sadly underwhelming due to their cold politeness—meeting many of the servants who worked at the palace and eagerly learning their stories, baking in the palace kitchens, attending the ballet, and being fitted for my gorgeous bridesmaid's dress.

Unfortunately, such wonders had been accompanied by the constant presence of *that guard,* something I especially loathed considering he and I were currently engaged in what promised to be a record-long silent treatment.

During my palace explorations with Eileen following my disastrous fight with Guard Alastar, I'd kept my eyes peeled for any sign of dragons, and while I hadn't seen any, I wasn't fully convinced they *didn't* exist at the palace. I doubted I could trust anything Alastar said to me on the matter. And now the very knave who'd caused my confusion was accompanying us to a waterfall in the Forest, a place Eileen had been particularly eager to show me, considering it was one of the places where she and Aiden's romance had developed.

Despite my annoyance with said villain, I fought the peculiar urge to glance over my shoulder at him as we walked through the Forest to the falls. After convincing myself that giving in would merely be to make sure he wasn't plotting something conniving, I succumbed to the pull. He stared back in his usual expressionless manner. The man was made of stone—incapable of showing any emotion, let alone *feeling* any.

"That guard's services are unnecessary, considering Prince Aiden is an excellent swordsman."

The prince cast me a rather impatient look. "It's *Aiden,* Rosalina," he corrected for what must have been the dozenth time. "There's no need for formality."

I grinned. Whoever would have thought that I, Rosalina, would ever have the honor of calling the crown prince by his preferred name?

"Of course dear Aiden is capable of protecting us." Eileen squeezed his arm, which was looped through her own. "But we're still expected to have our guards. Aren't you pleased Alastar is accompanying us?"

"*Pleased* is not the word I'd use to describe my feelings concerning the matter." Were heroines always so misrepresented in their stories?

The strange smile that filled Eileen's face whenever I complained about her guard returned. She exchanged her sly look with Aiden. They seemed to be exchanging that insinuating look quite often, and I was beginning to get a suspicion as to why, a reason I refused to acknowledge due to it being ridiculous.

Time for a change of subject. "How was your morning, Eileen?" For she'd spent it cooped up in royal meetings, just like a real princess.

Her mischievous expression immediately faltered, causing my heart to immediately extend to her in concern. Aiden rubbed her back soothingly. "You were wonderful today. Trust me."

Eileen forced a false smile. "I did my best."

Aiden frowned. "You don't need to pretend everything is alright, especially when I can clearly see it's not. Remember, no more secrets between us."

"It's just that..." She lowered her voice. "Did you notice your family's behavior? The king looked as if he disapproved of everything I did, and afterwards Seren said the most nasty thing."

Aiden's expression darkened. "What did she say?"

"It doesn't matter," Eileen said. "They clearly think I'm doing a terrible job. It's only been a week and already—"

"Shh, it's alright, sweetheart." He pressed a gentle kiss on her brow in assurance. "You're doing fine. You're still adapting, but soon you'll be a natural at this."

Eileen frowned. "So you agree I *haven't* been doing a good job?"

"No, I meant—"

"It doesn't matter." Eileen's sharp tone clearly indicated she was finished with their conversation. Aiden sighed and took her hand. Although they exchanged smiles, they seemed a bit strained.

I nibbled my nail worriedly, watching the fairy-tale couple as all sorts of unhappy scenarios played uninvited across my imagination. For once, I didn't want to dwell on the stories I was coming up with.

I slowed until I'd fallen back from the couple and Alastar had caught up. I immediately turned to him. "Are they fighting?" I whispered.

He performed his irritating eyebrow-cocking quirk again. "I'm pleased the royal guest has found her tongue again."

I'd forgotten about our silent treatment game. It appeared I'd lost that round, but it no longer seemed important. "Just answer the question." For my mind was swirling with all sorts of horrendous possibilities. What if their fight led to their estrangement? Eileen would be left heartbroken. Oh, no!

My concern must have shown in my face, for Alastar's expression softened. He glanced towards Eileen and Aiden, now conversing cheerfully as they swung their connected hands back and forth. "They appear to be in good spirits."

"They weren't a moment ago. Didn't you see them? It's a guard's job to observe, is it not?"

"But not to eavesdrop."

I gave him an exasperated look and he leaned closer, lowering his voice. "There's no need to worry. I was witness to how hard His Highness fought for his princess. He won't let her go so easily. Her Highness is merely trying to adjust to her new position, and His Highness is naturally concerned at how difficult it is for her. That's very different than fighting."

Yes, of course. He was right. I was being silly. The tension tightening my chest slowly eased. Alastar continued to study me.

"You're worried for Her Highness?"

"She's my best friend," I said. "Thus I want her story to be perfect."

"That'd be quite difficult, considering no book I've ever read unfolded quite that way."

An excited flutter filled my chest, further dispelling any lingering worry. "You're a reader?"

"Probably not as avid as you, I'm sure."

"But you do read." I wasn't sure why this excited me. Perhaps I hadn't been anticipating any commonality with such a stoic man. "And as such, you see that while stories have their obstacles to be overcome, they have no place in one's happily ever after. After all Eileen has been through, she deserves a wonderful ending." For Eileen had won the heart of a prince, the grandest ending imaginable to any story.

He gave me a peculiar look, one I wasn't sure how to decipher, but I was certain that he, being my antagonist, was silently teasing me.

I wriggled beneath his perusal. "Stop that."

He raised his eyebrow. "Am I guilty of yet another dastardly deed? First I thwart your efforts to explore the throne room, then I plant myself at the bottom of the stairs at midnight to await your arrival in order to nearly knock you over, then I concoct a scheme to get everyone to go along with an elaborate story about dragons. What's my crime this time?"

I glared. "Are you keeping track?"

"Such a feat is impossible considering your mind is impossible to keep track of."

"You're insufferable." Now that he'd eased my worries, I refused to linger in this man's presence any longer. I stomped ahead, biting my lip to smother several choice cursings too indelicate for a heroine to say in her story, but so help me, I was going to *think* them. As I did so, I kept my gaze forward and spent the rest of the walk pretending that the guard trailing us *didn't* exist.

It didn't work.

Soon, the path weaving through the trees opened up on its own to a tranquil clearing. My bad mood immediately dissipated at the magical vision before me. The gushing falls cascaded from the side of a small mountain, completely masked by the thick trees framing it, creating the illusion they spilled from the trees themselves. A shimmery pool hugged the fall's base. Sunlight peeked through the gaps in the branches and glistened off its surface, causing rainbows to dance in the shrouding mist, all while the waterfall itself gradually changed color.

I clasped my hands in delight as I soaked everything in. "This is *incredible.*"

As the servants who'd accompanied us began setting up our picnic, I scampered towards the waterfall and knelt on the grass surrounding its rocky outcroppings so I could peer into the pool—currently a light pink—where the reflection of my wonder-filled expression stared back at me. I leaned so close my nose grazed the surface.

"There's certainly something magical hidden within its depths. Perhaps it's the location of a buried treasure or the home of mermaids. Maybe even the water itself is enchanted. Oh, how *splendid.*"

Eileen giggled from her place nestled against Aiden's side as they cuddled at the base of a maple. "I just adore your stories, Rosie."

"They're not just stories. Truth exists in every tale, as you certainly know, considering your own had the most romantic happily ever after imaginable."

Eileen tipped her head back to beam up at Aiden. "Indeed it did."

He caressed her cheek and kissed her. My earlier worries concerning them immediately vanished. Their happily ever after was clearly going well. How could I have ever doubted?

I watched them with a girlish grin before returning my attention to the now-lilac pool to search for any signs of mermaids or buried treasure. The pool did seem a bit too shallow for mystical life—which was oh-so-disappointing—but that didn't discount the possibility of buried treasure or enchanted water. If there was something buried within its depths, perhaps a clue to its whereabouts existed in any secret markings on the surrounding rocks. I began exploring them earnestly.

"Looking for a marking of some kind? Or perhaps a map to a buried treasure?"

I stiffened at *his* voice and did everything in my power to resist humoring the speaker in question with a glance. "No," I lied stiffly, both surprised and frustrated he knew that was exactly what I was up to.

"You're a terrible liar, Miss Rosalina."

"It takes one to know one."

"Implying?"

I rolled my eyes. Emotionless *and* clueless. "That you're a liar."

"I'm not a liar."

I finally succumbed to the strange pull to glare at him. He was the picture of ease, sitting with his arm resting on a pulled-up knee, with that lip-twitching-so-not-a-real smile of his playing across his serious expression.

"Excuse me? You said there were dragons at the palace. If there aren't, how is that not lying?"

"Still sour about that? You sure know how to hold a grudge." Despite his accusing tone, his lips twitched again.

"The existence of dragons within the palace has yet to be proved or disproved, so you can't claim I'm a liar, whereas your terrible lying skills make you an open book."

"Heroines never lie. It's not ladylike."

Up went his eyebrow. "So you're not currently looking for secret markings?" He scooted closer to study the rocks thoughtfully. "What do these markings look like?"

I debated for a moment whether or not to humor him. "They could be anything," I finally relented.

"And when we find these ciphers?"

"Perhaps they'll lead to a secret treasure. I talked to a footman this morning whose father was a sailor, and he told me all about the adventures he went on sailing the ocean. I'm certain he discovered all sorts of treasures." The idea was positively thrilling.

"Ah, so we're currently in an adventure story. It's always one with you." He examined each rock with the utmost attention. "Frankly, it keeps me on my toes whenever I encounter you. I never know which tale we'll be playing out, although I do know that I'll likely be cast as the villain."

"It's obviously a role you were born to play."

"I must debate that point." He finally settled back. "I can't find any markings, Miss Rosalina. I think you're out of luck."

"I won't give up until I've looked myself." Perhaps they were invisible and were only illuminated under a moonlit night; that would be quite the twist.

I continued in my quest, all while the guard watched, his expression as serious as ever but merriment dancing in his eyes. It made him look almost…friendly, which was frankly a bit unnerving. I kept casting him glares, hoping to crack that rigid expression of his.

I finally settled back on my heels with a dejected sigh. "Well, this is most disappointing. This pool doesn't seem to contain mermaids or buried treasure. The only possibility remaining is that the water is enchanted; considering it changes colors, that's highly likely."

Alastar finally turned his focus away from me to study the shimmery pool. "Enchanted with what?"

I scooped some in my cupped hands and held it out to him. "Drink it and we'll find out."

"Is this how murders are conducted, Miss Rosalina, with seemingly innocent maidens offering poisoned water to unsuspecting heroes?"

"You're not the hero in *my* story."

"I noticed." He said this quietly, as if he didn't mean for me to overhear. Before I could question him, Aiden interrupted.

"Rosalina, when you're done talking with Alastar, we can start our picnic."

"We weren't *talking*; we were *arguing*."

Eileen and Aiden exchanged an amused glance at that, even though the fact wasn't at all humorous.

The servants handed Aiden, Eileen, and me a plate of food and we all proceeded to enjoy the bread, cheese, fruit, and strawberry tarts. However, Duncan and Alastar didn't eat anything, nor did the other servants. I repeatedly glanced towards Alastar. Wasn't he allowed to participate in the picnic? He may have been a guard, but that seemed rather unfair.

"Is something wrong, Rosie?"

I turned to Eileen. "Why aren't the servants eating? I'm sure they'd like some of this delicious food." Before she could tell me why, I stood and approached Alastar, extending my plate out. "Would you like some?"

He raised his eyebrow. "Are you in the need of a poison tester?"

"I want you to join the picnic."

"I'm a servant, Miss Rosalina, but thank you for your kind

offer."

"Servant or not, you should still be allowed to participate." I nudged my plate closer, waiting to see which baked good he'd select so I could satisfy my curiosity about which treat he liked best, but he made no motion to take any. "It wouldn't hurt to eat just one," I prompted. "How about this pecan bar. Is it your favorite?"

"I'm afraid not."

I sighed. "If pecan bars aren't your favorite either, what is?"

"I told you it's a secret, Miss Rosalina."

Uncooperative as ever. "Stubborn man." I slammed my plate down beside him and stomped back to the picnic basket. Another glance at Alastar revealed he *still* wasn't eating. For a moment we had a delightful stare down before he slowly picked up the strawberry tart and took a bite.

I smirked. "The Heroine Rosalina wins this round." And humming cheerfully, I filled up another plate for myself, determinedly ignoring the smirks exchanged between Eileen and Aiden.

Halfway through the picnic, Aiden kissed Eileen's temple before going over to converse with Alastar and Duncan, granting me the opportunity to visit with my best friend. I eagerly seized it.

"What do you think of the waterfall?" she asked me.

"It's enchanting. I never knew the Forest contained something so wondrous."

Eileen tipped her head back to stare at the canopy of branches above, which rustled in the gentle breeze, as if speaking to her. "The Forest is full of all manner of delights. I hope we can spend more time here together during your visit." She reached for my hand. "It's been wonderful having you at the palace with me."

I smiled. I'd loved being here these past three days. I'd not only been assured that Eileen was truly happy, but we'd been able to spend hours staying up late, talking and giggling, just like the many sleepovers we'd had over the years. Would this part of our friendship continue even after Eileen's marriage? How I hoped it would.

I glanced sideways at Aiden to be sure he was deeply involved in his conversation with the guards before I leaned towards Eileen's ear. "Are you and Aiden alright?"

She blinked at me. "Of course we are. What makes you concerned?"

I was wary of bringing up the tension I'd witnessed between her and her fiancé. My cheeks warmed. "During our journey to the waterfall, you two seemed...troubled."

She didn't answer for a moment before she slumped, as if the burden she'd been carrying had suddenly become too heavy. "I'm just worried about my upcoming duties as the new crown princess. I'm totally unfit for the task." She nibbled her lip. "It all sounds overwhelming, doesn't it? What if I do a terrible job?" She forced a smile. "But I'm sure it'll be alright. I'm just happy I get to be with Aiden, not to mention it's been wonderful being with you and mother again. Please be assured I'm perfectly well."

I released a whooshing breath of relief. "I'm so glad."

Her smile softened as she squeezed my hand. "You're such a good friend, Rosie. I really missed you. I felt rather isolated before you came, considering I don't know anybody, but now that you're here I'm much more at ease."

"I'm happy I can be of help."

We continued talking, exchanging stories we hadn't yet had a chance to share since our reunion, until Aiden came over and extended his hand to Eileen.

"Will you walk with me, darling?"

She beamed and allowed him to gently pull her to her feet. They left hand in hand, Duncan following a close distance behind, leaving Alastar as my sole companion since the servants had left to wash the dishes in a nearby stream. I spent the first ten minutes listening to the surrounding birds and pretending he didn't exist before I couldn't take our unbearable silence any longer.

"Do you know what I think?" I asked.

"Whatever it is, Miss Rosalina, it's sure to be unexpected."

"I'm convinced there's something hidden behind the waterfall."

"So we're still in an adventure story?"

I stole another glance at him. Despite his firm countenance, his eyes were dancing merrily. "Exactly. Thus, I'm going to explore." I stood to do just that, but before I could take a single step he seized my wrist. Unexpected warmth jolted up my arm from his touch. "Unhand me at once."

He gave me that stupid cocked-eyebrow look of his again. "*Unhand* you?"

I shrugged. "It makes for better dialogue."

His lips twitched in amusement he couldn't quite mask. "Most would have told me merely to let them go, but of course this is *you*." He shook his head. "I'm not going to honor your request to wade in the waterfall, not when there are hidden deep pockets which you could slip into."

I harrumphed. "Heroines are quite capable of taking care of themselves."

"That's certainly true, Miss Rosalina, but even the most capable heroine has need of a gallant knight once in a while."

"Not if it's *you*." I managed to tug my wrist free but the heat of his touch lingered, leaving my entire arm tingling. "Now I'm going exploring, and you can't stop me." I yanked off my shoes so I could wade into the pool, but he seized my wrist again to jerk me to a stop, his already serious expression even more rigid.

"No, Rosalina, I mean it. It's too dangerous."

I yanked myself away. "No need to worry yourself; I happen to be an excellent swimmer." I could at least stay afloat. I held up my dress and waded into the pool, shivering as the frigid water lapped around my calves. To my surprise, Alastar waded in after me. I narrowed my eyes.

"I just can't rid myself of you."

But his aggravating presence wouldn't deter me. I waded a few more steps, but before I could enjoy the fact that I was exploring a magical waterfall, I suddenly slipped, going under. Coldness pressed around me as I fought to resurface. In the struggle, I whacked my head against the rock. Pain laced my skull as I kicked towards the surface. I broke through right beneath the cascading falls, which pummeled over me in heavy rapids. I coughed and sputtered, but just as I was certain this was the end for the Heroine Rosalina, strong arms seized me by the waist and dragged me from the water to dump me unceremoniously on the bank.

"You nearly got yourself killed. Are you okay, Miss Rosalina?" Alastar's worry-filled face gradually came into focus.

"I did not," I snapped midst my wracking coughs, breathless sputters, and spitting out mouthfuls of water. "I just wanted to see what was behind that waterfall." I clutched my head and moaned. "Ow."

Alastar crouched down. "Let me look at that." He poked his surprisingly gentle fingers through my hair. "You have quite a bump."

"Great, I'm going to get amnesia and forget all my memories. I'll likely wander the Forest as a madwoman with no clue as to my real identity until I'm devoured by an escaped dragon that may or may not be one of the ones stalking the Sortileyan palace." And then I wouldn't be able to participate in Eileen's royal wedding, a thought even more unbearable than that of temporary amnesia.

Alastar actually chuckled. "How do you come up with this stuff?"

When I didn't answer, his fingers froze in my hair before trailing down my face to hook beneath my chin and raise my head up. I shivered at his touch and practically melted at the deep concern lining his eyes. *Hazel* eyes, and rather pretty ones, too.

"Are you in jest or is that a genuine worry?"

I shrugged helplessly. "One never knows."

"Then let me assure you that is a plot twist not in your future."

"In this chapter," I muttered.

"Not from this injury at the very least." He returned to it. "I believe you're safe from any negative consequences except for"—I hissed in pain at his prodding—"it being rather tender." He withdrew his fingers and I had the strangest notion to ask him to touch me again. "While I can't do anything for your injury, I can at least alleviate your other problem." He tugged off his cloak and draped it rather tenderly around my shivering frame. I tugged it more tightly around myself and was enveloped in the most delicious honey-lemon scent that made me slightly dizzy.

Warmth tickled my cheeks as I focused on the ground rather than him. "Thank you for coming to the aid of a damsel in distress, despite her claim of not needing a gallant knight."

I peeked up at him. A faint blush filled his cheeks. "You're welcome. Thank you for the food."

I smiled shyly. "Are there dragons in the Sortileyan palace, Alastar?"

He met my gaze with a crooked grin that sent a jolt of warmth seeping over me. Goodness, his smile was adorable. "Mm, well I've never seen any, but isn't it more fun to pretend there are? It makes for a better story, don't you think?"

I felt my grin widen. "That it does."

And it was in this manner that Aiden and Eileen found us when they returned—settling a temporarily truce...for this scene in our story, at least.

CHAPTER 5

Eileen sure knew how to write stories, for her happily ever after was utterly magical. Even in my dreams I could never have imagined attending such a grand occasion. The decorations were lush. Visions of lace and streamers of white flowers of all kinds—roses, daisies, jasmine—adorned the gilded ballroom where the reception was being held.

The wedding itself had been enchanting. Eileen and her Aiden stood beneath a floral archway woven with branches from the Forest, their hands clasped against one another's hearts as they exchanged vows, beautiful promises to love and cherish one another forever. I'd waited my entire life to find the man to speak such beautiful words to, the act of giving my heart in order for him to cherish it forever.

I embraced Eileen the moment the ceremony concluded. "I'm so happy for you." *Ecstatic* was admittedly the more accurate word. "I always believed you'd find true love. Everyone has a prince."

"As do you, Rosie." Eileen gave me one final squeeze before embracing her mother. Of course I had a prince—my heart fluttered as I remembered the storyteller's promise—although he was quite slow in coming. Perhaps I'd meet him tonight amongst all the prestigious guests attending the reception of the crown prince and his new crown princess. The splendid scene unfolded in my imagination—our eyes would catch one another's from across the crowded ballroom and time itself would stop as our hearts connected. I couldn't wait!

I caught sight of the King of Sortileya sitting on his gilded throne, watching the proceedings with a bored regality. Seated beside him was the Dragon Princess, Princess Seren. Both were frowning towards the newlyweds with clear disapproval for the union.

Aiden and Eileen wove through the crowds hand in hand as they received the congratulations of their regal guests, Eileen's expression full of joy, no sign of the slight uncertainty I'd caught glimpses of the past few weeks. Aiden leaned down to whisper something into her ear, likely the most romantic of endearments, evident by the way her blue eyes lit up at his words and her standing on tiptoe to brush her lips against his.

I sighed wistfully. So romantic. Imagine: Eileen was now the Crown Princess of Sortileya, and I, Rosalina, was her best friend. Surely this marked the beginning of my own grand adventure.

I turned away from the happy couple and flounced through the crowd, losing myself in the surrounding splendor. Nobles dressed in fine silks and ladies arrayed in glistening jewels swarmed around me and spun on the dance floor, their conversation and laughter mingling with the music from the orchestra. I mingled amongst the regal guests, getting a thrill whenever I introduced myself as Lady Rosalina, the new crown princess's best friend.

But after several minutes of mingling, the allure of being

amongst so many prestigious people began to wane. The conversations were all the same—discussing the lavish decorations, what so-and-so was wearing, and gossiping about titled individuals I didn't know.

I excused myself from a trio of gossiping ladies and wove through the crowds, searching for a familiar face so I could engage in more stimulating conversation to pass the time. I paused in front of one of the gold-encrusted full-length mirrors to admire my elegant dress, a gown of lilac satin that fell in lovely ruffles. I turned to see it from all angles before twirling, loving the way my dress swirled around my ankles. With my lush gown and my golden hair twisted in an elegant updo, I looked very much a princess myself. Oh, bliss!

I froze when my gaze caught sight of someone in the mirror, a handsome, golden-haired man. I swiveled around and frantically searched the crowds, but there was no sign of him. Where had he gone? I craned my neck, searching, and was just beginning to wonder whether the man I'd glimpsed had been trapped inside the mirror when I spotted him laughing jovially across the ballroom.

My heart fluttered as I hungrily stared at him, soaking in both the fine cut of his regal uniform and his chiseled features so I might sketch both of them onto my heart in order to keep the memory of him there forever.

As if sensing my gaze, he glanced over, and for one beautiful moment we stared at one another across the ballroom, just as I'd imagined in my earlier fantasies. I nearly melted when he flashed a dazzling smile and winked. Ooh, he was extremely handsome, deliciously so—the essential characteristic for one's true love. I had to meet him and see what other connections we shared. Immediately.

Introduction. I needed an introduction, but the proper way to secure one was to have someone already acquainted with this dashing stranger be the one to supply it, and I had no idea whom to ask. I couldn't ask Eileen, currently in the middle of her own celebration, which unfortunately left only annoying Gavin.

I began searching for him in earnest, but he was nowhere to be found. I gritted my teeth. What was the use of having a relation who was a member of the court if I couldn't even use him to my advantage? It was most vexing.

After several unsuccessful passes through the ballroom, combing my gaze across every face, I sighed in defeat and made my way to the refreshments laid in elegant and tantalizing arrangements on the surrounding banquet tables. Chocolate was the best way to quell even the most bitter disappointments.

I inhaled a chocolate pastry in three delicious bites. Still chewing the moist, fluffy goodness, I seized a gold-lined plate and filled it with all manner of chocolatey sweets before beginning another round of searching.

"What are you looking for, Miss Rosalina? Your prince?"

I stiffened at that familiar deep voice. *Him.* I turned to the stoic guard standing rigidly in his usual place against the wall, despite his not being on duty. While we'd settled a temporary truce of sorts at the waterfall the week before, a day hadn't passed when we hadn't exchanged our usual spar of words, a ritual made easier since he was always conveniently—or as I liked to look at it, *inconveniently*—around, guarding my primary companion.

But for once I wasn't annoyed to see him, despite him having caught me drowning my sorrows in dessert. "Alastar, I need you." I scampered over. He cocked his eyebrow.

"In need of an accomplice to hide your stolen goods? I caught you pilfering sweets." His lips twitched as he took in my full plate.

Why did guards have to be so observant? "I didn't pilfer anything; I'm a royal guest. Besides, everyone knows chocolate has magical properties to help mend the hearts of disappointed heroines."

"Are you a disappointed heroine, Miss Rosalina? From my observations, you've been floating through the reception as if you were the princess yourself."

My cheeks burned. How did he know that had been tonight's fantasy?

"For that, I won't share any of my sweets with you." I made an exaggerated show of enjoying a brownie oozing with frosted goodness. His expression remained rigid. I bit back a sigh. What was the point in riling a man when he appeared entirely unriled?

"Even off-duty guards are dull," I said as I investigated my spoils and selected a cookie. "You never react when you're supposed to."

His lips twitched. "I couldn't help but notice that you've seemed rather bored from all the shallow conversation."

Had he been watching me? A strange flutter tickled my breast at the thought, but I fought to appear indifferent as I delicately rolled my eyes and indelicately inhaled the entire cookie in two large bites, dribbling crumbs. "You're breaking our truce."

"I don't recall signing any contracts of late, Miss Rosalina. Now please don't keep me in suspense. If I'm to act as an accomplice in raiding the desserts, I'd like to know my role as soon as possible."

I fought against my smile. I could always count on Alastar to provide entertaining conversation. "I won't be requiring such a service." I extended my plate. "Take one."

His lips twitched as he selected a chocolate. "Bribing me?"

Perhaps a bit—I couldn't keep anything from him. "I've spotted a guest with whom I'd like an introduction."

"And you believe I, a mere guard, can supply it?"

"No, I need you to point me to one who can. Have you seen Gavin?"

"Sir Gavin left early, for he's being sent to Lyceria early tomorrow morning in order to negotiate some trade agreements."

Of course my slippery cousin—*fourth cousin*, I reminded myself—wasn't around when I needed him. Traitor.

That left me no choice but to rely on this guard, who shifted between villain and knight depending on his moods. Which role did he play tonight? I nibbled my fingernail. Perhaps I should offer him another sweet in order to get into his good graces.

"How disappointing. How will I ever secure an introduction now? I suppose you'll have to do."

"Your enthusiasm for my assistance makes me so eager to render it to you."

"Won't you help a damsel in distress?" I gave him my most imploring look, even batting my eyelashes. His expression didn't falter. Annoying. "If you can't supply an introduction, can't you at least give me his name?" The name of my true love was a start, at least.

"If you point him out and I happen to know him, then I'll be happy to..." His expression hardened. "Wait, *his* name?"

"Of course. I spotted the most handsome man when our eyes met across the dance floor; it just may be love, but how will I know unless I speak with him? You must help me."

He sighed and, expression still hard, turned to scan the crowds. "Where's this special man who's already swept you off your feet?"

I stood on tiptoe to search. "I can't see him. What if he's already left and I've forever missed my chance? Oh, this is awful." I wrung my hands at my horrible plight.

"I'm sure we'll find him. Then I'll arrest him."

I gasped. "*Arrest* him?"

Mischief flashed in his eyes. "In the course of my interrogation you can get all the information you need from him, including his name."

I searched his expression to see if he was serious. With his usual expressionless countenance, it appeared he was. Panic clawed at my heart. "Alastar, you can't do that. That'll ruin everything."

He chuckled. "I know."

Odious man. I continued craning my neck, searching, but the handsome stranger was nowhere to be found. I groaned in frustration. "I can't find him. Are you having better luck?"

"It'd be easier to assist in your search if I at least knew what the man looked like."

"He possesses all the essentials: he's tall, blond, handsome…"

"Of course he's handsome," Alastar grumbled, his bad temper seizing him once more. "Is that the only reason he's captured your interest?"

"Being handsome is a wonderful start, not to mention he did wink at me." I became all fluttery at the recollection.

Alastar had the audacity to snort. "Sounds like a scoundrel to me."

"He most certainly isn't. He's absolutely perfect and—oh! There he is, Alastar. Do you see him? Do you?" I seized his arm and pointed to the dashing man I'd just spotted in the crowds. Alastar's expression, if possible, became even more fierce. He gave the handsome man a skewering glare before the crowds once more swallowed him up.

"Of course," he spat. "*Him.*"

"Do you know him, Alastar? Please tell me you do."

"Not personally, but I recognize him as Crown Prince Liam of Draceria."

For a moment I stood frozen in shock as my mind scrambled to catch hold of his words. Then my excitement exploded. "A *prince*? Ooh, I *knew* it. Just like a fairy tale." It appeared Eileen wasn't the only one whose happily ever after included a dashing prince. Mine did as well, just as the story-teller had promised.

Alastar said nothing, only continued to glower. I frowned, both fascinated by his rare display of emotion and frustrated by it. "What's gotten you so ruffled? Stop pouting and introduce me."

"I'd rather not."

I pressed my hand to my hips. "Why not?"

"It's too presumptuous for a mere guard to approach a prince."

"But I'm practically royalty. Can't you make an exception?"

"You may be *practically royalty,* but I certainly am not. Now why don't you return to the reception?" With that, he walked away. I glared at his back.

"You aggravating, uncooperative, villainous man. Consider our truce over." I stomped away, seething, feeling a mixture of satisfaction at putting as much distance between me and my antagonist as possible and also a strange need to return to him and mend the rift that had sprung up between us.

I pushed aside that ridiculous notion and focused my attention on searching for the dashing Prince Liam—imagine, an actual *prince*!—but he remained lost to the crowds. What a tragic end to what had been a glamorous affair, and it was all *that guard's* fault. The aggravating man had a knack for getting under my skin unlike anyone I'd ever met.

No, I *wouldn't* think of him, not when he was thankfully no longer around. Alastar-free thoughts were the best ones to have at all times, especially at royal weddings.

Time for more chocolate. I returned to the refreshment table and began to eye the desserts for the one most likely to wash away my romantic disappointments. Before I could select one, a man appeared at my elbow, holding a glass of punch.

"Are you in need of refreshment, lovely lady?"

I swiveled around and my heart skittered to a stop. *Him.* His Highness Prince Liam. For a moment I stared, at a loss as to what to say. What introduction did one give a man after sharing a romantic connection across a crowded ballroom?

I finally thawed enough to shakily take his offered glass. "Thank you for your thoughtfulness, Your Highness." I curtsied and flashed my most charming dimpled smile, which he returned with a wide one of his own. I nearly melted. Ooh, he was positively handsome, not to mention he was already proving to be quite the gentleman.

"I felt I must come over and introduce myself to the best friend of the new crown princess," he said. "I'm Liam, Crown Prince of Draceria. It's a pleasure to make your acquaintance." He took my hand and kissed it. I thought I might faint. "And your name is?"

My name? Wait, what was my name? *Get it together, Rosie.* "My name is Rosalina, Your Highness."

"A beautiful name to match a beautiful girl. Now if you'll excuse me, I must find my sisters." He bowed and departed.

I stood in shock as I watched him get swallowed up once more by the crowds. It took several moments before I finally managed to float away from the refreshment table. The rest of the reception was a blur. I could think of nothing except for Prince Liam, his dazzling smile, and the special moment we'd shared.

So this was how happily ever afters started.

CHAPTER 6

"Not so rough, Rosie dear, you'll ruin the crust if you're not gentle."

I looked up from rolling out the dough for the crust of the apple pie we were baking, which I'd been pounding with an aggressive fervor, as if it were to blame for my melancholy. Since abusing the dough was out of the question, the next best method to venting my frustrations was to complain.

"When is she going to return?"

Mother didn't even need to press for details to know what had me in a bad mood. "I'm sure it'll be soon."

"Not soon enough. Eileen has been gone on her wedding trip for over a month—a month in which I haven't had a chance to see her."

It wasn't just missing my best friend fiercely that had me in a sour mood; it was being stuck at the bakery with nothing but dull, endless waiting to occupy my time. Bakeries were considerably more boring than royal palaces, especially when it had been raining for days.

My only consolation had been to bake treats to give out to our neighbors, for what better way to cheer someone up during a gloomy rainstorm than with my delicious peach cobbler? While I'd been giving out my treat, I'd kept an eye out for the storyteller in hopes I could extract more information about my prince to see if it was truly Prince Liam, but I hadn't seen her.

"She's on her honeymoon. Can you blame her for not hurrying back?" Mother cupped my chin with a flour-coated hand and gave me a reassuring smile. "But don't worry, she promised to send for you the moment she returns. Now be a dear and help me slice up these apples."

I sighed and obediently did so, first cutting them up before soaking them in lemon juice. As I did, my mind drifted back to Eileen's lavish wedding, exactly as I'd always envisioned a royal wedding to be: noble guests dressed in elegant finery, delectable cuisine, dancing, and best of all the fierce happiness of the bride and groom. If only my own wedding could be half as grand. My mind immediately imagined that enchanting future day hopefully not too far into my future.

"Rosie dear, you're daydreaming again."

I reluctantly emerged from my fantasies long enough to add the cinnamon, nutmeg, and brown sugar to the pie's filling before my mind drifted once more towards Prince Liam and our serendipitous meeting near the refreshment table. He seemed perfect for me in every way. If only we could spend more time together so I'd know for sure…

A knock sounded at the bakery door. Mother and I exchanged a perplexed look. When had a customer ever *knocked*?

"What on earth…" Mother murmured. "Rosie, would you—"

I was already halfway to the door, my curiosity compelling me to see who could possibly be on the other side. I yanked the door open and gasped at who stood there.

It was Guard Alastar.

I gawked at him—taking in his tall, broad form and his dripping brown hair, soaked with rain and plastered against his forehead—before I slammed the door in his face.

Mother emerged from the kitchen. "Rosie, what are you —" But her inquiry was cut off when Alastar knocked again. I tidied my hair and brushed the flour off my apron before reopening the door. "Who knocks at a bakery door?" I asked him.

"Who slams said door in a paying customer's face?" He responded in that deadpan way of his.

"Are you paying with coin or do you only deal in aggravating comments?"

His lips twitched. "Ah, Miss Rosalina, it's been a long month since I've been exposed to that delightful mind of yours, and yet…" He shook his head, leaving me literally dying to hear the rest of his unfinished thought.

"Aren't you going to finish your statement?"

"And deprive you of the opportunity of doing it yourself?"

I glowered. "You're as exasperating as ever."

"I do my best." He peered into the bakery. "Might I come in? It's a bit wet out here."

"No." I slammed the door again.

Mother frowned warily. "Was that a royal soldier? Whoever he is, don't leave him out in the rain. Open the door for him."

I was still rather upset for how he'd treated me at Eileen's wedding to obey her. "He's Eileen's head guard, a man who's nothing but trouble. I can't fathom how she can stand having him constantly around, for he's—for goodness' sake, what now?" Alastar was knocking again. I flung the door open with a sharp glare. "What do you want?"

"I'm here by royal command, and I'm not leaving until

I've accomplished my orders." He shoved his foot in the doorway to prevent my closing it on him again.

"And what royal command could you possibly be referring to? Eileen and Aiden aren't yet back from their honeymoon."

He leaned against the doorframe and peered around me into the bakery. "Might I come in to deliver my news? I'm not only cold, but whatever I'm smelling is intoxicating and I'm quite famished."

I snorted. "You're quite *famished?*"

He cocked that eyebrow of his. "Doesn't that make for better dialogue?"

A giggle escaped before I could stop it. I tried to smother it with my hand, but the mischievous thing slipped through my fingers. To my delight, Alastar smiled—not a half one, but a real smile. It was utterly adorable.

"I got you to smile," I said. "I didn't know you *could* smile."

"And I got you to laugh." He pressed his cold finger in my cheek. "You have a dimple."

"All heroines do." His smile softened me, especially considering he was rather soaked and I was beginning to feel sorry for him. I finally stepped aside to let him enter. "Go stand by the fire."

He did so, pausing to bow to Mother before facing the hearth and rubbing his hands in front of the crackling fire.

I snagged a pastry from the sample tray and shoved it into Alastar's hands. "Are pastries your favorite?"

He shook his head. I sighed. Would I ever figure out his favorite dessert?

I shoved my own pastry into my mouth. "Now, what's your message that compelled you to come all the way to Arador in the rain?"

"Knowing your affinity for the dramatic, I'd planned to descend on the back of a dragon and, after announcing my presence by trumpet, declare your message in the public square."

I rolled my eyes—never mind his story tickled my heart with delight. "What is it with you and dragons? Can't you be more creative?"

His lips twitched again. "I'm quite keen on the fiery beasts, considering they never fail to get a reaction from you; it's rather amusing watching you squirm."

I balled my hands into fists. "Please share your message before I kick you back out into the rain."

"Watching you try could prove rather entertaining." He took another bite of his pastry. "This is rather good. Did you make it?"

"Alastar, so help me—"

He chuckled—the oh-so-annoyingly-serious Guard Alastar actually *chuckled*—and admittedly it was rather fascinating.

He removed a gilded envelope from within his cloak and handed it to me with an exaggerated flourish and a deeper bow than was probably necessary. "You've broken my defenses, and shall now be rewarded. Your message, Miss Rosalina."

I snatched it from him before he'd even finished his speech and tore it open. I'd barely gotten a few words in before I squealed.

"For goodness' sake, Rosie." Mother—who'd been monitoring us rather closely, albeit a bit confusedly—wandered over. "What ever does it say?"

"A ball, I've been invited to a *ball*. Ah bliss, my life truly is turning into a fairy tale." I twirled and rammed into Alastar's firm chest. He *oofed*. "Oops, sorry Alastar. But did you hear? A *ball*!" I waved the invitation in his face.

"A ball? No, I hadn't heard. Why don't you shriek a bit louder?"

I rolled my eyes and returned my drooling attention to my gilded invitation, which I read over once again to make sure this wasn't a dream. Mother peered over my shoulder and gasped.

"A ball hosted by the Dracerian Royal Family? What an honor."

"The first of many honors now that my best friend is the new Crown Princess of Sortileya."

But it wasn't just the ball that had me aflutter with excitement—this was the perfect opportunity to see Prince Liam again and renew the connection we'd made at Eileen's wedding. The entire scene played across my mind's stage—a magical dance, long conversations, discovering each connection of our hearts the more time we spent with one another...I could hardly wait.

Despite such joyous thoughts, I nibbled my fingernail and glanced at Alastar. "What ever will I wear?"

"Is there a particular reason why you believe I'm capable of supplying an answer to such a tragic dilemma?"

Annoying as ever. "I only have a few days to prepare for what will certainly be the most magical day of my life. If you're not going to be helpful, then be so good as to leave and extend my acceptance so that I can begin getting ready." I shoved against his firm build in an attempt to get him to move towards the door, but of course he didn't budge.

"Does preparing for a ball really take *days*?"

"It does when we're busy at the bakery," I said.

He glanced around the empty bakery. "I see you're swarming with customers. Is it ghosts or just invisible people you cater to?"

"Goodbye, Alastar." I shoved against him again. Still he didn't move. "Move already. Must you always be uncooperative?"

He merely glanced down at me pushing breathlessly

against him. "I'm sorry to disappoint you, but I cannot leave until I've delivered my full message."

I immediately stopped pushing, grateful for the excuse to give up. "You mean there's more?"

He cocked his eyebrow. "Is there?"

"*Alastar*!"

He chuckled again and I allowed the sound to wash over me. "The royal carriage will pick you up tomorrow afternoon with Sir Gavin as your escort so that you may attend the ball with Their Highnesses three days hence."

I wriggled in excitement. If only it were tomorrow already. "I'm not sure I can wait that long to see my prince again."

Alastar had been half turned towards the door but paused to swivel around, his expression dark. "Your *prince*? And who might that be?"

"Why, Prince Liam of course," I said. "His family is hosting, after all." I leaned closer, too excited to keep my sweet little secret any longer. "I met him at Eileen's wedding after you refused to help me. He introduced himself to me and said the sweetest things. I'm sure this invitation came from him personally."

Alastar's countenance hardened in a way I'd never seen before. "I've fulfilled my duty and will now take my leave. I shall see you on the day of the ball."

My stomach jolted. "Don't tell me you'll be attending, too." I didn't want Alastar's presence to spoil my reunion with Prince Liam.

"Only because you want me to so badly."

Heat flushed my cheeks. "I do *not*."

His lips twitched, a welcome reprieve from whatever unpleasant emotion had previously eclipsed him. "I'll be sure to be there, not merely to guard Her Highness but as an eager audience for whatever adventure you'll find yourself in at your first ball. Besides, I wouldn't want to miss seeing your encounter with your *prince*."

He bowed and left. The moment the door closed behind him, I scampered to the window and pulled aside the drapes so I could watch him leave.

"Who was that man?" Mother asked. "You two obviously know each other. What exactly is your relationship?"

Alastar disappeared into the rain and I let the curtains fall back. "We're...*comrades*, of sorts, in battle."

"A battle of what, exactly? A battle of wits?"

"No, more of a battle of..." I thought about it for a moment before grinning. "...*stories*." And so far, Alastar was surprising me by proving to be a most formidable of allies... or foes; I hadn't decided which.

CHAPTER 7

"Don't be alarmed, Your Highnesses, but Miss Rosalina is about to burst."

I glared at Alastar, as stoic as ever, before peering back out the carriage window. The royal carriage was spacious and deliciously elegant, leaving me plenty of room to crawl all over the seats as I watched the passing scenery, which was much more exciting than Sortileya's woodlands.

Eileen smiled at my wriggling. "I'm pleased you're so excited, but then you've always loved dances."

"Are you fond of dancing, Rosalina?" Aiden asked.

"I find it delightful, but dancing isn't what I'm looking forward to the most tonight." I exchanged a sly grin with my dearest friend. "Should I confess, Eileen?"

"If you want. You're amongst friends."

That was debatable. I was determined to make Aiden my friend, considering he was so dear to Eileen's heart; Gavin was sort-of family, so he unfortunately fell in the friend category by default; and General Duncan—Aiden's personal guard and Alastar's brother—seemed nice enough. It was that Guard Alastar that was the problem.

But I refused to be deterred from a good story. I settled in my seat, rearranged the skirts of the gorgeous rose-pink ball gown Eileen had lent me, and leaned forward to begin. "In every 'once upon a time,' the heroine's happily ever after always includes true love, and where does she most often meet her heart's match?"

Eileen slipped her hand into her husband's and beamed up at him. "In the Forest."

"Yes, the enchanted Forest, but it was your *dance* with Aiden that deepened your love for him."

Eileen thought about it for a moment. "You're right, our dance helped me realize I couldn't live without him."

"Really?" Aiden's black eyes were lit with wonder. "I don't think you've ever told me that before."

I pressed my hands to my heart with a wistful sigh. "So romantic. Never underestimate the power of a dance. Stop that, Gavin." For he'd been pretending to hurl out of the carriage window. "You don't have a romantic bone in your body. I can't believe we're even related."

"Me neither," he muttered as he settled back in his seat. "Listen, I know you well enough to see exactly where this conversation is going. As such, forgive me for not showing the proper enthusiasm."

I folded my arms and lifted my chin with a challenging air. "If you know me so well, where exactly is it going?"

"You're going to inform us that you believe you're going to meet your true love at a dance. I've heard all of this from you before."

"I *know* I will," I said. "Hence I've never missed a dance, for one never knows which one her future husband will attend."

Gavin rolled his eyes. "You always have some far-fetched romantic notion as to how things will play out, and then they never go the way you expect. If you ever fall in love, I bet you end up meeting him in the most boring of all places...like a corridor."

Alastar cocked his eyebrow at that and I determinedly looked away from him. "I certainly won't meet the love of my life in a *corridor* but at a dance. And not just any dance, but a royal ball."

Gavin eyed my expression warily before groaning. "Oh no, I know what you're plotting: you plan on trying to ensnare an actual prince."

My cheeks burned. "What ever do you mean?" I squeaked.

"You've clearly set your sights on Prince Liam, which is why you're so excited to be attending the Dracerian Royal Ball, where he's sure to be in attendance.

My face enflamed further. How had he known?

Aiden frowned. "But he's betrothed."

"You were betrothed before you met Eileen," I reminded him, having heard the entire story from her personally. "But you broke it off to marry your true love. Why can't the same thing happen to me?"

"Because my situation was much different than Prince Liam's."

I didn't want to spend the remainder of the journey hearing Aiden dully outline the differences between two marriage contracts. Anyway, it didn't matter; whatever differences existed weren't enough to deter me. Already the possibilities began blossoming in my mind.

Eileen warily eyed my brightening expression. "Oh Rosie, you can't be serious. I recognize that gleam in your eyes. Please don't tell me you're really considering—"

"Of course I am," I said, unable to keep the secret any longer. "He's *perfect,* Eileen. We had the most romantic connection at your wedding and the loveliest conversation." I sighed at the memory. "I've always wanted to marry a prince and now I shall, just like you did."

"Don't get too excited, Rosie," Eileen said. "Liam is always charming. It's just his way."

I frowned at her. "But he winked at me."

"Liam winks at everyone, including me, but that doesn't mean he—"

"Liam *winks* at you?" Aiden demanded.

"He winked at me the first time I met him."

Oh no, Aiden threatened to veer the conversation off course with his overprotectiveness. "But Prince Liam's wink towards me was different, not to mention he also kissed my hand and stared deeply into my eyes. He's the one, I just *know* it."

"Life doesn't play out like your stories, Rosie," Eileen said gently.

"That's what Ferris told me after your disappearance, and you turned out to be alive and well, and not just that, but engaged to *royalty*—the greatest plot twist ever, I might add."

"That's different. This is love, and love can't be manipulated."

"I'm not *manipulating* love, I'm just helping it along," I said. "Now, won't you tell me all about him?"

I leaned forward and gazed at Aiden imploringly. He and Eileen cast a wary glance towards *that guard* before Aiden leaned back with a sigh.

"Very well, what do you want to know?"

"Everything."

"He's a fun-loving sort who enjoys uncovering secrets and coming up with whacky theories."

"A lover of stories," I clasped my hands. "I just *knew* he was the one. Ah bliss, this is going to be *splendid*."

Over the course of our carriage ride—during which there was an oh-so-welcome silence from that guard's corner—Aiden told me enough about Prince Liam for me to become even more convinced he was my prince.

"Ooh, I'm so anxious to see my future husband again and together dance the night away. When are we to arrive?"

Eileen glanced out the window. "Quite soon. There's the Dracerian palace now."

"Really?" I clambered to the window, where *that guard* sat. I crawled onto the seat between him and the window, and in my excitement accidentally elbowed him. "Oops, sorry, Alastar." I eagerly leaned out the window and squealed. "I see it, I see it! Oh, it's *beautiful*. I can definitely visualize myself living there. Look, Alastar." And without realizing the why behind my actions, I tugged him closer so he could peer out, too.

The poor man got a face full of satin and poofs from my ball gown as I stuck my head out the window in order to stare wide-eyed as the carriage jostled up the twisting road leading to the spectacular palace, a vision of marble and splendor, lit by dozens of torches that flickered in the starry night.

The heat of Alastar's breath tickled my ear as he leaned in close. "Don't fall out."

"I'm not going to fall out unless you decide to push me." I cast him a suspicious glance. "You won't, will you?"

Cue his cocked eyebrow. "Will I?"

Odious man. I rolled my eyes and returned to hanging out the window, subconsciously aware that I was practically in Alastar's lap and that the areas where my skin grazed his were strangely warm and tingly.

We couldn't reach the Dracerian Palace quickly enough, for I was certain that this was the beginning of my very own magical happily ever after.

"I'M IN HEAVEN, I'm in heaven, I'm in heaven," I muttered repeatedly as I gazed doe-eyed around me at the enchanting splendor of the Dracerian royal palace ballroom—with its glistening chandeliers, gilded marble, and garlands of flowers draping the walls. Dozens of nobles dressed in their finest silks and jewels stood conversing, the bells of their laugher dancing around the domed room.

Eileen squeezed my arm affectionately. "Isn't it lush? Royal balls truly are fairy-tale visions."

"Only they're far more grand than any fairy tale I've ever imagined." I soaked in the magical elegance surrounding me before I felt strangely compelled to share in this moment with one man in particular. "Don't you think so, Alastar?" I turned towards him only to discover he wasn't beside us. "Where's your guard?"

"Over there." Eileen motioned to the side of the ballroom, where Alastar and Duncan stood rigidly, alternating their attention between us and surveying the room for potential devious threats. I turned away with a disappointed sigh in time to notice Eileen exchange an amused smile with Aiden.

"What's that smirk for?"

"Nothing. Come, shall we greet the Royal Family?"

All thoughts of Alastar and the lush wonder of the glistening ballroom immediately vanished at the thought that I, Rosalina, was about to be formally introduced to the Dracerian Royal Family. Dazed, I allowed Eileen to loop her arm through mine and lead me towards them, where they sat perched on their thrones on a raised platform to oversee their guests.

The Dracerian monarchy were exactly as I envisioned—blond and extremely regal. They rose gracefully at our approach to greet Aiden and Eileen with fond smiles.

"It's a pleasure to see you again, Prince Deidric and Princess Eileen," the queen greeted.

Eileen curtsied. "The pleasure is ours, Your Majesty. Thank you for your generous invitation."

Midst their polite pleasantries, I eyed the other four royals—the three princesses, gorgeous and elegant in their layers of silk and jewels, as expected—and *him*, my future husband, His Royal Highness Crown Prince Liam. He was even more the perfect portrait of a prince than I'd remembered: wavy golden hair, large blue eyes, a firm chin, a dazzling dimpled smile, proper posture…not to mention he looked incredibly handsome in his dress uniform. Without a doubt, he was the one.

The princesses stepped forward to hug Eileen. "It's so good to see you again." Their gazes shifted to me. "Won't you introduce us?"

Eileen turned to me. "May I present my dearest friend. Rosie, these are the Princesses Rheanna, Aveline, and Elodie. Rhea, Aveline, and Elodie, this is my adopted sister, Miss Rosalina."

All three princesses gave me a sweet smile. "It's a pleasure to finally meet you, dear Rosie. Eileen has told us so much about you. I'm sure we'll become the best of friends."

I curtsied while gaping at them in an undignified, slightly dazed manner. The princesses of Draceria wanted to be friends with *me*? What a perfect beginning to my relationship with my future sisters-in-law.

"And this is Prince Liam." Eileen introduced him with unmistakable hesitation, as if she feared my response. "Liam, this is my best friend, Rosalina."

Prince Liam strode over with the perfect poise expected for his royal title. "I've already had the pleasure of meeting Miss Rosalina; it's wonderful to see you again."

He winked and my heart fluttered in excitement. He remembered our meeting! Did that mean it had been as memorable for him as it had been for me?

I scrambled for words, preferably something witty to impress, but I now found myself strangely tongue-tied, a rare sensation and one that felt strange to experience around my true love.

He seemed to be waiting for me to speak, and when I awkwardly remained silent, he bowed and gently kissed my hand. I nearly fainted at the romantic gesture.

"Unfortunately, I'm expected to meet several stuffy noble bores, but perhaps we can have another chance encounter at the refreshment table later this evening."

He released me and turned to be introduced to a group of noblemen who'd just arrived. Dazed, I allowed Eileen to lead me back into the crowds, feeling as if I were floating. What a wonderful meeting with my intended and his family. Our romance would undoubtedly be utterly *perfect*.

An hour later I wasn't so sure. Rather than being engaged in conversation with my prince, I'd instead trailed Aiden and Eileen as they tediously greeted one esteemed guest after another, all while shifting impatiently for the ball to officially begin. Were royals expected to talk with *everyone*? How tedious. When the music finally started, Aiden swept Eileen onto the dance floor, leaving me standing miserably alone on the sidelines, watching as Prince Liam danced with a dark-haired beauty rather than me.

"His intended." Gavin appeared beside me offering a glass of punch, which I gratefully accepted. "Princess Lavena of Lyceria, originally betrothed since infancy to the late crown prince and now to the new one, Prince Liam. Such a political match won't be abandoned so easily."

I studied the couple and noticed Prince Liam was not only not smiling, but he wasn't even looking at his intended, instead seeming to find the area above her head extremely fascinating. "His Highness doesn't appear enthralled."

"Indeed, he has no interest in the match, but one often has little choice in political arrangements."

"Aiden was part of an arranged engagement before he married Eileen, and that one was broken."

Gavin shrugged. "True, he was engaged to Princess Rheanna, an arrangement that was very difficult for him to break, but considering Sortileya is more stable than Lyceria and Draceria, their union wasn't as necessary as Prince Liam and Princess Lavena's is. It would be foolish for Prince Liam to throw it away, no matter how much he dislikes it."

I tightened my jaw. "You're saying that even if Prince Liam fell in love with me, our marriage would still be forbidden?" Oh, what a horrible thought.

"I'm just trying to protect you from inevitable heartbreak."

I angrily swirled my glass of punch. "True love conquers any obstacle."

"Real life isn't a story, Rose, and even if it were, why would Prince Liam fall in love with you?"

I flinched at his biting words. With a skewering glare, I stomped away from the most aggravating of cousins—*fourth* cousin, twice removed—and found myself drawn towards where Alastar stood guarding. He cocked his eyebrow at my approach, and although nothing else about his expression changed, unmistakable concern filled his eyes.

"Stomping at a royal ball? It looks like something has shattered all your hopes for a magical evening. What's bothering you, Miss Rosalina?"

"My evil cousin."

"Sir Gavin? How is he troubling you?"

I sighed, tears stinging my eyes as I relived Gavin's cruel words. "He says I'm unworthy of Prince Liam not only because I wouldn't be a prestigious match, but because he believes he couldn't fall in love with me."

Alastar's gaze snapped towards Gavin and narrowed darkly. "What an ungentlemanly thing to say. Please pay his words no mind, Miss Rosalina; your worth isn't deemed by your station. You're a charming girl."

I managed a small smile as I peeked shyly up at him. "Do you believe I'll find true love?"

"Certainly, Miss Rosalina, and probably when you least expect it. Speaking of which"—he frowned in the direction of Prince Liam, still dancing with his intended—"how was your anticipated reunion with His Highness?"

I sighed. "It was both magical and a disaster. I finally received the proper introduction I'd been waiting for, only to have my words abandon me."

"A rare event, indeed."

Despite his wry comment I brightened. "But at least he kissed my hand, not to mention he was utterly charming, as before."

Alastar's scowl deepened. "I see." He glared at Prince Liam again. "If he was so smitten, why aren't you dancing with your supposed prince?"

I pouted. "Unfortunately, he's currently engaged in his obligatory dance with his fiancée, which leaves me time to scheme on how to get him to dance with me again."

"I see." Alastar frowned as he studied my expression. "What do you think of him now that you've met him again?"

I sighed wistfully and Alastar's expression hardened.

"What's that sigh mean?"

"He's so princely, isn't he?"

"Define *princely*."

"Oh, you know," I said with an impatient wave of my hand.

"I'm afraid I don't. Please enlighten me."

"Well, just *look* at him." I motioned to where he spun on the dance floor with the utmost grace. Alastar did, his expression harder than ever.

"I'm afraid I'm failing to understand the definition."

I took a sip of my fruity punch. "He's blond, blue-eyed, has a dimple...it's no coincidence our features match."

Alastar cocked his eyebrow. "I had no idea true love was so superficial."

I scowled. "You're so unromantic, Alastar."

"I believe that attribute falls to you. I'm surprised you believe genuine affection grows from such shallow ground."

"I don't," I said. "While a handsome man is certainly ideal, I desire a deeper connection. I also want a compassionate man, as well as one who is fun and makes me laugh..."

"Makes you laugh, got it." Alastar stated it like he was committing my list to memory. I tilted my head.

"What are you up to?"

"I'm merely trying to understand your beliefs on love."

"If you want to better understand it, you'll need to witness true love in action, which you can do by observing my dance with Prince Liam. You must help me brew up ideas to make him ask me for a dance."

Alastar gaped at me. "You want me to help you ensnare His Highness?"

"I'm not trying to *ensnare* him," I said. "That's something only a villain would do, and I am most certainly not a villain. As the heroine, I'm merely creating the opportunity for him to realize we're a perfect match. Now help me come up with a way to secure a dance with him."

Alastar sighed and rested his chin on his fist in a pondering pose. "We can try telepathy so he can sense your desires, or perhaps a hypnotic spell would be a better choice."

I clasped my hands. "Oh, those are excellent ideas, but..." I frowned, considering. I'd never heard of those things actually working except for in stories, but I was willing to try anything. "I'll try telepathy first. The first dance is ending, so I best hurry." I turned towards Prince Liam and sent him earnest pleas to ask me to dance, pausing only to whack Alastar's arm. "Are you helping me?"

"The only assistance I can render is offering the suggestion, but I cannot in good conscience attempt to manipulate the mind of a Dracerian royal."

I drained the rest of my fruity punch. "You're no fun."

The final notes of the waltz trilled to a conclusion and my silent pleas increased. Prince Liam bowed to his fiancée without any enthusiasm before escorting her towards our side of the room. There he cast his eyes about, as if searching for his heart.

I'm right here, I silently screamed. *Pease dance with me.*

To my astonishment, not only did his gaze settle on me, but he approached and bowed. "May I have this next dance, Miss Rosalina?"

I gawked at him in shock. Amazing—telepathy had actually worked. My heart was doing cartwheels, for I, Rosalina, had been Prince Liam's first choice of a partner after his obligatory dance with his unwanted fiancée. Everything was going according to plan.

"Miss Rosalina?"

I shoved my empty punch glass into Alastar's hand before daintily placing my own in Prince Liam's with the grace befitting any princess.

"I'd be pleased to dance with you, Your Highness." And I gave him my sweetest and most adorable dimpled smile. He returned it and led me onto the floor. Even though I was about to have what promised to be the most romantic moment of my life, I couldn't resist glancing back at Alastar.

To my surprise, Alastar's expression had twisted into one that was rather sullen and grumpy as he glared after us, arms crossed, seeming rather upset that my most magical happily ever after was about to begin.

CHAPTER 8

Prince Liam was such an accomplished dancer, polished and fluid, just as a proper prince should be. I analyzed every aspect of our dance as he twirled me effortlessly from one step into another. He kept me at a polite distance, his hand—which was thankfully not clammy—clasping mine in a loose grip while his other hand rested lightly at my waist. I waited patiently for the heat of his touch to affect me in some way—whether through ripples or shudders, it varied in books—but I felt nothing from having his hand against my lower back. I frowned. Puzzling.

"Is something wrong, Miss Rosalina?" Prince Liam's blue eyes swirled with concern. Goodness, his eyes were lovely. Everything about him was handsome and regal. Now I needed to see whether our personalities matched.

I smiled. "I'm quite well, Your Highness."

He flashed a dazzling smile that I waited to make me weak at the knees. Nothing yet. Hmm…. "I'm pleased. You're a lovely dancer, Miss Rosalina."

I certainly was. I hadn't spent hours perfecting each move in front of a mirror—twirling with anything I could find, whether a pillow or a broom—for nothing. "Thank you, Your Highness. Your own dancing is exquisite."

He smiled politely and humbly at the acknowledgment, such solid virtues for a prince. "So you're Eileen's best friend?"

"I am." How I thrilled to have such a claim!

"She's a sweet girl," he said. "I met her while escorting my sisters to Aiden's competition for his bride and got to spend a lot of time with her." He glanced towards her and Aiden and sighed wistfully. "I wish I had any hope of experiencing love, but unfortunately my duty to my deceased brother's contract makes such a future impossible."

My heart swelled at his words. Prince Liam clearly wanted a love match. How could I encourage him to break his contract so that he could pursue a relationship with me like he desired?

Our spin across the dance floor put me in view of Eileen again. She sat hand in hand with Aiden, both watching my dance with Prince Liam a bit too closely and warily, as if they suspected I planned on laying a trap to ensnare him right here.

My cheeks warmed at their scrutiny. I hastily tore my gaze away and found it settling on Alastar, who also watched me rather intensely through narrowed eyes, all thoughts of acting as Eileen's guard seemingly forgotten. His expression seemed a bit graver than usual. Strange. The mystery behind his sour mood drew my attention to him again and again as Prince Liam and I twirled across the dance floor.

"Is something bothering you?" Prince Liam asked. "You seem a bit distracted."

"Do I?" Goodness, what was I doing? Here I was dancing with my prince, and I was gawking at the silly guard. I forced myself to look away from Alastar.

"Indeed. Perhaps I need to tell you something witty in

order to make you smile, lest no other woman will want to dance with me, considering they'd be under the false impression I'm a poor dance partner."

I forced myself to smooth out my expression. "You're a wonderful partner, Your Highness."

He grinned. "Be that as it may, I shall still endeavor to make you smile. See that duchess in the emerald dress?" He motioned with his chin to the woman dancing nearby. "She seems unusually pale. Do you think"—he made a show of looking around before leaning in close, lowering his voice to a whisper—"that perhaps she may be a ghost? I believe many of the neglected rooms in the palace are actually haunted. Perhaps she resides in one of those rooms. If we watch her closely, we might see her float up towards the chandelier."

I giggled.

"You have a lovely smile, Miss Rosalina. Still, you seem a bit distracted."

My eyes were once again drawn to Alastar, now openly glaring. Prince Liam followed my gaze and snorted.

"Wow, I've never seen Guard Alastar so sullen."

"He's always sullen," I said.

"Yes, but he's even more so now." Prince Liam's eyes twinkled, as if he found Alastar's strange moodiness amusing. "I suspect I know the reason. It appears I may not inherit the throne after all."

"Why ever not?" He had my attention again. Really, how could it have faltered so frequently? Prince Liam's conversation was quite pleasant, not to mention this really was a lovely waltz.

Prince Liam smirked and glanced towards Alastar again. "Having a royal guard for an enemy makes me concerned that my days are numbered."

"Oh, Alastar wouldn't kill you." The idea was ridiculous, even in the most dramatized story I could come up with.

"He might," Prince Liam said cheerfully. "Especially if I do something like this. Let's experiment." He pulled me closer. My stomach jolted, not the fluttery response I'd always expected to experience when dancing so near my heart's match.

"Please, Your Highness." I tried to subtly wriggle away so a few inches existed between us, all while wondering just what about our proximately had bothered me. Prince Liam paid no attention, too busy looking over my shoulder. He smirked.

"Success. He reached for his sword. He didn't draw it, but his hand is hovering over it rather threateningly. That was certainly interesting. I'd best be careful as I really don't fancy an early death." He flashed a bright smile. My heart fluttered. Finally, a response. It was truly a dazzling smile. "How are you acquainted with Guard Alastar?"

"We're enemies," I said. "He's made it his permanent mission to ruffle me. But I suppose in a way we're also friends." I frowned, analyzing our relationship from all angles. "I'm not sure what we are, to be honest."

Prince Liam cast Alastar another glance. "I think I have a pretty good take on the situation." And he left it at that.

We chatted easily and several times Prince Liam got me to laugh with his wit, but despite our engaging conversation, it was difficult to concentrate when I could feel the heat of Alastar's gaze following our every move. Soon I realized I hadn't experienced the magical connection I'd been waiting for that should have occurred as we danced in one another's arms. Disappointment rather than the flutters of true love filled my gut.

I glared at Alastar again, for he was certainly at fault. He always was. He merely cocked his eyebrow with a challenging look. I scowled. Yes, he'd undoubtedly done something to sabotage my first dance with my future husband on purpose. I wasn't sure *how*, exactly, only that he had.

"Is Alastar troubling you again?" Prince Liam asked, a bit too cheerfully.

"Indeed. He's rather..." I searched for an adequate word but couldn't come up with one that fit him. So I merely sighed. Prince Liam's smile widened.

"I see."

"Do you?" Is this what I'd been waiting for? A connection so strong that two soul mates could sense one another's thoughts?

"I do. Too bad Alastar's on duty. I'm sure he envies me now."

"Why would he?"

"And he's certainly taking great risk ignoring Princess Eileen," Prince Liam continued as if I hadn't spoken, which was rather un-princely of him. "I suppose he can't help it. You really are a lovely dancer, Miss Rosalina. I'm enjoying myself immensely."

And I was, too, even though I was still anticipating *more*. Desperate, I latched on to the subject I knew would create stimulating conversation.

"Your Highness, I've heard you're a lover of stories."

"Certainly, particularly secrets. Would you care to hear some juicy ones about some of our esteemed guests?"

At my enthusiastic nod, Prince Liam launched into several humorous stories that had me laughing with each twirl on the dance floor. When he wasn't entertaining me with his ridiculous tales, he asked me detailed questions about myself that left me no doubt of his interest.

All too soon, the last trills of the waltz faded, signaling the end of our dance. Prince Liam offered a deep bow, his startling blue eyes lingering. My heart leapt. Did we finally have a connection?

"Thank you for the pleasure of this dance, Miss Rosalina. It was a privilege to waltz with so lovely a partner."

I curtsied with all the grace and propriety required of a princess and returned his smile, making sure to angle my head so my darling dimple was clearly visible.

"The pleasure was all mine, Your Highness."

I rose from my curtsy, daintily took Prince Liam's offered hand, and allowed him to escort me off the dance floor. I smiled and nodded at the regal couples we wove through, pleased when their gazes lingered on me. To think that I, Rosalina, was being escorted by a prince at a ball! Oh, this entire experience really was just like a dream.

All too soon we reached the edge of the ballroom. Prince Liam swept into another bow and placed a kiss lightly on the back of my hand. I analyzed how long his lips touched my skin. Did he linger?

He didn't, and before I knew it, he'd released me. "I wish you a pleasant evening, Miss Rosalina. Enjoy the remainder of the ball." And with that, he disappeared into the crowd.

I stared after him, my heart both soaring and sinking. Our first waltz *seemed* to have gone well enough, but his hasty departure was admittedly troubling, especially with no promise of another dance; indeed, his departing words hinted at farewell. But surely he meant to seek me out again for another dance?

"You do realize you can't see His Highness anymore, don't you?"

I gasped and spun around to glare at Alastar, who must have wandered over after my dance ended for the sole purpose of annoying me. "I wasn't staring after Liam. I was merely…pondering."

"You mean plotting?" Up went his eyebrow. "And first names with His Highness already? Things must have gone very well. Was your dance everything you've ever dreamed about?"

I analyzed our dance from every angle. While Prince Liam had been the most polished of partners and the dance itself had been extremely pleasant, I couldn't help but feel it'd been *missing* something. But I certainly wasn't going to tell *him* that.

"It was...a start."

Alastar raised his eyebrow again. "How so? Feel any stirrings? He's so enamored he's already proposed?"

I scowled. "Now you're just making fun of me."

"No, I'm not." As usual, his expression was entirely serious. "You were quite specific on our journey here about the power of dances to bring together true love. I'm curious if the event you've always dreamed about actually occurred as you'd planned. It didn't appear as if anything romantic occurred, but as a bystander perhaps I simply missed it."

He'd voiced the very worry niggling the back of my mind, one I refused to sit down to tea with in order to analyze it further. "You seemed to have been paying a lot of attention."

"And you were paying a lot of attention to my attention. I'd even wager you watched *me* more than your perfect prince."

Heat engulfed my cheeks. I hadn't looked at him *that* often, had I? "You never answered why you were watching me so closely. You really shouldn't have been. You're not being a very good guard."

Alastar actually startled and spun around to search the ballroom for Eileen, as if realizing he'd lost sight of her. He relaxed when he spotted her in Aiden's arms on the dance floor.

His attention returned to me. "I'm performing my other duty of keeping you out of trouble. I also wanted to witness love at first sight. Unfortunately, I wasn't at all impressed."

"What's *that* supposed to mean?"

He frowned thoughtfully. "There didn't seem to be any…spark."

"Of course there was. Just because you failed to see our spark doesn't mean I didn't feel one."

He leaned his elbow against the wall. "And what exactly did you supposedly feel, Miss Rosalina?"

"I—" Again I had no answer. "The dance was quite lovely."

"I see. But the partner left a lot to be desired?"

"He's a prince," I said firmly.

"Is he really? Time to review my royal genealogies."

I glared. "He's handsome, charming, kind, funny, and a wonderful dancer…not to mention he entertained me with stories."

"Ah, your beloved stories. Did you enjoy His Highness's?"

"Immensely." Yet while they'd been entertaining, something had been…missing.

Alastar must have sensed my hesitancy, for his look turned to pity. "I'm sorry it didn't work out, but rest assured that—"

I cut him off with a gasp. "Are you suggesting we're not meant to be together?"

He arched that eyebrow of his. "You mean it's not obvious? Even if you were perfectly matched, you seem quite unenthusiastic about him."

"I am *not*." I folded my arms firmly across my chest, as if the act could protect my heart meant to be given to Prince Liam. "Our first dance might not have gone completely according to plan, but I refuse to give up so easily. True love is worth fighting for."

"Indeed it is," Alastar said solemnly. "So you're still willing to pursue His Highness even after tonight's disappointment?"

I sighed. "Well, there are other ways for my happily ever

after to begin—being saved from an evil curse, or rescued from a fearsome beast…"

Alastar held up his hand. "You stay here; I'll go fetch a dragon. With any luck, Prince Liam will rescue you before you're eaten. If not, then at least it'll make a spectacular show."

A giggle escaped me before I could stop it. Serious expression not faltering, Alastar turned and strode away. I scampered after him and seized his sleeve to tug him to a stop. "Don't disturb the dragon; can you imagine the havoc it would wreak at the ball?"

He glanced back at me, eyebrow lifted. "Good point. So you prefer the curse option? I can fetch my villainy textbook and look up something juicy. Would you prefer to fall into an eternal sleep, be turned into a frog, or be cursed with warts?"

Another giggle wriggled past my lips. "Ew, not warts. I can't become ugly."

"Isn't true love supposed to see one's inner beauty?"

I stared at Alastar as if seeing him for the first time. True, *he* wasn't particularly handsome, but there was something strangely appealing about him all the same that made it difficult for me to look away, especially when he continuously surprised me with his quick banter.

"Are you secretly a romantic, Guard Alastar?"

A blush caressed his cheeks as he cleared his throat and stared at the floor. "One does think about these things from time to time."

"You must have a lot of time to think, considering your position." I looked across the ballroom where another dance was currently underway, a dance which, disappointingly, no one had asked me to join. "Are you bored now?"

"I'm rarely bored, especially now. Even if you weren't so entertaining, I enjoy watching people." He gazed out over the elegant couples, swirling and twirling across the intricate marble floor, their jewels glistening in the flickering candlelight of the chandeliers. "Have you ever considered what each person's story is?"

I beamed. "Always. I love searching for clues to determine what each individual's tale could possibly be."

Alastar nodded towards an elderly couple shuffling a few feet away. "I've been watching that couple for most of the night. What story can you come up for them?"

"You mean you weren't only watching me?"

His fading blush burst to life again. "Considering you're a dear friend of Her Highness, I'm quite invested in your protection." He nodded back towards the couple. "If you enjoy love stories, observe them for a moment."

I did. The elderly man cradled his wife so tenderly while she gazed up at him as if he were the most handsome man in the world, despite age having robbed both of them of their beauty. The wrinkles marring their skin revealed their long life, likely filled with many magical experiences spent together. I sighed wistfully.

Behind them, Eileen spotted us from her place in Aiden's arms on the dance floor. She tapped him on the shoulder and motioned towards us. He glanced over with a knowing smile before he *winked* at me. My heart lurched as I realized what those conspiring looks meant...they believed I had a connection with *Alastar*. My smile melted away.

"What's wrong?" Alastar asked. "Have you spotted something dastardly?"

"I—" My face flared with heat and I found it difficult to look him in the eye. "It's nothing." Eileen and Aiden were wrong. Alastar was most certainly *not* my prince.

Luckily, I was spared any further explanation when the current dance ended and a dashing nobleman approached. "You've been standing here alone too long, lovely lady. Might I have this dance?" He offered his hand.

I wanted to point out that I hadn't been alone; I'd been with Alastar, and even though we hadn't been dancing it had been a rather pleasant interaction. But I really wanted to dance again. After all, this was a ball. I glanced uncertainly at Alastar. He smiled encouragingly.

"Have a good time," he whispered low enough so only I could hear him. "Perhaps *he* will be the one?" He winked. My cheeks burned as I placed my hand in the gentleman's clammy one.

Although the dance he swept me into was pleasant and he was a flawless partner, it wasn't quite magical. Maybe balls weren't all they were cracked up to be. I couldn't help but cast frequent glances towards Alastar, who, as with my dance with Prince Liam, watched me the entire time.

I DIDN'T GET a chance to visit with Alastar for the remainder of the ball, but thankfully I wasn't without partners. While I danced with an unfortunate number of lords and counts who either had clammy hands, bad breath, or two left feet, most of the dances were enjoyable, although all of them lacked the *spark* I'd spent every dance I'd ever attended searching for.

Prince Liam never asked me for a second dance, although I couldn't help noticing he did ask several other ladies more than once. A crushing feeling pressed against my chest at this disappointment. All hope was lost. My future now contained nothing more than spinsterhood and living out the remainder of my lonely, loveless days with a dozen or so cats.

I was just going over potential names for each of my future feline companions when Prince Liam approached me with his dazzling princely smile and proper bow. "Miss Rosalina, would you do me the honor of accompanying me into the midnight feast?"

I gaped at his extended hand, using every ounce of willpower to contain my ecstatic squeal. To think that the Crown Prince of Draceria had asked *me*, Rosalina, to sit with him at the feast! This was an honor far better than any second dance. My story was finally back on its proper course.

I beamed my adorable dimpled smile and curtsied. "I'd be honored, Your Highness."

I placed my hand atop his and allowed him to lead me into the grand banquet hall, nodding to all the guests who bowed and curtsied as we walked by. Prince Liam helped me into my seat directly across from Eileen with the grace of the finest gentleman. I glanced around at those sitting at this end of the table and an excited thrill rippled over me when I realized I sat in the section of *royals*. How fitting I should sit amongst them, considering I was a future queen myself. Ah, bliss!

Prince Liam glanced further down the table to where Princess Lavena sat and smirked as he leaned towards my ear. "Naturally, I was expected to escort her, but you were a much better choice. Thank you for helping me avoid the thorn in my side."

My imaginings about living my life in this spectacular palace after our grand wedding shattered and my elation faded. "Excuse me, Your Highness?"

"I was expected to escort Princess Lavena." He pulled a face. "I'll likely get scolded later for failing to do my duty, but that will be far easier to endure than a meal sitting next to *her*. Really, I can't imagine a lifetime of being shackled to her." He shuddered.

Oh, so it was like *that*. "I see," I said coolly. "So that's why you asked me?"

"You're pleasant company, much more so than *her*. There has to be a way to wriggle out of that arrangement. Do let me know if you come up with any ideas." He stirred our first course of soup with a pondering frown.

I tightened my jaw to keep from crying and sipped my own soup through pursed lips. It took several seething minutes to regain my composure. When I finally managed to do so, I raised my gaze to meet Alastar's, where he stood in his usual place against the wall, his constant presence strangely comforting. He raised an inquiring brow, eyes concerned, and I hastily looked away. I didn't need him mocking my failure to capture my prince.

The feast progressed over multiple courses: soup, salad, cheese, meat—divine cuisine presented on the finest gold-trimmed dishes, their mouthwatering scents rising in the steam to tickle my nose. With each dish Prince Liam easily conversed with those sitting around us and made several friendly comments to me, but I did little to return his efforts, not when he'd used me merely to avoid his unappealing fiancée. The thought twisted my stomach, causing me to lose my appetite. I moodily picked at my citrus roast duck.

Eileen frequently cast me concerned glances. "Are you alright, Rosie dear?" she eventually asked.

I sighed and slumped in an unladylike manner in my seat. I glanced sideways at Prince Liam, currently telling Aiden an animated story as he twirled his fork between his fingers.

"Rosie?"

I couldn't sit here a moment longer, not when I was on the brink of tears. "Do royals throw guests who leave feasts early into the dungeon?"

Understanding filled Eileen's expression; she knew I was serious when I wanted to leave before dessert. "Of course not, Rosie. Are you unwell?"

I nodded. Eileen started to stand, as if she meant to escort me herself, before a sly look eclipsed the concern in her eyes.

She glanced at Alastar and motioned him over. He obediently came.

"Dear Rosie is feeling ill," Eileen whispered to him. "Would you kindly escort her to her room so that she may retire for the night?"

He nodded and bowed before walking around the table towards me. I straightened in my seat, my heart pounding with each step of his approach. "May I escort you to your room, Miss Rosalina?"

That captured Prince Liam's attention. He glanced over, brows furrowed. "Goodness, Miss Rosalina, you're looking a bit pale. Are you alright?"

I forced myself to smile. "No need to concern yourself, Your Highness."

"Shall I escort you to your room?"

Why, so he had an excuse to leave the feast early? I suddenly didn't want to be around him a moment longer, not until I'd had a chance to have a good cry and plot my next step after this unforeseen obstacle.

"I shall be happy to escort Miss Rosalina," Alastar said with far more authority than I thought wise to direct towards a royal, but Prince Liam merely smiled as he settled back in his seat.

"I shan't deprive you of the opportunity; I do want to live another day." He winked cheekily. "I hope you feel better, Miss Rosalina. I look forward to seeing you tomorrow."

I gave Prince Liam a curious look before offering a grateful smile to my rescuer, who was giving the prince a rather fierce glower like he was on the brink of challenging him to a duel. Most puzzling.

"Alastar?"

His attention snapped to me and his expression immediately cleared. He helped me from my seat and escorted me from the dining room. The moment we were in the marble corridors I released a long breath.

"It was a long meal, wasn't it?" he said knowingly.

"The longest." And the walk back would be just as long. I wasn't sure how long I could go without bursting into tears.

He took in my crumpling expression and wordlessly extended his handkerchief. "Shall I look away, Miss Rosalina?"

I managed a breathless laugh. "This is the second time this evening you've helped a damsel in distress. You sure like to keep me on my toes, Alastar; I never know whether I'm dealing with a villain or a gallant knight."

"I'll perform whatever role you need me for, Miss Rosalina, and right now it's clear you need a knight." He tried again to hand me his handkerchief, but I waved it away.

"No thank you, that won't be necessary." We'd reached the grand staircase, which we began to ascend. If I could just hold on a bit longer…I scrambled for a conversation topic, the perfect distraction from my burning tears on the brink of escaping.

When I couldn't think of anything to say, Alastar came to my rescue once again. "I know you're disappointed and I'm deeply sorry about that, but please don't worry; your story is only beginning. Even if one chapter is going poorly, the next one is bound to be full of unexpected surprises."

We finally reached my room, where Alastar bowed, a friendly smile in his eyes as he bade me goodnight. I watched him go until he'd disappeared around the corner, leaving me feeling considerably lighter from a mere stroll. When Alastar wasn't being villainous, he was actually rather sweet.

CHAPTER 9

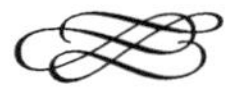

Once again I couldn't sleep, my mind swirling, both with memories of my first royal ball and the fact that I was spending the night in another magnificent palace—and unlike the increasingly familiar Sortileyan palace, the Dracerian palace remained an unexplored mystery. I beamed girlishly into my pillow at the thought.

My smile vanished almost the moment it arrived, and I sighed as the disappointments I'd struggled to keep at bay once again washed over me, the real reason for my frustrating insomnia. Prince Liam was all I'd imagined my prince to be, but not only had our dance been strangely void of any romantic spark, but his escorting me into the feast had merely been to avoid his fiancée. So humiliating!

My misery was on the verge of sinking me into despair when a sudden thought occurred to me—I had been looking at this all wrong. Prince Liam hadn't used me to snub his fiancée; he'd been drawn to me in his moment of need...and wait! I bolted upright with a gasp—his actions had been a cry for help! He wanted *me*, Rosalina, to save him from his detested match. It was all so clear now. How could I have missed it?

I fell back against the pillows, my mind now fully awake and swirling frantically. Despite the thrill of realizing Prince Liam's wishes to be with me over Princess Lavena, he was still entangled within the bounds of honor and contracts, and it would take some doing to help him escape.

I nibbled my nail, considering. There had to be a way for me to get him to override his duty in order to follow his heart...but what? For he *needed* to; of that I was quite certain. We'd finally found one another, and no matter what obstacles got in our way, we would overcome them. I wouldn't fail him again.

Unfortunately, this firm resolution chased sleep even further away. I tossed and turned a good deal more, making the royal bedclothes a tangled mess, before I sat up with another sigh. By the moonlight streaming through the window to illuminate the clock, I could see it was extremely late. Did I dare venture from my room and walk the corridors of this palace at night?

I debated within myself for a moment before finally concluding that wandering the Dracerian palace would make for not only a grand adventure but a juicy recounting later. That decided, I pattered from bed and slipped from my room. Unlike the night I'd explored the Sortileyan palace, I had a specific destination in mind. Where did one go when their story wasn't going exactly as planned? The library, of course.

It took me ten minutes of purposeful walking to realize I hadn't the faintest idea where the library was, and ten minutes more to conclude that I was completely and hopelessly lost.

"Oh bother," I grumbled as I glanced around the shadowy corridor adorned with all manner of ornate rugs, tapestries, suits of armor, paintings, and expensive vases that all seemed identical to the ones found in the past several dozen hallways I'd explored. "Must royals collect so much useless stuff that fails to provide adequate landmarks? It's really quite annoying."

"Are you really blaming the decorations for your latest plight?"

I shrieked and spun around to see Alastar leaning against the wall, arms crossed, eyebrow in its designated position arched above his eye. It raised further at my yell.

"Shh, don't wake the dragons."

I pressed my hand against my frantically pounding heart. "You scared me."

"My apologies," he said gravely. "It wasn't my intention to scare you; hence I've been trying to be as stealthy as possible as I've followed you."

"You've been *following* me?" My heart escalated at the thought.

"No need to be accusing; it wasn't for any vile purpose—although knowing you, you'll undoubtedly construe it as such."

"Then what are you doing up? Are you meeting someone?"

He titled his head. "Am I?"

My settling heart flared to life again. He wasn't, was he?

He chuckled. "I spotted you several minutes ago when you stomped grumbling and cursing past the gallery on the third floor. I knew you were lost and would need my assistance when it finally occurred to you that whatever scene in *The Story of Rosalina* you were currently experiencing wasn't going according to your careful plotting."

I folded my arms across my chest. "How do you know that getting lost in the Dracerian palace wasn't exactly what I had in mind for tonight's adventure?"

Cue his eyebrow lift once more. "Forgive me for misunderstanding; I had no idea you were bent on becoming victim to the labyrinth of these treacherous hallways. I'll leave you to it, then. Good evening, Miss Rosalina." He bowed and walked away, whistling as he did so. It took me a dazed moment to get over the fact that the serious Alastar was *whistling* before panic set in.

"Wait! Please don't go, Alastar." I ran after him and tugged him to a stop. "I lied. Of course I didn't plan on getting lost. Please don't leave me here alone." A strange thrill rippled over me when I touched him, an almost *frightening* feeling. Alastar stared at my fingers curled around his elbow before raising his gaze to mine.

His lips twitched. "I figured as much."

His gaze lowered once more to where I held him, his expression puzzled, as if he couldn't figure out why I clung to him for dear life, despite my reason being obvious: he'd certainly vanish the moment I let him go, leaving me to my own devices.

"Are you seeking an escort back to your room?"

"That would be lovely, but first may we take a detour?" I tugged him down the corridor. "I want to go to the library."

To my surprise, he obediently followed. "What prompted this spontaneous late-night visit?"

"If you must know, I'm researching story elements."

He cocked his eyebrow. "Oh? *The Story of Rosalina* not going as planned?"

"Obviously not, considering Prince Liam isn't in love with me...*yet*."

"Perhaps love doesn't always come immediately," he said. "I believe love happens gradually. Perhaps a single portion of one's heart can be taken at first sight, but it seems to take repeated moments of obtaining one another's heart piece by piece before anyone can finally have the whole of it."

I paused a moment and allowed that rather romantic picture to fill my mind before I shook my head. "That's not how it works in stories."

"This may come as a shock—perhaps you should sit down—but life doesn't play out the way it does in books."

"Then you need to read different books," I said.

"Hence a midnight trip to the library for a bit of research in this latest scheme of yours?"

"Finally, we're on the same page."

"Hmm." He was silent for a moment, as if pondering something deep. "Well, if it's the library we're heading to, is this a bad time to point out that we're going in the wrong direction?"

I glared at him, but the effort was half-hearted. "Why didn't you tell me so earlier?"

He chuckled. "For being thoroughly lost, you seemed quite determined to be the one leading. I was getting the impression that the library was a red herring and you were really luring me to the dungeons to feed me to the dragons, considering that's the direction we're currently headed."

"You can't fool me with that story again; there aren't any dragons in the palace," I snapped impatiently. "And even if there were, feeding you to them would give them indigestion."

He snorted, and for that brief moment he was almost smiling. He rearranged his expression almost immediately, leaving me yearning to see his almost-smile again.

"Good call, for dragons are rather cranky when they've eaten something that doesn't agree with them. They'd likely burn up the entire palace in their rage."

I finally succumbed to the battle I'd been fighting from the moment I'd encountered him tonight and smiled. I wove my arm back through his, nestling a bit closer than I meant to, but unable to pull myself away from his cozy warmth as he turned around and led me up the hallway we'd just come down.

We walked in silence, but it was surprisingly comfortable, as if walking through the palace corridors on the arm of a royal guard in the middle of the night was a perfectly normal thing to do. After several rather pleasant minutes, Alastar glanced down at our connected arms.

"Is there a particular reason you're massaging my arm?"

I startled, noticing too late my fingers had been unconsciously rubbing the crook of his elbow. My cheeks flamed. "I—oh, I had no idea I was doing that." I started to withdraw my arm so that I could cut off the offending body part and bury it and myself alive, but Alastar seized it in order to rewind it back around his.

"It's quite alright; I was just checking. You can leave your hand there." His own hand lingered on top of mine long after he'd put my own back.

Our silence now became unbearable. My face burned as my mind scrambled for an explanation for why I'd been caressing Alastar's *elbow* of all things. While I was properly mortified, Alastar himself seemed perfectly at ease, which only made my embarrassment more acute.

A distraction—I needed a distraction. I grasped on to the first conversation topic I could think of midst my humiliation. "Why are you awake at such an hour?"

"To act as your escort. Every heroine is in need of a gallant knight to protect her from the perils of the palace after midnight."

I tilted my head skeptically. "Is that really the reason?" A strange thrill rippled over me at the thought he'd stayed up this late for *me*.

He glanced down at me with his typical emotionless expression before he sighed and returned his gaze straight ahead. "In truth, I am often awake at night, considering I usually find it difficult to sleep."

"Really?" What a most unexpected dialogue response.

"Let me guess: you believe I was cursed as an infant by an evil witch."

"That's exactly what I was going to say. Perhaps it was the same curse that made it so you couldn't smile."

He chuckled, and it fascinated me just as much as the first time I'd heard it. I found myself smiling again.

"Why can't you sleep? Was it really the curse of an evil witch?"

He shrugged. "It's as good an explanation as any, although I suspect it's because I keep such sporadic hours as a guard that my internal clock has become skewed. I used to try and fight it, but now on nights when sleep eludes me, I go on long walks instead."

"That's a rather dull reason. I much prefer thinking that you were cursed by an evil witch." I tapped my lips thoughtfully. "Or perhaps you wander the corridors at night because you're a secret spy against the crown. Your current quest: steal a stone from the Dracerian vault, a stone that allows you to manipulate the minds of others. Your target: the Prince and Princess of Sortileya themselves…"

I launched into an epic story, complete with all manner of obstacles and grisly details. By the time I'd finished, Alastar was grinning.

"That was spectacular, Rosalina."

His praise made me feel light and fluttery. "Why, thank you. I promise I won't inform Aiden and Eileen of your secret quest."

"I would appreciate that, considering I don't want to lose my post guarding Her Highness. Ah, it appears we've arrived at our destination." He paused outside some double doors and held one open with a bow. "After you, Miss Rosalina."

I stepped into the vast library and tipped my head back with a contented sigh as I took in all the books stretching from the floor to the domed-glass ceiling, where moonlight tumbled through to bathe the shelves in silvery light. A balcony twisted around the second story to provide access to the volumes on the upper shelves.

"Libraries are one of my favorite places," I breathed. "So many books. I'm itching to explore."

I wandered up and down the rows, stroking the spines reverently, as if a mere touch would allow me to hear each book's whispers of the stories contained within its pages. Alastar eventually appeared beside me with a flickering candle. I smiled my thanks and returned to browsing the books.

"Aren't books wonderful? It's so magical how each volume contains stories written with the same twenty-six letters, yet the tales of adventure, mystery and romance are so varied. One never knows quite what to expect when one turns the page, but whatever it is--and no matter what obstacle the heroine encounters--she experiences a happily ever after in the end." I sighed contentedly.

I glanced at Alastar to gauge his reaction to my monologue; his serious expression had softened to one that was quite tender. "Is that why you believe life is a story? You want a happily ever after?"

"Life *is* a story," I said. "Each day we live adds another page to our tale, each bringing unexpected surprises. Everyone you interact with is a character, each adventure a chapter, and to receive a happily ever after, one must do all in one's power to seize it. That's what I'm quite determined to do, despite there being an unnecessary complication."

"You mean the fact that Prince Liam didn't instantly fall in love with you?"

"Exactly." I sighed. "I don't quite understand it. After all, we're perfectly compatible, not to mention I'm cute, sweet, charming...everything a hero can expect from a heroine. Did I do something wrong?"

I shyly peeked up at him through my lashes. His expression softened further as he reached a hesitant hand out and rested it on top of mine, causing a strange flutter to fill my stomach.

"No, Rosalina, you didn't do anything wrong. It's just that love can't be forced."

"I'm not forcing it," I said. "Prince Liam has given me enough glimpses of his true feelings for me to know that the seed of love has already been planted. It just needs to be nourished in order to blossom, allowing us to be together after I save him from his betrothal."

"Just remember that even if your story doesn't go as you expect, that doesn't necessarily mean it's not a happily ever after." He squeezed my hand before releasing it, leaving my fingers itching for him to touch them again.

Silence settled over us as I continued perusing the shelves, but it was difficult to concentrate with my awareness of Alastar's presence as he dutifully followed me with the candle, not looking the least bit sleepy or impatient.

"Have you read this?" I pulled my favorite book from the shelf and tipped it so he could see its title.

"*Tales of Magic and Romance to Enchant the Heart?*" Up went his eyebrow as his gaze met mine. "Must have missed that one."

"Oh Alastar, that's the most tragic news I've heard all day." I slammed the book into his chest. He *oofed*. "Your current quest should be to become less stuffy, and your first assignment in attaining that goal is to read this."

He flipped it open and scanned the contents, his expression twisting as he did so. "These look...delightful." He didn't sound the least bit enthused.

"They are. This one is my favorite." I traced my finger down the page to point to "The Tale of a Princess and a Magical Wishing Well."

"Princesses and wishes. That should keep me on the edge of my seat."

I whacked him. "Stop sounding like you're about to be tortured. It's a delightful story."

He appeared doubtful. "Is it sappy?"

I wrinkled my forehead. "Meaning…?"

"Is there a lot of ridiculous staring into each other's eyes and kissing and whatnot?"

I twisted a lose strand of my golden hair around my finger and avoided his eyes. "I don't recall."

He groaned. "That means there *is*."

"Stop complaining and just read it," I said.

"I'm afraid I won't be able to fulfill that wish of yours, or do you really intend for me to steal this from the Dracerian royal library?"

I nibbled my fingernail, deliberating. "Very well, you'll have to borrow my copy. I'll bring it the next time I visit."

"Can't wait," he said wryly.

I took the book from him and scanned the table of contents. My breath caught as my gaze traced over a story title I'd forgotten about: "The Tale of the Witch and the Love Potion." I gawked at it as the beginning of an idea flickered to life.

Alastar groaned. "Uh oh, something is brewing in that mind of yours, and I'm almost afraid to ask what it could possibly—"

"Alastar," I shrieked. "That's it!" I tapped the story that had caused my brilliant epiphany. His brow furrowed.

"'The Tale of the Witch and the Love Potion?' Are you a witch, Rosalina?"

"No, but I do have a recipe for a love potion."

His mouth fell open. "You can't be serious. Does such a thing even exist?"

"Of course it does. My family has a book of magical recipes you bake into desserts, and one is a love potion. It's such an obvious solution I can't believe I didn't consider it earlier."

His puzzlement twisted into alarm, and if I hadn't been so fascinated to see him openly showing emotion, his expression would have annoyed me.

"Oh no. Please don't tell me you're truly considering..."

"I certainly am," I said smugly as I slid the book back in its place on the shelf. "I'm going to brew up a love potion to give to Prince Liam so he can have the strength to overcome his arranged engagement in order allow himself to fall madly in love with me."

CHAPTER 10

Goodness, Prince Liam was remarkably attentive this morning. He must have sensed that I'd concocted the most delicious plan that would allow us to finally be together, meaning our hearts were already beginning to connect. He'd scarcely spoken to anyone else throughout breakfast, engaging me in an interesting discussion of books we'd each read as we dined on the delectable spread. With each of Prince Liam's coy smiles and flirtatious winks, any lingering doubts concerning his feelings vanished —this was the behavior of a man who'd found his true love. How fortunate that woman was *me*.

I dreaded my upcoming departure—how tragic that I was being torn from my love so soon after we'd just found one another—but we'd no sooner finished breakfast than Prince Liam gave me a dashing smile that caused my breath to hitch.

"It's a shame you're leaving so soon. I've thoroughly enjoyed your company."

My heart became aflutter with excitement. He loved spending time with me and dreaded our parting! "I feel the same, Your Highness. If only I could remain longer."

He twirled his fork as he leaned back in his seat. "Perhaps that can be arranged." He winked at me, causing my settling heart to flare to life again. Oh, he was definitely interested. This was only confirmed when he swiveled to face Eileen and Aiden. "Rosalina hasn't had the privilege of a tour. Might I give her one before your departure?"

Aiden rolled his eyes. "Really, Liam, you want to subject her to your infamous grand tour?"

Prince Liam pretended to look affronted. "Infamous? Just subject yourself to a tour given by the servants—or, if you're brave enough, my father—and you'll better understand how thrilling mine is. Theirs will lull you to sleep with their rambles about every dull fact from past royals, whereas mine is full of all manner of juicy secrets and exciting stories." He leaned closer to me and lowered his voice. "How about it, Rosalina? A private tour, during which I'll show you all the secrets of the palace?"

I could scarcely breathe with him so near. I found myself lost in those eyes of his. Oh, but he was incredibly handsome; he'd completely cast me under his spell. I mutely nodded my consent.

"Excellent. I knew you were one for adventure." He stood and offered his arm. I nearly knocked my chair over in my eagerness to accept it, my hand curling perfectly around his elbow. I smiled in anticipation and was pleased when he returned it. "Shall we?" He led me from the dining room, making a special effort to pass a glowering Alastar on the way out.

I couldn't help looking back at him. I hadn't had a chance to speak with him since he'd kindly escorted me back to my room the evening before. "Alastar looks upset."

"Does he?" Prince Liam glanced over his shoulder and smirked. "He does. Poor bloke, forced to stand around all day while I get to escort a beautiful maiden. He undoubtedly envies me."

I became fluttery once more. I, Rosalina, was the beautiful maiden on Prince Liam's arm! Despite the sheer magic of my circumstances, Alastar's scowl nagged at me for the first several corridors until it faded away as Prince Liam launched into his tour.

"Now, you may think this is an ordinary hallway," he said mysteriously. "But this particular hallway happens to be haunted."

A delighted thrill rippled up my spine. "Haunted, you say?"

"Yes. Strange noises emanate from it every night, decorations are often discovered mysteriously rearranged...clearly, it's the work of ghosts, and I have a theory as to which type of ghosts. Would you like to hear it?"

"Absolutely." I fluttered my eyelashes and was pleased the gesture was well received; his grin widened as he leaned down to whisper into my ear.

"I find it highly probable that two of Draceria's past queens are having a squabble even beyond the grave about how this particular corridor should be decorated."

I giggled and he seemed pleased he'd gotten me to laugh. And why shouldn't he? Surely a man enjoyed making the woman he cared for happy.

The tour continued. Prince Liam showed me all sorts of rooms, each accompanied by a story told with theatrical gestures that I doubted could be found in any of the royal histories, but which delighted my imagination. He told me of dramatic battles, scandalous secrets, unsolved mysteries... even the simplest rooms had a captivating tale attached to it. I was certain that there was no place more fascinating than His Highness's home, soon to be *my* home.

Prince Liam's storytelling was interrupted when, upon

leaving a parlor that was said to contain a map to a hidden treasure woven in an ancient tapestry, we spotted Princess Lavena at the end of the hallway. He immediately tugged me behind the thick drapes of a tucked-away alcove.

We were forced to stand rather close due to the confined space. Heat pulsed between us and it became difficult to breathe. I peeked up at His Highness, expecting him to be giving me the smoldering look I'd always read about heroes giving beautiful maidens. Perhaps he'd use the opportunity to steal a kiss?

But no. He wasn't looking at me, but trying to subtly peer through the slit in the curtains to watch his unwanted fiancée. A minute crawled by, and when I was certain I'd faint from our proximity, he released a whooshing breath of relief.

"She's gone. Thank goodness she didn't spot us. Disaster averted." He led me out from behind the drapes and re-looped my arm through his.

"You really dislike her, don't you?" I said.

He scowled. "There's no one I dislike more. She's a vile, spoiled woman who will make my life a misery the moment we take our vows and become bound to one another. No man deserves such a sentence."

My heart wrenched. No, he couldn't marry her! He deserved someone better than that...one who would love and cherish him as I would. "Is there no way out of it?"

"Other than her demise? I'm afraid not. Not that I haven't tried."

"Perhaps if you fell in love with someone else, you'd be allowed to marry her instead?" I smiled up at him, hoping he'd see that *I* was the woman he was meant to fall in love with.

"In an ideal world, that would be the perfect plan," he said. "Perhaps you and I should elope and I'll finally be free."

He winked at me before leading me into a state room, but I scarcely heard whatever humorous story he rattled off about the royal who'd commissioned this room, my mind eclipsed by his recent words.

Me. He wanted to marry *me*. He'd essentially just *proposed.* I thought I'd float away in my joy. To think I was so close to becoming a princess, living my happily ever after in a palace with my prince. Oh, bliss!

The rest of the tour passed in a daze, and all too soon Prince Liam returned me to Aiden and Eileen, who'd spent their wait conversing with Prince Nolan of Lyceria and Prince Liam's sisters.

Prince Liam released my arm with obvious reluctance. "I very much enjoyed my time with you, Miss Rosalina."

"As did I, Your Highness."

He flashed his princely smile. "I wouldn't expect anything else." He glanced sideways towards Princess Lavena, who watched us through narrowed eyes. He glared right back before pressing a lingering kiss on my hand. "I eagerly look forward to our next meeting."

I stared after him as he left, my heart soaring at his romantic parting words. I scarcely noticed Eileen sidle up to me. "I take it you enjoyed his tour?"

"Oh Eileen, it was magical." I pressed my hand to my heart with a wistful sigh. "He's so...so..." Words couldn't express how perfect the morning had been, what with the prince's attentions...and his near marriage proposal!

"He is charming," Eileen said. "I'm glad you enjoyed yourself."

Enjoyed wasn't an adequate enough word to describe the bliss I was feeling. I followed Eileen and Aiden to the waiting carriage in a daze, floating with each step. I was jerked rudely back to earth when Alastar helped me into the carriage with a tight, almost painful assisting grip that compelled me to look at him.

I frowned at his glower. "What's wrong, Alastar?"

"How was your *grand tour*?" he asked drily. I lifted my eyebrows in surprise, but nothing could dampen what had likely been the best morning of my life.

I beamed as the wondrous memories returned to dance across my mind. "Positively wonderful."

His eyes narrowed. "I see."

"His Highness is the most charming man I've ever met, not to mention humorous and incredibly handsome and— "

He snorted. "Yes, you've mentioned how handsome he is. Many times." He clambered into the carriage after me and slammed the door before settling back in his seat, arms crossed and glaring.

I frowned at this grumpy Alastar, both fascinated by his open display of emotion and rather annoyed by it. Why was he always so moody? Was he trying to ruin my perfect day?

I exchanged a puzzled look with Aiden and Eileen, who were looking at Alastar with a mixture of confusion and pity. No answers would come from them. Not that I needed them. Alastar wasn't my concern; my prince was. As the carriage rolled out of the palace gates, I closed my eyes and repeatedly relived the memory of the grand tour with Prince Liam, revisiting every single detail, especially His Highness's smiles and the sweet way he'd looked at me—as if I was his heart's match. I sighed wistfully. Perfect.

Alastar's dark tone pierced my daydreams. "His Highness is nothing but a flirt."

I opened my eyes to glare at him, but before I could retort, Alastar continued.

"His attention towards you was nothing special. I've witnessed His Highness's behavior on many occasions, and he never misses the opportunity to pay attention to a pretty girl."

"Alastar's right," Aiden said. "While his intentions are innocent, I wouldn't read too much into Liam's attention."

"He paid me more than a bit of attention," I snapped. After all, he'd essentially proposed.

"Then he undoubtedly felt guilty about upsetting you last evening and was trying to make it up to you," Alastar said.

No, it was very obvious that he yearned for me to rescue him from his arranged engagement so that he could marry me, his true love, and nothing Alastar said would cause me to doubt what I knew to be the truth. He didn't know what he was talking about; after all, he hadn't witnessed the tender moments the prince and I had shared.

Ignoring him, I re-immersed myself in my lovely daydreams, this time lingering on the thrill I'd experienced being pressed so closely to him while we'd been hiding from his dreaded fiancée, a moment that had been followed by his romantic words: *"Perhaps you and I should elope and I'll finally be free."*

I sighed happily. We were meant to be together. And I now knew how to save him from his arranged marriage. The love spell was definitely the solution. Nothing else would be strong enough for him to stray from his duty and follow his heart.

I couldn't wait to return to the bakery and begin this newest quest—securing the heart of my prince.

THE ONLY CONSOLATION in being forced to leave magnificent palaces and return to my dull life was I would now have the chance to obtain our family's magical recipe book. Upon my return to Arador, it took three days before the opportunity to steal my loot from its locked cabinet finally arrived.

The bakery had just closed and Mother and Father had left for market, leaving me, Master Thief, the perfect moment to pick the locked cupboard with my hairpin. Unfortunately, there were always foes lurking to dissuade a heroine from her goal—in this case, my pesky older brother. Before I could even sneak into the kitchen and begin my heist—

"What are you up to, Rosebud?" Ferris stood in the doorway of the parlor, watching me with suspicious eyes as I wriggled with impatience to make my move to snatch the book of magical desserts from its hiding place.

"Nothing," I said hastily.

His eyes narrowed. "I highly doubt that. The mischievous Rosalina is never up to *nothing*."

I locked my jaw to keep my swarm of brilliant retorts from escaping their prison and causing trouble. Allowing him to goad me into one of our epic fights—which ranged in length from hours to occasionally days—would rob precious time from my quest. I had a happily ever after to achieve.

Without a word, I picked up my copy of *Tales of Magic and Romance to Enchant the Heart* and walked right past him to sit on the parlor chair. I turned to "The Tale of the Witch and the Love Potion" for inspiration. I curled up in front of the hearth with a plate of day-old cherry tarts and immersed myself in my story.

Unfortunately, I couldn't shake Ferris so easily. He leaned against the wall and watched me for a good ten minutes before he finally straightened with a sigh. "This is boring. I'm off to my mate's."

"Have fun," I said as I casually turned my page. He slowly backed from the room, and a minute later I heard the jingle of the front door. I waited several minutes more before I crept over to peer through the slit in the drapes. No sign of him. Excellent. I scampered into the kitchen and careened right into Ferris.

"Ah ha, I knew you were up to something."

It took every ounce of discipline to school my features. Older brothers were the worst. "You haven't left yet?" I made a show of putting on the kettle on the hearth to serve as my alibi in venturing into the kitchen. "Would you like some tea before you go?"

Ferris continued to frown at me before sighing once again. "Fine, I give. I don't care what you're up to, even though you have that 'Rosalina is about to make trouble' gleam in your eye. I'm leaving now, for real."

"Have a good time." When he left, I tiptoed to the kitchen window to watch until he disappeared down the road. Finally. That delay had taken too many unnecessary pages of my story.

After a successful lock-picking, I pulled *Enchanted Sweets and Delights* from its hiding place and took it to my room. I sat cross-legged on my bed, eased it open on my lap, and frantically turned the pages, searching, searching...there! "A Spell of Love." I grinned. Perfect.

My smile faltered as I scanned the page. Goodness, what a complicated recipe. The list of ingredients was vast, many rather unusual. I could raid my parents' stock for the more common ones, and a few might be found in the Forest, but the others...I nibbled my fingernail as my gaze lingered on some of the rare flowers. Perhaps those could be found in the Sortileyan palace gardens, which I was fortunate to have access to.

It'd likely take at least a month before I succeeded in my quest. What a bother. And I'd been hoping to be able to whip the spell up this afternoon so I could take it with me on my next visit to the palace.

~

By the time Eileen and Aiden invited me for another stay two agonizingly long weeks later, I'd managed to procure over half the ingredients, all carefully measured in labeled jars. After our usual hug in greeting, Eileen's brow furrowed as she took in my bulging satchel.

"What do you have there, Rosie?"

I grinned and pulled out *Enchanted Sweets and Delights*, having been forced to lug it from the bakery since the book was enchanted with a spell that prevented me from copying any of the recipes out, which would have been so much easier. "I have a plan."

Eileen frowned. "Oh no, not *that* book."

I pouted. "Why the wary tone? You know this book is perfect for helping achieve happy endings, considering we baked truth cakes from it for your own romance."

Eileen blushed at the reminder, but her firm countenance didn't waver. "While those admittedly worked, magic is still rather dangerous to meddle with. What are you planning on baking?"

I flipped to my bookmarked recipe. She gasped.

"Oh, Rosie, you can't possibly be serious."

"Of course I am," I said. "I need to do all I can to ensure my happily ever after—hey!" Eileen had seized my book and proceeded to show the recipe to Aiden before I could snatch it back.

His eyes widened. "Would such a recipe actually work?"

"From personal experience with goods baked from this book, it likely will," Eileen replied. "And thus we can't risk her even trying. You do realize who this love spell is intended for, don't you?"

Aiden's mouth fell open. "Rosalina, you're not seriously considering—"

"Of course I am," I repeated, prickled at the negative reception my ingenious plan was receiving from my best friend and her husband. From his usual place against the wall, I also sensed *that guard*'s disapproval, but I didn't even spare him a glance.

"You can't spell Liam," Aiden stated firmly. "Manipulating anyone's heart is dishonorable enough, let alone that of a royal bound to a political contract."

I ignored this argument, for he was unaware of the connection Prince Liam and I already shared, especially during his humorous tour of the Dracerian palace, where it was clear he was beginning to realize how perfect we were for one another.

I snatched my book back and scanned the recipe. "While I've successfully acquired half of these ingredients"—I patted my stuffed satchel—"some will admittedly be a bit more difficult. Despite that obstacle, I have no doubt I'll succeed."

"Rosalina..." Aiden's tone was hardening. I continued to ignore him.

"The entire process of tracking these down makes this just like a real quest, a natural part of any story. I predict it'll take no more than a few weeks. Is Prince Liam scheduled to visit within that timeframe?"

"*Rosalina*, I'm serious. You will not spell Prince Liam."

I snapped the book shut and pressed my hand to my hip. "I'm your wife's best friend and thus don't deserve to be scolded by your Dark Prince persona, Aiden."

He sighed and rubbed his temples.

"Don't worry, dear, I'll talk to her." Eileen rested her hand on his shoulder and his hardened expression softened at her single touch. He reached up and squeezed her hand before returning his wary glance to me.

"I'll leave your mischief in my wife's capable hands. If you'll excuse me, I have a meeting to attend. I'll join you the moment it finishes." He kissed Eileen goodbye, and despite my annoyance at his using his Dark Prince wiles on me, it warmed my heart to see his usual doting on my dearest friend.

"I'm so glad I'm not expected to attend that meeting," Eileen said when Aiden left. She looped her arm through mine. "How about a walk through the gardens?"

Perfect, an opportunity to search for some of the needed flowers for my love spell. "A stroll sounds lovely. Just let me grab something from my room first." Carrying that enchanted golden ball would be the perfect lucky trinket to carry during my quest to find ingredients for my love spell.

Once I was back—the bauble safely in my pocket—we were forced to walk past *that guard* while exiting the parlor. I used the opportunity to finally steal my first glance at him since arriving. He was frowning with disapproval. No surprise. He leaned down to my ear as we passed him, the warmth of his breath caressing my neck, causing me to shiver.

"You can't force true love, Rosalina."

His words pierced my heart. For some reason, his disapproval bothered me the most.

CHAPTER 11

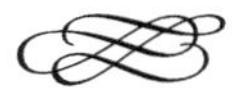

"You can't really be serious, Rosie," Eileen said the moment we stepped out into the glorious sunshine and blossom-scented air.

"I most certainly am."

"Then I must do my best-friend duty and talk you out of this nonsense before you create an epic mess for yourself."

She led me down a cobblestone path that wove through manicured flowerbeds of blossoming lilies, irises, and buttercups, but the beauty of our surroundings did little to soften her disapproval.

Several ladies of the court also out strolling nodded politely to Eileen as they walked past. She waited until we were out of earshot before continuing. "Surely you must realize that forcing someone into thinking they're in love with you is not only morally wrong but would be completely unsatisfying."

"If he didn't care for me at all, then it would be," I said. "I'm merely encouraging affections that already exist between us."

Eileen frowned. "I hate to be frank, but I didn't notice any connection between you two at the ball. "

I flinched at the painful reminder that what was supposed to have been the most romantic night of my life hadn't turned out like I'd dreamed it would.

"I admit that at first I was rather disappointed, but I later realized that as one of the hosts, Prince Liam had a duty to attend to his other guests. But he did escort me into the feast, a very telling sign of his interest. And did you see how he doted on me during breakfast the following morning? He did it even more during our private tour of the Dracerian palace." Not to mention he'd essentially proposed.

Eileen laid a gentle hand on my arm, as if about to impart terrible news. "I did, Rosie, but I'm afraid the attention he gave you wasn't any different from the attention I've seen him give other women. You're misinterpreting his personality to fit what you *want* it to mean, when really being friendly is just his way."

My stomach jolted at her words, but I refused to listen to them. She was wrong—she *had* to be. "I can tell the difference between when a man is being charming and when he's being flirty, and Prince Liam was the latter."

Eileen frowned skeptically. "If you're so certain, then why are you brewing up a love spell?"

"Because he's being slow in confessing his love, and strong heroines take their story into their own hands," I said. "The spell is merely to encourage him to choose love; I wouldn't give it to him if I didn't believe he felt something for me."

"You seem determined to make yourself fit with Liam solely because he's a prince," she said.

"Because marrying a prince is the most incredible thing that can happen in any story. You should know, considering it happened in yours."

"Yes, but I didn't fall in love with a prince; I fell in love with Aiden."

"In your case, it turned out to be the same thing."

She sighed. "Believe me, him being a prince was an unfortunate turn of events."

I gaped at her, baffled at such a ridiculous comment. "Well, if someone like you—who didn't even want to marry a prince—married one, then why can't I? The village storyteller even said so."

"The storyteller?" She rolled her eyes. "Oh Rosie, don't be ridiculous, you know that dear woman is called the storyteller for a reason. Thus you shouldn't take any predictions she makes seriously."

"She said you were alive and you are," I said. "If she was right about that, then she's right about my finding a *prince*. That was the word she used. My story will have the same outcome as yours."

Eileen pursed her lips and for a blissful moment dropped the subject entirely. Unfortunately, I couldn't get away from her meddling so easily.

"I watched you for most of the ball, during which both Aiden and I noticed you *do* have a connection with someone."

She glanced behind us. Curious, I did too, and saw Alastar following us from his discreet guarding distance. I gasped and snapped my head back round, my cheeks already flaring with heat.

"*Him*? Don't be ridiculous, Eileen."

Her expression was entirely serious. "I'm not."

"There wasn't any connection between us."

"Really? Because you spent a lot of time looking at him, talking with him, and even *laughing* with him. It was the first time I've ever seen him laugh."

I snorted. "Which is exactly why he's not the man for me; he's far too serious."

"I wouldn't discount him so quickly, especially when you can't deny you're drawn to him. What other explanation do you have for your behavior towards him at the ball?"

The heat already filling my cheeks burned. "I—we were just...plotting together."

Eileen raised her eyebrow and I hated the reminder of that guard, whom I was quite determinedly doing my best *not* to think about. "*Plotting*?"

"Yes, making up stories together. He...plays along."

Eileen's lips twitched, another reminder of Alastar. Was she mimicking his quirks on purpose just to aggravate me? "If that's not a connection, dear Rosie, I don't know what is."

I shook my head. "He's just a guard. He's *your* guard."

"I don't mind if you have feelings for my guard."

"*Feelings*? That's absurd. I feel nothing towards *him*. He's my foe." I frowned. No, I didn't consider him that, not anymore. "Or perhaps my friend. Nothing more."

"Friendship is a start," Eileen said brightly. "And if you're anything like I was, it may take you some time to realize your feelings extend deeper."

"No time in the world would make me realize nonexistent feelings," I snapped. "You're just trying to sway me from spelling Prince Liam, but consider your efforts thwarted."

Eileen sighed. "Rosie, you must realize that spelling Liam could result in several political ramifications for both Draceria and Sortileya. You simply can't go through with it."

I nodded simply to appease her and it worked, for nothing more was said as we thankfully moved on to other topics as we strolled the grounds for an hour. Considering we were no longer discussing specific guards I *didn't* have feelings for—although I admittedly remained acutely aware of his trailing presence—we passed a very pleasant afternoon.

Aiden eventually returned. Eileen's entire expression lit

up as she ran up the path to meet him. They embraced before Eileen looped her arm through his and walked on ahead, leaving me alone.

Well, not entirely alone.

I allowed the royal lovebirds to walk farther ahead before I darted down a side path, withdrawing my scribbled list of ingredients and referring to the included illustrations, an aid that would help me track down some of the more unfamiliar flowers. The thrill of the quest made it like a game.

I consulted my list. Seven different-colored petals plucked from azalea flowers. Azaleas—how perfect for a love spell, for they not only symbolized femininity but were often used to showcase one's romantic feelings. Luckily, I didn't have to search long before I discovered the flowers growing in patches in the next garden over. After waiting for a group of strolling nobles to disappear down the path, I started snipping away at the myriad of colors.

"I saw that."

I yelped as I spun around to face my discoverer. "I didn't do it."

Alastar cocked his eyebrow as he took in the garden sheers in my hand, evidence of my crime. I hastily shoved them behind my back, but it was too late; I'd been caught red-handed.

"I didn't do it," I repeated, my voice cracking in betrayal.

Alastar made a show of glancing around the garden, checking for other potential suspects. We were alone.

"Perhaps I'm seeing things, Miss Rosalina, but I could have sworn I just witnessed you snipping one of the royal plants with those sheers you're now determinedly hiding behind your back. Correct me if I'm wrong, but I do believe this is sufficient evidence to prove that you *did* do it."

I gnawed at my fingernail as I tried to come up with a

plausible cover story. "What are you doing spying on me anyway? Aren't you supposed to be guarding Eileen?"

"They wanted time alone and told me to take a break."

I pressed my hands to my hips. "And you chose to spend it watching me?"

A light blush tickled his cheeks. "I wasn't spending my break *watching* you; I was merely checking up on you. The way you scampered off naturally raised my suspicion, one that I can clearly see was valid."

Alastar removed my satchel from my shoulder and peered inside. His eyebrow rose, for my bag was stuffed with the pilfered azaleas. Thank goodness the golden sphere I'd borrowed from my room was in my pocket else I'd be in even more trouble; Alastar already had ample evidence to arrest me.

I groaned, burying myself and my guilt in my hands. "It's the dungeon, isn't it? I'm going to wither away in the darkness for the rest of my tragic days."

"Not to worry, Rosalina, Prince Aiden is merciful to those who pilfer from his gardens. Your punishment will likely only be—Rosalina?"

Embarrassingly enough, I'd started *crying*. "Please don't take me to the dungeon."

Alastar's expression immediately softened. "Of course I won't, Rosalina. I'm sorry I frightened you; I thought we were playing out another story."

I peeked up at him through my blurry tears. He handed me a handkerchief, but I made no motion to take his offering.

"You missed your cue," he said. "You're supposed to accept a handkerchief when a noble knight offers it to a lady in distress." He pressed the handkerchief into my hand, but I immediately released it, letting it flutter to the ground. He sighed as he stooped down to retrieve it and gently wiped away my tears himself. "I can't keep up with when we're in a story and when we're not. I thought you were playing. I didn't mean to frighten you. Please be assured that, stealing from the royal gardens or not, you mean too much to Her Highness for the prince to ever punish you. After all, you're practically royalty."

I managed a half smile. "You're right, I am."

"Exactly." He finished drying my eyes and pressed his handkerchief back into my hand. This time I kept it, now inexplicably wanting to cherish this token forever. Alastar searched my face, his own anxious. "Are you alright?"

I nodded. "As exciting as I'm sure a sojourn in the dungeon would have been to read about in any other story, I'm quite relieved it won't become a setting in my fairy tale. Dungeons are too dreary for innocent, beautiful damsels such as myself."

"Beautiful, yes—but innocent?" Alastar's lips twitched.

"Of course I'm innocent; I'm sure the head gardener would attest to that. Certain perks come from baking his favorite apricot bars." I brightened hopefully. "Are apricot bars your favorite treat?"

"I'm afraid not."

I slumped. How disappointing. Would I ever figure it out?

Alastar once again looked in my bag of stolen plants. "Whether the head gardener turns a blind eye to your explorations or not, I must do my duty as a royal guard and investigate the crime I witnessed. What's been going on here?"

"Isn't it obvious? I'm *questing*."

I again started walking up the garden path, but with his much longer stride, he easily caught up. "You can't force love. It's impossible. Even if your spell miraculously works—which frankly, I have my doubts—then the love it creates would be concocted by magic and wouldn't be real. Is that really what you want?"

"Of course it'll be real," I said. "For Liam is my prince. The spell will simply nourish the budding feelings he already has for me so he has the strength to break away from his duty to his engagement contract in order to marry me instead."

Alastar rolled his eyes. "Rosalina, this isn't a game. If you managed to succeed, not only would you be forcing an unsuspecting man to give his heart away not of his own volition, but you'll create a mess with great political ramifications. You're truly determined to be the villain in your story."

I skidded to a stop with a gasp. "You take that back."

He folded his arms across his chest. "No. I won't, not when it's true."

I stomped my foot. "Take it back."

"No."

I glared at him. "How dare you cast me as the villain, Alastar."

"You're casting yourself in such a role. Now, if you don't mind us taking a brief detour down this pathway here"—he took my elbow and gently turned me onto the path in question, which twisted alongside a well-maintained hedge—"I can check on Her Highness."

"She's with the prince and hence doesn't need your protection."

"Be that as it may, I'm still on duty." It only took a moment to find Eileen, curled up beneath a blossoming cherry tree with Aiden, snuggling and…I smiled in delight. They were stealing kisses midst their conversation.

Alastar nodded to himself before leading us away. "She seems to be doing well."

I giggled at such an understatement. "Indeed; I've heard kissing is quite nice, not that I would know." I sighed. "It's one of the greatest disappointments of my own fairy tale to have never been kissed."

Alastar guided us down a pathway lined with tulips in a

rainbow of colors. "If I understand how the delightful mind of Rosalina works, the reason you haven't been kissed is because you're waiting for true love."

I pressed my hands to my hips. "Is that a problem?"

"No need to get ruffled. Believe it or not, I admire that sentiment."

"Do you feel the same way? Have you ever kissed anyone?" And a strange anxiousness tightened in my chest at the thought that Alastar had indeed kissed someone before.

He tilted his head. "Have I?"

Oh no, he had. I sharpened my glare. "That's what I asked. Have you?" Oh, please say that he hadn't.

"Would it bother you if I had?"

An inexplicable wave of emotion crashed over me, sending an unexpected pang to my heart. "You *have*? Who?" My mind worked frantically before settling on a likely woman. "Is it Eileen's handmaiden?" She was rather beautiful. "Not that it matters," I added hastily. "I'm merely curious."

He titled his head, studying me with a rather intense expression before understanding lit his eyes. "Ah, I see." He started walking again, leaving me staring after him. It took me a dazed moment to get my legs moving so I could hurry after him.

"See what?" I demanded the moment I caught up to him, panting. Of course he didn't answer. I seized his arm and dug my heels into the path to pull him to a stop. "For goodness' sake, answer me, Alastar. What's the meaning behind your cryptic response just now?"

Amusement danced in his gaze. "What do you think, Miss Rosalina?"

"I haven't the faintest idea, hence I'm demanding to be told at once."

He became preoccupied with a bush of blossoming roses,

tracing his fingertip along the petals of a pink rose with the utmost concentration before he finally raised his lit gaze to mine. "I simply…have a hunch."

"About what?" I pressed. His lips twitched as he returned his attention to the flower, now tracing its stem.

"That, my Rosie flower, is a secret, and correct me if I'm wrong, but you don't strike me as one who's particularly good at keeping secrets."

A strange pleasure rippled over me at his use of my nickname before I pushed it away and tightened my jaw. It was true that I was a terrible secret keeper. How could one keep silent when one had a juicy story just dying to be told? It was impossible. But I couldn't let Alastar know that, else I'd never uncover his secret.

"I *can*. Occasionally. It's been known to happen if the secret is boring enough, and considering this is your secret, that shouldn't be a problem."

His lips twitched again but he still didn't look at me. "What of your own secrets? Are they boring or thrilling ones?"

"Mine are fascinating, of course."

Finally, he looked up, his face aglow. "As I suspected. Then I'm afraid I must disappoint you and keep this secret to myself, for it's not my own, but *yours*." With that, he turned and walked away.

I stared after him in a daze before scampering after him. "It can't be my secret, for I haven't told you any."

"Not intentionally," he said brightly. "But you did share one with me just now. I suppose it couldn't be helped. As I suspected, you're *terrible* at keeping secrets."

"But if it's my own secret, you should have no qualms about sharing it with me."

He shook his head. "As you're about to discover, I'm *excellent* at keeping secrets."

"Apparently so, for you have yet to tell me whether or not you've kissed someone before." I bounced restlessly on my heels, anxiously awaiting his response.

"You do seem eager to know. Are you perhaps jealous?"

"Of course not," I answered hastily.

His lips twitched into one of his half smiles, his eyes dancing. "I do love this secret of yours. Very well, I'll humor you. I'm afraid that aspect of my own story is still a mystery."

It took a moment for his meaning to hit me. "Does that mean you've never kissed either?"

He raised his eyebrow. "Does that surprise you?"

"Not in a bad way." And for some inexplicable reason I smirked triumphantly, quite pleased with Alastar's answer yet unsure why. He eyed my smirk with one of his own, the look in his eyes as if he was keeping not just one secret but a multitude of them, ones I desperately wished he'd share.

I paused in our stroll when we passed a clump of lovely daisies. I promptly knelt down and picked some.

"More pilfering?" Alastar asked.

"These are for my maid, Eloise. She seemed rather sad this morning, and I thought these would cheer her up."

His expression softened, and the way he looked at me caused my heart to flutter in pleasure.

After I'd finished gathering my bouquet, Alastar led us back around to check on Eileen again. She was still thoroughly involved with her husband, so we didn't linger. As we strolled away, I gazed longingly back at the couple and the adoring way Aiden looked at my dearest friend.

"Do you think anyone will look at me like that one day?"

Alastar met my gaze, his own strangely smoldering. "I do."

"I sure hope so." We took a path lined with artistically trimmed shrubs. "Do you like being Eileen's Head Guard? It seems rather boring."

"I like it very much," he said. "Not only is it impossible for it to be boring with all of the unexpected things that come from your mouth, but it's the greatest honor I've ever received."

I crinkled my nose. "How?"

Alastar's already serious expression became even more so. "It's no secret the princess is who His Highness values above everything else. To think he's entrusted her care and protection to *me*..." He shook his head, dazed. "Despite our years of friendship, I still couldn't believe it when he approached me with the task. To have such trust from him..." He seemed to have no words.

I sighed. "You must be the most trustworthy person in the kingdom for Aiden to entrust Eileen to your care." And I'd liked pretending he was a villain. "What was your life like before you became a royal guard?"

"You really want to know such trivial details about a mere guard?"

"Of course I do, for I'm discovering that you're not merely a guard—you're also a villain, a fellow wanderer, an adventurer, and a noble knight, all rolled into one."

His lips twitched upwards into a full smile. "Noble knight? Have I changed parts again? You'll have to excuse me so I can fetch my lines from my room."

I giggled and looped my arm back through his. "I like to keep you on your toes."

"Believe me, Miss Rosalina, no one has ever done so the way you have."

"Then my scheme is a success." I smiled up at him and to my delight he returned it. Like his previous smiles, it was adorable. "Now, won't you tell me more about yourself?"

"Very well, I'll humor you. One of my most treasured memories is of being curled up on my mother's lap as a boy as she read to me. This led to a lifelong love of stories, as they always remind me of her. I find that making up stories is an excellent way to pass the time when one is standing guard all day."

I could just picture the tender, homey scene he described. "That sounds lovely. Was your mother also a servant at the palace?"

"She was the lady-in-waiting to the late queen, His Highness's mother, for she came from a noble lineage before she married a guard far below her station. They were so happy together that I knew she never regretted it."

"How did she die?"

Sadness filled his eyes. I rested my hand lightly on his arm. "In the illness that struck Sortileya several years ago. It spread from the capital to several of the surrounding villages, taking many lives, including my parents. I'm fortunate it didn't take me or my brother, Duncan."

"Is that why you're always so sullen?"

Alastar frowned. "Do you believe I'm unhappy?"

"Well, you never smile," I said. "It's rather disappointing. I like smiles."

"No wonder. You have a beautiful smile yourself."

My cheeks warmed at his praise. "As all heroines do."

"No, there's something different about yours...sweet, genuine, and a bit mischievous at times." He reached out, as if about to trace my lips with his fingertip, but caught himself and dropped his hand. Strange disappointment filled me. What would it have been like to feel him touch me? "And you have an even lovelier imagination."

My disappointment faded as warmth blossomed within me, causing me to feel I'd swallowed the sun. "You really think so, Alastar?"

He paused and gave me an earnest but tender look. "I do," he murmured. "You're absolutely enchanting."

I lost myself in his hazel gaze, a pleasant sensation I'd

read about but had never before experienced for myself. It was a lovely feeling.

As we approached the palace doors, the tenderness eclipsing his usual serious expression faded, leaving me yearning for it. "My break is nearly over. I must leave you now and return to guarding Her Highness. Shall I take your satchel with me? I assume you won't be needing it anymore."

He looked deeply into my eyes and slowly brushed his knuckles along my cheek. I shuddered and leaned against his fingers, finding myself unconsciously wanting to bridge the distance between us to quench my sudden need to be closer to him. A strange energy passed between us, one that I ached to explore.

Alastar lowered his gaze to his stroking fingers. "Rosalina?" he whispered. "You're not really going to spell Prince Liam, are you?"

With those words, whatever hypnotic spell had settled over us vanished. I yanked myself away. "I have to, Alastar, and no one—especially not you—is going to stop me."

I held my satchel close to my body and ran up the palace stairs, nearly careening into the footman as he opened the door for me. I fought the mysterious urge to look back at Alastar with every step away I took, but I couldn't escape the feelings he'd caused me to feel, ones that, while tender, were emotions I didn't want to understand.

CHAPTER 12

I squinted at the faded recipe in *Enchanted Sweets and Delights* and silently cursed for not having had the foresight to bring more than one candle. For I, Rosalina, finally found myself alone in the palace kitchen, about to practice baking up a love spell in order to create my completely perfect happily ever after. Ah, bliss!

The kitchen door squeaked open. Without even turning around I sensed who the intruder was. Sure enough, it was Alastar who spoke. "As I suspected: the heroine has snuck down to the kitchen as part of the latest scheme she has up her sleeve."

My grin widened as I spun around to face him. His flickering candle illuminated his usual serious expression and the merriment dancing in his eyes. "How did you know I was here?"

"When you hurriedly said good night to Their Highnesses and scampered off, I knew you were up to mischief. It wasn't difficult to deduce that you'd gone to the palace kitchens in order to practice your ridiculous plot."

His gaze lingered on the dozens of empty bowls waiting

to be used and the flour I'd already spilled all over the counter. He joined me and leaned against the counter.

"Are you up to the mischief I think you are?" His gaze settled on a basket, stuffed to the brim with rolls hot off the hearth. He raised his brows. "Perhaps not. What do we have here?"

"Freshly baked orange rolls," I said brightly. "I just whipped them up and thought I'd give them out to the guards tomorrow."

"Guards aren't allowed to eat while on duty," he said.

I rolled my eyes. "I know that. I was going to wrap them up and tuck them into their pockets while they're standing guard as a tasty treat for later. Although"—I nibbled my fingernail—"admittedly the delicious aroma may distract them from their duty." As I spoke, I plucked a roll from the basket and slipped it into Alastar's own pocket. "Are orange rolls your favorite treat?"

His lips twitched but he didn't answer.

I sighed. "I'll figure it out eventually."

"I hope that you do." He pulled out the roll and tore off a piece, but hesitated before putting it into his mouth. "These aren't spelled, are they?"

"Of course not, but they are my great-grandmother's famous recipe. Aren't they delicious? They're our most popular item back home in the bakery."

"They are good." He took another bite. "But they're not my favorite." He popped the rest of the roll into his mouth. "Now that you've thoroughly distracted me, might I inquire what mischief you're concocting now that you've finished baking your famous rolls? You can't be lingering in the kitchen at such a late hour for no reason."

I folded my arms with a scowl. "I'm not going to tell you."

"Ah, a secret. In that case, I'm going to discover what it is very shortly." He glanced at the clock. "I give you a minute.

No worries, I can wait." He settled back to whistle cheerfully. Aggravating man.

Since he expected me to tell him, naturally I became determined not to. But that was the problem with secrets; the ones that one was supposed to keep were the most slippery and difficult to hold on to. I mashed my lips together, determined to keep it inside where it belonged, but this only aggravated it further. The secret banged against my lips, begging and pleading for release. Stubborn thing. But it wouldn't vanquish me, for I had a battle with a certain guard that I was determined to win.

He waited with annoying guard-like patience and far too much amusement as the war—Rosalina vs. The Secret—raged within me. He smirked and leaned towards my ear. "Don't fight it."

His words broke the dam I could no longer maintain and the secret tumbled out. "I'm practicing my love spell."

The moment the words escaped I ached to snatch them and shove them back inside where they belonged, bound and chained and locked away. I slapped my hand over my mouth, as if the action could revert the damage.

He arched his eyebrow. "The love spell?" He leaned towards my book to study it and groaned. "Oh no, I was hoping that wasn't the one you were planning on baking. I thought you didn't have all the ingredients?"

"I *almost* have everything I need, but considering Prince Liam is visiting in a few days, I'll probably only have one practice session to fine tune some of the more difficult aspects of this love spell so I can bake it just right when the time comes; love can be a tricky thing."

"Practice would be wise; otherwise you'd inadvertently turn Prince Liam into a frog."

"I'm not going to turn Prince Liam into a frog, Ali."

His eyes narrowed. "What did you just call me?"

"Your name is such a mouthful," I said. "As much as my own full name is perfect for a storybook heroine, Rosie is much more adorable. You're in great need of a nickname, too, and Ali is just perfect. Perhaps it'll help loosen you up a bit; Alastar is such a stuffy name."

He stared at me, his face expressionless as usual, and like always, I found it annoying. How could I get any hint of what he was thinking when his countenance was always so stoic? It was so guard-like and utterly aggravating.

"*Ali* isn't a name that seems appropriate for a guard," he finally said. "Not when it's rather…feminine."

"If your masculinity is so fragile, I could shorten your name in another way. Would you prefer *Star*?"

He pulled a face and I smirked in triumph.

"Ali it is! The serious guard finally gets a nickname. It's a new chapter in your story, Ali."

He continued staring at me, but while his expression naturally didn't change, something flickered in his eyes. Was that…amusement? "Is that so, Rosalina?"

I pulled a face. "Won't you call me Rosie?"

He smiled, a real one. "It would be my honor to call you Rosie."

"Good. Now that we've settled that, I must get back to what I was doing."

I bustled over to the cupboard to fetch the cocoa while he frowned skeptically at my recipe book. "Is this the first time you've baked a spell?"

"No, I've baked plenty of spells—all in secret, of course." My cheeks warmed. "My parents disapprove of my baking spells. They're the first in generations to refuse to bake from this family heirloom, despite having a pantry stocked with the most common magical ingredients."

"Naturally, your parents' disapproval doesn't stop you."

The teasing glint in his eyes softened. "Do you enjoy living in a bakery?"

"I do." I blinked, slightly surprised by my own answer, and even more so when I realized it was true. "Being surrounded by delicious smells and treats, experiencing the thrill of creating pastries and breads, meeting a variety of interesting customers, and having plenty of time to brew up wonderful stories midst the hours of kneading…it's wonderful."

Ali frowned at *Enchanted Sweets and Delights*. "Do you ever sell anything created from this?"

"Oh, no. When I bake from it, I only do it for myself, although admittedly I sometimes get dismal results. In the week following Eileen's disappearance, I tried and failed a dozen times to bake a spell to eliminate grief, but I could never manage it."

Ali's expression sobered. "I can't imagine how much pain you must have been experiencing during that time."

"It was the darkest time of my life." I pushed the memories away and forced a smile. "Thankfully, my story has taken a much brighter turn, especially considering my life is about to include true love." I tapped the love spell recipe and Ali's frown deepened.

"Rosie, you really aren't going to go through with this, are you?"

"I *am*," I snapped. "And neither you nor Eileen is going to thwart my happily ever after. This is my story, and thus I'm the one who determines how it'll go. Now give me your candle; mine is starting to burn out."

He made no motion to do so, so I snatched it from him and set it beside my book to better illuminate my page.

"Now make yourself useful and help me."

He cocked his eyebrow. "You want me to assist you in

getting yourself into a predicament that I firmly disagree with?"

I pressed my hands to my hips. "Of course I do. Are you going to be a good friend and cooperate?"

The annoyance marring his expression softened as he leaned closer, grazing my arm as he did so. I shuddered. "You consider me a friend, Rosie?"

"Of course I do."

He smiled—full on *smiled*. I hadn't even been sure that was possible. "Excellent, then we're finally on the same page. I've considered you a friend from the moment we met, but you were stubbornly determined to think the worst of me."

"How could I form a good opinion when you were doing devious things like knocking me down the stairs and threatening to feed me to the dragons?"

His lips twitched again as he shook his head. "I think you need to reread the beginning of our story, for I seem to recall things didn't happen in quite that way."

"Maybe not, but you have to admit my version of events makes for a better story. Now, no more stalling. I need to get started, and you need to help me. Put this on." I shoved a floral apron I'd discovered in one of the drawers at him. He raised his eyebrows at it.

"This is not the type of *thing* a royal guard wears. If my fellow guards ever got wind of this, I'd never live it down."

I scowled at his non-moving and thus non-cooperating form. "For goodness' sake." I seized the apron and tugged it over his head. He tried to wriggle away, but I yanked him back by the apron strings, spun him around, and tied it around his waist. "There."

He glanced down at himself, expression horrified. "Please assure me I don't look as ridiculous as I feel."

I rested my chin on my fist and surveyed him before my

giggle escaped. "Oh Ali, you look so pretty and frilly in your flowery get-up."

He closed his eyes and groaned, looking as if he were being tortured. "Please don't make me wear it, Rosie, I'm begging you."

"I didn't realize such a baby was allowed to join the ranks of the royal guard. Is His Highness aware you whine over your masculinity?"

"As a fellow man, he'd sympathize with my plight of being forced to wear this...*thing*."

I rolled my eyes. "Drama, drama, drama. Like it or not, that's your costume for this scene. Now stop complaining and help me; it's only getting later." I consulted the recipe book. "Let's measure the flour first. I already put it away. Has your deflating masculinity impacted your ability to find it for me?"

He stared at me for a moment before he left with a grumble to do my bidding, muttering something about deceptively innocent-looking heroines being bent on his torture. My lips twitched as I watched him explore the kitchen.

"My assistance is likely more of a hindrance, for I haven't the faintest idea where to find the flour."

"Keep looking; I'm sure it's around here somewhere."

He did, making a mess as he yanked open cupboards and drawers in his search. "It's not."

I watched him squirm a bit more before I blinked innocently at the counter. "Oh, silly me, it's been here the entire time."

He growled as his stomped back over. "You're villainous, Rosie."

I arranged my face in what I hoped to be the epitome of innocence. "What ever do you mean? I'd truly forgotten I hadn't put the flour away after all. Do you really think that I,

Rosalina, would lead you on a wild goose chase just for my own amusement? Wait—Ali, what are you doing?"

For a wicked grin was slowly spreading across his face. He approached slowly, backing me into the edge of the counter. My heart hammered, but not in a frightened way, more in anticipation at this delightful twist in the scene we were playing out.

"What scheme have you concocted against a poor innocent damsel?"

"One word, Rosie: *revenge*." He seized me in his firm grip—goodness, his arms were so warm as they held me cozily against his chest—and hoisted me up. I immediately flailed in my attempt to escape, kicking my legs against his shins, but aggravatingly he didn't loosen his hold.

"Put me down this instant, you fiend."

"Not until I've gotten my revenge. Now, where's that flour you sent me to find…ah, here it is. Look, Rosie, I found it. And I know just how to use it."

I shrieked as my over-imaginative mind concocted all sorts of devious ways flour could be used as a tool for revenge. Sure enough, Ali dumped a fistful of flour over my head and proceeded to rub it into my hair.

"Ali!"

He laughed, a deep, warm sound that sent a ripply shudder over me from my head to my toes. How I loved his laugh, especially the way his chest rumbled against me as he did so, and suddenly I stopped fighting, feeling the strangest contentment to stay in his hold forever.

Ali paused. "You're being strangely quiet, Rosie, especially considering you were just attacked. Did I go too far? Are you upset?"

I tipped my head back. His usual mask had cracked, revealing a face marred with worry, as if he truly thought he'd done something wrong.

"It's quite alright; you didn't upset me."

His worry twisted into wariness. He furrowed his forehead. "You're up to something. The question is: what?"

I wriggled in his arms. "If you're brave enough, put me down and you'll find out." The truth was I didn't want him to release me at all…although if he held me much longer, I was certain I'd faint from how strangely dizzy I was suddenly feeling with waves of sensations rippling over me. He set me down gently and I immediately ducked beneath his arms, seized a handful of flour, and threw it into his face.

He gaped at me with a look of utter betrayal as he rapidly blinked at me through his flour-covered face. "So this is the game you want to play?"

"Who says it's a game?"

He nodded gravely. "Well, if playing will keep you out of mischief, then I'll happily participate in this nonsense with you."

He threw a fistful of flour at me, I threw more back at him, and it escalated into a full-fledged flour fight, complete with all manner of delightful cheating, foul plays, spectacular hits, and laughter. Eventually, we settled onto the flour-coated floor in stitches. I loved watching Ali laugh; it lit up his entire expression.

I leaned against Ali's firm chest and tipped my head back. "You're surprisingly fun for someone so serious."

"Aren't characters in novels always full of surprises?"

That got me giggling again. "I love how you play along." From the beginning, he'd always gone along with my nonsense. It was wonderful.

His hand lightly traced up and down my arm, leaving a flour trail and causing me to shiver. "Not exactly, for you're always several steps ahead of me; it's all I can do to keep up."

"You'll keep trying, won't you, Ali? We must always remain friends." For I was anxious for this relationship of ours—whatever it was, for it was *wonderful*—to never, ever end. I knew I'd always need my co-writer to put up with my stories.

"For you, Rosie, always." He smiled down at me, so sweetly. I smiled back, and in that moment, a strange energy surged between us, similar to the one we'd experienced together in the garden, one that pulled me closer to him and made me want to stay close to him forever.

I blinked rapidly and severed our gazes, breaking the strange spell. I shouldn't be thinking about *him*, especially when I had such an important task awaiting me. I shook my head to clear it and glanced around the flour-covered kitchen.

"We've made quite a mess in here, haven't we?"

"You mean *you* made the mess and dragged me into it, just as you always do."

I smirked, but it vanished almost immediately as worry clawed at me. "Cook will have me hauled to the dungeon if she discovers this." I gnawed at my fingernail as I glanced around the kitchen again.

"Don't fear, Rosie; you'll not be carted off to the dungeon on my watch. We'll clean the kitchen until it's so spotless Cook will never know what happened." He stood, extended his hand—a pleasant flutter filled my stomach as it enveloped mine—and helped me to my feet.

Despite our spectacular mess, it only took us half an hour to scrub all the evidence of our flour fight away. When I'd put away the broom and Ali had put away the mop, I yawned and stretched. "How late is it?"

"Very late."

I pouted. "I was afraid you'd say that."

"I suppose this means you won't get a chance to bake up mischief tonight."

I brightened. "But there's always tomorrow." I fiddled

with my apron strings. "If you can't sleep again, will you rejoin me for more midnight baking adventures?"

He grinned and my heart soared to see it. "Definitely, Rosie. Someone has to keep an eye on you for whatever plots you're brewing in that imaginative mind of yours."

I returned his smile, pleased that my story comrade was so willing to continue playing his part, even if I was still unsure what story we were writing together.

I couldn't wait to read in order to find out.

CHAPTER 13

I sat beside the lovely pond dotted with lily pads and cattails, hidden behind the palace's majestic hedge maze, the perfect place to spend in celebration of my recent victory. I'd just completed a successful day of questing, which was perfect considering Prince Liam was coming tomorrow. Memories of our pleasant time together at the Dracerian palace filled my mind. I couldn't wait to see him again.

I reached inside my bag to brush my fingers across the leaves plucked from a rare glowing-laurel fern—whose leaves changed colors every few minutes—which I'd discovered in a secluded area of the royal grounds, hidden amongst regular ferns. It quivered at my touch, as if it were alive. An excited glee overcame me whenever it shifted to pale rose, the color the love spell specifically instructed it should be when added to the recipe.

As I withdrew my hand, my touch grazed the smooth metal of the golden ball I now frequently carried with me everywhere. I pulled it out and examined it closely, just as I'd done before I'd once again stolen—or rather, *borrowed*—it.

Without a doubt it had helped me locate my second-to-last ingredient as I'd traipsed the gardens this afternoon, leaving me only one ingredient away from success.

I tossed it into the air and caught it, admiring the way the golden sunlight glistened off its surface. So pretty. This was most definitely an enchanted object such as was common in fairy tales. No doubt it would lead me to something fantastic.

A loud croak coming from nearby caused me to momentarily pause. A large frog rested on a lily pad and watched me with rather knowing bulging eyes for an amphibian, as if something about my actions fascinated him. I tilted my head, studying him curiously. In the very same fairy tale about the princess and her golden ball, she too encountered a frog, one who turned out to be a prince in disguise. What a delightful twist that one should be here now.

"Good afternoon," I said politely just in case this frog really was a prince and I was sitting in the presence of royalty—never mind he was rather green and currently covered in warts and slime.

The frog merely continued staring.

"Are you acquainted with these gardens, Your Highness? For I'm on a quest and am in need of one final ingredient. Do you happen to know where I might find a lueur moonflower?

The frog made no response. How rude. I glared.

"Do you not know, or are you refusing to tell me?"

The frog remained unresponsive save for his yellow throat puffing in and out as he croaked. I harrumphed as I resumed tossing and catching my golden ball, a bit more aggressively than before.

"If you're a prince, then you're being most impolite by refusing to help a damsel in distress when she's in dire need of your assistance in—oh no!" I fumbled with the golden ball, but it slipped through my fingers and rolled down the sloping lawn to plop into the pond.

I gasped. I, Rosalina, had just lost an enchanted object pilfered from the royal family. I scrambled down the bank to peer into the blue-green water for any sign of my lost object. Only my pale, wide-eyed reflection stared back at me. I nibbled my fingernail. Did I dare risk putting my hand inside? I had no way of knowing what sort of water this was —normal water, enchanted water, or water that would result in dastardly injuries from a single touch.

The frog croaked again, as if he were laughing, and I glared at it. "Now look what you made me do. You're supposed to *help* princesses, not cause trouble. No spell-breaking kiss for you."

"Do my ears deceive me? Is Rosie blaming someone other than me for the predicament in which she currently finds herself?"

My heart gave a strange leap at the sound of that voice. I turned to see Ali leaning casually against the back wall of the hedge maze, arms folded with a teasing look in his eyes. He made a show of glancing around. No one but us—and the obnoxious frog—was here.

"If you don't mind my asking, who are you talking to?"

Ali was the last person I wanted to see right now. Friend or not, as a guard, it was his duty to punish criminals such as myself. Oh horrors, how had I ended up in such a plight? Why couldn't I have left that golden ball alone?

"Why do you want to know?" I asked, my shaking voice betraying my guilt.

"I find myself quite invested, considering I heard there's a kiss in store for this mysterious individual."

My cheeks flared with heat. So he'd heard everything. Of course. This nosy man always seemed to find me at my worst and took great delight in tormenting me over that fact.

"I'm not kissing anyone but my true love. I was conversing with this frog, who is quite likely an enchanted prince. Everyone knows the only way to break such spells is by a kiss, but I refuse to waste one on the likes of him. I was just telling him so when you arrived."

He stared at me with a deadpan expression, leaving me no clues as to what he was thinking or feeling. For some reason it bothered me more than usual.

"Let me see if I understand the situation correctly," he finally said slowly. "You're conversing with a frog in case it's a prince in disguise?"

My eyes narrowed. "Is that a problem?"

"Not at all. I just want to be sure I have the story straight so I don't fumble my lines."

He pushed off against the hedge wall and approached. My heartbeat escalated the closer he came and I found myself smoothing my hair, which had been rumpled in my frantic dash to peer into the pond. He squatted on his heels beside me, his gaze first on me before sliding to the frog.

His lips twitched. "I hate to ruin your story, but that's not a prince."

"How do you know?" I asked hotly. "It very well could be."

"Because that's a *female* frog."

My jaw tightened as I studied the frog more closely. "How can you tell?"

"Female frogs are bigger than males."

It bothered me he knew the difference. "You seem awfully informed about frogs. Perhaps you're on your own quest to find your princess in disguise and break her spell."

"My princess isn't in disguise, but in plain sight," he said with a rather smoldering look. My heart flared. He couldn't be talking about *me,* could he? "Thus I won't be kissing random frogs. Now, won't you tell me what's troubling you? I heard your squeal from the next garden and my curiosity led me here to see if I might be of assistance."

"I'm currently a damsel in distress."

"Are you ever anything else?"

I tore out a handful of grass and threw it at him. His serious expression didn't even falter except for his lips twitching, as if he found my tantrum amusing. Odious man.

"Once more you're determined to play the villain in *The Story of Rosalina*," I accused.

"Ah, but you're wrong—I'm here to help a fair maiden in her time of need." He peered into the water. "I heard a splash, so I'm assuming you've just dropped something. What is it? Something that's not yours to lose, I'd wager?"

My cheeks burned as my confession tumbled out. "Oh Ali, I know I shouldn't have taken something so priceless from my room, but it was so pretty and I needed it for my quest. Now I've lost it. *Oh*!"

I buried my face in my hands. He rested a light hand on my shoulder. "Don't worry, Rosie. I may not be a prince, but I do strive to be a gallant knight."

I peeked through my fingers in time to watch him reach into the pond. "Wait, Ali, the water could be enchanted or—"

Too late. He submerged his arm and fished around, his brow furrowed. I bit my fingernails and held my breath, waiting...

He withdrew the golden ball with a crooked grin. "Success. Your stolen object, My Lady."

I released my breath in a whoosh. "Thank heavens. I didn't fancy the gallows."

"Once again you come up with the most extreme scenarios." Despite having retrieved the golden ball, he didn't return it, but began to toss and catch it as I'd been doing. "So what quest were you on that you needed this golden ball?"

"I believe it's enchanted and will lead one to true love, so I've been searching for the last ingredients for my love spell. I only have one left."

Ali fumbled and nearly dropped the ball. "You *what*?"

"I'm only one ingredient away from succeeding in my quest."

"You mean from ruining your life and the lives of others." His free hand clenched into a fist. "For the last time, Rosie, you can't spell Prince Liam. There will be consequences that even you with your vivid imagination can't imagine. I don't want to see you hurt."

I folded my arms. "I can do what I like in my own story, and you shan't stop me."

Alastar said nothing for a moment before he sighed. "Speaking of stories...I'm glad I found you so I could return your book." He retrieved *Tales of Magic and Romance to Enchant the Heart*, which I'd lent him several weeks ago.

My bad mood melted away and I clasped my hands in delight. "Ooh, have you finally read it? Do tell me what you think of it."

"Hmm...well, as predicted, it's sappy. Do you really enjoy reading about such superficial love?"

"It's not superficial," I snapped, already immensely disappointed in his reaction.

"The affection seems rather shallow. Shouldn't genuine love focus more on one's inner beauty? I must admit I'm disappointed to learn you enjoy reading about such meaningless love when I hoped you'd be one who looked deeper."

A vulnerable look filled his eyes. I tilted my head, studying it. "It bothers you, doesn't it, when people fail to see beyond appearances."

He suddenly seemed quite preoccupied with the ground. "I'm just afraid...I mean, most people judge a book by its cover without even bothering to read the book."

Sympathy washed over me as I discovered this rare insight into Ali. "Are you afraid women will judge you by your cover and choose not to read your story?"

His blush deepened as he kicked his toe into the dirt. "I've been told that I possess a less than attractive cover. I've always been compared to my brother, and not in a flattering way."

I considered Duncan's appearance. He was, admittedly, dark-haired and handsome, and yet...not particularly appealing to me. I stared at Ali, who was definitely not classically handsome, but how I loved being around him.

"You don't look much alike," I ventured. Ali sighed defeatedly.

"So I've been told. It's never bothered me too much before until...*recently,* I suppose." He stared into the pond, avoiding my eyes.

"If it means anything, *I* find you attractive."

His gaze suddenly snapped to mine, his hazel eyes wide. "You're just saying that; I know I'm not handsome. It shouldn't matter. It *doesn't* matter." He let out a long sigh. "It didn't used to matter." He peeked back at me, cheeks crimson, eyes rather shy. "You really think so?"

I rested my chin on my hand to study him. "Yes."

And I did. While he certainly wasn't handsome in the traditional sense, I didn't seem to mind. He was fun, sweet, and imaginative, with the most gorgeous eyes that were literally the windows to his soul, not to mention he had the ability to make me smile. His features were rough and serious while also soft and gentle, especially in his lip-twitching smiles. I nodded, confirming my own opinion.

"Definitely. I like the way you look, especially as I've read your book further and am enjoying it immensely. I want to keep reading it." I stepped closer and lightly traced around his eyes. "Your eyes are my favorite, especially when they show your emotions and help me read you better."

His eyes lit up as his lips curved up into a real smile. It pleased me how much my words touched him. "You're really very sweet, Rosie flower."

Just as before, a strange thrill rippled over me at this nickname. "As are you. It's the reason we're friends despite my deciding early on to hate all guards forever."

Up went his eyebrow. "Why is that?"

"Because when I first came to the palace, I thought all royal guards were the Dark Prince's minions bent on performing his evil deed, which you demonstrated when you thwarted my attempts to explore. Thus when I met you, it was your role that prevented me from initially reading your book and why I cast you as the villain."

"So I was the wrong genre. I'm glad you finally decided to give me a try anyway."

"And I'm glad you gave me a try, even if fairy tales aren't your preferred genre." I sighed.

"I didn't dislike your favorite book by any means; I'm just surprised that the romance is so superficial."

"But it's not," I protested. "You need to read it more closely."

"Then perhaps I should give it a reread before I return it."

I smiled, pleased by his willingness. "Which was your favorite story?"

He lightly traced my lips, as if memorizing the shape of my smile. I shuddered. "I didn't like 'The Tale of the Witch and the Love Potion' at all, as I knew I wouldn't, but I really enjoyed 'The Tale of the Princess and Her Prince in Disguise.'"

"Ooh, that one is splendid, even if the heroine is a bit daft. I mean, who wouldn't recognize true love when it's staring her right in the face?"

Cue his eyebrow lift. "I couldn't have said it better myself." Ali extended his hand. "Come, I want to show you something."

I rested my hand in his and allowed him to help me up and loop my arm through his. "Where are we going?"

"You'll see." He led me down a secluded path I hadn't yet explored. Hidden deep behind the hedge maze was the most enchanting tree I'd ever seen. The leaves were shimmery, almost gold, and the fruit growing from its boughs was almost translucent in appearance.

I stared in wonder. "Wow, what kind of tree is this? I've never seen anything like it."

"Legend says this is an enchanted tree whose fruit reveals one's true feelings, no matter how deeply one suppresses them." He plucked a fruit from the tree and used a dagger from his boot to cut it in half. He held a piece out for me while keeping the other for himself.

I stared first at it, then up at him. "What's this for?"

"I thought it'd be wise for you to see the secrets of your heart before following through with your disastrous plot."

I hesitantly took the fruit. Without breaking eye contact with me, he took a bite from his own piece. I watched him with bated breath. "Does it work?"

He swallowed and examined the fruit before meeting my gaze once more. "I do believe it does. Everything seems a bit more clear now."

"In what way?" I leaned closer, eager for his answer. He motioned towards my own half.

"Don't leave me in suspense. Eat yours."

I did. The fruit was a unique and juicy explosion of sweet flavor with a hint of tartness. Ali's gaze intensified as he gave me a searching look, as if hoping to discover something.

"Well?"

A stirring of *something* prickled my heart as I met his eyes, but I found myself pushing it away, focusing determinedly on an image of the dashing Crown Prince of Draceria. "I still think Prince Liam is my prince."

He sighed and frowned at the half-eaten piece in my hand. "You got a bad piece of fruit."

I folded my arms. "No I didn't; we ate from the same piece. If you don't like what's in my heart, why did you ask?"

His frown deepened as he searched my gaze. "If you searched your heart, you'd realize what a mistake you're making. Do you enjoy ending up in messes of your own making, Rosie?"

I tightened my jaw. "Falling in love is anything but a mess. Obstacles are a part of every story."

He nodded, as if I'd said something deeply profound. "Indeed they are, but you seem to be a heroine who inadvertently creates her own obstacles." He took another bite. "Keep eating; maybe you'll see sense before you do something completely foolish."

I threw my fruit half at him. It bounced off his chest rather satisfyingly. "You keep changing roles in my story. Why do you continuously switch back and forth between friend and foe?"

He glanced disappointedly at my fallen fruit before meeting my gaze again, his own intense. "*I* don't change roles; *you* keep changing the part you want me to play. I keep hoping one day you'll select the one I desperately want to be for you."

That strange energy passed between us again. Despite my annoyance, I found myself stepping closer, drawn towards *him*. "And what role is that?" I whispered.

"I think you already know. Sometimes one keeps secrets even from themselves." His expression hardened. "You're so blinded by the way you're determined your story should play out. Your terrible plotting will lead to nothing but an *un*happily ever after." His expression slowly transformed from anger to a strange desperation. "Can't you see what a huge mistake you're about to make?"

I met his anxious gaze head on. For a moment we stared at one another, the strange energy that seemed to frequently fill our interactions burning between us. I forced myself to remember Prince Liam and his desperate need for me, of the storyteller's prediction, all to give me the strength to say my next words.

"*The Tale of Rosalina* will end how I've determined it will, Ali."

He winced. "You're clearly determined, but don't be surprised when a few...obstacles show up." He tore his gaze away and examined the golden ball. "You say this leads to true love?"

Thankfully, the venom from his voice had disappeared. I swallowed. "Indeed."

"And how does it work, exactly?"

"I'm not sure. That's why I've been carrying it around with me."

"In hopes it'll lead you to your prince?" He examined the ball a bit more before raising his gaze to mine. His eyes swirled with a tumult of emotions along with a secret, one I was desperate—but somehow afraid—to discover. "Perhaps you've already found true love but are merely too blind to see it. Have you considered that plot twist?" He raised his longing gaze and bridged the remaining distance to shove the rest of his enchanted fruit into my hands. I shuddered as our fingers touched. "The spell on my fruit is working, so perhaps if you eat mine, things will become more clear."

He spun around and walked off. As I watched him disappear around the hedge maze, I took a tentative bite and a myriad of foreign emotions immediately swirled through me, ones I had no name for, but ones that were warm, tender, and beautiful. They seemed to intensify when Ali paused to glance over his shoulder and our gazes met once more.

For the first time since coming up with this brilliant plan to get my story back on its proper course, a pinprick of doubt tickled my heart. I reached into my satchel to stroke my recently acquired laurel-fern leaf waiting patiently to be used in my love spell. For some strange reason, rather than thinking of Prince Liam, the image of the longing swirling in Ali's eyes filled my mind instead.

With a gasp, I allowed his fruit half to slip through my fingers to the ground.

CHAPTER 14

I encountered Eileen in the hallway. "I was just looking for you," she said. "I'm in desperate need of a break after the tedious meeting I just endured. Can you keep me company while I prepare for tonight's state dinner?" She sighed, as if the thought of attending the dinner completely overwhelmed her.

I was in no state to be good company, but without even waiting for an answer, she looped her arm through mine and led me to her bedroom so I could sit with her as she got ready. Normally, I adored playing dress up, but even the gorgeous gowns of satin and lace couldn't tug my thoughts away from my confusing encounter with Alastar, the strange feelings I'd felt when I'd taken a bite from the fruit that may or may not have been enchanted, and the intense look in his eyes when he'd looked at me, almost as if he...but no, that couldn't be true. Could it?

"Rosie?"

I blinked rapidly and turned towards Eileen, who was now wearing a violet gown and sitting in front of her vanity having her dark hair arranged by her lady's maid. Weariness filled her eyes, reminding me of her own trying day. Only my concern for my best friend was enough to tug me away from my confusing Alastar-filled thoughts.

"Was it really such a stressful day?"

"Every day seems more stressful than the last," Eileen said.

I ached to assure her; I hated seeing my dear friend so distressed. "But you're doing so well. I've been watching you."

She sighed wearily. "I certainly hope so. I am trying. Before I married Aiden, I knew being a princess would be difficult, but I admit it's more so than I imagined—countless duties and events, constantly being on display, always having a guard trailing you…it's quite exhausting at times."

My brow wrinkled. While admittedly the reality of royal life was far different than how it was portrayed in books, Eileen almost made it sound like she didn't even *like* being a princess. "But surely you still enjoy being a princess, right?"

"Not yet, but I'm sure in time that'll come. I love Aiden. He makes it worth it." Eileen glanced at me with a rather knowing look, the kind only a best friend could give. "Enough about me. You're being uncannily quiet. What's bothering you?"

How could I possibly answer when I myself didn't understand the emotions swelling within me? Confusion, hurt, remorse…all from fighting with Ali. While no one was in favor of my brewing up a love spell, his disapproval bothered me the most. And then there had been that strange look he'd given me…not to mention the foreign feeling I'd experienced when looking at him…my heart fluttered just thinking of it.

"Oh."

I glanced at Eileen. "What?" I squeaked.

"You're thinking of a certain guard. Well, I shan't disturb

you." She turned back towards the mirror, but her reflection revealed her knowing smirk.

My cheeks burned. "I'm not thinking of *him*."

"Aren't you?" Eileen's expression was far too innocent. I tightened my jaw.

"No."

"Then why are you blushing?"

I muttered a very un-heroine-like curse at my betraying face, and Eileen's smirk widened. Once more, my attempts to keep a secret had failed dismally. "Ali and I got into a fight."

Eileen raised bow eyebrows. "*Ali*?"

Cue even warmer cheeks. "It's my nickname for him."

"That's rather—*ow*!" Eileen winced as her lady's maid accidentally poked her with a hairpin.

"My apologies, Your Highness," the maid muttered. Eileen smiled as she waved the apology away and resumed our conversation.

"Your nickname for him is sweet. Does he like it? I imagine he does."

"He doesn't like it in the least." I managed a small smile at the triumph of ruffling that aggravating man.

"Oh, I'm quite sure he does," Eileen said brightly, ruining my moment. "But that doesn't matter. What did you and *Ali* fight about?"

My half-smile vanished in an instant. "You can't call him that. Only *I* can."

"Forgive me." For some reason Eileen looked far too pleased at my snapping at her for such a trivial offense, only to me it didn't feel trivial at all. "Please don't keep me in suspense. What was your argument about? You normally get along so well."

I snorted at that. When had Ali and I ever gotten along? "The love spell," I said. "He's determined to thwart me."

"I daresay he is." Her lips twitched, an annoying reminder

of the man I was trying and failing to *not* think about. "Poor Alastar. I imagine he's particularly set against your scheme."

She said nothing more, but it didn't matter if she had; I wouldn't have heard her words, for at that moment I noticed her lady's maid had stilled halfway through her task of arranging Eileen's hair. I met her gaze and she glared at me. My brow furrowed. Why was she so hostile?

Eileen noticed her servant's pause and looked up. "Is something the matter?"

"Of course not, Your Highness; forgive me." She resumed her work with a blush, but she poked the pins into Eileen's hair with far more force than before, as if our conversation had distressed her, which was strange, considering we'd only been speaking of Ali...

My breath hooked as a possibility dawned on me, one that was impossible to rid myself of once it had taken root: this maid was interested in Ali. Was he interested in her as well? I suddenly became eager to find out.

I narrowed my eyes at the maid, analyzing. She was annoyingly beautiful. Brunette, green-eyed...were those traits Alastar found appealing? Suddenly my own lovely appearance looking back at me in the mirror seemed utterly lacking. Maybe Ali didn't like blondes.

Wait, why did I care whether Alastar preferred blondes or brunettes? The feelings from the garden returned—intense, beautiful, and utterly bewildering—but they were mingled with something more—a sharp, burning feeling that slowly seeped over me like poison.

"Rosie?"

I didn't respond to my friend, only continued glaring at the offending maid, who seemed even more concentrated on arranging Eileen's hair. I managed to tear my gaze away and it met up with Eileen's in the mirror.

Her expression softened. "Thinking of him?"

I couldn't *stop* thinking of him. His earlier words occupied my thoughts, making it impossible to focus on anything else. What had he meant that the enchanted fruit had worked for him? He'd said it with such passion, as if it truly had illuminated precious feelings.

And then a possibility occurred to me, causing me to gasp. Could he possibly…hold a *tendre* for me?

I'D EXPECTED my first official state dinner to be a grand affair, but so far, it had been nothing but dull, dull, dull. Although admittedly, making my grand entrance with the crown prince and princess had been a thrill, not to mention I looked every bit a princess myself, as Eileen had lent me a beautiful pink formal gown.

Only one thing marred the moment: Ali and the puzzle about what he felt for me, which still occupied my thoughts. I'd no sooner entered the banquet room than I began frantically searching for him, finding him standing rigidly in his usual place against the wall. My heart gave a strange leap. My bitterness concerning our recent fight melted away at seeing him, and a strange flutter filled my heart—similar to the one I'd felt in the garden.

I analyzed the feeling. What was it? It was almost as if…I was *attracted* to Ali, or found I liked him more than a friend, feelings which were ridiculous, of course. After all, he was just a guard, far from being a handsome prince. Besides, I knew what *true love* felt like, considering I'd felt it with Prince Liam. The emotions I felt for both men weren't even close to being the same.

Still, I experienced a strange urgency to flounce by him so he could get a full view of me in my princess finery. I lifted my chin, delicately took hold of my gown, and walked gracefully past him, making sure my skirt grazed his legs as I glided by. I couldn't wait to see his reaction. I glanced coyly over my shoulder…

Nothing. He kept his gaze straight ahead, his jaw tight, not even acknowledging me with his usual eyebrow lift or lip-twitching half smiles. I frowned. After his earlier display in the garden, I'd been so sure that perhaps he harbored a little crush on me. But then why was he ignoring me? I tightened my jaw and swiveled away, determined to ignore him in return. I refused to let him ruin my first state dinner.

Unfortunately, Ali's help wasn't needed to make this the most tedious meal I'd ever participated in at the palace. I could see why Eileen struggled with being a princess at times. The dignitaries were all old and stuffy, speaking in a dry monotone on the dullest of subjects. My few attempts to liven up the conversation with entertaining stories received blank stares from the dignitaries. After the third attempt, I gave up and resigned myself to sitting in silence, suppressing my frequent yawns and stealing peeks at Ali, who didn't glance towards me once the entire meal.

He certainly wasn't showing any interest in me. In fact, he almost appeared *uninterested.* It was most confusing…and frustrating.

I hoped to escape the tedium when the dinner concluded, only to find myself trapped inside a stuffy parlor filled with these same dignitaries droning on about dull political matters. Soon even my overactive mind—which normally never seemed to run out of stories—had been lulled to sleep.

I glanced longingly out the window. It was such a sunny evening. If I were at home in Arador, I'd spend such a day not cooped up as I was now, but instead in my favorite meadow, with a basket of day-old pastries and a stack of my favorite fairy tales. Even if I was expected to help my parents in the bakery, there we could at least exchange stories as we went through the familiar, comforting motions of baking. A sudden homesickness swelled within my breast. I never thought I'd find my common girl life more exciting than any moment I spent in a palace.

I tried passing the time thinking of Prince Liam. But even while immersing myself in my favorite daydream of our utterly romantic palace tour, I found my mind drifting, instead finding myself repeatedly trying to engage Ali's attention, but he remained aloof and distant. He'd clearly not gotten over our fight. Or perhaps he'd decided he no longer liked me—if he even had in the first place.

The political conversation still swirled around me. I fought to suppress another yawn and glanced sideways at Eileen to see if she was experiencing the same struggles to stay awake. No sign of boredom filled her face. Instead she sat with perfect posture and unwavering attention, responding with graceful, intelligent comments. Aiden frequently smiled at her, his eyes filled with such tenderness, clearly extremely proud of her. The sweet display gave me my first smile of the evening. Despite Eileen's frequent worries, she was doing a wonderful job.

I glanced at the clock. Only a quarter of an hour had inched past. How much longer would I be expected to endure this? If only I could sneak into the kitchens, where I could help the servants clean up and spend the evening exchanging stories, just as I'd passed many evenings at the palace—but unfortunately I was expected to remain.

I prayed for something to break up this monotony, and a miracle occurred in the form of a dark-haired parlor maid arriving, bearing tea and sweets. Excellent. Eating would provide a much-needed distraction. I immediately—but daintily—dove in. Ooh, raspberry custard, delicious. Could this be Ali's favorite treat? I'd no sooner taken a bite than my gaze drifted back towards him. I stiffened. He still wasn't paying attention to me, nor to Eileen. Instead, he was fixated on the maid. My eyes narrowed. Why was he watching *her*?

She handed a cup to an aging ambassador sitting close to where Ali stood guarding and glanced at him to bat her eyelashes. For a moment they stared at one another before she smiled coyly, flirtatiously, and he lifted his eyebrow back.

I nearly choked, and then I was coughing, but despite the noise attracting the attention of nearly everyone in the room —including an icy glare from Princess Seren--it didn't even warrant a glance from Ali. Instead he remained fixated on the maid, his eyebrow still raised, a gesture he'd given me dozens of times but which I now realized meant nothing special.

I was never going to share my famous brownies with that parlor maid ever again.

The maid finished her task and left the room, pausing only to give Ali a lingering look. My jaw tightened. So it was like *that*. The two obviously shared a tender relationship. Was it just the two of them, or did Ali also toy with Eileen's lady maid? He'd wasted no time after I'd admitted that I considered him handsome to think himself a lady's man. He probably now raised his eyebrow and twitched his lips at every girl that came along, the rogue.

The burning pain had returned, and I finally recognized it for what it was: *jealousy*. Yes—I, Rosalina, was envious that a mere guard seemed to be interested in multiple women, none of whom were me. Well, I refused to allow him to steal my affections now. Whatever *spark* had transpired between us in the garden had clearly only been a flirtatious game to him and meant nothing. I wouldn't allow that confusing encounter to distract me from my *real* prince.

I shoved away every strange, fluttery feeling I'd ever felt for that guard and forced myself to focus on Prince Liam, the only man for me. My spell was almost ready, and then I'd finally win the heart of my prince, giving him the strength to finally break his forced engagement so he could cherish me--and only me. That was the only happily ever after I wanted, and nothing—especially any unwelcome feelings for that slippery guard—would cause me to stray from my chosen course.

CHAPTER 15

After my long and arduous quest, I, Rosalina, had finally succeeded in creating my love spell. Prince Liam had arrived earlier in the day, and seeing him again had only confirmed he was the prince for me. In his absence, my thoughts had admittedly wavered slightly—undoubtedly Alastar's doing. But when I greeted Prince Liam and he kissed my hand with his usual dimpled smile, my destiny had once again become clear.

I beamed at the chocolates, perfectly round and the most delectable-looking dark brown. They looked so delicious I was tempted to sample one myself. I clasped my hands and squealed. What a brilliant success.

"Do you want to wake the entire palace?" Ali grumbled.

I spun around to see him standing in the doorway. I unconsciously ran my fingers through my tangled hair, damp and wild from having spent a good portion of the midnight hours melting chocolate over a hot fire. "How did you know I was here?"

"I followed the scent of mischief and naturally knew you were the source."

At the mention of mischief, I subtly scooted so my body hid my chocolates. "Mischief?"

"Indeed." I expected his lips to twitch as he studied me but instead his expression was rather sullen; he undoubtedly hadn't gotten over our recent fight. Despite by own lingering annoyance, I still experienced the sudden urge to get lost in his eyes—a rather strange notion—so naturally I severed our gaze and stared at the chocolate-splattered floor instead. But hard as I tried, I couldn't resist the strange lure pulling me to Ali for long. I peeked up at him through my flock of golden hair to discover him no longer looking at me but studying the splotched floor with a puckered brow.

"What's been going on here?" he asked.

"Nothing," I squeaked, sidling over a few more inches to make sure my chocolates were completely masked from view. He cocked an eyebrow.

"I sincerely doubt that. What are you hiding, Rosie?"

I gnawed my lip, fighting the curse that was anxious to escape at the predicament I was quickly finding myself in. "I'm not hiding anything."

He stepped more fully into the kitchen, eyes suspicious. I wriggled beneath his scrutiny. "The guilt filling your eyes, your rigid posture, and the chocolate all over the floor indicate otherwise."

I growled in frustration, a very unappealing heroine moment, to be sure. "Why are you so observant?"

"I'm a guard, Rosie. It's my job."

I sighed and reluctantly scooted over so he could see my arrangement of beautiful chocolates all lined up in darling rows on the tray.

He gawked at them. "You didn't."

"I did! Aren't they delightful? I've never made anything so perfect."

The only advantage to having been discovered was it gave

me the opportunity to brag, and since Ali had been rendered temporarily speechless, I swelled myself up in preparation to tell the entire tale.

"When we squabbled about this the other day, I only had one ingredient remaining that was being stubbornly elusive. After baking up a tracking tart last night, I was able to find it in the Forest this morning. Naturally, I didn't waste a moment and immediately whipped up these chocolates as soon as the kitchen was free. It was quite the adventure—mincing all the ingredients small enough to stir them seamlessly into the chocolate as it melted over the smoldering hearth, but look how splendidly they turned out!"

Ali listened to my recitation without altering his expression. When I finished, up went his eyebrow. "What a stirring account of how unhappy endings are created."

My heart lurched. "Whatever do you mean?"

"This path will undoubtedly lead to a very unhappy Rosie."

I pressed my hands to my hips. "If this was the wrong path, the chocolates wouldn't have come out so splendidly. See?" I seized the tray and held it out to him for his inspection, waving it beneath his nose. "Don't they look tasty?"

He cocked an eyebrow. "You're offering me a love spell? You want me to fall in love with you?"

Heat flared my cheeks. "Of course not." What a ridiculous notion. He was obviously trying to charm me just like he charmed the palace maids, but I refused to fall for it. I slammed the tray on the counter.

"Even if I ate one of your spelled chocolates and it actually worked, it wouldn't create real love."

"You're so unromantic," I snapped. "Don't you believe in love?"

Although his expression didn't falter, the look he gave me was intense. "I do, more than you know, but I don't believe such an emotion can be created through magic. Even if these worked"—he tipped his head towards my rows of chocolates —"it would merely create a façade of love, an infatuation, which isn't true love at all. I'm surprised that you—a girl with the most romantic heart I've ever encountered—don't want something *real.*"

I flinched. "Of course I do, but I must do *something* to hurry things along in winning my prince, for unfortunately, my true love's unwanted marriage is imminent, and only a love spell will give him the strength to break away from his duty."

"Prince Liam isn't your true love," Alastar said. "The more you come to know His Highness, the more you'll realize how ill-suited you two are. If you spell him only to realize he's not *the one*, you'll find yourself in a bundle of trouble."

My jaw tightened. "That's not going to happen. He's my prince and I'm his princess."

"No, he's *a* prince," Ali corrected. "But marrying a title isn't enough to guarantee the happily ever after you desire. One day you'll finally realize that and will be quite unhappy that you're stuck with him." His grave expression settled into determination. "As your friend, it's my responsibility to intervene."

I narrowed my eyes. "*Intervene?*"

"Yes. Since you have continually ignored my advice to not bake the love spell, you've left me with no other choice."

His eyes honed in on the chocolates. I gasped and stood in front of them like a shield. "You wouldn't!"

"Wouldn't I?" He stepped closer. "My duty is first to the crown, which includes protecting Prince Liam from your scheme."

"Thwarting the heroine's goal isn't a noble act, but an evil one."

He advanced another step, then another, taunting me

with his slow approach. I pressed my back against the edge of the counter, desperate to protect the spelled chocolates I'd worked so hard on.

"It pains me to be temporarily cast as your antagonist, but I find myself quite invested in your happily ever after. Thus I must take drastic action."

"Drastic action?" My voice shook. "Your scheme better not be to steal my love spell." By the gleam in his eyes, I knew that was precisely his dastardly intention.

He took another slow and deliberate step, as if he delighted in extending my torture as part of this villainous game.

"Don't steal my love spell. Please, Alastar."

He froze. "*Alastar*? Are we back to formality?" He sounded rather disappointed.

"Villains don't deserve nicknames."

"But don't friends?"

"If you steal my love spell, we're no longer friends and never will be ever again."

His normally rigid expression actually crumpled. "We *are* friends, Rosie."

"Rosalina."

He sighed. "Very well, Miss Rosalina."

My formal name sounded so wrong passing Ali's lips—no, *Alastar,* I corrected myself. He deserved no nickname from me.

"We are friends," he continued. "That's why I must stop you." He finally closed the distance between us. "I know you, Rosie. You won't be satisfied with anything less than the most perfect of happy endings. Being trapped in a loveless marriage with a prince you scarcely know won't make you happy."

"It will, for Prince Liam will be in love with me," I protested.

"He'll be *infatuated,* Rosie. I know you don't want that, and as your friend I don't want that for you, either. Hence, you've left me with no other alternative."

He grabbed me by the waist and hoisted me away from the counter in order to seize the tray of spelled chocolates. I shrieked and pounced, whacking him with my fists. Pain laced along my wrists as I hit him over and over, but my efforts were futile; he was too strong. In no time at all, he'd swept my dozen chocolates into his satchel.

"Give those back!"

"Calm down, Rosie; you don't want to wake the entire palace."

"I'll wake up anyone who'll come to my rescue and lock you away as a thief." My tears escaped and his expression twisted.

"I'm sorry, Rosie."

"Don't call me that," I stuttered, finally giving up on hitting him and burying my face in my now throbbing hands. "You're evil, Alastar. I do believe I hate you." I never should have let that rigid guard weasel his way into my affections; it made his betrayal even worse.

"I'm sorry for that, too. It pains me to be your antagonist." He brushed my shoulder, but I flinched away and glared.

"You've ruined my happily ever after."

"Believe it or not, I've just saved it. I hope one day you'll realize that." He carefully took my hands in his large, calloused ones and examined them. Despite my anger, I shuddered at his touch. The reaction frightened me. I tried to yank away, but his hold was firm. "Oh dear, your hands are red. Do they hurt?"

"All because of *you.*" I fought to ignore the pleasant sensations rippling across my skin as he massaged the backs of my hands with his thumbs. They somehow hurt less with him touching me. "You're the most evil villain that's ever existed. Release me at once."

He obediently, albeit reluctantly, did. I seized the opportunity and dove for his satchel, trying to yank it away, but once again he was far too strong. He pushed me away both forcibly and surprisingly gently.

"I'm sorry, Rosalina." His normally stoic expression was a mask of regret—or rather *false* regret; villains experienced nothing but villainous emotions.

"You're not sorry. From the beginning, you've done everything in your power to continuously thwart me at every turn."

"One day you'll finally understand that we're on the same team." He bowed and strode from the room, taking the spell I'd worked so hard on with him.

"I won't be thwarted," I called to his retreating back. "I'll do whatever it takes to obtain my fairy-tale ending."

He paused in the doorway to glance back. "As will I, Rosie."

He disappeared, leaving me with my heart wrenching and glaring after him with clenched fists in the middle of the messy kitchen scattered with chocolate-covered pots and pans I'd used to create the most perfect and now stolen love spell.

But losing Ali was far more painful, a loss made more torturous considering he'd been a villain in disguise this entire time.

IF ALASTAR BELIEVED he could foil my fairy tale so easily, he'd missed an essential Heroine Rosalina character trait: *determination*. I avoided him all the next morning as I plotted my next move—for there *would* be a next move; that was guaranteed.

"Alright Rosie, the suspense is driving me mad," Eileen said at breakfast. "What's happened between you and Alastar? You're glaring at him like—"

"—like he's a dastardly fiend."

"Exactly. Wait, what?"

"That guard is a menace." To my annoyance, he made no acknowledgement of the sharp dialogue I was using to attack his character; he merely continued staring rigidly ahead, which only angered me further. "Throw him in the dungeon, Eileen, and let him rot."

"*What?*" She exchanged an alarmed and thoroughly puzzled look with Aiden. "What ever for? Did you two get in a fight?"

"No, I merely unmasked the traitor. He's a thief."

Eileen raised an eyebrow, and I hated the reminder of the guard I was quite determinedly not looking at...until I skewered him with another glare, silently cursing when he didn't even flinch.

"You heinous villain, I worked hard on those."

He still said nothing. Eileen and Aiden exchanged another look before Aiden turned to Alastar. "Is it true you stole from Rosalina?"

"Yes, Your Highness, it is."

Aiden's expression hardened as his fierce Dark Prince persona settled over him. "Stealing is not condoned, Guard Alastar."

"Of course not, Your Highness."

"And yet you stole from our guest, the dearest friend of Her Highness?"

"Yes, Your Highness." He was as stoic as ever, without even the hint of cracking under his prince's interrogation.

My hand tightened on my butter knife. "May I suggest the dungeon?"

Aiden sighed. "Such an extreme won't be necessary, Rosalina."

"But he's a thief!"

"Indeed." His frown deepened. "This behavior is most unlike you, Alastar. I demand an explanation."

"I stole spelled chocolates intended for His Highness Prince Liam."

I skewered Alastar with a glare. First a thief and now a traitor; Alastar was proving to be the King of all Villains.

Aiden's mouth fell open and Eileen spun on me with a gasp. "Oh, Rosie, I thought we told you to not spell Liam."

"But I need to spell him. He's my prince." I turned imploringly towards Aiden. "Tell Alastar to return the spell so that I can."

Aiden sighed heavily. "Rosalina..." He shook his head and then turned to *that guard*. "Thank you for your interference, Alastar."

He bowed. "Of course, Your Highness."

"*What*!?" I slammed my hands on the table, shaking the cutlery. "You're condoning a thief? What kind of monarchy is this?"

"Please, Rosalina, calm yourself," Aiden said sternly, the force of his black eyes causing me to sink several inches in my seat. "His job is to protect the crown, even if it means stealing forbidden love spells from over-excited girls. I will not have anyone connected to me or my crown do something so dishonorable."

Eileen laid a hand on Aiden's arm. "Dear..."

Aiden turned a rare frown towards her. "Please don't tell me you approve of her attempting to spell a member of the Dracerian Royal Family, darling."

"Of course I don't, but please scold her as a friend, not as the prince."

Aiden intertwined his hand with hers. "Very well, love." He turned back to me, considerably less fierce and regal. "I apologize for my harshness, Rosalina, but please understand that I cannot allow you to spell Prince Liam or anyone else while within these palace walls. Am I understood?"

"Yes," I grumbled, slouching further in my seat.

Eileen forced a smile that didn't quite reach her eyes. "Excellent. Now that that's settled, I'd like to discuss today's plans. Would you like to visit the waterfall with me, Rosie?"

"Will *he* be joining us?" I asked, not even sparing that guard a glance.

"Of course he will."

"Then no thank you."

Eileen sighed. "This is ridiculous, Rosie. Don't avoid me because of Alastar."

I folded my arms and stuck my chin in the air. "If he'll be there, then I won't be."

Hurt filled Eileen's expression. She turned her wounded expression towards Aiden, who sent me the deadliest of glares for inflicting pain on his beloved wife.

Even though it was childish, I remained undeterred. I spent the remainder of the day continuing to avoid Eileen—and thus Alastar—and plotting until I finally came up with a brilliant plan to take back what was mine: I'd sneak into the scoundrel's room, steal back my spell, and thus restore my story back to its proper course.

AFTER EILEEN and Aiden left for the waterfall—taking that thieving guard with them—I put my plan into action. It'd taken some snooping in the royal library to uncover a map of the palace in order to locate the guards' quarters—and considerable more time spying outside the guards' rooms in order to learn which one was Alastar's—but naturally I, Rosalina, had succeeded.

I made my way through the labyrinth of corridors, encountering no one except for the parlor maid who'd been openly flirting with Ali the other evening. I froze, my heart flaring at her presence so near Ali's door. What was *she* doing here? If I hadn't been trying to be stealthy, I'd have confronted her. As it was, I hovered behind the corner and watched her suspiciously until she disappeared down the other end of the hall.

I tiptoed towards Ali's door and tentatively jiggled the knob. Excellent, a spot of luck: it was unlocked. Cleverness was obviously not in his bag of villain tricks.

I slipped inside and for a moment simply basked in the fact I was inside Ali's room—or rather, *Alastar's*. I looked around hungrily. His room was simple and impeccably neat, with no sign anyone lived here. I poked around in hopes of discovering something about my foe. Unfortunately, that quest ended most disappointingly. I paused, blinking rapidly to tug myself from my curious snooping. I couldn't afford distractions. I had a mission: locate my spelled chocolates.

I expected to have to tear the room apart, but to my astonishment they were in the first place I searched—beneath the mattress. What an obvious hiding place. Clearly he'd greatly underestimated my determination, taking no thought to hide them in a more secure location. Alastar really was the worst villain ever. But no matter; I had what I wanted.

I unwrapped them from their cloth prison and admired them. They looked even more perfect in the sunlight streaming through the window, exactly like chocolates one would purchase in a candy shop. I, Rosalina, was amazing. I carefully wrapped them back up, but before doing so, I did something quite clever.

Now, an ordinary heroine would take the batch in its entirety, but I was more crafty than that. I wrapped two chocolates in my handkerchief and tucked them into my bosom. I slipped the rest of the chocolates into my satchel and tiptoed from the room, escaping unnoticed. I was just congratulating myself on a scheme well done when someone cleared his throat behind me.

I closed my eyes with a heavy sigh. Of course *he'd* catch me. How did he always know when I was up to something? But a heroine encountering obstacles during a quest was, unfortunately, an essential element in any story. I suppose things had been a bit too easy up until this point.

I slowly turned around and plastered on a fake smile. "Fancy seeing you here, Ali—*Alastar. Guard* Alastar."

"I was going to say the same thing, Miss Rosalina, before you stole my line." He gave me a searching look. "What is a prestigious guest such as yourself doing in the servants' section, specifically outside my bedroom?"

"Just...wandering the palace, as usual."

"Seems out of character to see you engaged in such an activity at any time other than midnight." His eyes narrowed and I wriggled beneath his penetrating stare.

"I'm not doing anything wrong. Eileen granted me free rein of the palace." My voice shook, betraying me. "What are *you* doing here? Slacking in your guarding duties?"

"Not in the least," Alastar said. "Her Highness decided not to go to the waterfall after all, due to missing her best friend, who is currently avoiding her for childish reasons. I was sent by Her Highness to plead for you to get over your annoyance with me, commanded quite forcefully to do whatever it took for us to resolve our squabble, and told to inspire the proper guilt in order to cajole you into joining Her Highness for tea in the garden."

The intended guilt at my being a terrible friend prickled my heart; Eileen didn't deserve to suffer because of Alastar's mischief. "Tea in the garden sounds lovely. Let me just...go to my room for a moment." I'd taken no more than a single step when Alastar stepped forward.

"What's in your satchel, Rosalina? Spelled chocolates stolen from my bedroom, perhaps?"

I stared wide-eyed at him. What did a heroine do when the antagonist detected her scheme? Only one thing.

I turned and bolted down the corridor, but Alastar easily caught up to me and seized me from behind. I immediately shrieked and fought to break free.

"Let me go, you fiend! Unhand me, you villain! Release your prisoner, you dastardly scoundrel!"

"Trying to decide which bit of dialogue sounds best?" Alastar's breath tickled my ear as he whispered into it. For a moment I stopped fighting in order to savor his firm, warm arms wrapped so snugly around me.

Goodness, what was I *thinking*? This was exactly how villains kidnapped unsuspecting girls—by luring them in with their charming wiles before revealing their true dastardly colors—and I was anything but a stupid heroine.

I jammed my elbow into his stomach, but although he *oof*ed, his confining hold didn't loosen; the only damage seemed to be my throbbing elbow. "Are your abs made of steel?"

"I'm a guard, Rosie, and thus am expected to maintain a well-built physique, which I understand most girls seem to appreciate."

I froze and a strange burning tightened my chest. "Which girls? I knew you were having flings with half the palace maids."

He chuckled and had the audacity to give me a snuggle. "Oh Rosie, you certainly have an imaginative mind." My entire body shuddered and I cursed my body's reaction, ill-timed in a moment when Alastar was definitely the scene's antagonist. "Your reaction means we're still friends after all."

"We most certainly are *not*."

"We are, even when you become furious with me for doing this." He reached into my satchel and snatched my wrapped chocolates. I shrieked and made to grab them, but he easily held me away.

"Why do you have to be so strong?" I panted. "It's especially annoying when you continually use your strength to thwart the heroine's goal."

"I look at it more as helping the princess." He set me down and tucked my chocolates under his arm. "I recommend studying lock picking in the royal library, for I'm never leaving my door unlocked again."

"I can't believe you were foolish enough to do so in the first place."

"Well, I figured you'd want these back."

"Hence it was idiotic not to lock your door."

His lips twitched. "I clearly underestimated you."

I made another futile attempt to steal the chocolates, but after a wrestling match—which I unfortunately lost quite horribly—I figured I'd given enough of a fight for Ali not to be suspicious of my giving in so easily.

"You may have won this battle, but the war isn't over, Ali...*Alastar*."

"Indeed, I know it's not," he said, his tone far too cheerful for him currently being threatened by a very determined heroine. "I'm looking forward to your next plan of attack. It will definitely keep me on my toes, I'm sure."

"It certainly will. Prepare for your demise." I flounced away, smiling the moment my back was turned at the knowledge of the two spelled chocolates safely hidden in my bosom. What would follow next in my tale would be a spelled prince, a royal wedding, and my living the rest of my happily ever after in the the Dracerian palace, for my formidable foe, the dragon Alastar, had been successfully vanquished, and as such wouldn't be able to meddle in my story ever again.

CHAPTER 16

I hadn't seen much of my prince since he'd arrived at the palace a few days ago due to his being trapped in boring meetings with Aiden, but he was much more princely than I'd remembered. I admired each of his regal features hungrily as we sat together in the parlor—wavy golden hair, startling blue eyes, engaging conversation, and a charming smile…there was no doubt about it: he was *the one*.

Perhaps I was making more progress in our romance than I'd initially believed, for he cast me frequent glances throughout tea. My spelled chocolate waited in my reticule, in a pretty box tied with an aqua ribbon, for the perfect moment to give it to him. Unfortunately, Ali—*Alastar*—had so far foiled my actually doing so by monitoring me a bit too closely. Aggravating. Why would he be suspicious when he thought he'd stolen back all my chocolates?

I sent him several glares until Liam turned to talk to Aiden, giving me the opportunity to stomp to where Alastar rigidly stood at his usual place against the wall. "You're supposed to be watching Eileen, not me," I hissed.

"She's asked me to keep you out of trouble," he said.

This time I glowered at my so-called friend, who'd noticed me talking to her guard and smiled back a bit too innocently.

"Did she, now?" That was a decidedly non-best-friend action for her to have taken, and behind my back nonetheless.

"Naturally, for it wouldn't do for you to cause mischief when a prestigious guest is visiting."

"I'm not causing mischief; I'm *plotting*."

"Meaning you're about to carry out something devious."

I rolled my eyes. "You are, as usual, annoying." I flounced back to my seat. As I settled against the satin cushions, Eileen leaned forward with a conniving smile.

"How is dear Alastar doing?"

"He's obnoxious, as usual." I took the opportunity to send him another delicious glare. He didn't react as he continued watching me with the intense attention only a guard could give. "Why did you ask him to watch me?"

Eileen sipped her tea with a bit too casual of an air. "I figured he'd be doing it anyway, so he might as well not be shirking his duties in doing so. Besides, I recognize that gleam in your eye—you're up to something."

I tightened my jaw. Why did everyone always assume I was up to mischief? Writing stories was anything but.

A reprieve from the awkwardness of that accusation came when the maid Eloise entered the room with a fresh tray of tea and sweets. I smiled at her and was thrilled when she returned it. She was the maid who cleaned my room, and whenever I happened to see her, I made it a habit of sitting on my bed and keeping her company while she worked.

She glanced at Aiden and Eileen—who hadn't even looked up at her entrance—before pointing to her bulging apron pocket, where I glimpsed the note I'd written for her and left on my pillow with one of my famous sugar cookies. Excellent, she'd received my treat.

I glanced at Alastar to see if he'd taken notice of the maid, but his gaze remained riveted to me. Despite not wanting him to watch me because he was suspicious, this thought still cheered me. At Eloise's departure, I attempted once again to find a way to capture Liam's attention. I sensed Eileen's gaze and turned to find her smiling.

"Is she one of the servants you've befriended?"

"Yes, Eloise," I said. "She's a lovely person who has adorable twins. She let me play with them the other day when you and Aiden had that long meeting. I love babies. When are you and Aiden going to have one?"

My question yanked Aiden's attention from his conversation with Liam. A rare blush filled his cheeks, but Eileen's expression lit up. "I'm not sure. Hopefully we'll be blessed with a child soon." She reached for Aiden's hand and he leaned over to whisper in her ear, leaving Prince Liam without a conversation partner. I saw my chance and scooted into the seat next to him.

"Prince Liam, it's a pleasure to see you again. It's been far too long since we last conversed."

"Indeed it has, Miss Rosalina." A strange smile played across his face. He cast a glance over my shoulder at something and I turned around to see that it was Alastar. I glared at him once more before turning back to my prince.

"How were your travels, Your Highness?"

"Quite pleasant. I always enjoy the journey to Sortileya. Such beautiful scenery."

"I imagine," I said. "Draceria is also picturesque. There's nothing quite like your kingdom's rolling green hills."

"Sortileya's own forests are quite stunning."

"I thoroughly agree."

And just like that, our conversation ground to a halt. I bit my fingernail as I struggled to come up with *something*, but what did one talk to a prince about? Politics, perhaps, but that topic was a real bore. The weather? No, Rosie, too cliché.

As I deliberated, I noticed Eileen and Aiden frowning at me, as if they sensed I was laying a snare for Prince Liam when really I was only luring him to his happily ever after.

We're only talking, I mouthed to Eileen before turning back to Prince Liam, who studied me closely. But the moment we made eye contact his strange look settled into an easygoing grin. He had a perfect princely smile, complete with gleaming white teeth and that adorable dimple.

I struggled to find something to say. It was strange having my words so stubbornly elusive when normally I never ran out of things to talk about. I glanced sideways back at Prince Liam, looking at me almost expectantly. My cheeks warmed. Desperate for a distraction, I seized a lemon tart from the tea tray. "These are divine."

"I agree. I always eat far too many sweets when I visit Aiden. I suspect he's trying to fatten me up because he's jealous about how good-looking I am. But I can't help being the most popular prince in the five kingdoms." Prince Liam winked, a gesture which, as usual, caused my heart to flutter.

"Don't worry, Your Highness; no number of conniving acts from the Dark Prince could ruin your princely fame."

Prince Liam laughed and I smiled, pleased he found me witty. But unfortunately, this topic quickly ran its course, leaving me once more scrambling for another. Goodness, why was it so difficult talking to my intended? Hopefully, conversation would be easier after he'd taken the love spell. I ached to give it to him now, but Aiden and Eileen were being especially attentive of our conversation.

Topic, Rosie, think of a topic…*any* topic. "Have you heard

any good stories lately, Prince Liam? You always have such entertaining ones."

"Unfortunately, nothing new since we last spoke." Prince Liam snagged a lemon tart and shoved the entire thing in his mouth in a very unroyal manner. "Father keeps me busy with all manner of dull royal duties, not to mention my fiancée, Princess Lavena, is currently visiting for a few weeks. Hence it was a great relief when I was expected in Sortileya for meetings. As much as I detest them, they provide me the perfect excuse to leave, not to mention the company is much more pleasing here." He gave me a wink.

He'd come to see *me*! How spectacular.

Aiden shook his head with a chuckle. "Still avoiding Lavena? You can't evade your fate forever."

"Perhaps not, but I can delay it for as long as possible. It's unbearable thinking I have to marry that horrid woman." He shuddered. "There has to be a way out of that dreaded arrangement, but I have yet to discover an escape clause."

This was going splendidly. He was avoiding Princess Lavena in order to spend time with me. Luckily for him, my love spell would be the answer to all his worries. I immediately plotted my next move.

"You seem to be enjoying the lemon tart, Your Highness. Might I interest you in some chocolates I baked? It's an old family recipe." I slipped it from my reticule and held it out to Prince Liam.

Prince Liam smiled and untied the ribbon. "Thank you, Miss Rosalina, this is most thoughtful." He lifted the lid to reveal the chocolate nestled inside. "Mmm, I do love chocolate."

Alastar leapt forward. "Rosie, you little scamp. Don't eat that, Your Highness."

Prince Liam paused with it halfway lifted to his mouth. "Why, is it poisoned?" He winked at me.

Eileen and Aiden looked up at Alastar's cry. Eileen's eyes widened. "Rosie, is that—"

I gave her a *look* to tell her to keep quiet and not interfere, but it was nowhere near the piercing death glare I sent to Alastar. Eileen spun on her husband.

"Aiden!"

He leapt from his seat. "Liam, don't eat—"

Prince Liam popped the chocolate in his mouth. "Why is everyone so ruffled? Jealous that Miss Rosalina chose *me* to share her sweets with? Hmm, this is quite tasty. I'm quite... enjoying...it..."

His chewing slowed and a blank expression settled over him. I waited with clasped hands and bated breath. How long did it take for a spell to go into effect? What would happen if it didn't work? What if I'd done something wrong? Oh dear, I hoped I hadn't inadvertently poisoned the heir to the Dracerian throne.

"Prince Liam?" I asked hesitantly. He swallowed and blinked rapidly before settling his gaze on me. For a moment, he merely stared, his look smoldering, as if he'd never quite seen me before now.

His mouth fell open. "Oh Rosie, never has such beauty as yours graced my vision. Indeed, with your hair flowing as waves of gold and your eyes the color of sapphires, no creature who ever has ever lived could ever outshine you. You're finer than any jewel."

Ooh, bliss, love compliments! I eagerly leaned closer. He did too and cupped my face. Such a romantic gesture, even if his hand was a bit clammy.

"Oh my dear, darling Rosie, you're so beautiful. How could I have been so blind as to not see that there's no one more worthy of my heart than you?"

I couldn't resist casting Alastar a smug look. His expression was horrified. "What have you done, Rosie?" he hissed.

Prince Liam gently turned my face back towards himself. "Please don't look at anyone else but me, dearest Rosie. I can't survive without staring adoringly into those gorgeous eyes of yours for as long as possible. They're windows to your beautiful soul, which matches mine in every way."

Wow, such poetic phrasing, although the love spell was a bit more potent than I'd planned. I tried to glance at Alastar in order to measure his reaction to Prince Liam's...*intensity*, but before I could manage it—

"Don't look away from me, Rosie." Prince Liam flung himself off the sofa, dropped to his knees, and seized my hand to plant a wet kiss on it. "Dearest Rosie, never look away from me ever again. I couldn't bear it."

Aiden gaped at Prince Liam practically drooling at my feet while Eileen covered her mouth in horror and Prince Liam's personal guard stared at him in bewilderment. "Rosie, you didn't— "

"Win the heart of the prince?" I said with a smirk. "I most certainly did."

"Indeed, dear Rosie," Prince Liam gushed. "My heart is only yours forever. Please allow me even a piece of yours to always treasure, for you're my crown jewel."

I pressed my hand to my heart. My love spell had actually *worked*! Now my happily ever after was back on its proper course. A royal wedding and a castle awaited me in my blissful and magical future.

Aiden groaned as he rubbed his temples. "I can't believe this." He pierced me with the full force of his hardened black eyes. "You have to reverse it."

"Would you really wish for me to lose love now that I've found it?" I asked. "Just look how happy your friend is. You don't want to break his heart, do you?"

"Yes, Rosie, I'm so happy now that I've at last found my true love. I never knew true happiness until you entered my life." Prince Liam pressed kiss after kiss along my knuckles, all while I smirked triumphantly, Aiden and Eileen continued watching helplessly in horror, and Alastar scowled darkly from his place against the wall.

I tried not to pay him any attention, but midst my prince gushing praises at my feet, I couldn't help but steal several glances at Alastar, all while experiencing an emotion that almost felt like...*regret,* as if I'd just lost something precious.

I TOOK A DEEP, wavering breath. "Come on, Rosie, you can do it." But despite my best attempts to convince myself, my hand remained frozen on the doorknob. Goodness, it shouldn't be this difficult to leave my room. By the way I steeled my resolve, one would think I was going into battle rather than encountering my prince under a love spell that had worked perfectly...a bit *too* perfectly, actually.

I frowned at that thought and the secret hope that followed that I could slip away before encountering Prince Liam. My forehead furrowed. Why would I *not* wish to see my prince, especially considering we were a perfect match and he now finally realized it? Perhaps it was merely because his affections were rather...startling. Yes, that had to be it, but surely I'd grow used to them. He was my true love, after all, and as such, nothing would get in the way of my determined happily ever after, even if so far it wasn't exactly what I'd had in mind.

Ever since Prince Liam had eaten the spelled chocolate during yesterday's tea, he'd been following me around like a lovesick puppy, never letting me out of his sight for even a moment, all while gushing compliments that surprisingly had quickly grown wearing.

And then there had been dinner. I squeezed my eyes shut

at the memory. Oh goodness, *dinner.* No moment could be more awkward than having a man gape open-mouthed at me, watching every movement I made so *hungrily,* without bothering to touch his own food. The worst had been when he'd actually *drooled,* right into his soup. Eileen nearly choked while Aiden buried his face in his hand with a groan, all while I died a slow, agonizing death of mortification.

Prince Liam's drooling gaze wasn't the only one I'd felt throughout dinner. Several stolen peeks revealed that Ali—or rather, *Alastar*—appeared to be exclusively watching me, with a rather intense look that seemed to say, "Is this really what you want to live with for the rest of your life?" And I couldn't help but privately admit that Prince Liam's...*obsession* would take some getting used to. Perhaps the love spell would lose some of its intensity over time.

A note slipped beneath my door just then. Although the handwriting was unfamiliar, I immediately knew who it was from. This was my first love letter, but despite having spent my entire life yearning for one, Prince Liam's words left me feeling strangely...*empty* as I read them:

Never have I hated the night until it separated me from my very heart. I'm longing for you.
Your Adoring Liam

Multiple hearts had been drawn around the single line, but they did little to add emotion to the empty words. I tossed it onto my desk before trudging back to the door, knowing Prince Liam was undoubtedly waiting on the other side for me to emerge. He'd likely stand there all day until he saw me, which meant hiding in my room would do absolutely nothing except cause me to waste away with hunger.

With a steadying breath I yanked the door open to reveal

Prince Liam, unsurprisingly waiting with wide, hopeful eyes, which lit up the moment he saw me.

"Darling! I didn't think it was possible, but you're even more beautiful this morning than when we were forced to part last evening. Good morning, my love." He swept a kiss across my hand.

Why did his sweet words feel so shallow? In books, such sentiments caused the heroine's heart to flutter. He was *supposed* to make me feel that way—after all, my heart had fluttered as our eyes met across the ballroom at Eileen's reception—but there was definitely no fluttering occurring within my heart now. As it was, it took everything in me to stifle my groan.

"Good morning, Prince Liam."

"Liam." He offered me his arm, which I took after a strange moment of hesitation. "There's no need for formality between two whose hearts are one. And yes, it's a wonderful morning, for the unbearable night that separated us is finally over. What a horrible night it was. I thought of you the entire time, of course, and dreamed of you most longingly. Did you like my love letter? I hope it pleased you, for I so want to please you. Please tell me I did." He gave me a pathetically hopeful look. I forced myself to smile.

"It was quite lovely."

He brightened. "I'm so glad you liked it. I shall compose you infinitely more in our future together." He suddenly jerked us to a stop. "What's wrong, darling? Why are you frowning?"

I didn't realize I had been until he mentioned it. I forced another smile. "No reason at all. Please don't worry yourself."

He traced my frown with his fingertip, and it felt nothing like when Alastar had traced my smile during our time beside the pond several days earlier. "How can I not worry about my precious petal? Perhaps food will cheer you up."

He led me into the private dining room. A chorus of good mornings greeted us, seeming slightly insincere with the way Eileen and Aiden exchanged wary looks when they saw me on Prince Liam's arm.

Just like last night, Aiden and Eileen had arranged for us to dine with Prince Liam away from the king and Princess Seren—seeming keen on keeping his condition a carefully guarded secret for as long as possible—but although his lovesick behavior was hidden from their scrutiny, we couldn't escape the attending servants, who gawked at Prince Liam with every infatuated action he performed; his personal guard in particular seemed to be having a difficult time containing his bewilderment. Undoubtedly, the gossip about Prince Liam's condition would quickly spread and soon reach His Majesty's ears. By Aiden's dark expression, he feared the same thing.

I quite determinedly didn't look at a certain guard as Prince Liam helped me into my seat, although I was strongly aware of his presence. Prince Liam had no sooner assisted me than he scampered eagerly to take the one across from me. Oh dear, I couldn't bear to endure another meal of his gawking. Would every meal be like this for the rest of my life? I gnawed at my nail at the thought.

Obviously, drooling royals weren't far from the mind of a certain individual, for *that guard* suddenly broke his protocol of remaining a silent and invisible presence in order to speak up.

"Shall I fetch His Highness a bib, Prince Aiden, considering he's once again sitting across from Miss Rosie?"

Eileen snorted into her juice but Aiden's hardened disapproval didn't even falter. "Thank you, Alastar, but that won't be necessary. Will it, Liam?" He gave him a sharp look.

Prince Liam sighed. "I suppose not, but how can I not stare at this most lovely of women? Rosie's beauty is like the sun. Can you expect me not to bask in her presence after an entire night without her?"

Aiden blinked at him—for once, in all the time I'd known him, seeming at a loss for words.

"It was the longest night of my life," Prince Liam continued. "Immediately upon waking, I wrote of my torment in a love letter for my Rosie. Shall we share it with them, love?"

I became extra occupied with my poached eggs and bacon. "I don't have it with me."

"You don't?" Prince Liam gasped so sharply you'd think I'd left an essential body part behind rather than a piece of paper. "But I thought you were planning on cherishing it forever."

"I didn't want to get it dirty," I said hastily, praying that my white lie would wriggle me out of this mess before Prince Liam burst into tears, which he looked precariously close to doing. To my immense relief, his expression cleared.

"So thoughtful, darling. It's quite alright; I have it memorized. Would you all like to hear it?"

Oh, please no. He wouldn't really.... "Prince Liam, that won't be necessary."

"It's *Liam*, my sweet," he said. "And of course it is, Rosie. Shouldn't our love for one another be declared openly?"

Already my face flamed as Prince Liam swelled up to share what would likely be one of the most humiliating moments of my life, all while Eileen wore an expression bordering between curiosity and dismay and Aiden became extra preoccupied with his food, his jaw tight. I was immensely grateful I wasn't facing *that guard*; the thought of his reaction bothered me more than all the rest.

Prince Liam cleared his throat and recited with the utmost tenderness, "The words I penned my petal this morning: 'Never have I hated the night until it separated me from my very heart. I'm longing for you.'"

An awkward silence that was anything but reverent followed, broken only by a snort from *him*, which made the situation all the more humiliating. Eileen cast Alastar a puzzled look while the meaning behind his snort gnawed at me. Was he unmoved by romantic sentiments? Was his heart made of stone? And why wasn't he bothered by Prince Liam's affections? Shouldn't he be? And if he wasn't, why not? Because for some reason, I felt he *should* be.

And the fact that he apparently wasn't caused inexplicable anger to bubble within me. I turned to glare at him and his twitching lips. "Is something amusing?"

"Oh, just—" He snorted again and I narrowed my eyes.

"You find such romantic sentiments humorous?"

"It's just so…*ridiculous*."

Prince Liam gave him a scathing glare, as if any insult towards a poem about me was a slander to my character.

"Not in the least," I snapped, despite that having been my exact thought when I'd first read the love note. Why did such sentiments seem so romantic in books but so out of place in the real world?

Alastar cocked his eyebrow. "Oh? You're truly moved by such shallow words?"

"They weren't *shallow*," I said. "His note was perfectly romantic."

He snorted again. "If you say so, Rosie."

"*Rosalina*." I twisted back around so I could avoid looking at him. Prince Liam had the most peculiar look on his face that bordered on amusement. It cleared the moment our gazes met, a gesture that was strangely still absent of any flutters I was still waiting for. How long did they take to arrive when one was with their true love?

"You really enjoyed the letter, my sweet?"

"Oh yes," I lied, determined to do so for no other motive than to bother a certain guard. "Very much."

"Excellent. I shall write you another before the morning ends."

"How...lovely. I mean...that sounds wonderful." That response was sure to rile that guard.

The rest of breakfast stretched endlessly and was almost as unbearable as yesterday's dinner. Once again Prince Liam spent the entire meal gawking, but thankfully he didn't drool again—I likely would have died of humiliation if he had.

Unfortunately, the rest of the meal didn't fare much better. I was left with Prince Liam reciting accolades to my unparalleled beauty. I promptly tuned him out to daydream up other places I'd rather be than here. There were so many wonderful options—from exploring the dungeons at midnight to being kidnapped by an evil witch and carried off on her broomstick. I'd just settled on curling up next to a sleeping dragon as a nice alternative to enduring this visit when Prince Liam once more demanded my attention.

"You're daydreaming again, my darling love. Won't you share the thoughts of that delightful mind of yours?"

"Just thinking about dragons." Despite my annoyance with him, my gaze instinctively darted sideways to Alastar's. His lips twitched and I managed a half-smile back. Unfortunately, Prince Liam noticed our exchange and his eyes narrowed as he once again tried to tug my wavering attention back to him.

"What about dragons?"

"Just how pleasant it would be to be currently sleeping next to a particularly hungry one."

Prince Liam seemed thoroughly perplexed while Alastar snorted and winked, clearly knowing exactly why I'd been thinking of starving dragons and how pleased I'd be to offer myself up as a tasty morsel for them to enjoy.

The endless meal continued. Despite it thankfully remaining drool free, Prince Liam embarrassed me in other ways, particularly when he shushed Aiden right in the middle of speaking. "Hush up, Aiden, Rosie looks like she's about to say something."

I most certainly hadn't been. I glanced up, my mouth still full of my recent bite of toast, which I hastily shallowed. "I wasn't, so please allow Aiden to finish his comment."

Prince Liam waved that idea away. "Who cares about *his* comment; I'd much rather hear yours. I want to hear every thought that passes through your pretty head."

Aiden raised both eyebrows in shock. I doubted he'd ever been shushed by anyone his entire life. My jaw tightened. "I wasn't going to say anything, Prince Liam."

"Liam," he corrected. "If not, then please do, my sweet, so that I can hear the melodious sound of your voice."

I gawked at him for a moment before I glanced incredulously at Alastar, whose normally expressionless face clearly radiated, *I told you so*. Oh, how I hated his annoying tendency to rile me. I'd play this tedious game with Prince Liam, just to wipe that smirk off Alastar's face. I glared at him before turning back around to smile extra sweetly at Prince Liam.

"What shall I say that'll please you?"

He closed his eyes and clutched his heart. "Anything. Indeed, those words you spoke just now...sheer poetry. Please give me a moment so I can commit them to memory."

My determination to play along evaporated immediately and I glared at Alastar again. He gave me another knowing look, which I responded to by sticking my tongue out at him. Instead of the gesture annoying him like it was supposed to, his lips merely twitched in his Alastar way of smiling. Throughout the remainder of the meal, I felt him monitoring me. I refused to warrant him a single glance.

When at last the tedious meal finally drew to a close, Eileen cheerfully turned towards me. "What are your plans for today?"

Before I could even open my mouth to answer, Prince Liam did so for me. "Spending time with me, of course. We're to spend every waking moment together." He took my hand while I bit the inside of my lip to suppress my sigh. There went what had initially promised to be a pleasant morning.

Eileen glanced sideways at Aiden—whose expression had darkened once more—before forcing a smile. "Oh, how...lovely."

"Indeed," I said through my teeth. "But Eileen, surely you want to spend time together—*just us girls*—after lunch?" I gave her a desperate look.

"Of course, Rosie. I always welcome time with my dearest friend. In the meantime, I shall occupy my time with my dear husband."

At least one of us would have a good time. No, Rosie, I scolded myself, time alone with Prince Liam would undoubtedly be more romantic than this embarrassing breakfast. After all, this was what I'd been fighting for—an opportunity to be courted by my true love. My encounter with the storyteller at the bakery had specifically told me to keep my eye out for a *prince,* not to mention His Highness and I were practically engaged after his near marriage proposal during the tour of his palace, so time alone with him would surely be *happy,* wouldn't it? And hopefully less intense.

We all rose from the table. As I passed Alastar on my way out of the dining room, he grabbed my wrist to gently tug me to a stop. The heart flutters I'd been waiting for with Prince Liam overcame me at this single touch, a surge of heat encircling my wrist.

"What do you want?" I demanded.

Up went his eyebrow. "Hostile, hostile. I just wanted to explain the meaning of my laughing at His

Highness's...*delightful* letter to you. I didn't mean to make light of romantic gestures of the heart or to offend you."

"Then it's too bad you managed to do both."

"Come on, Rosie." Prince Liam tried to tug me away, but Alastar grabbed my wrist again to keep me there; my body reacted the same way it had the first time. Ignoring Prince Liam's protests, he leaned down to my ear and I shuddered as his warm breath caressed my skin.

"Prince Liam's letter was wrong—night can never separate true love." Disappointment lined his expression as he pulled away. "You haven't taken a stroll for several nights."

"Because we're enemies now."

"Even if you're determined to pretend you now hate me, I thought you'd now be more willing to take a late night stroll with me. You could lead me down to the dungeons to feed me to the dragons in order to conveniently eliminate me from your life. With no witnesses to the murder, no one would be any wiser."

My lips ached to curve into a smile. I covered the offenders with my hand so Alastar wouldn't see them, but by the triumph in his eyes, I knew that he had. "Perhaps I want to torture you a bit before knocking you off."

"How will you torture me, Rosie?"

"You'll just have to wait and see." I smiled exaggeratedly at Prince Liam, who waited with wriggly impatience. "Shall we go for a romantic stroll through the gardens, Liam dear?"

He lit up and offered his arm. I sensed Alastar's frown behind me as I took it. I stole one final glimpse at him as I left and wished I hadn't, for fierce pain filled his gorgeous hazel eyes. Despite my determination to hate him forever, this hurt me for reasons I couldn't put into words.

CHAPTER 17

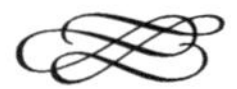

I nibbled my fingernail as I looked around my bedroom a few days later, now resembling a garden with the dozens of flower bouquets and potted plants gifted to me by Prince Liam, their perfume suffocating and making me feel faint. Love notes and sappy poems also littered nearly every surface, all full of empty praises. It was surprising how quickly flattery could feel so *unflattering*. Surely, true love consisted of more than just this? It had to.

Surveying the surrounding chaos, there was no doubt the love spell had worked...a bit too well. Prince Liam—who'd extended his visit in Sortileya just to court me, a thought that no longer thrilled me as it once had—scarcely left my side. Not sure how else to spend the time, we spent hours upon hours strolling the gardens.

While we always found things to talk about—especially when we discussed books we'd read—conversation wasn't quite as stimulating as what I'd always imagined conversing with my true love would be like—I'd expected more than common interests; I also wanted *depth*. While Prince Liam was certainly charming, always friendly, and also enjoyed stories, he limited himself to unusual ones he'd heard, whereas I ached for a storytelling partner, one who could weave tales seamlessly with me. I didn't find that in him, which meant that the fairy tale I'd planned for myself wasn't turning out at all like I'd always imagined.

I'd been cooped up in my room too long. Was it finally safe to leave? I tiptoed to my bedroom door and opened it an inch to peer out. Prince Liam still paced restlessly, waiting for me to emerge. Deep down I knew it wasn't a good sign that I'd taken to avoiding the man I'd determined to make my intended, but I couldn't worry about that now; I had a prince to slip away from.

Prince Liam paused with his back facing me, staring down the hallway. "Good afternoon, Alastar."

My stomach gave a strange flip at the name, and I risked opening my door a few more inches to catch a glimpse of the guard, the one that had served as my life preserver this past week. He'd offered encouraging almost-smiles in his typical Alastar way, or wry comments that caused me to smile in return. Whenever he excavated one from me, his eyes lit up, as if he were an avid collector of my smiles. It was during these moments I could admit how much I missed him—our midnight strolls, our bantering, everything. This aching only increased the longer we spent apart.

I continued watching Ali through the crack in the door. He bowed in acknowledgement of Prince Liam's greeting before his gaze flicked towards mine. By the slight widening of his eyes I knew he'd noticed me peeking out at him. How embarrassing, but despite having been caught, I didn't feel inclined to duck away.

"Good afternoon, Your Highness. Seeking Miss Rosalina's company?"

Prince Liam gave his usual love-sick sigh. "How could I possibly yearn for anyone else's?"

"Indeed." Ali tightened his jaw. "Is she resting in her room?"

"She is. I can't bear our separation, so I'm waiting out here for her so I may see her the moment she emerges."

I risked opening my door further, grateful for the well-oiled palace hinges as it swung open silently. Prince Liam kept his back towards me, but while Ali faced me, his expression didn't betray any hint that he saw me.

I wondered if I could risk recruiting Ali's aide for my escape plot. Aside from his frequent efforts to sabotage my love spell, he'd proven himself more friend than foe throughout our acquaintance. Would he be willing to play the part of a noble knight now?

When I caught his attention, I pointed to myself, made a walking motion with my fingers, and pointed down the opposite end of the hallway before clasping my hands to give him my best "I'm a heroine in the gravest distress" pleading look.

His expression still didn't falter, but by the look in his eyes, I sensed his acceptance of his new accomplice role. Excellent. If my escape succeeded, I'd bake Ali a batch of cinnamon banana muffins in gratitude.

"How will you spend your romantic afternoon with Miss Rosalina?" Ali asked Prince Liam, playing his part as my accomplice well via distraction.

"Quite likely another garden stroll. How fitting I spend time with my own flower in the wondrous outdoors, considering Rosie is the most beautiful flower of all."

"Indeed she is."

I'd slipped from my room and was just quietly closing the door behind me when Ali's agreement caused me to freeze. My heart flared to life as my gaze sought his, seeking an explanation, but once again he betrayed no emotion, leaving me burning with curiosity as to his meaning behind such a comment.

"She's like my ray of sunshine after an endless night," Prince Liam continued. I rolled my eyes as I crept down the corridor on tiptoe, only increasing my pace when I breeched the corner. From there I hurried down the hallway.

"Rosie petal?" Prince Liam's voice drifted from the corridor I'd just escaped from. Drat, he must have seen my attempts to slip away. I had to hide before he found me. Where would the prince be least likely to look for me? I flung open a random door and discovered a cupboard. Perfect.

I settled comfortably amongst the brooms and waited. A moment later, his footsteps passed my hideout. I breathed out a sigh of relief at having succeeded in my escape but stayed still in case he returned. The thought niggled my mind that I likely shouldn't be trying to hide from my future husband—and how once we were married, I'd *never* be able to get away from him—but I hastily shoved it away. Prince Liam was perfect for me. I reminded myself of this over and over, despite my beginning to no longer believe it.

Time slowly ticked away while I told myself stories, but even those quickly became tedious. I was just second-guessing the wisdom in shoving myself into such a confining cupboard and wondering how many more pages I'd be trapped here when the door suddenly flung open.

"Rosie! There you are. I've been looking everywhere for you."

My stomach sank. How had he found me? I peeked up at him and offered a weak, "Good afternoon, Your Highness," all while silently cursing his uncanny skill at hide-and-seek.

His blue eyes widened as he took in my surroundings. "It's Liam, my sweet, and goodness, what are you doing in *here*, darling?"

"Hiding from the dragon."

I waited for him to play along like a certain guard would have done, but Prince Liam only laughed as he offered his hand. "There are no dragons, dearest." He helped me to my feet and looped my arm through his before I could brew up another escape plot. "I'm so relieved I've found you. I missed you fiercely. Now that we're reunited, shall we go for a stroll through the gardens?"

Of course he'd suggest that. We literally did nothing else together. "That sounds quite nice," I lied. "But how about we do something else instead. Perhaps we could go to the kitchens and bake."

He flashed his princely smile. "But petal, a flower such as yourself deserves to be somewhere where your beauty can truly shine."

I sighed. The gardens it was. I braced myself as if we were heading for the gallows rather than the warm sunshine and splendor of the outdoors. It was amazing how quickly I'd grown to loathe the once-wondrous royal grounds. We'd only gone a few steps when Prince Liam suddenly reached for my hand.

I yanked mine away with a gasp. "What are you doing?"

"Holding your hand," he said. "It seems appropriate, considering how we feel for one another."

He was right, for if we were soul mates as I'd believed since the moment we'd met, hand holding seemed natural. Still I hesitated. I'd never held a man's hand, but I'd always imagined the moment as magical as one's first kiss. Shouldn't the moment be more special?

Oblivious to my doubts, Prince Liam took my hand. I waited for this romantic gesture to stir the deeper feelings I'd been yearning for—ones which had been strangely absent up until this point—but still they didn't come. Instead, I noticed all sorts of other things, like how after only a few steps, His Highness's hand seemed rather hot and sweaty. I ached to wriggle free from his firm grip and wipe the feel of his hand away.

Once again, this was not how I'd expected my happily ever after to go, but then again, everything on this path to true love had been rather underwhelming up to this point. Perhaps it'd get better with a bit more time; it just *had* to.

Just as we reached the entrance hall and before we could step outside, Aiden arrived with Eileen on his arm. He froze when he saw us together, his expression fierce. "What's going on?"

Prince Liam beamed. "I'm spending time with my Rosie petal."

"I see." Aiden tightened his jaw. "Have you forgotten we had a meeting a half hour ago, which I was forced to reschedule because of your absence?"

Prince Liam blinked at him. "A meeting?"

"Yes, a meeting," Aiden snapped. "While you've always been irresponsible, ever since your infatuation, it's gotten entirely out of hand. I suggest you stop mooning over Rosalina and start taking your duties more seriously."

Prince Liam's eyebrows rose in shock, the most coherent expression I'd seen from him since the spell began. "Of course. If I can manage to find a way to leave Rosie—"

"Find one." Aiden's look became dangerous. Prince Liam glanced at me, seeming on the brink of laughter, not an expression I'd expect from one being so thoroughly scolded by the Dark Prince.

"He doesn't understand our love," Prince Liam whispered. "I must leave you, darling petal, but please be assured my thoughts will be only focused on you."

"They should be focused on the meeting." Aiden stood watching, arms folded.

Prince Liam sighed. "Fine, I suppose I can spare a few thoughts on the meeting. Until afterwards, petal." He kissed my hand and departed. Aiden watched him go through narrowed eyes before he turned the full force of his gaze to me.

"Rosalina," he hissed, taking a menacing step closer. "This has gone on far too long. You will unspell Liam."

I shrank beneath the sharpness of his disapproval. "But Prince Liam is my true love. I can't just—"

"Enough," Aiden snapped. "You will reverse that spell. He's not only betrothed to a princess, but his infatuation is causing him to shirk his duties, and I won't stand for it. The only reason I've allowed it to go on for this long is because I was convinced it would fade, which it clearly hasn't. Enough is enough."

"Dear." Eileen rested a calming hand on Aiden's arm. He glanced down at her, his expression still hard.

"What is it?"

"You're clearly in no state to speak calmly. I'll talk to Rosie. You go to your meeting."

He released a long breath. "Please talk sense into her, because if I have to be the one to deal with this, she won't like it..." Aiden swept a hasty kiss across Eileen's cheek before leaving with long, agitated strides.

Eileen immediately turned to me, her grave expression speaking volumes. "This can't go on, Rosie. If word of Liam's condition leaks out, it could cause not only problems between him and his betrothed, but also for Aiden. You need to reverse the spell."

She launched into a myriad of reasons why, but as much as I tried to pay attention, my mind quickly drifted. She didn't need to remind me of the potential consequences of my situation—I knew I'd created quite the mess, and the situation was made all the worse considering I wasn't sure how to wriggle myself out of it.

~

I SAT in the parlor with Eileen, nursing a cup of tea a parlor maid had just handed to me—the very maid I was certain Ali fancied. My hand tightened around my cup as the increasingly familiar envy festered within me. I yanked my gaze away and took in the parlor, anything to distract myself. It was my favorite room in the palace—a vision of soft pastel rose walls, cream rose-carved molding accented in gold, and vases of blooming roses. My best friend sat curled up on the loveseat with her sketchbook perched on her lap and several pencils tucked into her hair.

I sipped my tea as my mind drifted to the last several days. While I'd finally achieved everything I'd always wanted, something was…missing. I was so lost in my thoughts that it took me a while to notice that Ali wasn't at his usual guarding post. My heart jolted. Wait, where was he?

I stroked my finger along the rim of my cup as I frowned at the strange guard standing against the wall in Ali's place. "Where's Ali?" I asked casually.

Eileen smirked but didn't look up from her drawing. "He's training with a regiment of guards."

Training? How annoying. I pursed my lips. "When will he be finished?"

Eileen shrugged. "I don't know; Aiden deals with the guards."

"Do you think he'll be back by tonight to guard you at dinner? What about for tomorrow's picnic excursion?"

Eileen finally looked up with a mischievous glint in her eyes. "It's strange how often you notice Alastar, considering his job is to be invisible."

"I don't; I just noticed he wasn't here," I replied hotly.

"And you sure talk to him quite often," Eileen continued, laughter in her eyes. I knew exactly what she was thinking—

that I harbored feelings for Ali—but I refused to acknowledge anything to her. "And whenever he's not around you talk about him."

"I do not."

She raised her eyebrow like *he* always did, only his was much cuter. "Are we not currently discussing Alastar?"

"No, we're not. I just wanted to know where he was."

"Hmm." A smile tugged on her lips as she returned to her picture. "Rather than Prince Liam?"

I pursed my lips. I didn't care where Prince Liam was, as long as it wasn't with me. I returned to my tea. For the next minute I wriggled about on the sofa, trying to keep my next burning question firmly in my mouth where it belonged. Unfortunately, this battle against my slippery tongue was one I always seemed doomed to tragically lose.

"What type of guard training?"

Eileen smirked but didn't look up. "Whose guard training, Rosie? Forgive me, I'm not sure to whom you're referring."

"Ali, of course," I snapped.

"Oh, the guard we're determinedly *not* talking about?"

My cheeks burned. "I'm just asking a question."

"I see." Her mischievous grin widened as she glanced up. "I'm afraid I don't know the details except that all the guards go through routine training exercises. Aiden would know more. We could ask him."

"No, don't!" That would be utterly mortifying.

"But aren't you curious?"

Not *that* curious. "I'll simply ask that elusive guard next time I see him…if he ever returns to his post."

I glared accusingly at the replacement guard standing where Ali was supposed to be. Even with his absence, strange feelings continued poking my heart, encouraging me to examine them. I pushed them away. The storyteller had mentioned only a prince, meaning I had no reason to be thinking of Ali…but for some reason, despite not wanting to think of him, the man refused to leave my thoughts.

"Still thinking of Alastar?" Eileen asked. My cheeks flamed.

"*No,*" I lied, sipping my tea through pursed lips. "Why would I?"

"I just thought you'd want to think of your *prince,* is all. You two are very well matched, don't you think?"

"Ali isn't my prince!" But even as I denied it, the emotions swirling within me intensified, bathing me in warmth. It was an extremely frightening sensation. I seized a cookie from the tray to dunk into my tea; splotches splattered my gown. "Ali is as un-prince-like as anyone could possibly be. For one thing, he doesn't look the part of a prince; not only is his hair the wrong color but so are his eyes. Hazel, Eileen. Princes are to have blue or green."

Eileen's forehead furrowed. "Alastar has hazel eyes?"

"Such pretty ones, just like honey. Not that I've noticed. I most certainly *haven't.*"

Eileen gave me a searching look. "Indeed not." She suddenly ceased drawing and flipped to a blank page.

"What are you doing?"

"Inspiration has just struck, and I must remain on good terms with my muse. Now tell me, Rosie, what other things about poor Alastar deem him unworthy of being your prince?"

I shoved my now thoroughly soaked cookie into my mouth, dribbling crumbs. "Princes are to have dazzling smiles—a dimple being an added bonus—but Ali is far too serious and never smiles at all. Well, he does, sort of; his lips twitch when he should be smiling, so I know he feels something behind his stoic mask, but pretends not to. And he doesn't laugh, either. Instead he lifts his left eyebrow to mock me. He's also the opposite of a gentleman; instead of treating me like a lady, he feels the need to ruffle me." The warmth in my chest deepened and I smiled. "Yet he always goes along with my stories, as if we were cowriters in a never-ending tale..."

And I continued, sharing moments of his humor, his sweetness, his patience putting up with my antics, his ease in understanding me as if he could read me as no one else could, the way he always had just the right thing to say to me, everything. As I spoke, Eileen's hand rapidly caressed the page.

"What are you drawing?" I asked.

"I'll show you in a minute; I'm almost done."

I paused. How strange I'd managed to come to know so much about this particular guard after repeatedly ignoring him. How had this happened? The familiar stirrings I'd experienced several times since eating the supposed enchanted fruit returned, causing my heart to flutter. What were they? Whatever they were, I shouldn't be feeling them, not when I had Prince Liam's affections and Ali likely fancied that parlor maid currently waiting on us. And yet...

Eileen made a final touch to her picture and turned the sketchbook around. "What do you think?"

My breath caught. Ali stared back at me. Eileen had captured him flawlessly—from his serious expression to the mischievousness filling his emotional eyes. I gaped hungrily as my eyes traced over every feature, unnecessary considering I already had his face memorized.

I had to have this. My motivations behind this fierce need could be analyzed later in the sanctity of my room—or better yet, buried too deeply for me to study them too closely. No matter what scheme I had to concoct, I would obtain Ali's portrait.

"I—" Strange shyness caused me to lower my gaze to my crumb-filled lap. "Can I have it?"

"Of course. I drew it for you." Eileen crawled off her chair and handed it to me with the same majesty as if she were bestowing one of the royal jewels, only this was far more precious to me, a treasured possession I'd aways keep near my heart.

After my visit with Eileen concluded, I stared hungrily at my newly acquired portrait as I walked down the corridor. It truly was a perfect likeness, as if Ali had been trapped on the page. To think I could carry him about as a storytelling companion in my pocket. I sighed contentedly. Oh, bliss.

Oof. I rammed into something. At first I wondered if it was Ali, for he was the one I usually encountered while wandering the palace. But it was far worse.

"Darling!" Prince Liam gushed. "Did I harm you, my petal?" He ran his hands along my arms, as if the gesture would soothe away any pain from our collision. I flinched away.

"Forgive me, Prince Liam; I wasn't watching where I was going."

"Liam," he corrected, stroking the back of my hand. It took every ounce of willpower not to shudder. I tried to tug my hand away but his grip was firm, possessive. For an awkward moment we stood there, him gaping sappily and me wriggling uncomfortably beneath his unwanted attentions.

"I'm sorry, I must go. We'll see one another later."

His hold on my hand tightened, his desperation to keep me close even though I wanted nothing more than to be as far away from him as possible. "Rosie, my love, don't torment me so. It's been an age since we last saw one another."

"We saw one another only an hour ago." It was utterly unfair I'd run into Prince Liam again when I still hadn't seen Ali all day.

"That's too long, Rosie. We must make up for lost time."

I couldn't quite suppress my groan. "Might I suggest commissioning Eileen to draw a portrait of me for when we're separated?" Which would hopefully be as often as possible.

His gaze settled on the portrait in my hand. "Excellent suggestion, my Rosie. Is this one?" He snatched the portrait. His expression went through an interesting journey—from his lips twitching to devastation filling his eyes to contempt hardening his features.

He raised his wounded gaze to mine. "What's the meaning of this, Rosie petal? Why are you carrying the portrait of another man?"

"Give it back." I tried to grab it, but he held it out of reach.

"Are you in love with him?"

My face flared with heat. "I most certainly am *not*." I ignored my frantically pounding heart and the message it seemed to be trying to tell me. Now was not the time for self-reflection; I had a thief to apprehend. I managed to snatch back Ali's portrait. I carefully smoothed out the edges.

Prince Liam watched, looking on the verge of tears. Then he was on his knees at my feet. "You clearly treasure that portrait. You must love him. Oh, Rosie." He crawled closer, backing me against the wall, and seized my hand. "Please love me, Rosie. I'm your prince."

This was getting utterly ridiculous. His attentions were smothering me, threatening to drown me. I clutched Ali's portrait protectively against my heart. "Please, Your Highness," I stuttered, on the brink of tears. "Please stop."

He didn't. I looked to Prince Liam's accompanying guard, who made no move to assist me; he didn't even seem to notice my plight, his baffled expression locked on the prince with a look like he considered the heir to his kingdom's throne to have gone mad.

Panic constricted my chest. It appeared I was left to my

own devices. My mind scrambled to formulate a plan. I'd just settled on pretending to faint when my knight appeared at the end of the corridor. I'd never better appreciated good timing in stories than when I saw Ali appear at this perfect moment to rescue me, the damsel in distress, from the annoying dragon.

His face was damp from exercise and his hair rumpled from his training, but no one had ever looked more handsome, especially when he skewered Prince Liam with a suspicious glare. "There appears to be trouble."

"*Ali!*" His name came out around a sob. Prince Liam twisted around to glare at him.

"*You*. You're trying to steal my Rosie's heart away from me."

Ali cocked an eyebrow at him. "I haven't stolen anything, Your Highness, not when Miss Rosie's heart is reserved for her prince." He gave me a searching, almost challenging look. I leaned back against the marble wall and gave him my most pleading expression.

He immediately softened and stepped forward. "Your Highness, perhaps you need a breath of fresh air to ponder your love for Rosie."

"Excellent. She shall accompany me." His hold on my hand tightened.

"No thank you, Prince Liam. I would rather…not."

Prince Liam looked as if my refusal had crushed his heart. "Do you no longer love me? Your heart must have been stolen by that guard, considering you have a portrait of him."

I'd been quite determinedly hiding Ali's portrait behind my back. "What portrait?" I squeaked.

Prince Liam reached behind me and snatched it to show Ali, whose eyes bulged as he took in the picture before turning a questioning look to me. "Rosie? What—"

My embarrassment was so acute I was on the brink of

being engulfed in flames. Ali stared at me for a moment, almost…longingly, an incredibly soft and sweet look, so unlike Prince Liam's lovesick drooling. Then he smiled, actually *smiled,* shaking his head in wonder before he turned the full force of his serious-guard persona on Prince Liam.

"Your Highness, please return Rosie's property and give her space. She seems quite overwhelmed by your adorations."

Prince Liam looked almost desperate. "No matter how much affection I bestow upon my petal, it's never enough."

I closed my eyes in disgust at his words. Would this nightmare ever end?

"Look at her, Your Highness; she appears unwell. Please give her some space." My eyes were still closed, but I heard Ali's tone sharpen and could imagine the disapproval on his normally stoic expression. He played a dangerous game being so forceful with a royal, but I was infinitely grateful, especially when Prince Liam sighed in acquiescence.

"Very well." I opened my eyes as he returned Ali's portrait and I clutched it protectively to my heart. Ali unfortunately noticed, which served as more fuel to add to the fire of my humiliation, humiliation which only grew as Ali stared at it before raising his questioning gaze to meet mine with a tender smile. It was official—this was the day I died of utter mortification.

Prince Liam stood and kissed my hand; I winced as if his lips were poison. "We'll unite later, my sweet. In the meantime, I'm composing a new love poem for you. It'll be ready by dinner."

Which meant I'd likely have to read it out loud. I sighed wearily. "How…lovely." I clutched Ali's portrait closer to my heart, as if the gesture could give me strength to endure Prince Liam's affections.

"Indeed it will be, Rosie petal. I'll be counting down the minutes until our reunion." He stared at me for a bit longer before he finally released my hand and took his leave, walking backwards down the corridor in order to keep his sappy gaze on me for as long as possible. When he reached the end of the hallway, he blew me a kiss, but before he could disappear around the corner, Aiden arrived with Duncan trailing him, expression hard.

"Liam, where have you been? You've missed another meeting."

Prince Liam's expression cleared and his eyes widened. "There was a meeting today?"

"Yes, and it was our last meeting before your return to Draceria tomorrow," Aiden snapped. "I reminded you several times in case your mind was occupied with a certain girl." He glared at me and I withered beneath it.

"I'm sorry, Aiden, I didn't mean—"

Prince Liam swallowed his apology at another dark look from Aiden. "It's not entirely *your* fault." He glared at me again and my stomach jolted. I instinctively took a step closer to Ali, needing his strength for what was to come.

Eileen appeared around the corner and I nearly sobbed in relief at her timing; only she seemed able to calm her husband when his Dark Prince persona overcame him. Her eyes widened as she took in his dark expression.

"Goodness, dear, what ever is the matter?"

Aiden ignored her and tightened his jaw as he gave me another accusing look. "Rosalina, I need to speak with you."

Beside me Ali stiffened, and when I stole a peek up at him, he looked almost guilty. My heart pounded furiously in my chest. Whatever Aiden had to say to me certainly wouldn't be good.

CHAPTER 18

"Did you hear me, Rosalina? I need to speak with you. Now."

I pressed my hand to my pounding heart in a feeble attempt to calm it, something that felt impossible with the rather frightening way Aiden looked at me.

I took a wavering breath before lifting my chin bravely. "Of course, Aiden."

He nodded curtly before gesturing towards a nearby door. "We'll take this discussion somewhere more private."

He strode into the room and I slowly trudged after him, my mind racing as every unpleasant rumor I'd ever heard about him swirled through my mind. I forced myself to push them away.

Eileen followed me in, and Alastar and Duncan took their usual guarding positions against the wall. Aiden spun on Prince Liam when he also followed us into the room. "This is to be a private discussion, Liam."

Prince Liam stared at him for a moment before looking towards me. "But I can't possibly part from my Rosie."

Aiden closed his eyes with a look very much like he was

praying for patience. "Do it anyway." His hardened tone left no room for argument. Prince Liam's eyebrows rose before he obeyed, backing slowly from the room in order to keep me in his line of sight. The moment he left, I nervously perched on the edge of an armchair while Aiden began pacing like an agitated predator. I wriggled in my seat, waiting, casting Eileen a few panicked looks. She frowned at her husband, perplexity lining her brow.

It took me several minutes to summon my bravery. "What is it, Aiden?" I squeaked.

He didn't speak but simply stared at me, the force of his black eyes enough to keep me pinned in my seat. After what seemed like an eternity, he finally spoke. "This has gone on long enough, and I won't tolerate it a moment longer."

"Tolerate what?" I managed.

"Dealing with a spelled prince, one who misses important meetings and is pining for a silly girl who isn't his intended. What were you thinking?"

I winced. "Well…I just wanted to encourage Prince Liam's feelings towards me—"

"In case I didn't make it clear before," Aiden interrupted, each word deliberate and slow. "Prince Liam is bound by a political contract betrothing him to Princess Lavena of Lyceria."

"Well, I figured he could break it and—"

"You don't just *break* contracts," Aiden said. "It isn't done."

"You broke yours."

Aiden's eyes narrowed. "My situation was drastically different from Liam's," he said. "That likely didn't occur to you, nor did the fact that if Liam could easily get out of his contract, he would have done it by now. He detests the match."

I opened my mouth to tell him that falling in love with

me would give Prince Liam the perfect opportunity to finally wriggle out of it, but Aiden's hand snapped up, silencing me.

"Since you clearly don't seem to understand his situation, let me outline it for you once more. Prince Liam is engaged to Princess Lavena, an arrangement that is to be a great benefit to both Draceria and Lyceria. They've been engaged for years under contract. Their marriage will create a coveted union between both kingdoms...and you just tampered with it. Do you understand what you've done? If word of this gets back to the King of Draceria, there could be dire consequences—our relations with Draceria could crumble, trade agreements could fall through, our economy could suffer—all due to your selfishness."

Unease knotted my stomach.

"Aiden, please stop." Eileen stared wide-eyed at her husband, as if she'd never seen him before. He ignored her and stepped closer in order to loom over me. I shrank in my seat.

"You spelled a foreign prince while under *my* charge, meaning I'm going to have to take responsibility for your ridiculous actions. I told you not to spell him, yet you disobeyed me."

"I—I just wanted him to fall in love with me," I stuttered.

"Only because *you've* decided your story has to play out that way," he said. I winced at his hard tone. "You recklessly pushed forward with absolutely no regards for the consequences to you or anyone else. But there are consequences, whether you want there to be or not. This isn't one of your fantasy worlds; this is real life, and it's high time you got your head out of the clouds."

"Aiden!" Eileen's alarm was riveted to me. My lip trembled and tears burned my eyes, but I would not cry. I was supposed to be a brave heroine, one who, at this moment, was facing quite a formidable foe. Eileen saw the emotions I battled and settled beside me in order to wrap her arm around me before turning to her husband. "Aiden, please, try to contain yourself."

His eyes narrowed at her. "*Contain myself*? Don't you realize how serious this is?"

"Of course I do, Aiden, but Rosie is still my friend."

"I don't care," he snapped. "You have to understand the difficult position she's put me in. Your friendship doesn't change the fact that she tampered with a political contract, which will harm our alliance with Draceria. We rely on them for forty percent of our trade. If they learn what's happened, our foreign relations—"

"I know, Aiden," Eileen said. "But try to scold her gently."

"I've already tried that, and look at the mess she's created for all of us." He rubbed his temples, as if warding off a headache. "I can't believe it. She's spelled the Crown Prince of Draceria. If my father ever gets wind of this…what a disaster." He took several long, deep breaths before straightening and once more giving me his serious Dark Prince look. "This is what's going to happen: you're going to reverse the spell."

I bit my lip. He made it sound so easy. "But—"

His hand snapped up again. "No, Rosalina, I don't care if you've deluded yourself into believing he's your path to happily ever after. He's *not*. As such, you *will* find a way to reverse that spell, or so help me—"

"No, that's not what I meant. I don't know how."

He frowned. "Excuse me?"

"I don't know how to reverse the spell." The tears I'd fought to hold back finally escaped. Eileen's arm tightened around my shoulders.

Aiden leaned closer, his dark eyes flashing. "Then I suggest you go back to your bakery and figure it out. And don't return until you've created the counterspell."

His words slowly sunk in and my stomach jolted in horror. "Are you…sending me away?" He couldn't be serious. Banishment only happened to vile villains in all the tales I'd ever read. How then could it be happening to *me*?

"That's precisely what I'm doing."

At his words, Ali fidgeted uneasily behind me. "Your Highness, if I may—"

"Not now, Alastar," Aiden snapped, not even warranting him a glance.

"But Your Highness, there's something I need to—"

"I said *not now*." Aiden glared at him until he snapped his mouth shut then turned the force of his disapproving dark eyes back to me. "You will leave the palace and not return until you've found a way out of this mess."

A crushing weight pressed against my heart. "But—*but*—"

Aiden stared me down. "No arguments, Rosalina. This isn't a story or a game of make-believe; this is a political arrangement you've endangered, an interference that'll result in political ramifications. I forbade you from creating a love spell. You disobeyed and must now suffer the consequences. You will return to Arador until you come up with some way to unravel this mess you've created."

He made it sound like I'd gone against a direct order, whereas I'd always considered his cautions against the spell as disapproval from my best friend's husband, not a command from the prince himself. I gaped at him, speechless, but while my words had become lodged in my throat, luckily my ever-faithful best friend had plenty to say.

Eileen leapt to her feet and glared at him. "Aiden, stop it."

He finally turned his fierce attention away from me to stare at her. "What? She's left me no choice."

"I understand you're angry, Aiden, but Rosie is my friend. I know what she did was wrong, but can't we discuss this before you send her away?"

He frowned. "I'm the crown prince and you're the crown princess, both bound by duty to the kingdom. There's no room for personal relationships in—"

"I don't care," Eileen said. "I don't want you to be a prince right now; I want you to be my husband."

Aiden's expression hardened. "Why are you defending her? Don't you understand how serious this is?"

"I do, Aiden, but—"

"No, you clearly don't. If you did, you wouldn't be siding with your silly friend."

Eileen's eyes narrowed. "My *silly friend*?"

"I've allowed your relationship with that girl to blind me to my duties long enough," he snapped. "I have a responsibility to my throne and my people. I should have put a stop to her scheme the moment she concocted it, but I tiptoed around her actions because she's *your friend*, one who spends far more time inside her head than in reality. Enough is enough. I don't care who she is, only what she's done. Don't you understand the dire consequences of this if the King of Draceria finds out?"

Eileen folded her arms across her chest. "Of course I do, but I don't think—"

"No, I don't think you really do." His voice was escalating. "The best friend of the Crown Princess of Sortileya has conspired to damage a union between two other kingdoms. I now have to figure out how to smooth everything over while also facing the reality that a foreign prince was spelled under my roof with no current way to reverse it."

The arguments swirled and tension pressed against me, smothering. Desperate for a reprieve, I turned to the one who always seemed to ease my worries. Alastar watched the confrontation with wide eyes. He sensed my gaze and met mine, his own filled with remorse.

Aiden took several deep, steadying breaths. "I know this

is all new for you," he said slowly. Eileen's jaw tightened. "I know she's your friend. But that doesn't matter right now. You need to understand the obligations that come with the throne."

"I'm doing my best," she said.

"I know that, Eileen," he said, his tone finally softening. "You've been doing wonderfully, but there's still much you have to learn. In situations like this, you can't let your heart rule your head."

"Rulers are to have compassion, are they not?"

"They also have to do what it takes for the benefit of their kingdom, even at great personal sacrifice."

"As if I haven't already sacrificed enough," she snapped. "Now I'm expected to sacrifice not just my old life but my best friend, too?"

"That's not what I'm saying," he said, exasperated.

She pressed her hands to her hips. "Then what *are* you saying?"

"I'm merely saying that, friend or not, Rosalina has created a huge mess, one that *we* now have to take responsibility for."

I looked back and forth between Aiden and Eileen, my heart tightening. I felt as if all I'd believed about romance was shattering before my very eyes. How could this be happening? The perfect fairy tale couple was *fighting*. Eileen had found her prince and was now supposed to be living happily ever after. This wasn't happily ever after at all.

And it was all my fault. I'd ruined my best friend's story, making me a villain. I didn't realize I was sobbing until the fighting couple blurred from my tears. "Please stop fighting," I managed weakly.

Eileen's hardened expression softened. "Oh, Rosie." She pulled me into a hug. "It'll be alright."

"It will only be alright when she reverses that love spell," Aiden snapped.

She glared at him, and for a tense and horrible moment they had a stare down. "I understand, Aiden."

He released a whooshing breath. "You do?"

"Yes." Her tone was crisp. "Rosie has put the Sortileyan crown in a precarious situation with the Dracerian throne."

He nodded, his hardening tone softening into relief. "Yes. Rosalina has tampered with a serious contract."

"So she has." Eileen's expression was eerily detached. "Because of her actions, you're asking her to return to Arador in order to find a counterspell."

"Yes, darling." Aiden took her hands in his and gave them a squeeze. Eileen slowly tugged her hands away. Aiden's forehead furrowed. "Eileen—"

She lifted her chin defiantly. "If she has to return to Arador, then I'm going with her."

His mouth fell open. "Wait, what?"

"I'll be going back to Arador with Rosie." She headed for the door, her skirts swirling in her strange, calm anger. "Come, Rosie, we should pack."

I didn't move. I stood frozen, as did Aiden. He gaped after her before thawing and hurrying towards her. "What are you saying, Eileen?"

"I'm overdue for a visit to my mother, don't you think?" she asked, her voice airy. "It's been far too long since I've seen her, but I've been so busy with princess duties lately I haven't had a chance."

"Sure, we can visit your—"

"*We* are not going to visit my mother; *I* am." She kept her back to him so he didn't see her wobbling chin. But I did. The sight of it was like a knife digging into my heart.

Aiden didn't speak. He merely stared at her back, a wall

between them, before gently reaching out to stroke her back. "Eileen..."

She flinched away and spun around, her teary eyes narrowed. "You've made your point perfectly clear that *my silly friend* has caused you all sorts of princely problems."

Aiden bit his lip. "I'm sorry, I shouldn't have called her that."

"It's not me who needs your apology."

Aiden glanced at me, his expression twisted in remorse. "My apologies, Rosalina, that I allowed my frustrations to hurt you." He turned back to Eileen, as if hoping everything would be smoothed over with a simple apology. How I hoped they would be. After all, fighting didn't belong between a couple living out their happily ever after.

Eileen folded her arms across her chest. "I'm still leaving for Arador. You've clearly outlined the precarious situation, and I wouldn't dream of taking you away from the palace at such a critical time."

"But Eileen—"

"Apparently, royals are meant to rule with their head, not their heart."

Aiden just stared at her. Eileen's lip trembled.

"I'm sorry for the circumstances we now find ourselves in, but not as much as I'm sorry I'm not the princess you had in mind when you married me."

"Eileen, I—"

"Because I know I've been a disappointment." Eileen's eyes were glassy with unshed tears. "But I can't stand here and be the logical consort you need me to be. I love Rosie. She's my best friend. I can't let her go back to Arador alone. But I promise that while I'm there, I'll help her find a way to reverse the spell."

Aiden's regality crumpled. He cupped her chin. "You're

not a disappointment, Eileen. I never intended for you to feel that way."

"I still need to leave."

He stroked her cheek. When she didn't pull away, he bridged the distance that had sprung up between them and rested his forehead against hers. "Are you—" He swallowed before trying again. "Are you unhappy in this life with me?"

She sighed and wrapped her arms around him. "I'm not unhappy with you, but I'm overwhelmed by the life you came with. It's been such a huge adjustment. Can't you see that?"

He lowered his eyes. "I did, but I pretended not to. I didn't want to admit that marrying me thrust you into a life that's as difficult as you feared."

"More so, I must admit," she said. He flinched. She cradled his cheek. "I need some time away from palace life. I need to go to Arador with Rosie, and you need to stay here."

He sighed and reluctantly released her. "Then at least take Alastar."

Eileen rolled her eyes. "I don't need Alastar to accompany me."

"Yes, you do. You can't travel to Arador by yourself. At least grant me that request. Please, Eileen." His tone was hardening again, but in a different way than before—not with anger but in desperation. He no longer looked like the Dark Prince but instead like a man who felt estranged from his wife…an estrangement that was my fault, just like the political mess he found himself in.

"I can take care of myself," Eileen said. "I've spent my entire life in Arador without a guard trailing me."

"Yes, but that was before," he said. "You can't go to Arador without a guard. You're a princess now."

She sighed. "Yes, I suppose I am. But right now I don't want to be a princess."

Aiden flinched again. He opened his mouth to retort but

closed it again when words didn't seem to be forthcoming. With a groan of defeat, he spun around and slumped towards the window and rested his hands on the sill, crumpled and defeated.

Eileen stared at his back, and when she finally turned away her face was streaked with tears. My heart wrenched. "Eileen, I—"

She shook her head, dismissing me, and strode towards the door. I slowly followed her, guilt gnawing at my heart, all while the scene I'd just witnessed played repeatedly in my mind. I, Rosalina, had single-handedly created a political mess between three kingdoms, all while destroying my best friend's fairy tale ending.

I was the vilest of villains.

CHAPTER 19

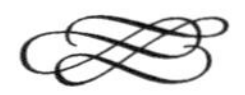

"You're leaving?"

I sighed. "Yes. As I've already told you, something has come up and I must return to Arador for a while."

Prince Liam just continued to stare with a blank expression. "But Rosie petal, you can't return to Arador." He squeezed my hand, which he hadn't relinquished since I'd given him the devastating news of my departure.

"Prince Liam..." I began.

"*Liam,* my sweet." He lifted my hand and pressed a kiss to it.

"Liam, I'm sorry this news upsets you, but I need to return home."

He considered the matter before he brightened. "I have it: I'll come with you."

My stomach clenched in horror. That would undoubtedly be an utter disaster. My imagination—for once unwelcome—flared to life: Prince Liam trailing me around Arador, his gaze lovesick and drooling while he spouted love sonnets...panic swelled, tightening my chest. He *couldn't* follow me. I was already being forced to endure the humiliation of being banished to the bakery by the crown prince, like a toddler being sent to her room for a time-out. Having everyone know of my love spell would escalate an already mortifying situation.

Besides, it'd be impossible to search for a reversal spell with him around. Right now I didn't want to think about my own fairy tale but rather Eileen's, considering her story was currently experiencing the most tragic twist—a twist that *I*, the dastardly villain Rosalina, had caused—and I was desperate to do whatever it took to make amends. If I could just reverse the spell, could Eileen be reconciled with her own prince?

I glanced towards her, standing rigidly in the entrance hall with Aiden beside her, his arm around her waist. Despite the affectionate gesture, they weren't speaking to one another, the tension from their recent fight still cloaking them.

And it was all my fault.

Prince Liam continued to lament our separation until Alastar—who stood rigidly nearby, waiting to escort us to Arador at Aiden's insistence—broke his role of being a silent and invisible guard in order to come to my rescue.

"Your Highness, I hate to be the bearer of disappointment, but I feel compelled to remind you that only yesterday I heard you inform Prince Aiden that you were soon expected back in Draceria for royal duties."

Prince Liam frowned at Ali—whose face was as usual expressionless, but whose eyes contained a meaningful look I couldn't decipher—before he sighed.

"As much as it pains me to admit it, he's correct." He took my hand again, squeezing my fingers as his startling blue gaze seeped into mine. "But don't fear, darling; even if we're separated physically, you'll never leave my thoughts or my heart."

I tried to smile, but my lips weren't cooperating.

"Despite our separation," he continued, "I'll continue to assure you of my devotion."

I wished he'd release my hand. His own was rather sweaty. I sent Eileen a pleading look, and she managed to thaw from her dazed stupor. She shook off Aiden's embrace. "It's time for us to depart."

I followed Eileen out into the sunshine and down the steps to the awaiting carriage, Prince Liam remaining devotedly at my side. He pressed my hand, which he still had yet to relinquish, against his heart. "I'll think of you every moment."

The driver opened the carriage door and Aiden helped Eileen up, keeping his hold on her hand. "Eileen?" he murmured. She finally met his gaze. For a moment they stared at one another before they embraced. "Have a good time. I'll miss you."

"I'll miss you, too."

He kissed her cheek before reluctantly releasing her and stepping aside so I could enter the carriage. I turned to Ali to seek his assistance, but Prince Liam did the honors instead. "I'll write you five letters a day," he said.

I almost groaned at the thought. "I'd hate to distract you from your royal duties."

He considered. "How thoughtful, darling. Very well, three letters a day, but don't ask me to do anything less; I couldn't bear it."

I sighed and managed to finally yank my hand free. Ali climbed in after me and the door closed. I wiped my hand on my gown. The carriage started moving. Prince Liam jogged beside it. "I'll count down the moments until our reunion. We'll be together soon, my love."

The carriage blessedly picked up speed and he fell back.

He blew me kisses until we'd rolled out of the gates. I sighed and leaned back on the velvet seat in relief.

"That love spell's much more potent than I thought it would be; I have no idea how I'm going to reverse it. What if he misses me so much he follows us?" I peeked out the window and was relieved to see that so far he hadn't.

Eileen made no comment. She pressed her face against the glass to watch the passing scenery. In the window's reflection I could see the tears she couldn't hold back any longer.

My heart wrenched. "Eileen?"

She sniffled and didn't say anything. I tried again.

"Eileen, I'm so sorry about—"

She wiped her wet cheeks but didn't look at me. "Not now, Rosie. I need some time."

The silent treatment—a punishment I thoroughly deserved for having ruined her life. The guilt twisted my heart, made worse by the fact I had no idea how to atone for my mistakes.

I glanced at Ali, sitting rigidly on the opposite seat, arms folded and his usual serious expression in place. I waited for him to lift one of his eyebrows or for his lips to twitch, anything to indicate I wasn't in as much disgrace as I feared.

His face remained frozen. Unsurprising, considering I *was* in disgrace. I may have narrowly avoided Prince Liam following us to Arador, but he still believed himself in love with me, and as desperately as I'd fought for him to feel those emotions, they'd come at far too high of a cost.

It was the quietest carriage ride I'd ever endured, a torturous silence that was only broken by Eileen's occasional sniffles. She cried the entire three-hour ride back to Arador, her fingers wrapped around the pearl necklace that had been a gift from Aiden, meaning she was thinking of him and missing all I'd broken between them.

With every turn of the carriage wheels and each tear I saw trickle down Eileen's cheek, my remorse grew. I was not only a dastardly villain but a terrible friend. Eileen had been blessed with a fairy-tale romance, and I, in my selfishness in trying to create my own, had destroyed hers. Regret squeezed my insides, suffocating and making me feel utterly helpless. How could I ever fix this?

My hands twisted and untwisted in my lap as my mind spun frantically, but for once I didn't welcome this visit from my imagination. A story played across my mind—my best friend dying of a broken heart, a grief-stricken Aiden feeding me to the dragons in revenge…no, too extreme. I forced myself to push away such a drastic possibility and allow a more likely scenario to fill my thoughts instead—arriving in Arador as the banished, disgraced castoff from the royal family, where I'd live out the remainder of my days in lonely misery.

I startled when Alastar reached across the space dividing our seats and rested his hand over mine to still their shaking. He didn't say anything, just gave me an assuring look, as if promising me everything would be alright, but how could it possibly be after the mess I'd created?

The carriage rolled into Arador and stopped in front of Eileen's cottage at the edge of the woods. She didn't even wait for the driver to assist her before she opened the door. Ali immediately moved to follow her but froze at Eileen's teary glare.

"No, Alastar, I don't want you accompanying me."

"But Your Highness, I'm under orders to—"

"Please, don't address me by my title, not here. For just a few days, I don't want to be a princess but just Eileen." She ignored the driver's hand and jumped down. Ali scrambled towards the door before she stopped him with her hand. "No, Alastar, I mean it."

"But His Highness ordered me to—"

"I don't care," she snapped. "Aiden isn't here; *I* am, and as such I give the orders, and I'm ordering you to stay. You will stay with Rosie. Guard her or guard nothing—I don't care."

Before she could close the carriage door, I asked my burning question, a gauge to measure how upset she was with me. "Do you want me to visit you soon?" I asked hesitantly.

She didn't even look at me. "No, thank you." And with that, she slammed the carriage door rather forcefully and stomped up the path to her cottage. My heart wrenched. Our friendship was clearly over.

Ali stared after her, looking rather disgruntled. "Orders or not..." He hoisted the door open even after the carriage started up again, but I seized his arm, tugging him to a stop.

"Leave her be. She doesn't need a guard right now." Or a best friend, apparently. "What she needs is a good cry with her mother."

He grumbled but obediently settled on the seat with a sigh, his surrender. "If His Highness learns I strayed from my post..."

"Eileen won't tell him and neither will I. I'm not too keen to displease him any further." For at this point in my story, being thrown in the dungeon seemed far too likely a scenario should I fail in my newest quest.

"His Highness would never throw you in the dungeon," Ali said.

"He will if I don't come up with a counterspell." I gnawed at my fingernail. "Ali, what am I going to do?"

"You're a resourceful heroine. I'm sure you'll come up with something."

The carriage stopped in front of the bakery, the setting for the next dark chapter in my story: confessing to my family I'd spelled a crown prince into thinking himself in love with me. Ali disembarked first and extended his hand, but I made no move to take it, frozen in fear. What if my family hated me for what I'd done?

"Come now, Rosie, you're a brave heroine. It's time to face the dragons."

Ali's lips quirked into one of his half smiles that did wonders for my nerves. I shakily placed my hand in his. Warmth seeped over me as his hand enfolded mine, sending a wave of calm over me. Even after I'd descended, I made no move to pull away.

"Don't worry, Rosie; your family will stand by you…as will I. Together we'll come up with a solution."

His hazel gaze seeped into mine as he gave my hand an assuring squeeze before releasing it. I ached to ask him to keep holding my hand—for I needed his steady strength I'd come to rely on—but his comfort had given me the fortitude I needed.

With a steadying breath, I entered the bakery, where I hoped my family would not only stand by me, but together we'd come up with a solution to the plight I'd created for myself and everyone else, even though at the moment that seemed an impossible feat.

CHAPTER 20

Father frantically searched *Enchanted Sweets and Delights* as I hovered, gnawing my fingernail. "There has to be a reversal spell in here *somewhere*," he said.

"What if there isn't?" Despair squeezed my chest at the thought. If only life were like a story, so that when it wasn't going as expected, one could choose to stop reading rather than being forced to endure each miserable chapter of what was certainly going to become an unhappily ever after.

Mother wrapped her arm around me. "Don't panic, dear, we'll figure something out."

"We'll fix the problem, even if there isn't a reversal spell," Ferris said from his place rummaging the cupboard for mixing bowls. "The solution seems obvious: all we need to do is whip up a poisoned tart, give it to the prince, and—"

"*Ferris*!" Mother gaped at him, horrified.

He lowered his eyes sheepishly. "I was only joking, Mother."

"*Never* joke about something like that again." She turned back to me. "Now don't worry, dear. Every spell has a counterspell—it's one of the foundational rules of magic—

although admittedly they're trickier to make and not always successful."

I groaned. "What if ours doesn't work?" Hopelessness once again threatened to swallow me whole. "I'll be thrown in the dungeon for sure."

"Quite likely," Ferris chimed in. "Then I'll finally be an only child."

"Don't tease her like that, Ferris; Rosie is upset enough as it is."

Father continued frantically combing the recipe book, muttering to himself, before he grinned in triumph. "There, I knew there'd be a counterspell. There always is."

I nearly tripped over my skirts in my eagerness to see it for myself. My breath hooked as I hovered over his shoulder and read the glorious words, "Love Reversal Spell." I released a relieved sigh. "I'm saved."

"Assuming it works," Ferris added unhelpfully. I glared at him.

"It'll work. I'm an expert at creating spelled treats, as seen in the success of the first one." Some of the despair pressing against me slowly eased. We'd found a reversal spell. Life wasn't over. Now all that was left was to make it. "Let's bake it immediately."

Father looked up from scanning the ingredients. "Hmm, it appears we're missing two of the ingredients, princess."

The elation I'd been feeling came crashing down. "We are?" Why did obstacles have to repeatedly appear in one's story?

"Yes. We're out of crushed dragon scales, which can easily be purchased at the apothecary at the other end of Arador. However, the enchanted water will be more difficult to track down."

I nibbled my fingernail in thought before an idea occurred to me. I brightened once more. "There's enchanted water in the Forest. Eileen took me to a waterfall that changed colors. All I'd have to do would be to…oh." I didn't want to go to the Forest without Eileen, certain I'd get lost if I ventured there on my own, but Eileen currently wasn't speaking to me.

Mother rested an assuring hand on my arm that did little to quell the panic once again rising in my chest. "I'm sure she'll be willing to help you. Best friends can't stay away from each other for long. In the meantime, you can fetch the dragon scales. Are you willing to go right now?"

Before I could answer, a knock sounded on the door, despite the bakery being closed. My droopy heart immediately flared to life. There was only one person I knew who knocked on the bakery door…. "Ali!"

I scrambled from the kitchen to hoist the front door open, where Ali stood. I beamed up at him, taking in his tall, broad form. Even though it had only been a few hours since he'd left me at home, feeling compelled to return to his post standing outside Eileen's cottage, it felt as if it had been far longer.

I managed to tear my gaze from his face to notice he held a bouquet of blooming roses. I gaped at the flowers, my heartbeat escalating. "Are those for me?"

"Yes," he said.

My heart swelled further, on the brink of flight at the utterly romantic gesture. I peeked up at him with a girlish smile. "From you?"

His cheeks darkened. "I'm afraid not. I found them on the doorstep."

My soaring heart immediately crashed in disappointment. I'd never considered the idea of Ali giving me flowers, but now that I did, it was one I rather liked, and it was crushing that he hadn't satisfied this new secret longing.

"Who are they from?"

Ali shifted from foot to foot, looking almost guilty, as if aware he'd disappointed me. "A certain lovesick prince."

I groaned, my mood darkening further. "I see." I snatched the elaborate bouquet and returned glowering to the kitchen.

Mother's eyes widened when she noticed the roses. "What a lovely bouquet. Who's it from?" Her gaze immediately darted towards Ali.

"A spelled Prince Liam. Who else?" I set the offensive bouquet down unceremoniously and glared at it, never mind it truly was lovely—an arrangement of roses in all colors, a flower whose expense should have immediately alerted me they hadn't been from Ali. The fact that I'd allowed myself to get my hopes up only darkened my mood further. I sighed. It seemed my life was full of nothing but one disappointment after another.

Ferris surveyed the bouquet from all angles before grinning mischievously. "There's a note. This ought to be good." Before I could stop him, he snagged the piece of gilded parchment and unfolded it.

"Don't you dare read that." I made to grab it but he held it out of reach.

"Don't you want to hear sweet nothings from your besotted prince, Rosalina?" He cleared his throat and with an exaggerated theatrical flare he began to read:

My Dearest Rosie Petal,

"Rosie petal?" He sniggered before continuing.

It feels as if universes are separating us rather than mere hours and miles. I'd sacrifice all my wealth and title just for a glimpse of your smile, for you are my finest jewel. I miss you fiercely.

Your Adoring Liam

Silence followed Ferris's reading, during which I determinedly avoided Ali's eyes. Ferris examined the note before raising his gaze to mine, for once no ounce of teasing filling his expression. "This is serious, isn't it? You really did spell the Crown Prince of Draceria."

"Finally you understand the extent of my dire circumstances." My anxiety was rising again, suffocating. I released a strangled sob and buried myself in my hands.

Mother rubbed my back. "Don't despair, dear; everything will be alright. We have a reversal spell; now we just need the two remaining ingredients. Why don't you go purchase the dragon scales now? It'd be good for you to get out of the house. Guard Alastar, would you please accompany her?"

My gaze snapped up in time to notice Mother's mischievous smirk. For some reason, my heart started beating wildly at the thought of Ali and me alone together. "Oh, I doubt he'd want to," I said. "He has a duty to guard Eileen."

"Despite my attempts to ignore her wishes for the sake of her safety, she's unfortunately quite forcefully forbidden me from approaching her or her cottage for the remainder of the day; she wants time alone with her mother." Ali released a heavy sigh. "The moment His Highness learns I strayed from my post..." He shook his head.

"I told you, he won't learn of it," I said, hoping my words were true. I'd hate to see anything happen to Ali as a result of the mess I'd made for everyone.

"Considering I'm currently off duty, I'll happily accompany you to purchase an ingredient," he said. "Besides, I'm eager for a grand tour of Arador from one who knows all the fantastic stories about this charming village."

I managed a small smile. "I do know of several wonderful tales, but I'm almost afraid to share them, considering it's my love for stories that entangled me in my current plight."

"You only find yourself in trouble when you attempt to manipulate your own," he said. "But not to worry; I'm becoming an expert at reining your imagination in before it gets too out of control."

"Not when you play along."

His lips twitched, and for a moment we simply stared at one another before Ali held out his hand. I rested mine in his, marveling at how perfectly it fit. He enfolded mine before bowing to my family. "I'll watch over her."

"I'm sure you will." Mother's eyes twinkled mischievously as she looked back and forth between us before exchanging a strange smile with Father, as if the two were speculating and were rather pleased at whatever conclusions they'd come up with. Did *everyone* suspect my relationship with Ali was deeper than it actually was?

Ferris, however, surveyed Ali with a rather fierce and protective look, once again no trace of his usual teasing on his expression. "I don't think it's wise to let Rosie accompany that guard alone," he said. "We don't know anything about him."

"Don't be ridiculous, Ferris," Mother said. "He's Eileen's personal guard. Obviously, he's a man that can be trusted." She gently pushed me towards the door. "Have a marvelous time, you two."

"I still think they should have a chaperone," Ferris said coldly, sizing Ali up as if he was going to challenge him to a duel.

"They'll be fine," Mother said with a wink towards me that made my cheeks warm.

The moment we stepped outside into the warm sunshine, a wave of calm washed over me. It was such a beautiful day. The breeze was soft, pleasant, and caressing, tangling my hair. I was finally home again and away from the palace and Prince Liam. I breathed out a contented sigh.

"Are you ready to be the leader on today's adventure?" Ali asked.

"I'm not sure that's wise," I said. "Whenever I take control of a tale, things end up quite the mess."

"We are in a mess," he said, and my brow furrowed at his use of the word *we*. "But no matter the obstacles in any story, the heroine and her hero always overcome them. Now, we're visiting the apothecary for an ingredient in a reversal spell?"

I nodded and pointed down the crowded street. "The apothecary is in that direction."

"Lead the way." He looped my arm through his, and I led him into the bustle of the market. Hustling villagers crowded the street, already full of an array of stalls selling all sorts of wares—fresh produce, haunches of meat, spices, homemade goods and trinkets—and filling the air with the clinking of coins and the murmurs of bartering.

I was keenly aware of Ali's presence beside me and felt a thrill at being escorted through my home village by *my* royal guard. I felt the strangest inclination to drop his arm in order to hold his hand. I curled my own into a fist to resist this impulse and distracted myself by sharing my memories of Arador. It was difficult at first, as if I were stirring my imagination from slumber. I wasn't even sure I wanted it to return, but once it'd awoken and stretched a bit, it began to dance through my mind and breathe life into my words.

We paused in the middle of a story about a secret princess who had taken refuge in a shed from an ogre who'd been chasing her—which was really an elaborate recounting of when Ferris had accidentally locked me in a farmer's shed, where I'd been trapped for three hours—when we paused beside the floral stand, bursting with an array of cheerful blossoms in a rainbow of colors. As I was admiring each of the arrangements, Ali briefly disappeared, returning with a flower he'd purchased.

"For you." He held out a single iris, its lovely purple and white petals aglow in the sunshine. I stared at it in awe as I lightly traced its petals. *Ali gave me a flower*. My heart swelled in happiness. This gesture was so much sweeter than Prince Liam's elaborate bouquet.

"It's lovely, Ali."

"I'm happy it pleases you." He tucked it behind my ear, his fingers grazing my cheek as he pulled away.

"Why an iris?" I asked breathlessly.

A blush dotted his cheeks. "Irises are considered a royal flower. With your love for fairy tales, I thought you'd like that."

I sighed and let my fingers—which had been caressing the petals of the flower in my hair—drop. "I used to. Now I'm not so sure."

We began walking again, weaving through the people and the stalls. I looked around the familiar cobblestone paths and quaint grey stone buildings as if seeing them for the first time. Whereas I'd always considered Arador a boring place to have grown up, now each shop we passed triggered a happy memory, as did the familiar scents drifting through the street —the floral perfume of the floral stand we were leaving behind, the aroma of bread drifting from our own bakery, the spices being sold from the stands, the meat from the butchers, and my favorite roasted chestnuts, which Ali purchased for us to share as we continued our trek to the apothecary.

I had a lovely time pointing out various places and people to Ali, telling him story after story about various memories I'd developed over the years. His expression softened with each tale. "It sounds like you've had a lovely life in Arador."

I came up short, blinking rapidly. "I guess I have." I glanced around Arador once more, as if seeing it for the first time. "It's been a wonderful place to grow up." To think I used to hate this simple village, when now it seemed so charming and freeing after the confining elegance of the palace. I recognized each villager and reveled in their smiles and friendly nods in greeting, as well as their cheerful laughter. I envied their contentment, something I'd never been able to find here before. Could I ever come to share in it? Perhaps I was already beginning to.

Excitement bubbled in my chest when I spotted my favorite building. "The library. Oh Ali, I have to show you it."

He obediently escorted me there, where we explored the tiny building, lined with books. We spent a cozy hour visiting all my favorite stories, our quest to the apothecary forgotten as we traced our fingers along the spines, pulling out books to immerse ourselves in the scent and feel of their leather and musty pages. I was delighted to discover Ali and I had read some of the same books. Each commonality we discovered strengthened the connection I already felt with him, one I ached to explore further with each passing moment.

"Can I ask you a question?" I queried as we finally realized the lateness of the afternoon and stepped back outside to resume our walk to the apothecary. "Is royal life usually how it's been during my visits with Eileen?" I asked this hesitantly, not wanting his confirmation to shatter what was left of my dreams.

"It's not a storybook, if that's what you're asking," he said. "I've watched Prince Aiden shoulder many responsibilities and duties over the years, but there are wonderful things about it as well." He glanced down at me with sweet understanding. "You've been disappointed in the reality, haven't you?"

"I admit I have. I want to imagine there's something marvelous to be found outside the pages of a book. Is that silly?"

"Not at all," he said, so kindly. "But I do think you have a tendency to spend so much time trying to find what you expect to see that you fail to notice what's really in front of you."

I nibbled my nail, considering. "Perhaps you're right. I've always hated the village I grew up in because it wasn't a palace, but today I feel as if I'm seeing it with new eyes."

"The memories you shared with me were always a part of you, even if you didn't recognize it."

He was right. I once again took in the village, small and simple to be sure, but full of so much life and joy. I smiled. "Arador may not be a palace, but it has its own charms."

"And your imagination will allow you to have the most grand adventures wherever you are, even here."

"My imagination and I are currently not on very good speaking terms."

"That's too bad," Ali said. "Your imagination is charming. It may be a bit impulsive and needs to be tamed, but you should never get rid of it."

I smiled. "Thanks, Ali." I untucked the iris from my hair and twirled it by its stem, admiring it. It was so lovely, somehow the most beautiful iris I'd ever seen. I peeked up at Ali, watching me with an intense look.

"Do you like it even if it's not a bouquet of roses?" He looked so vulnerable in that moment, as if both desperate and afraid to hear my answer.

"I like this much better. Besides, irises are my new favorite flower." I tucked it back in my hair, earning me another one of his almost-smiles I was coming to love.

We arrived at the apothecary, a dank room with herbs and strange plants dangling from the eaves. I browsed the crowded shelves until I found the crushed dragon scales. I started to pick it up, but Ali rested his hand over mine to stop me. Warmth rippled up my arm.

I slowly met his gaze. "What is it?"

"Rosie, I—I need to tell you something."

I waited. He shifted from foot to foot. I'd never seen him so agitated. He opened his mouth to speak but remained silent. "What is it, Ali?" I asked gently.

"I—nothing." He was silent a moment. "I'm sorry, Rosie."

"For what?"

He fiddled with the jars lining the shelves, avoiding my eyes. "I only wanted to help you, but because I'm going about it in the wrong way, I'm hurting you instead."

"You're doing nothing of the sort. It's not your fault I allowed my imagination to author my love story, an action that ruined my best friend's own fairy tale." The guilt for that offense returned, sharp and prickling.

"Their fight wasn't your fault, Rosie," he said gently.

His words felt empty, especially considering I knew they weren't true. I sighed. "Do you think there's a way out of the predicament I've created for myself?"

He shifted again, looking rather uncomfortable. "I do. There's always a way. I—" Again he didn't say anything. I tilted my head, studying him.

"You're behaving rather out of character. I suspect an imposter."

My teasing earned me one of his lip-twitching smiles. It pleased me to see it. I plucked the crushed dragon scales from the shelf, and this time Ali made no motion to stop me.

After I'd purchased the dragon scales, we stepped back outside. The afternoon was melting into evening; the sun hung low on the horizon, casting the village in a sheen of golden-rose light. For a reverent moment, I allowed the loveliness of the setting sun to bathe me.

"Oh Ali, I never knew Arador could be so beautiful."

"It truly is a lovely place." He rested his hand on my lower back to guide me back towards the bakery. I nearly jolted at the contact. I took several breaths trying to school my heart, now pounding wildly.

For several minutes we walked in silence, allowing me to look around my village once more and savor its simple charms, all while marveling at the wonderful time I'd spent here. I never knew any moment in Arador could be so pleasant. Perhaps it was Ali's presence that had made it magical.

The spell was broken when he glanced down at me with a vulnerable look. "I've missed you, Rosie. It seems like you've been with Prince Liam almost every waking moment. I didn't realize how much I'd come to rely on our interactions until they were stolen from me. You do like to take things of mine, don't you?"

I furrowed my brow. "What else have I stolen from you?"

"Something very precious." He paused before hastily adding, "Do you miss His Highness? Having spent so much time with him the past week, I'm worried you find my company dull by comparison."

In truth, I hadn't thought about Prince Liam at all. "I can't say that I do. In fact, I'm rather relieved to be free of him for a while."

"But aside from the fact that you shouldn't have spelled him for ethical and political reasons, I thought his courtship was what you'd always dreamed about?"

"Well...it admittedly didn't go as well as I thought," I said. "Although he's undeniably charming." Despite how annoying his attentions admittedly were, it was still somewhat flattering that I'd received them from a real prince.

Ali cocked an incredulous eyebrow. "Indeed. If that's all that's needed for a relationship, I'm in trouble when I eventually start courting."

I froze, the tranquil afternoon we'd spent together instantly darkening. "You're planning on courting someone?"

"I'm hoping to." He gently tugged on my arm to resume our walk, but I'd been transformed into a statue by an evil spell and wouldn't be able to move ever again.

"Has someone caught your fancy?" My heart plummeted at his nod, a nod which confirmed what I'd until now been merely suspecting. "Oh." I remained rooted to the spot, but while I stood unmoving, inside my heart was a hurricane of emotions. "I see."

His frown deepened. "Are you alright?"

"Is it one of Eileen's ladies you fancy?" They were all annoyingly beautiful, her handmaiden in particular.

"No."

"Then it must be that parlor maid, the one you couldn't keep your eyes off during the recent state banquet."

He scrunched his forehead, as if trying to remember, before rolling his eyes. "Oh *her*? She flirts with everyone, but I assure you her attentions were unwelcome."

My heart lifted at that bit of news, but I wasn't fully appeased. "Then..." I struggled to come up with another position on the royal staff but I found it impossible to even breathe, let alone think coherently. Ali gently tugged on my arm again, and this time I managed to thaw enough to stumble after him. "Then who do you want to court?"

"That's a secret, Rosie."

More secrets? "Won't you tell me?" For I'd never wanted to know a secret as fiercely as I wanted to know this one.

"Perhaps one day you'll wriggle it out of me."

We continued our stroll, but I suddenly no longer wanted to be on Ali's arm; instead I needed a secluded hiding place where I could break down and cry.

"Are you alright, Rosie?" Ali gazed down at me with concern. I bit the inside of my lip to keep my tears at bay. I refused to cry in front of him.

"I'm fine."

"You never could lie to me, Rosie."

I glared at him, for he was the perfect target for the agony now racing through me for reasons I didn't quite understand. "Stop reading me like an open book."

"I admit I'm too curious not to when you so conveniently leave it open. Might I suggest getting a lock? Although I must confess I hope you don't."

His gaze was smoldering, intensifying the strange feelings igniting my insides, causing me to yearn for him to read every single page of my story for the rest of our lives.

"I don't want to get a lock," I whispered. He stepped closer and touched my cheek. I leaned against his fingers.

"Rosie..." He said my name both like a caress and as if he was in fierce pain. He stroked my cheek, each touch causing me to melt as he stared into my eyes. "You have the most lovely eyes," he whispered gently. "They're like an ocean, brimming with life, mischievousness, and *stories*."

He smiled at me, another *real* smile, this one soft and tender. His words danced through my mind. I had ocean eyes that were full of stories. Never had a compliment touched me so deeply.

"You agreed with Prince Liam the other day when he called me beautiful," I said. A blush caressed his cheeks and his expression softened.

"You are beautiful, not just you but your imagination. I noticed it the moment we met. Whenever we're not together, I miss not just you but your stories, *our* stories."

He suddenly dipped down, as if he meant to...but he couldn't, not Ali. Despite whatever was happening seeming utterly impossible, without conscious thought I leaned upwards to meet him. But he suddenly pulled away with a gasp, causing my heart to crack.

"Forgive me, Rosie." He stumbled backwards, glancing towards the horizon, where the sun was sinking further. "It's getting late. I need to return you to the bakery and check on Her Highness."

It took me a moment to find my voice, and once I had, it took even longer for me to still my pounding heart enough to take his arm. We didn't speak for the remainder of our walk. The moment we arrived at the bakery, Ali bowed, cheeks still crimson, and departed without another look back.

Later that night, as I lay awake staring up at my ceiling, my mind revisited the scene with Ali over and over again, trying to make sense of not only what had almost happened, but of the lingering disappointment that it hadn't.

CHAPTER 21

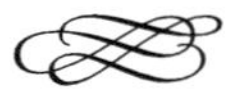

"Rosalina, you have another *love letter*," Ferris drawled.

I didn't even look up from the dough I kneaded. "Throw it into the fire."

He naturally chose to ignore this request. His snigger was followed by the sound of his unfolding the letter with exaggerated slowness. I gritted my teeth. Of course he couldn't let this golden opportunity to harass me pass. Older brothers were the worst.

"Oh, that's a surprise."

Ferris's comment tickled my curiosity, despite my fiercely trying to focus on the bread. I couldn't bear to hear another sappy poem gushing about all my supposed virtues and beauty that Prince Liam couldn't possibly really believe considering he was under the influence of magic.

"Hmm, this really is unexpected."

Ferris again. I bit my lip to keep my curiosity firmly inside where it belonged, but it escaped anyway. "What is it? Is the prince's latest poem less sappy than the last several he's sent?" That would be a miraculous feat.

"It's not from Prince Liam."

"What?" I swiveled around. "Who's it from?" A strange hope flared to life in my heart, one I was afraid to examine too closely in case I was wrong.

Ferris made a show of examining the signature. "Let's see, it appears to be from...ah, him."

I bounced impatiently on my heels. "Who?"

Ferris looked up with a knowing smirk. "Guard Alastar."

"*What*?!" My heart flared and I snatched the letter to hungrily read it...only to see that it wasn't from Ali at all but Prince Liam. I spun on my cruel brother, who was grinning quite wickedly. "Ferris!"

He chortled. "My suspicions are confirmed. I knew you fancied him."

My cheeks flamed. "I don't *fancy* him." *Fancied* seemed a word far too inadequate for...for...for whatever existed between Ali and me, something I couldn't quite put my finger on. The excitement that had filled my heart deflated.

"Yes you do." His smirk widened. "I don't see why. He's really not that good-looking, certainly not the type of prince you've been dreaming about your entire life."

I glared at him, my flour-coated hand balled into a fist, crumpling the offending letter. "Don't you dare say that about Ali." He was perfect.

His wicked grin widened. "A bit defensive, are we? I knew you liked him." His sniggering faded, replaced with a rare serious expression. He rested his hand on my arm. "It's my duty as your big brother to make sure anyone you fancy is worthy of you."

"I don't *fancy* him," I said again. "We're just friends." But somehow those words, too, felt inadequate on my tongue. The warmth in my cheeks deepened. "Ali and I are *good* friends," I clarified. Hmm, that didn't seem quite right either.

As if his name had been a summons, the bakery door

opened, the bell above it ringing merrily to signal someone's arrival. Considering it was the rest day and the bakery was closed, I hoped that meant it was...

Eileen walked through the bakery and appeared in the kitchen, Ali behind her. I stared at my best friend, hungrily searching her grave expression. I hadn't seen Eileen since our arrival in Arador and was alarmed at her puffy eyes that signaled long, restless nights, likely filled with crying.

Eileen smiled at me, though it was clearly forced, as it didn't quite reach her eyes. My heart tightened. She was clearly still upset with me, as she should be, considering I'd ruined everything.

"How are you, Eileen?" I asked hesitantly.

"Fine," she clipped in a tone that dismissed further questions.

Ferris sidled over with a look like he was about to create mischief. Sure enough, he gave Ali a strange smirk. "Rosalina enjoyed your love letter this morning."

I shot him a glare, which was likely rather ineffective considering my face was already burning with a mortifying blush.

Ali's eyebrows squashed together. "My...what?"

"Rosalina thought this morning's letter from Prince Liam was from you. You should have seen the way she eagerly scampered over to—"

"Ferris!"

He merely sniggered.

"Be grateful you're an only child," I mumbled to Eileen. To my delight, she managed a small smile, causing my heart to flare in hope that she didn't truly hate me after all.

I finally felt brave enough to glance at Ali, only to discover he wasn't looking at me, but was tracing his finger in the powdery flour marring the counter with exaggerated concentration, seeming almost embarrassed.

I forced myself to turn away from Ali back to Eileen, who was now staring out the window, lost in her melancholy.

"Have you heard from Aiden?" I asked.

She blinked as she turned back to me, as if I'd pulled her from somewhere far away. "Aiden? Yes, we've exchanged letters. He's worried about me."

"I'm glad." I wrung my hands. "Do you also exchange tender words?"

She shrugged. "A few."

"So...you two are doing well?" How I hoped so. I *needed* them to be. I couldn't bear the thought I'd destroyed my friend's happily ever after.

Eileen said nothing, not the best of signs. I took a wavering breath.

"Eileen, I'm really sorry about—"

"It's not your fault," she said crisply. She turned away and began wandering the kitchen aimlessly. I nibbled my fingernail and glanced at Ali again, aching for one of his assuring looks, but he was quite determinedly avoiding my eyes as he drew swirl after swirl in the flour.

"Aiden is quite anxious to know whether you've made any progress on the reversal spell," Eileen said.

"Oh." Of course she was only here to check up on me. A friend who ruined her best friend's marriage didn't deserve visits made in friendship anymore. "I've found the recipe, but I'm still missing one of the ingredients—enchanted water located in the Forest."

"Then we shall go to the Forest's enchanted waterfall this afternoon."

I searched her expression to see whether this offer to help was given because she wanted to be in my company again or was purely based on her royal duty to do whatever it took to reverse the love spell.

"I hope the spell works," I said.

"I'm sure it will," Eileen said. "You've gotten in all sorts of messes before, and yet things have always worked out."

All my previous mishaps over the years were nothing compared to the mess I found myself in now. Aiden had been right to banish me.

Eileen looked around the kitchen, her gaze lingering on the three bouquets that crowded the counter. Her lips twitched, another promising sign. "I see Liam is as attentive as ever?"

"This is nothing," Ferris said. "You should see the parlor… Your Highness." He added the title hastily. Eileen raised an eyebrow.

"I see. Well, I should update Aiden and then we can track down the final ingredient. Do you mind if I use the writing desk in the parlor?" Without even awaiting my reply, she started towards the next room. Ali naturally followed her, but in the doorway she turned to him. "No, Alastar, you don't need to accompany me."

"But Your Highness—" he objected.

"No tragic fate will befall me writing a letter," she said, sounding thoroughly exasperated. She started to turn but paused to give me a half smile. "Unless that writing desk is haunted and swallows its victims whole?"

I could see she meant for me to play along, but as was usual of late, I wasn't in the mood to do so. "No, it's an entirely ordinary writing desk."

"I see I'm not the only one in need of cheering up." Concern filled Eileen's expression. She glanced back at Ali. "You'll stay here and keep Rosie company." Although her command was firm, a bit of life flickered in her eyes as she glanced between us. "I'm sure Ferris has things to do as well."

He looked back and forth between Ali and me with another uncharacteristically protective big brother look. "But they—"

"Excellent." Eileen's interruption caused Ferris to cut his protests short. "I'm sure you have duties to attend to that will take you far away from the kitchen."

I expected him to ignore her request, but instead he gave her a sloppy bow and left. Eileen smiled, this one finally looking real. "Maybe there are perks to being a princess after all." And humming, she left the kitchen.

Silence filled the space between Ali and me. I shifted restlessly from foot to foot, stealing several glances at him. He finally looked up, but his gaze was captured not by my own but by my hair. "You have flour in your hair."

My cheeks warmed as I caught the ends of my hair with my still flour-covered fingers. "Do I? I've been kneading bread."

"You do. Here."

He stepped forward, closing the distance between us, and suddenly I was enveloped in his warm, intoxicating presence. He smelled just like my favorite honey-lemon muffins, and suddenly I found it strangely more difficult to breathe. It became even more impossible when Ali touched my hair, a gesture that caused my stomach to flip and my heart to patter wildly.

His brow furrowed. "Looks like I've made it worse." He frowned at his own flour-coated fingers.

I giggled. "There's no hope for me, then. I shall be a flour-covered heroine for this chapter of my story."

A smile tugged on the corners of his mouth. "Ah, there's one of your delightful comments I've missed. It's been far too long since I've seen you."

I tilted my head. "We saw one another yesterday." When we'd almost...my face burned. His own face became swallowed in a blush.

"Mm, only a single day? Perhaps a villain has cast a spell on me to make it seem far longer."

His fingers returned almost hypnotically to my hair, which he stroked between his thumb and forefinger with the utmost attention before he seemed to catch himself. His already rosy cheeks deepened to crimson and he yanked his hand away, as if he'd been burned, leaving me yearning for his touch.

Another awkward silence settled over us, each second feeling like an eternity as I searched for anything to say to him. "How's Eileen?" I asked.

"Overall well, so please don't be distressed over her."

That was a best friend's job, even a former best friend. I frowned. "Don't lie to me. I can clearly see she's not well."

"She's admittedly out of sorts, but she stopped crying yesterday, so that's progress."

Dread pooled my stomach. Did that mean Eileen had been crying most of her time in Arador?

"And she seems to be enjoying her time with her mother," Ali continued. "Although I can tell she misses His Highness."

His words were like another stab to my already guilt-ridden heart. "If they don't make up soon, I'll be responsible for breaking my best friend's heart."

"Not in the least, Rosie," he said, his tone far more gentle than I deserved. "Everything will be alright. You're a good friend to be worried about the princess, but you should be focusing on this spell of yours."

He met my gaze and smiled, one that was so sweet and felt extra special, for it not only cracked his usual rigid expression, but felt like it had been saved just for me. My heart gave a strange flutter.

"Are you ready to go to the Forest, Rosie?" Eileen had appeared in the doorway, her finished letter in her hands and a strange smile directed towards me.

I suddenly realized just how close Ali and I had been standing. Too late I hastily scooted backwards several feet to put the appropriate distance between us. "You really don't mind taking me?"

"Of course not." Her smile grew. "I haven't been inside the Forest in so long, what with *royal duties* getting in the way." She pulled a face. "Let me just find Ferris and have him see that this letter is delivered to the palace."

I nibbled my nail nervously as I glanced out the window, which gave us a view of the swaying trees. "What if we get lost?"

"We won't," she said. "The Forest has always loved me, but now that I'm its sovereign, it also respects and obeys me. It'll lead us to the final ingredient and then you can finally create the reversal spell." She looped her arm through mine and tugged me outside into the warm sunshine.

THE MOMENT we stepped into the Forest, the trees swayed excitedly, the wind pulling Eileen closer to them and caressing her hair as if giving her a hug. She giggled as she tipped her head back to smile up at them with undeniable fondness.

"I've missed you, too. I wish I could linger, but we're in need of enchanted water from the waterfall. Can you take us there?"

The trees rustled again—seeming rather excited to be of service—before the path before us wriggled into a new position, twisting deeper into the Forest and out of sight.

I frowned at it warily. "Will that path really lead us to the waterfall?"

"We'll never know unless we take it; that's something I've learned."

Eileen gently tugged on my arm as she stepped confidently onto the path, Ali maintaining his usual respectful distance behind us. I followed, keeping a close eye on the trees. Sunshine tumbled through the leafy canopy above us, dancing around us in glittery pools, making the Forest feel truly enchanted. The knots twisting my stomach slowly eased.

Occasionally, the path would shift in a new direction as the Forest gently guided us. Eileen seemed to be in no hurry as she followed the Forest without hesitation. I searched her expression, taut and missing her usual vibrancy. Guilt returned to gnaw at my heart.

I reached out and brushed my fingers on her wrist. "Do you hate me?"

She glanced towards me, her eyebrow raised. "Hate you? Why would you think that? You're my best friend."

"One who doesn't deserve to be your best friend any longer." The tears I'd been fighting to keep back escaped. "I've ruined your happily ever after."

She blinked at me, seeming confused, before her rigid posture crumpled. "You didn't ruin my happily ever after."

"That fight between you and Aiden was all my fault."

Eileen carefully stepped over a log strewn across our path before glancing back at me. "You didn't cause our fight; *I* did, because I've neglected to confide in my husband."

I stared at her, stunned. That hadn't been the response I'd been expecting. "What do you mean?"

She sighed. "I mean I've been discontent for quite some time, but I was afraid to tell Aiden for fear of hurting him. We were both worried about how I'd handle this drastic change in my station, but nothing could have prepared me for how difficult it's been." She shook her head. "With all the challenges I've faced, I can't understand why you *want* to marry a prince."

"Because in storybooks—"

"Life isn't like one of your stories, Rosie," Eileen said gently.

I now realized she was right, but despite my own life turning out very differently than the fairy tale I'd always planned, I still yearned to believe that portions of them could be real. "That's not true," I protested. "In your story, an enchanted forest led you to your true love, who happened to be a prince who swept you away to live in a castle."

"But you've forgotten to read beyond my happy ending," she said, her tone becoming serious. "I may have married a prince, but his family doesn't approve of me and his court constantly judges me because I don't measure up to their high standards, not to mention learning how to be a royal is an arduous process. I miss the freedom I used to enjoy, especially the days I'd spend exploring the Forest and drawing. Now there's little time for that as I'm swamped with royal obligations I'm not even good at. What's worse, I fear I'm disappointing Aiden and that he regrets marrying me." Her eyes shone with unshed tears.

"Of course he doesn't." I gave her hand an assuring squeeze. "He loves you."

Eileen frantically wiped her eyes. "I know that, and I love him. But is love enough?"

"Of course it is," I said, baffled that she could even consider otherwise. "Love is the most powerful force in the entire world."

Eileen tilted her head. "Then why were you so willing to settle for less than true love just so you could become a princess?"

My stomach jolted. I lowered my gaze to the leaf-strewn path we walked. "I thought I loved Prince Liam, but now...I don't think I ever did. I was merely in love with the idea of being in love with a prince."

"I think you allowed yourself to get caught up in a fairy

tale," she said kindly. "Liam is handsome and charming—everything a prince should be—but he isn't *your* prince. You've been looking so intently for a man who's a prince on the outside that you've failed to recognize your true prince based on who he is on the inside. But I'm confident you'll soon find your true love, likely in the most unexpected of places." She looked up at the trees, a soft smile on her face. "Being here brings back so many memories of when I first met Aiden. I was rather blind to love myself, but now that I've finally recognized it, I know that it will see me through any difficulty. It's the reason I made the choice I did. But it's still hard at times."

"Do you ever regret it?" I asked.

Eileen didn't even hesitate. "Never, even if our life together isn't at all like your fairy tales."

"What's it like instead?"

She stared out across the sea of green surrounding us like a cocoon. "Stories always end when the heroine finds her happily ever after, but I've come to learn that happily ever after is different than I expected. It's not the end of a story but the *continuation* of it, and like any story, it's full of ups and downs, moments of happiness woven through moments of sorrow."

"So sometimes you're unhappy?" I asked hesitantly.

She shook her head. "Not at all. I'm very happy with Aiden. The longer we're together, the more I love him, but..." She bit her lip. "Every day brings a new set of challenges. I knew I never wanted the princess life and I was right, but while I never asked for this royal life, I care for Aiden too much to allow anything to keep me from him. Love is about sacrifice. Aiden sacrificed getting a polished princess for a bride, and I sacrificed the simple life I love. Although it's hard, I don't regret my decision. I chose the right path for me—now you need to do the same for yourself." She gnawed her lip. "I just hope Aiden hasn't regretted his decision either. I've been thinking about him ever since our fight. I know I've hurt him. I can't wait to return to him and apologize."

We continued the remainder of the journey arm in arm and in silence, this one full not of tension but of contentment. The woods were so peaceful; I couldn't believe I'd never explored them with Eileen before now. The more the paths twisted and led us, the more I trusted they'd take me where I needed to go. Could I place as much trust in my own uncertain journey and muster the faith required to allow my story to write itself?

Soon, the path opened up into the clearing with the waterfall of enchanted water, whose turrets fell in colorful streams, creating a mist that glistened in the sunlight.

Returning here brought back memories from my first visit, when I'd wanted to investigate the falls for mystical life and buried treasure, only to fall in and be saved by Ali. My cheeks warmed at the memory of his firm arms wrapped protectively around me following his daring rescue, the worry that had filled his stoic expression, how that moment had been a turning point in what soon after quickly developed into one of my dearest friendships. I shyly peeked back at Ali, who by the look in his face was also lost in his reminiscences. How fitting that this was the location for the final ingredient in my love reversal spell.

Eileen noticed my backward glance and lowered her voice. "You two are a good match, don't you think? He plays along with your imagination yet also grounds you." Eileen settled on the bank next to the frothy pool and I followed, my heart beating wildly.

"He's a good friend," I ventured.

Eileen raised her eyebrows. "Only a friend? Really, Rosie, you need to stop focusing on what you think your story should look like so you can recognize what it already is."

Feelings stirred in my heart, ones that I'd fought to suppress for fear of examining them too closely. After my recent disaster with "love," I was afraid to give it another try.

I ran my fingers through the cool water, currently a light lilac. "I admit I'm rather confused on what my story should be, considering I got it so wrong the first time."

"Well, that's the beauty of being the heroine of your own fairy tale—when it doesn't go as planned, simply rewrite it." She handed me a glass jar.

I dipped it into the enchanted pool, now a lovely shade of rose. The water glistened within the jar, a reminder of its magic. Magic had gotten me into this mess, so surely it'd get me out.

Even after I'd tucked my final ingredient away, Eileen and I lingered, soaking our feet in the shimmery pool, making crowns from the wildflowers growing in the clearing, and laughing and talking, just like we'd always done. Despite my mistakes, nothing had changed between us. That thought was incredibly comforting.

As sunset began to caress the treetops, Eileen reluctantly pulled her feet from the pool to tuck them beneath her. "We should probably return to the real world now, shouldn't we?"

For once, the real world was exactly where I wanted to be. I was anxious to return to my bakery and begin baking the reversal spell in order to put my happily ever after back on its proper course. I stood, brushing off the loose blades of grass from my dress.

"We should. But this was fun. We'll have to come back sometime."

"Definitely. Spending more time here would help me handle my royal duties better; the Forest rejuvenates me." We walked towards the trees, but before a path could appear before us, another opened up several yards away, coming from the opposite direction. We turned just as Aiden entered the clearing.

Eileen's breath hooked. They stared at one another, wide-eyed, for a long moment. I held my breath waiting, hoping…

"What are you doing here?" Eileen squeaked.

Aiden took a tentative step forward. "I'm here to see you."

Eileen's forehead furrowed. "But how did you know I'd be here?"

Aiden patted a nearby tree with a smile. "I have my sources." The tree ruffled its leaves smartly. Eileen gave a strangled sound that was a mixture between a laugh and a sob.

"The Forest told you I was here?" She was silent a moment. "Then it did what I asked it to do."

He grinned. "Interesting. We both made the same request of it."

Eileen released another choked sob and ran to him. He met her halfway and seized her in a tight embrace, burrowing his face against her hair.

"Eileen, Eileen, Eileen…" He murmured her name over and over. She tipped her tear-streaked face up to smile up at him.

"You're here," she murmured.

"I am," he said. "The moment you suggested coming to Arador I wanted to come with you, but I thought you needed time…away from me."

"Not you," she insisted. "Never you. I missed you."

He released a long breath. "And I missed you. I thought of you the entire time you were gone, worrying…" He cradled her cheek. "Darling, are you really so unhappy in this life with me?"

"Of course not, Aiden. I'm so happy with you." She bit her lip. "I just feel like I'm a disappointment as a princess to you and the king. Royal life is so foreign to me."

"I know it has been a big adjustment, but please believe me, you're doing a wonderful job." His assuring grin became mischievous. "You can't doubt you're the only one for the role, considering you won that Princess Competition of mine."

Eileen laughed. "We both know that competition was rigged."

"Naturally." His arms tightened around her to nestle her even closer. "The moment I met you I knew you were the one for me. Please let that be enough."

"It is, Aiden." She snuggled closer. "You're the right path for me. I've never regretted it, and no matter how hard things get, I never will."

He released a sigh of relief.

"And you want to know a secret?" Her expression became mischievous. "I actually missed life at the palace. I guess I'm adjusting better than I thought I was."

He nestled against her hair. "I'm so glad."

I watched the sweet, utterly romantic scene with a full heart. Everything was alright between them. Their reunion served as a reminder that nothing could separate true love. Hopefully that meant that a love reversal spell could separate two who *weren't* in love. Now that Eileen's happily ever after was back on its proper course, it was time to fix mine.

CHAPTER 22

Upon our return from the Forest, Father and I baked the reversal spell, measuring each ingredient carefully to ensure it would have the desired effect. When the toffee had cooled, I carefully wrapped the enchanted treats and tucked them into my reticle for our return trip to the palace.

The following day, I wriggled anxiously in my seat in the rose parlor as I awaited Prince Liam's arrival, casting several glances towards the door where he was due to appear any moment now. I was only distracted from my restless waiting by Ali, who seemed especially grave today and failed to meet my gaze.

Eileen looked up from conversing with Aiden and reached over to squeeze my hand assuredly. "You made the spell perfectly. I'm sure it'll work."

I took a steadying breath, trying to believe her. I'd never made a spell with so much precision and I was quite confident I hadn't made any mistakes, but would it be enough? How I hoped that it would be. Spelling the Crown Prince of

Draceria had not only been wrong, but I could finally admit, however reluctantly, that we weren't an entirely good fit.

I tensed as the door opened and a footman entered. "Crown Prince Liam of Draceria here to see—"

"*Rosie*!" Prince Liam nearly knocked the footman over in his haste to reach my side. He knelt at my feet and seized my hand, staring up at me with eyes wide with adoration. "Oh, Rosie petal, it's been far too long since we last saw one another. I nearly died without you. How was your trip to Arador? I've only just returned from Draceria, where I thought of you every moment of the day."

I sighed. The potency of the spell seemed more off-putting now, considering the wonderful distance I'd had from it. Since my right hand was currently being repeatedly kissed by the lovesick prince, I tried to wriggle the reticule free one-handed. "Your Highness, I've brought a gift back for you."

"A gift from my Rosie?" He lit up.

I managed to extract both my hand and my reticle, which I opened to reveal the spelled toffee I'd painstakingly created. "I baked another treat especially for you."

He eagerly held out his hand, palm up, and I started to hand it to him...but hesitated. Did I really want to do this? Part of me still wanted to believe a life with Prince Liam was how my story should go, considering I'd imagined that ending for myself for so long and the storyteller had caused me to believe in it. It was a hard admission to make that it was wrong, for doing so would destroy my lifelong dream of my own prince in my own castle.

But I now realized the cost was too high. If I continued this course, I'd receive my prince and castle—and with it the duties that came from being a princess, only unlike Eileen, I wouldn't have the joy of being in love with my husband.

I searched Prince Liam's blue eyes. I didn't love him, only

the fantasies I'd created of the life he'd give me. And that wasn't real love—not the kind I read about and wanted. I may not get the storybook ending I'd always imagined, but I could still find my own happily ever after.

My gaze was drawn towards Ali, still in his usual guarding post, staring intently at me. The sweet look in his hazel eyes gave me the resolve to place the toffee in Prince Liam's hand.

He got up off the floor and settled beside me, smiling at my toffee as if it were a precious jewel. "Did you make this, my Rosie?" And he continued to admire it.

I shifted impatiently. "Aren't you going to eat it?"

"Eat a gift you made? I think not. How could I eat something so perfect? Instead I'll keep it forever."

Alarm filled my heart. This wasn't part of the plan. "But Your Highness, I made it especially for you."

"Which is why I'll cherish it." He pressed the toffee to his heart.

My panic swelled, but before it could eclipse me, an idea struck. Princes always seemed moved by damsels in distress. I conjured up some tears, which wasn't difficult when I considered the consequences should I fail to unspell the Crown Prince of Draceria.

Prince Liam's eyes immediately widened in alarm. "What is it, petal?"

I buried my face in my hands. "I worked so hard to make you a treat I hoped you'd like, and now you won't even eat it."

Prince Liam immediately began fluttering about, stroking my arms soothingly. "Please don't be upset, Rosie. I didn't realize it meant so much to you. Of course I'll eat your treat if it'll make you happy."

My gaze snapped up in time to watch him pop the toffee into his mouth. Everyone watched with bated breath, waiting in anticipation as Prince Liam chewed slowly, swallowed.... "Mmm, that was delicious. Thank you, Rosie."

I held my breath as I continued watching him, searching for any indication that the love spell was fading, for the sappiness to leave his eyes, anything...but nothing happened. "Prince Liam?" I asked hesitantly.

"*Liam*, my sweet." He brushed another kiss along my knuckles.

"Do you still love me?"

"Of course, my Rosie petal. How could you ever doubt my love towards you?"

I sank back in my chair in defeat and exchanged an alarmed look with Aiden and Eileen. Aiden moaned, burying his face in both hands. "Maybe it takes time for it to work?" Eileen whispered. We continued to wait anxiously but were left disappointed as Prince Liam continued to stare doe-eyed at me, no sign that his infatuation was melting away.

Aiden snapped to his feet, burrowing his fingers in his hair as if he meant to yank it out. He paced the parlor several times, clearly agitated. Prince Liam glanced at me and raised his eyebrows, the first sign of his old self rather than the spelled version. My heart swelled in hope...before it was dashed again when he leaned towards my ear.

"He's obviously jealous I possess the love of one who bakes such delicious treats."

My eyes burned with tears, these ones real. I buried my face in my hands, the hopelessness crushing me. If the reversal spell hadn't worked, what was I going to do?

Eileen appeared at my side. "We'll figure something out," she whispered.

"How?" I glanced towards the lovesick prince, who lit up when our gazes met. He was most definitely still spelled, which meant I was back where I started—on my way to an unhappily ever after with no way out.

Horror curdled my stomach at the realization: I was a character trapped in a story I no longer wanted to be in, and I had no idea how to break free from a plot rapidly spiraling out of control. The parlor was suddenly much too confining. Escape—I needed to escape.

I yanked my hand from Prince Liam's burning grip and leapt to my feet, ignoring the wounded look now filling his eyes.

"Rosalina?" He attempted to reach for my hand again but I jerked away. I'd had enough of this ridiculous charade.

I bolted from the parlor and darted down first one hallway, then another, before I dove behind a curtain. I pressed myself into the corner, panting for breath as all the tears and frustrations of the last several weeks came pouring out. The love spell had worked...far too well. And now I couldn't undo what I'd done, despite desperately wanting to. I'd become the tragic heroine in my own story and there was no escape. I whimpered and slid down the wall to curl my legs to my chest and bury my face against my knees.

I stiffened when I heard footsteps approaching. No, I simply couldn't bear it if it was Prince Liam. I pressed myself deeper into my corner in hopes it would swallow me whole. Being forever trapped in the walls as an eternal decoration seemed a better fate than another encounter with my spelled albatross.

I held my breath and waited, hoping the footsteps would pass my hiding place. To my horror they paused directly in front of me. The curtains slowly parted. I didn't even need to look up to see who it was.

"So you found me," I mumbled into my knees.

"Were we playing hide-and-seek?"

I peeked up at Ali. Despite his wry comment, no trace of amusement lined his features. They softened further as his gaze took in my crumpled expression.

"I'm sorry, I should have knocked before barging in."

Normally, I'd have responded with a witty comeback as part of our usual word spar, but I was a defeated heroine and in no mood to play today, not even with Ali.

"You may come in," I said with a sigh.

He slipped behind the curtain and settled himself beside me on the floor. Heat pulsed in the close space between us.

My cheeks warmed. "How did you know I was here?"

"After your hasty escape, I heeded Her Highness's orders to come after you. As to how I knew you were behind this curtain..." He leaned closer and I caught a whiff of his delicious honey-lemon scent. "...I believe you need to pick better hiding places, Rosie."

Once again I didn't have it in me to retort. I leaned my head back against the wall. "If Eileen is the one who sent you, why didn't she come herself?"

"She seemed to believe you'd prefer to see me," Ali said carefully, as if unsure of his own words. "She had a most mischievous smile as she made the suggestion."

How could Eileen possibly want to play matchmaker at a time like this?

Earnestness filled Ali's eyes as he scooted closer, awashing me in the heat of his touch. "Would you like me to sit with you for a while?"

I nodded numbly. We sat in silence for a while before he was the first to break it.

"Rosie?"

He said my name so tenderly, in a way that made me certain he understood everything I was feeling. My tears escaped. I reburied my face in my knees, but Ali wouldn't allow that. He wound his arm around me and pulled me gently against himself.

I burrowed against his warm chest. "Why didn't the spell

work? I don't understand; I know I followed the recipe exactly."

"I'm sure there's a logical explanation," he said.

"There is: I'm doomed to an unhappily ever after. I've ruined not only my life but Prince Liam's as well. You were right, Ali; I am the villain in my own story."

"Of course you're not." Ali's arms wound more securely around me. "Just because you're experiencing a dark part of your fairy tale doesn't mean the story is over."

He gently brushed my tears away with his thumb, his eyes full of tenderness. I searched his gorgeous hazel gaze. I used to fancy I favored blue eyes or even green in a man, but not anymore. Now I adored hazel, especially Ali's eyes, not only beautiful but full of such sweetness.

"I've made such a mess of things." I said. "Nothing is going as I thought it would. I plotted for Prince Liam to be spelled and he is, but..."

Something lit in Ali's eyes. He leaned closer. "But..."

"He isn't my prince. I now realize he never was." I couldn't look into his eyes, couldn't admit how wrong about everything I'd been.

Ali cupped my chin, encouraging me to look up at him. "If he's not your prince, is there someone else?"

My heart beat wildly and I found myself leaning towards his touch, and yet...I furrowed my forehead, trying to sort through my jumbled feelings. "I don't know."

He leaned back with a disappointed sigh. "It's alright, Rosie. One day you will."

"How do you know?"

"Because you're terrible at keeping secrets, especially from yourself. Thus I have no doubt you'll eventually sort everything out."

"Then why is everything so confusing now?"

"I believe you're currently experiencing a common trope

in many stories where the heroine begins her tale with one goal in mind, only to discover during her quest to obtain it that it's no longer what she desires."

"But I still long for true love. That hasn't changed." Although that dream had never felt less obtainable than in this moment. More tears trickled down my cheeks and Ali wiped these away too, the gesture so sweet I only cried harder.

"I know you do," he said. "Perhaps the key to breaking His Highness's spell has nothing to do with magic. What's the most powerful force in any fairy tale?"

I gasped. "True love."

He smiled. "Exactly."

He was right: true love could break any curse, no matter how powerful and sinister. But my elation at the idea quickly faltered. "And where am I supposed to find true love?"

"Like anything worthwhile, it has to be discovered."

"Great. When you find a treasure map leading to it, please let me know."

He frowned. "I don't think anyone can help you on that quest of yours."

"Then I'm doomed." I reburied myself against his warm, cozy embrace. "This is the tragic end of *The Tale of Rosalina*, an ending full of tears and heartbreak, with no happily ever after in sight."

Ali began rubbing my back. I nestled closer with a strangled sob. "Don't you think it's a bit early to be making such a denouncement? A true heroine fights through her obstacles and doesn't give up."

I shook my head. "I no longer believe a fairy tale romance exists for me, else the reversal spell would have worked."

"Of course it exists." Ali moved his stroking touch from my back to my hair. "As the noble knight in *The Tale of*

Rosalina, I'll do everything I can to help the fair maiden obtain her happily ever after. Can you trust me, Rosie?"

I stole another peek up at him. Sincerity radiated in his sweet expression. "Why do you believe in my happy ending?"

"Because even when the heroine experiences obstacles in her tale, they never last forever. And when they eventually end, what happens?"

I finally managed a smile. "She achieves her happily ever after."

Ali nodded. "Exactly. Even if you don't believe in yours right now, I'm confident one day you will again. After all, it's an essential trait that makes you my Rosie flower." He embraced me, tightly and tenderly. I melted against him and allowed him to hold me for this chapter of my story, one I strangely felt would never be long enough.

And despite my story being in the darkest of chapters, I felt a flicker of hope ignite in my heart.

CHAPTER 23

The dark, shadowy corridors had become incredibly familiar, like friends, almost more so after midnight than they were during the day. I'd snuck out of my room later than usual, for Prince Liam had taken it upon himself to pace outside my door every evening, as if hoping to catch one last glimpse of me before he retired for the night. Even after he'd finally abandoned his near-constant post and returned to his own room, I'd cautiously peeked around every corner before venturing into the hallway so I could evade him should he still be up and wandering the palace.

I became more at ease when Ali appeared as the corridor I currently wandered met up with his, as if he knew I'd arrive at that time and place—and perhaps he did, taking his cues from the invisible script of whatever scene in our story we were currently playing out. He fell into step beside me. I beamed up at him and he smiled warmly in return. I was glad he was here; evening wouldn't be complete without our midnight stroll.

We wandered passage after passage, no particular destination in mind, walking in contented silence. Who would break it first? Everything seemed to be a delightful game between us. Each interaction we shared left me eager to discover what scene we were currently acting in, for we were cowriters in this tale, a tale that was *us*.

I peeked up at him only to discover his sweet smile. He'd been smiling more and more lately, and even though it was becoming increasingly familiar, it still filled me with joy to see it.

"How would you like to explore a part of the castle you've never seen before?" he asked.

"That sounds like a grand adventure."

Ali held out his hand. My breath hitched. For a moment I just stared at it. He wriggled his fingers. "Step one: you're supposed to take my hand."

Slowly, I did. The moment I rested mine in his, his fingers gently enfolded my hand to cradle it within his own. Ripples of heat pulsed up my arm. How could I experience such a reaction from a mere touch? But it wasn't a mere touch at all but an incredibly heavenly one.

"You're holding my hand," I murmured.

He tilted his head. "Is this as precious an experience for you as your first kiss? I'm not taking away anything from your fairy tale, am I?"

I shook my head. While I'd always considered my hand being held as sacred as the act of true love's kiss, I didn't mind sharing this experience with Ali. I peeked through my lashes to stare into his not-so-handsome-but-somehow-incredibly-handsome face. "This is exactly how I imagined the experience would be."

He gave my hand a gentle squeeze before leading me down the hall. "Then let's commence tonight's adventure to discover a most spectacular secret of the palace...or rather, *secrets*."

I shivered in anticipation and allowed Ali to lead me down several corridors on different levels of the castle. Wherever he planned on taking me took awhile to get to. I didn't mind. How could I when we were strolling hand in hand—*hand in hand,* imagine *that*—through a palace after midnight. No matter how many times we'd embarked on our nightly wanderings, it had never lost its thrill, but this particular midnight stroll was better than all of the others combined. For I, Rosalina, was walking *hand in hand* with Ali through a moonlit palace. Oh, bliss!

My forehead wrinkled in puzzlement as I considered this. Ali was a royal guard, not the prince I'd always expected to share this moment with, yet somehow I felt every bit a princess. What an unexpected plot twist.

Despite how much I relished Ali's hand intertwined in mine and delighted in the warm sensations rippling over me from the gesture, my ever-simmering curiosity soon got the better of me. I tugged on his hand when I couldn't stand the anticipation a moment longer.

"Ali, I'm going to burst. What's the secret you're determined to torture me with?"

He chuckled and the warm, reverberating sound went straight to my heart, appeasing my wriggling impatience. "I knew sooner or later your curiosity would get the better of you. You've made me wait a torturous amount of time for your secret, so I thought it only fair..."

"A secret is too precious to toy with in such a way."

"*Secrets* in this case, Rosie, and since I'd very much hate to make you actually burst before discovering them, I shall put you out of your misery." He walked a short distance further then pulled me to a stop in front of a wall covered by an ornate tapestry depicting a gruesome battle scene that I couldn't help but stare at even as I simultaneously wanted to tear my gaze away. "Here it is."

I frowned at the tapestry for a moment more before gazing quizzically up at him. "The secret is the tapestry?"

"Is it?"

I should have known it wouldn't be that easy. Ali always kept me on my toes. I smiled to myself. It was one of the things I liked most about him.

"Smirking at the tapestry won't get it to reveal its mysteries to you."

"That's what *you* think." I cleared my mind from all the rather pleasant Ali thoughts filling it in order to focus on the task at hand.

The scene depicted knights battling a ferocious dragon, and the dragon was clearly winning. It was a fierce beast made up of fiery gold and flaming red threads that hovered in the air, breathing orange fire at the struggling valiant knights. I studied every inch of the tapestry, determined to unlock its secrets, but no matter how long I stared at it, it seemed to be an entirely ordinary tapestry, hanging on an entirely ordinary wall that was part of an entirely ordinary corridor. Ordinary, ordinary, ordinary.

After several minutes of intense study—during which Ali watched with far too much amusement—I spun on him.

"Are you tricking me? This appears to be an entirely ordinary tapestry."

"Giving up already? That's unlike you. I went through all the trouble of securing His Highness's permission to share this with you. If you're unable to decipher its secrets..."

"No!" I squinted at the tapestry again, searching for any secret codes or hidden symbols that might have been woven into the fabric of the gruesome tale it portrayed, which would reveal the location of something quite fantastic. Surely this was a worthy quest, considering Ali seemed quite insistent that I discover its meaning.

I peeked sideways at him. Anticipation filled his gorgeous

hazel eyes as he waited for me to figure out *something*, which meant I had all the information I needed to uncover this secret before me.

Think Rosalina, think. I cycled through all the tales of castles I'd read over the years—until the most fantastic possibility lit my mind. I gasped. Could it possibly be true? I glanced at Ali for confirmation, and even though I hadn't spoken my hunch out loud, it was as if he read my mind in that unique way only he could.

"*Really*?" I squealed.

He nodded.

"But I thought it was a made-up story, like the dragons wandering the palace..." Now that I knew the *what*, all that remained to be discovered was the *how*.

I yanked aside the tapestry and ran my hand along the smooth marble wall, combing my fingers for a hook or a knob. Nothing. But I was undeterred. I got on my knees and ran my fingers along the crease where the wall met the floor. Still nothing.

"Ali," I complained.

"Heroines never give up, Rosie. You'll be so pleased to have found it without my help."

He was quite right about that, but I was naturally too stubborn to admit it. I let the tapestry fall back and sat back on my heels to stare up at it.

My gaze lingered on the dragon, flying in front of a palace, as if guarding a secret. I gasped as I remembered words Ali had shared during our first midnight wanderings. *"Dragons guard the secret passageways."* I stood and pressed my thumb on the guarded door stitched into the tapestry, and the wall behind it slid open. I slid the tapestry aside to discover the dark tunnel that had been hidden behind the wall.

I gawked at it for a moment in disbelief. I, Rosalina, had

just uncovered a secret passage in the Sortileyan Royal Palace. I squealed and covered my mouth with my hands to smother it as I bounced up and down.

"Ali! Ali, I did it! I found a secret passage! Nothing so thrilling as this has ever, *ever* happened to me. Ah, bliss!"

He chuckled as he wove his fingers through mine. My hand instinctively tightened around his, squeezing all the feeling from his hand as a way to channel my intense excitement.

"Don't tell me the adventure is over quite yet. Shall we see where it leads?"

"You mean we can *explore* it?"

"Of course. It would be cruel to have you discover a secret passageway and not allow you to explore it to your heart's content," he said. "Besides, knowing you, you'd sneak back here and do it even if I forbade you and inevitably become lost in the labyrinth within the walls."

He reached for an unlit torch hooked onto the wall and lit it. The torch flickered to life, bathing us in its orange glow.

Ali bowed and waved his hand. "Would you like to lead the way?"

I seized the torch and tugged him into the passage. The wall slid shut behind us with a *thud* that reverberated through my bones. A nervous thrill rippled over me. "What would happen if we got lost in these walls and never found our way out?"

"Then we'd die a horrible death and become ghosts who stalk the palace at night."

"And perform spectacular hauntings on the royal residents for generations."

Ali smiled. "I take it you don't mind such a fate?"

"As tragic as it is, it's not too terrible of a way to end the story." Especially if I could be a ghost with Ali.

I plunged forward in my explorations of the stone

passageway—dank, damp, and incredibly twisty. I kept a firm grip on his hand as our footsteps echoed and the flame of our torch bathed the grey darkness in flickering pools of light.

"Where does this lead?" I asked some minutes later.

"It would spoil the surprise to tell you," he said. "Although I'll mention that all the passageways are connected in one big labyrinth."

"And should we take a wrong turn…"

"Then I'll chortle like the villain I am as we suffer an untimely demise."

I squeezed through a narrow spot and the coldness from the surrounding walls pressed against me. "Do you know these passages well?"

Cue his head tilt. "Do I?"

"You better."

"You're not resigned to your fate of dying tragically within these walls and becoming a ghost?"

"As spectacular as that would be, no, I'm not."

His lips twitched. "Very well, I'll ease your worries: I know them quite well. Prince Aiden and I spent hours of our childhood exploring them. Still, I'm only confident enough to guide you to specific locations, a few of which I'll take you to tonight."

I allowed Ali to guide me through the musty, twisting corridors within the walls, leading me to rooms that were locked from the outside at night. The passages were a maze I couldn't even begin to figure out, but Ali guided me confidently—either leading the way or, when I wanted the illusion of leading, giving calm instructions behind me about where to go next.

In this manner we found our way to the library with its array of thousands upon thousands of volumes cast in shadowy night, to the conservatory whose symphony of perfumed flowers penetrated the air, to the garden bathed in moonlight and stars. Each time we entered a room, the wall closed behind us and I thrilled to discover the secret knobs that would allow it to swing open again.

"I think that's enough for one night; it's getting quite late," Ali said once we'd slipped back inside after visiting the gilded throne room.

"But I want to see more." Our whole evening together had been taken right out of a storybook and I didn't want it to end.

"You will. There's one place in particular I want to take you, but we wouldn't have time to do it justice tonight."

Anticipation filled me to my usual bursting. "Will you show me tomorrow night during our next midnight stroll?"

He gave my hand an assuring squeeze. Once again I experienced a strange fluttering from the simple gesture. "Of course. Adventures must be seen through to their completion."

I smiled as I allowed Ali to lead me back through the passageways towards our final destination of the evening: the hallway outside my room, where we'd have to momentarily part ways. Even though I knew I'd see him tomorrow when he accompanied Eileen and me on whatever outing she had in mind, it wouldn't be the same as being alone with him now.

So I relished this moment—Ali's surprisingly soft calloused hand securely wound through mine and the rippling warmth that cascaded from my heart, seeping over me like a wave of sunshine. The unexpected twists of the passageways leading me along an unfamiliar route seemed symbolic of the course my story seemed to be taking—I wandered blindly down a corridor with no idea where I'd end up, but wherever it turned out to be, I was sure it'd be somewhere thrilling, especially considering Ali was leading the way.

CHAPTER 24

"Ali, if you don't tell me where you're taking me, I'm going to assume it's somewhere dastardly and scream, waking up the entire palace. Then you'll be thrown into the dungeon, to my great satisfaction."

This was our third night exploring the secret passageways. Each midnight venture had been filled with pleasant memories spent in Ali's company as he led us to the most thrilling places within the palace—from grand state rooms to long-forgotten nooks and crannies. Our nighttime adventures had been a much-needed reprieve from the monotony of palace life during the day, considering it was still filled with Prince Liam's unwanted attentions.

I pushed aside thoughts of the annoying prince and smiled up at Ali mischievously. Despite what I had considered to be a delicious threat, Ali didn't look the least bit frightened. Instead, his lips merely twitched.

"Scream away, Rosie, but I think you'll find the royal guards will be on my side."

I grinned. He had me there. "Well, if you won't tell me where we're going, can we at least get there sooner? I've been bursting with curiosity all day wondering where our adventure would lead us tonight."

"Hold out a bit longer, for we're almost there. About a minute more, I'd wager."

True to his word, the secret passage began to slope downward. Ali held my hand more securely as he carefully led me down to where the passage ended at a solid wall. He grinned at me over his shoulder.

"Here's a riddle: where is the most magical place in a palace?"

I shuddered in excitement, immediately knowing which room lay beyond the wall.

"Would you like to do the honors?" Ali pointed to a hidden notch. I pushed against the wall to slide it open to reveal...

I gasped in wonder as I stepped into the vast ballroom, which glistened in the night as if it'd been dipped in magic. The intricate marble floors were bathed in pools of bright silver moonlight, which not only danced across the surface but glistened off the dozens of crystal chandeliers. These were nowhere near as beautiful as the diamonds of stars filling the velvet sky, which shone through the windows lining the walls and the glass-domed ceiling above us. It was a wonder to behold, as if I'd stepped into an enchanted otherworld of starlight.

"Oh..." I breathed, for there were no words to describe the enchantment now surrounding me. "Oh, Ali..."

"Magical, isn't it?" He stood so close behind me I could feel the heat of his body seeping into my back. I instinctively leaned against him—allowing his warmth to enfold me like an embrace—and tipped my head back to stare into his hazel eyes, lit like the surrounding stars.

"It is."

His arms wound around me from behind to nestle me

closer, and I melted further against him with a contented sigh. I allowed myself to bask in his embrace for a moment before I twisted around in his arms to hook my arms around his neck. Soon I inexplicably found myself running my fingers through his hair to satisfy my strange urge to touch him, all while my mind swirled in confusion.

This hadn't been how my story was supposed to go, but now that it was, I couldn't imagine it unfolding in any other way. It was always supposed to be *Ali*'s arms I was enfolded in—so securely and comfortably, as if he meant to keep me close always—*Ali*'s lips that caressed my cheek, *Ali* whom I was pressing myself closer to, just so I could bask in his warmth, *Ali* whom I felt the strange need to always remain near.

Ali was as far from a prince as anyone could possibly be. He was a *guard*—untitled, unwealthy, and very much unroyal. But whatever foreign beautiful thing this was, I didn't want it to stop, certain that forcing myself to pull away would cause my heart to shatter.

A strong feeling burned within my breast, one that made my head foggy. What was this incredible-beyond-sheer-belief emotion that made my heart swell to bursting and cause it to soar? Why was my body reacting to such subtle touches from this guard? Could it possibly be…

My breath caught at my epiphany.

Ali's lips had wandered to my brow, caressing my forehead with an aching tenderness. My fingers curled around his uniform to keep him close, and I whimpered with a need I didn't know how to express.

There was only one way to know for sure what I was feeling—the very method used in hundreds of fairy tales, and what more perfect place to explore this cascade of blissful emotions than in a ballroom? Surely a dance would untangle the knot that was now my very confused heart.

"Ali, will you..." I could barely get the words out through the breathlessness that had overcome me. "Will you dance with me?"

He nestled against my hair. "You want to dance, Rosie flower?"

"This is a ballroom, after all, and dancing at midnight beneath the stars sounds positively..." I couldn't finish, the thrill of the idea of dancing in such an enchanting setting with Ali filling me to the brim.

"...magical," Ali supplied before pulling away. "I'm no prince, Rosie. Didn't you want to meet your prince through a dance?"

It wasn't that I wanted to use this dance to *meet* my prince, but to confirm what my heart had been whispering to me for ages, whispers I'd stubbornly ignored for far too long. "Dance with me," I pleaded. "Please, Ali."

Without another word, he hooked his hand around my waist—sending a jolt of heat up my spine—and pulled me into a tuneless waltz.

The dance was everything I'd ever read about and more—everything that I, Rosalina, had ever dreamed. A princess meets her prince at a royal ball, where they fall in love during a single dance. It was the stuff of fairy tales, and as I'd always believed, there was truth found in fairy tales, especially considering this dance was one straight from the pages of one.

Ali wasn't the smoothest dancer by any means. In fact, to be honest, he was quite terrible. My feet were trod on half a dozen times as he twirled me first into one wrong step, followed immediately by another. I'd always imagined my prince to be a flawless dancer.

I quickly realized it wasn't the steps that made a dance so utterly and completely perfect but the gazes, the touches, and most of all the feelings. Ali's touch was like fire, making me feel like I sat curled up in front of a warm hearth; it was his gaze, smoldering as it seeped into mine, fusing a connection between us as we explored one another's eyes; and it was the feelings, ones I now had words for but was still afraid to admit.

Ali pulled me even closer and I allowed myself to snuggle in his perfect hold as he leaned down to my ear. "Here's another secret of mine: I've never met anyone like you."

How I relished hearing such a sentiment from *him*. For a moment I had no words, afraid that my newest discovery from the magic of dancing—a discovery which left me breathless—would come tumbling out if I so much as opened my mouth.

"Do I make a good heroine?" I finally asked.

He burrowed his face against my hair. "The perfect heroine in any story I hope to be a hero in."

"Are you the hero in my story, Ali?"

He pulled back and his gaze seeped into mine. "Am I?"

At his question, the truth exploded within me, the truth that had always been in my heart but which I'd refused to acknowledge.

I, Rosalina, was in love with the Royal Guard, Alastar.

We ended the most romantic of all dances by gradually slowing to a stop before Ali settled on the floor directly below the glass-domed ceiling, gently pulling me down beside him. I all too happily joined him, needing to remain in contact with the man I now realized had completely stolen my heart.

Looking back on all our experiences together, I realized it had happened exactly as Ali had told me he imagined true love to occur: bit by bit, as he stole portions of my heart until he possessed the whole of it. I stubbornly hadn't realized the process had been taking place until my heart was firmly in his cherished possession.

The object of my affection lay beside me, entirely unaware of the dramatic change that had occurred within me. He gazed up at the starry night while I lay nestled beside him, his arm looped around me and my head resting on his chest.

I analyzed our position. He was holding me close. He must care for me. Perhaps tonight he'd finally share the feelings of his heart, giving me the confession of love I'd waited my entire life to experience. Now would be the perfect time for him to make his confession. I waited with bated breath... but he remained silent.

"Are you alright, Rosie?"

Was I alright? I'd just made the most important and amazing discovery and I was overwhelmed with wonderful soaring sensations. It felt as if our midnight dance had ended ages ago, for I was currently experiencing a hundred lifetimes in the span of only a few minutes. How did one return to earth after such an experience?

"Rosie?" Concern laced my sweet Ali's tone as he sat us up and peered down at me, his gaze both tender and worried. "Has your voice been stolen by an evil sorceress?"

For once I couldn't play along, the sudden shyness cloaking me making doing so impossible. I looked away. His rough yet still unbelievably smooth fingers hooked beneath my chin to raise my head and reconnect our gazes. My heart hammered in anticipation. Was he about to confess his love?

"Rosie?" His thumb stroked my cheek and I seriously thought I'd melt from the overwhelming sensations. I rested my hand over his and closed my eyes, leaning against his soft touch.

"Oh, Ali..."

Even though my eyes were closed I sensed his smile, so attuned I was to its presence. "Your voice has been returned. I was getting rather worried." He looped his arms back around me to pull me snuggly against his firm chest. "It's unlike you to be so quiet. Did I do something wrong? Was it the dance? I know I'm a terrible dancer."

I silently shook my head. The dance had been absolutely perfect.

He lightly traced around my closed eyes with his fingertip until I opened them to see his normally serious expression seeped in concern. "Then what is it?"

I love you. I ached to tell him but I could barely think, let alone make such an admission. Now would be the perfect time to share it, while we were bathed in starlight in a ballroom in a royal palace at midnight, but somehow I just couldn't. Not yet. Not until I was completely assured he loved me, too.

I leaned against him and relished the feeling of his arms tightening around me. I tipped my head back to gaze at the stars. "So beautiful," I murmured. "This is truly enchanting. It makes me believe that magic truly does exist."

"Don't tell me my Rosie ever had doubts."

I smiled. "Not doubts, but...one hopes that things that can't be seen turn out to be real."

"Much like your stories?" His fingers were now caressing my hair. "Do you have any tales about the stars?"

I sighed. Made-up stories almost seemed so silly now compared to the one I was currently living. "Not at the moment."

"I don't believe it." He twisted and untwisted a strand of my hair around his finger. "You always have a story, Rosie."

And so I did.

Once upon a time, in a ballroom bathed in the enchantment of moonlight and starlight, a heroine and her hero shared a magical and perfectly romantic dance, during which the heroine came to realize she'd lost her heart.

"Not all stories are meant to be shared," I murmured.

His brow furrowed. "You have a secret, Rosie, and I see this is one you're determined to keep. The only logical explanation for such an impossible feat is that you're an imposter."

I managed a smile. "Perhaps I am. I don't feel like myself any longer." Did love change a person? I felt I'd been turned inside out—and it wasn't an unpleasant feeling by any means.

Ali's concerned gaze caressed my face, so tenderly. "Something has changed, but I can't quite figure out what. You're normally an open book, but you've not only closed yours but locked it as well."

"That means you only need to find the key—a noble quest for a gallant knight."

An earnest intensity filled his entire expression. "I'll never stop looking until I have."

I rested my head against his chest and allowed him to hold me. In this moment, I knew for a certainty I'd found my prince, a man who'd been in disguise but who was everything I'd ever wanted in my prince. While my story hadn't gone entirely as planned and I'd had to rewrite many chapters, there was still a plot element I was determined to have—that of my true love professing his love for me. Only then would I know for sure whether I possessed the heart of the man I loved.

CHAPTER 25

I spent the next several days hidden away in my room, poring over volumes of fairy tales taken from the royal library's vast collection. It took hours perusing them and studying their secrets with a religious fervor to create the perfect plan for how to obtain a confession of love. I researched tale after tale, exploring the methods used by heroines to capture their heroes' hearts. I painstakingly wrote down each foolproof tip—staging an opportunity for the object of my affection to perform a dramatic rescue on my behalf, batting eyelashes, demure smiles, accidental touches, compliments on his manhood, staring at his lips, and seeking uses for his brawny strength. Success was assured.

I gasped at the knock on the door. My list fluttered to the ground and my elbow bumped into my teetering stack of books as I bent to retrieve it, knocking them over. Oh bother.

"Rosie?"

Eileen. I dropped to the floor and scrambled around, gathering my books in a wild frenzy. "Yes?"

"Can I come in?"

"If you must."

The door opened and Eileen entered. "'If I must?' What a way to greet your best friend." Her bewildered expression took me in, kneeling on the floor amidst the chaos I'd created. "What are you up to? I've scarcely seen you for days, inexcusable with your visit nearing its conclusion. I've come to convince you not only to leave your room but to possibly extend your stay."

She bit her lip, looking as if she feared I'd want to leave as soon as possible with my lovesick prince still driving me insane, but I now had a greater incentive to stay, even if it meant putting up with Prince Liam.

"Of course I'll extend it." After all, I needed more time to extract a confession of love from Ali. "I need to stay longer in order to...oh, bother."

I'd picked up one book too many and my entire armful toppled. The breeze created by the falling books caused my list of flirting advice to blow towards Eileen. She picked it up, brow furrowed. I gasped and scrambled over to grab the incriminating evidence.

"Oh, please don't read it."

Too late. "*Flirting Advice from Literature's Greatest Heroines —A Romantic Guide Compiled by Heroine Rosalina, Seeker of Her Happily Ever After.*" She raised her gaze to mine. "What's going on, Rosie? I thought you were trying to discourage Liam's affections, not encourage them."

I gnawed at my fingernail as I remembered my lovesick prince. I'd been receiving love notes three times a day since I'd locked myself in my room, and they'd immediately gone straight into the fire. "I don't want Prince Liam's attention but rather his inattention. Unfortunately, the love spell hasn't worn off." At this point I was beginning to fear it never would.

Eileen's eyebrows rose. "Such interesting techniques you have here. Who are you trying to woo, Rosie?"

I fought to maintain an innocent air. "Who says I want to woo anybody?"

Eileen smiled girlishly. "Oh Rosie, you can't hide anything from me. I know it's Alastar. I must say you've been quite slow to realize you care for him. It's driven me and Aiden mad."

"*Aiden* knows?" How mortifying that even the Dark Prince knew of my ignorance to recognize my true love. Did the entire palace also know? How could everyone have known my true feelings when I'd kept my most precious secret hidden even from myself? I covered my face in my hands. "What a daft heroine I've been."

"Don't be too hard on yourself. It took me a while to realize that I loved Aiden."

"So you don't mind me wooing your guard?"

"Rosie, it's obvious you already have his heart."

"I hope so, but I can't be sure until he professes his love for me."

Before Eileen could comment, a note slid beneath my door. She picked it up and grinned girlishly as she read it.

I sighed. "I'm so sick of Prince Liam's love notes. Just toss it into the fire."

"You might want to read this one first."

I seized the note and my heart fluttered when I saw the signature—it was from my real prince.

Dearest Rosie,

I've pondered your recent and rather agonizing absence and have entertained several possibilities: either you've been cursed by a wicked warlock, you're lost within the secret passageways, you've become a tasty snack for a dragon, or you're avoiding me. Whatever scenario has befallen my damsel in distress, I'll be your gallant knight and find a way to either break your curse or rescue you from becoming a ghost trapped within the palace walls.

I miss you.

Ali

I happily gaped at my delightful note, far better than all of Prince Liam's love notes combined. Eileen wrapped her arm around me for a side hug. "I believe you've already succeeded in your quest. Simply share your feelings with Alastar rather than this nonsense." She nodded towards my list of flirting advice.

"I've already rewritten so many of the chapters in my story; this one needs to go as I've always dreamed: my true love confessing his undying love for me."

Eileen sighed. "Must everything be so complicated? There's no need to play games."

"But Ali and I always play games."

"I can't deny that." Eileen shrugged. "Well, if your silly quest will get you to leave your room so you can spend time with me and a certain guard you're head over heels for, then so be it."

I froze with my hand on the knob. "Is Ali right outside the door?" My heart fluttered in hope.

"No, I asked him to wait in the garden for me." And she led me from my bedroom so the quest "Win the Confession of Ali's Heart" could commence.

The moment we stepped into the gardens, Ali hurried up to me, not even glancing at Eileen, let alone bowing; Eileen only smiled in amusement at his faux pas before quietly slipping away.

"I see you found your way out of the passageways," he said. "I was about to organize the royal guards to search for you."

Seeing him again was like eating a feast after a long period of starvation. Flutters overcame my heart just being in his presence. "It wasn't the passageways that I'd succumbed to but the curse of an evil warlock."

"If I'd known earlier, I'd have embarked on an epic quest to discover the counterspell to save you. Thankfully, you've rescued yourself and had no need of a knight. I'm relieved it was only a curse that befell you rather than a dragon consuming you."

I giggled. Oh, how I'd missed him. "Luckily, I was able to avoid the palace dragon."

He eyed me warily and broke from our playful script. "Obviously, you're whole and unspelled, so does that mean you've been avoiding me?" He actually bit his lip in worry at the possibility.

"There were some important matters I needed to attend to." And speaking of, it was time to implement the first bit of advice I'd excavated from my precious fairy tales. I tipped my head back and batted my eyelashes. Surely, he'd melt at such an adorable romantic gesture and thus feel compelled to share the feelings of his heart.

Instead of melting like he was supposed to, his brow furrowed. "Do you have something in your eye, Rosie?"

I stopped immediately, my cheeks flaring with heat. "It must have been the dust from all the books I've been reading." Not to be deterred, I tried another tactic and offered him my most alluring smile.

"Are you alright, Rosie? You don't look well."

Defeated again. Why weren't these fairy-tale-tested flirting techniques working?

"Perhaps you need a brisk stroll through the garden." He tipped his head down the path and motioned for me to follow. I waited for him to reach for my hand in order to hold it like he'd done a few nights previously, but he determinedly kept his arms clasped behind his back. My heart cracked.

We walked in silence. I suddenly felt both uncharacteristically shy around Ali and rather lost. How did one interact with the love of their life? Things had been so easy before I'd realized just how dear this man was to me. Now I was afraid of saying the wrong thing and inadvertently sabotaging everything.

"Did you read any interesting stories while you were immersed in your world of words?" he finally asked to shatter the silence.

I avoided his eyes. "Not really."

He tilted his head, waiting for me to elaborate, but it was hard to be imaginative when glaring at Ali's unavailable hand, one I desperately wanted to hold.

He frowned. "Hmm, you seem different ever since our midnight dance. I know you, Rosie—you're hiding something. Won't you please tell me?"

My secret burned on my tongue, one I wanted to share but couldn't until he professed his love first. But I refused to let my secret conquer me, for this was a battle I was determined to win.

Focus, Rosie. What were more of those flirting tips? But it was impossible to concentrate with Ali so near, bathing me in his intoxicating warmth.

"You smell like lemons," I blurted. *You smell like lemons*!? Oh, what a ridiculous thing to say.

He gaped at me as if I'd lost my mind, which I likely had. "Pardon?"

"You smell like honey and lemons," I stuttered. "Just like my favorite muffins."

He continued to gape at me for an agonizing moment before he chuckled. "It's a defense mechanism against dragons."

"Of course it is." I instinctively leaned closer, succumbing to the battle that had been raging in me since being in his presence again. "Are you sure it isn't pollen for a Rosie?"

His breath hooked and his gaze locked with mine. A fierce intensity passed between us. "I desperately hope so."

We stared at one another for a blissful moment more before I lowered my gaze to his lips, flirting tactic number three. To my delight this one worked. He leaned down and I stood on tiptoe to meet him…

"Alastar, where's Eileen?"

Ali yanked away from me, cheeks crimson, and swiveled around to face Aiden, who'd arrived with Duncan guarding closely behind. He watched us with a frown.

"The princess?" Ali stuttered.

Aiden's frown deepened. "Yes. Where is she? You're on duty and should be watching her."

Ali looked around the rose garden where we stood, scanning the manicured paths. There was no sign of Eileen. "I—"

Aiden's eyes widened. "You mean you don't know?"

"I—no, Your Highness, I'm afraid I don't."

Panic and anger filled Aiden's face. He looked ready to spring into a frantic search when Eileen strolled casually into the rose garden, her sketchbook tucked under her arm. Before she could even greet us, Aiden seized her in a tight embrace.

"What is it, Aiden? Is something wrong?"

"Where were you?" he demanded.

"I just went to fetch my sketchbook," she said. "It's been awhile since I've had a chance to draw, and these gardens are too lovely to remain unsketched for long." Her brow furrowed as she took in Aiden's expression. "Were you worried about me?"

"Alastar lost track of you, which is inexcusable," Aiden nestled her close and began rubbing her back.

"It was more I purposely lost track of Alastar," Eileen said.

"He was spending time with Rosie, and I thought they could use a moment alone in order to—" She gave me a mischievous look and my heart tightened with guilt.

Her explanation was clearly not enough to satisfy Aiden. He snapped his attention back to Ali and glared. "Your duty is to watch the crown princess and to ensure no harm befalls her, not to fraternize with her friend."

Ali bowed his head. "You're right. I forgot my place. My apologies, Your Highness."

"An apology isn't good enough. Eileen could have been hurt."

Eileen rolled her eyes. "Aiden, I was only gone for a few minutes."

"I know, dearest, but you are the future queen, meaning there's always the possibility of harm befalling you. Alastar's first duty is to the crown." His glare sharpened. "He hasn't been paying close attention for weeks. I cannot tolerate this any longer. I'm afraid he's going to have to lose his post."

Ali flinched but nodded humbly. "I understand, Your Highness. Please forgive me for failing to protect the princess."

Panic knotted my insides. I'd distracted Ali and now he was being punished for it. Once again I'd made a muddle of everything. "No! Please Aiden, don't send Ali away. It was my fault. I was trying to—I mean, I was distracting him because —" My cheeks burned.

Aiden frowned at me. "Rosalina, it's only due to your friendship with Eileen and my friendship with Alastar that I've tolerated the situation for this long, but things cannot continue like this." He turned to Alastar. "I'm sorry, but your behavior has left me no choice."

Ali merely nodded in acquiescence while horror swelled within my breast. "Please give him another chance. I promise I won't talk to him while he's on duty."

Eileen rested her hand on his arm. "Please Aiden, don't punish him. It's my fault for leaving without telling him."

Aiden shook his head. "He should have noticed you'd disappeared, whether you told him you were leaving or not."

"Yes, dear, I know, but don't be too harsh on him. He's been a wonderful guard and remarkably attentive considering the circumstances…" Her eyes flicked towards me and I wanted to sink in shame that my presence had been causing trouble for Ali. Eileen rested her hand on Aiden's cheek. "Please give him another chance. For me."

He searched her eyes for a moment before sighing, relenting. He glanced at Ali. "I don't want to punish you, Alastar. You've been a loyal friend, which is why I've entrusted you with Eileen's protection."

"You have every right to be upset, Your Highness," Ali said solemnly. "It was the greatest honor to be granted the position to protect the princess, and I have treated it lightly as of late. Forgive me."

Aiden stared at Ali for a long moment. "Despite the circumstances, I'm still inclined to give you another chance." His expression became serious. "But I'm warning you—this is the last time this lack of attention will be tolerated."

Ali bowed, and when he straightened, I gave him a relieved smile, expecting him to return it, but he hastily looked away, his jaw taut, as if angry with me that I'd nearly cost him his job. My heart sank. This wasn't how the story was supposed to go, for if Ali loved me, surely he'd understand I hadn't meant to hurt him. It seemed that tragedy struck whatever I touched.

CHAPTER 26

True to his word, Ali guarded Eileen with rigid and unwavering attention, not even glancing in my direction whenever we were together. Although I yearned for the relationship we'd built between us, I understood the reason for his inattention—he wanted to prove to Aiden he was still worthy of the position to which he'd been entrusted. But when his behavior continued long after he was off duty, my panic escalated, especially when I no longer found him wandering the palace at night, no matter how many corridors I traipsed through.

On the third night of his absence, a horrific thought filled my heart—he was obviously avoiding me. The only explanation I could conjure up as to why was that he didn't share my tender feelings like I'd believed. Perhaps that was why he'd never confessed his love for me. I must have mistaken his affections, just as I'd been wrong about Prince Liam's. Horror curdled my stomach at the thought. Now nothing remained for me except for living out my spinsterhood in Arador with my cats.

I entered the dining room for breakfast. Out of habit, I glanced over at Ali's usual guarding place and startled—he wasn't there. Instead, Duncan stood in his place. I frantically scanned the dining room but there was no sign of him. My panic rose—Aiden must have sacked him after all.

"Eileen, where's Ali?" I demanded.

She paused in buttering her toast and glanced towards the wall, as if just noticing her usual guard wasn't at his post. "I don't know."

How could she not know? I turned to Aiden, sitting at her right. "Where's Ali? Did you let him go? I thought you were going to give him another chance. He's been unwavering in his promise not to talk to me." A bit too much so.

"He approached me last evening requesting time off," Aiden said. "He didn't say why." But the look he gave me caused me to suspect that *I* was the reason. Ali must not be able to bear being around me any longer. My stomach tightened in despair.

I scrambled from the table over to Duncan. Surely my prince's brother would know his whereabouts. "Where's Ali?"

Duncan continued looking straight ahead, "I couldn't say, Miss Rosalina."

"Did he leave the palace?"

No response. I released a huff of frustration.

"He did, didn't he? He must be avoiding me." The thought was unbearable. "Do you know when he's coming back?"

"I couldn't say, Miss Rosalina."

He was no help, but I refused to be deterred. I tried a different tactic. "I'll bake you your favorite lemon bars if you tell me."

Rather than being tempted by my offer, he merely gave me a *look* of disapproval that clearly revealed his training as a guard to not accept bribes from desperate heroines. Stubborn guard. I couldn't believe one of my treats had failed me in my time of need.

I turned my efforts to interrogating the other servants around the palace, which also yielded no results. Each morning that followed, Duncan remained at Ali's post, confirming my greatest fear—he'd left the palace in order to get away from me.

My heart broke. True love had been within my grasp, but it had been suddenly snatched away. This heartache became even more unbearable as I was forced to continue to endure the lovesick attentions from the wrong prince, whom I'd been avoiding as much as possible. My story had transformed from a fairy tale to a tragedy.

I trudged to my room, in need of a good cry, and discovered a note awaiting me just inside my bedroom door. My heart leapt when I recognized the handwriting. *Ali*! Was this a love note or nothing more than his farewell letter to me? My hands shook as I tore it open.

Dear Rosie,

I must speak with you. Please meet me at the enchanted tree near the hedge maze.

Ali

I reread the note three times, my heartbeat escalating with each perusal. The delight at the thought of seeing Ali again competed with my fear at what he could possibly want to speak to me about.

I braced myself and turned to leave in order to find out, but paused when my gaze settled on my nightstand, where my last spelled chocolate remained hidden.

A plan formulated in my mind should my meeting with Ali not go well. I, Rosalina, would not be the tragic heroine in my story. I would keep fighting until I'd obtained my happily ever after.

My heart beat wildly as I slowly approached the shimmery tree, aglow in the glistening sunlight, where Ali stood with his back to me. I paused to stare at him, as if my study would allow me to read ahead in this scene to see if it contained the confession I'd longed for…or the unhappy ending I feared.

The only way to know would be to continue reading. I took a wavering breath and hesitantly stepped forward. "Ali?"

He spun around to face me. For a moment we merely stared at one another. Then in three strides he was in front of me and I was in his arms for the most wonderful embrace, one I never wanted to end.

"Rosie…" He nestled his head against my hair.

I burrowed against his firm chest in relief and sighed happily as his arms tightened around me, as if he wanted to keep me close. Already this scene was going much better than I'd anticipated. "I've missed you, Ali."

"And I've missed you."

I tipped my head back to search his eyes, radiating with an incredibly gentle look, which despite his recent avoidance, gave me hope that this conversation would go in the direction I desired.

"Then why have you been avoiding me? Are you angry I got you in trouble with Aiden?"

"I haven't been avoiding you; I just needed some time away to think about things."

"About what?" I asked breathlessly. How I hoped it had been about me.

He cradled my face, a promising sign. "I've been thinking about our future and trying to decide what to do. Ever since you came to the palace and into my life, I've been distracted.

I tried to ignore you so I could be the guard worthy of protecting the princess, only to find the task impossible. Prince Aiden was right—our situation can't continue like this. But I can't bear ignoring you any longer."

My heart tightened. Once again, I'd inadvertently hurt him. By the look in Ali's eyes, I knew he was about to tell me he couldn't serve as Eileen's guard anymore…which meant he was leaving.

No matter what, I couldn't allow that to happen. My fingers curled around my remaining piece of spelled chocolate. "Will you do something for me?"

"I'll do anything for you, Rosie flower."

I held out my hand to present him with my love spell. He stared at it in astonishment before raising his bewildered gaze to mine.

"That's—"

"The last of my love spell. Please eat it."

He gaped at me before swallowing. "You want *me* to eat it?"

"Yes, so you'll fall in love with me."

Ali's eyes widened. "You want *me* to fall in love with *you*?"

"Oh, *please*, Ali." I wrapped my arms tightly around him, clinging to him with the determination never to let him go until he was mine. "I'll die from heartbreak otherwise. It's the most romantically tragic way for a heroine to go, but please don't make me experience it. I just want you to love me. Please eat this, Ali."

He was silent for an agonizing moment. "You won't trick me into eating it?"

I shook my head. "I couldn't do that to you. I want you to choose to. I know it wouldn't be true love, but at least spelled love from you is better than no love at all, for I could at least imagine that your love for me was real."

He was silent a moment more, and when I snuck a peek into his face, he seemed utterly bewildered. "Oh, Rosie..." He attentively ran his fingers through my hair, causing shivers to ripple over me from his soft touch. "I can't take your love spell."

"Why not?" I was crying, but my ridiculous blubbering was worth it when Ali once more wiped away my tears before hooking his finger beneath my chin to raise my gaze to meet his. His eyes smoldered not only with intensity but with the secret I'd been trying to excavate from him for weeks.

"I won't take it because"—he took a deep breath—"I don't need it."

I gaped at him. "You don't...*need* it?"

He shook his head. "No."

"But—" I wrinkled my forehead. "If you don't take it, how can you fall in love with me?"

Ali cradled my face, his touch soft despite his calloused hands. My heart flared to life, pattering so wildly I was certain he could hear it.

"Oh, Rosie," he murmured as he leaned down and rubbed his nose along my jawline. "I don't need your silly little love spell to fall in love with you. I've already been spelled."

My breath hooked. "You have? You mean you took—"

"No, Rosie, I didn't eat your enchanted chocolates. I didn't need to." His hazel gaze penetrated mine, smoldering. "I fell in love with you on my own."

My heart fluttered as the beautiful confession I'd been waiting for enveloped me. "You love me?"

He smiled. "More than anything."

The chocolate slipped from my hand as I squealed and pounced on him, hugging him fiercely. "Since when, Ali? Do tell me before I burst from utter happiness."

"Almost from the very beginning. You cast your spell on

me the moment you opened your mouth and shared the thoughts of that delightful and imaginative mind of yours. I immediately knew my heart was in jeopardy."

"The beginning?" I gaped up at him incredulously. "That long?"

"That long." His lips caressed my cheek and I shivered, my hold on him tightening.

"What's happening?" I whispered.

"The hero and heroine are at long last coming together," he said.

I hooked my arms around his neck to stare adoringly up at him. "This wasn't how the story was supposed to go, you know."

"This is exactly how it was supposed to go," he said. "Aren't stories full of twists and turns and all manner of delightful surprises?"

I traced each of his features with my fingertip, lingering in particular on his lips. "And princes in disguise?"

His lips twitched beneath my tracing finger. "Is that my role, then?"

"Definitely. You've always been my prince; it just took me a while to figure that out." I sighed. "What a fool I've been. You were right in front of me the entire time and I couldn't see it."

"I'm easy to miss considering I'm not particularly princely." He bit his lip. "Are you disappointed?"

I lifted his hand and pressed a kiss first on one fingertip, then another. "No."

His eyes widened in wonder. "And we didn't meet in the way you wanted, either; I recall your mentioning that the thought of meeting true love in a corridor the most boring of all scenarios. Not to mention our story played out quite differently than you anticipated."

"None of that matters as long as we've found each other.

Now that we have..." Heat tickled my cheeks as I leaned closer, staring at his lips.

"True love's kiss." He leaned down and captured my lips with his own, and I gasped at the beautiful sensations now encompassing me.

I'd read about hundreds and hundreds of kisses in my fairy tales, but reading about something and experiencing it were completely different things. Mere words were inadequate to describe the sheer wonder of feeling someone so dear caress my lips, love's most beautiful waltz.

I moaned as I kissed him back, wrapping my arms more securely around his neck to burrow my fingers in his hair to pull him closer. My prince's arms tightened around me and lifted me off the ground. Warmth, tenderness, sweetness...a fluttering of delightful emotions beginning in my heart cascaded over my entire body, sheer magic.

All too soon it was over. Ali had no sooner broken our most-perfect-of-all-kisses than I found myself murmuring, "*Wow.*"

He chuckled. "That sums it up quite nicely." He stroked my cheek, his eyes boring into mine. "I love you, Rosie flower. You're the perfect heroine for my story."

His words were like an embrace from the sun. It wasn't until I'd heard them that I realized just how long my heart had been aching for them. "I love you too, Ali." My forehead furrowed. "This is certainly an unexpected twist. I truly didn't see this coming."

"Love is like that; it sometimes sneaks up on you when you least expect it." He leaned down to lightly kiss me again.

"Ours is the most perfect of all stories," I murmured. "Love at first sight for the hero and a prince in disguise for the heroine. Can it get much better?"

"It can," Ali said as his lips caressed my neck. "For this is *our* story. And we'll live happily ever after."

We lost ourselves in another perfect kiss, as all kisses from one's true love always are.

CHAPTER 27

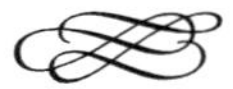

As we basked in this most magical of moments enfolded in one another's arms, I suddenly jerked away. "Prince Liam! He's still spelled. Oh no, what am I going to do?"

He rubbed my back soothingly. "If our true love's kiss hasn't broken the spell, perhaps you should tell him you spelled him."

I gasped in horror. "Are you out of your mind? I couldn't do that."

He stroked my cheek. "I'm not in jest, darling. You should be honest with His Highness about what you did."

My cheeks burned at the thought. He lightly traced my blush, eyes incredibly tender.

"I'll be right by your side; we'll slay the dragon together."

And despite my terror for the upcoming battle, I knew I could face the fearsome beast, for now that I'd found my prince, I knew every obstacle in my fairy tale would be conquered thanks to my gallant knight.

Several minutes later when we stood outside the parlor where Aiden and Eileen were entertaining Prince Liam, I wasn't so sure. I stood paralyzed, my breath coming up short and feeling on the brink of a faint.

Ali gave my hand a reassuring squeeze. "True love breaks any spell," he reminded me. "Trust me."

I searched his sweet expression. It was hard to believe I used to think him stoic when his emotions were revealed in subtle ways—in the lines of his features, the way his mouth twitched, and especially his eyes, which currently shone with absolute adoration.

I trusted this man, utterly and completely. He read this feeling in my eyes and squeezed my hand again. "Let's conquer your dragon, flower."

With a deep breath, I opened the door. Clinging to Ali's hand, I shakily entered the dragon's lair, where my lovesick foe sat. His eyes lit up when he saw me, while Eileen immediately took in me and Ali's clasped hands with wide eyes.

She squealed. "Please tell me this means you two have finally gotten together." At my nod, Eileen seized Aiden in a side hug. "Finally, finally, *finally*. I told you, Aiden. I told you they'd get together. It took forever."

He grinned with obvious approval. "I didn't doubt you, my love. They had an obvious connection from the beginning."

I exchanged a shy yet adoring look with Ali. Meanwhile, Prince Liam gaped at our entwined hands with a crumpled look. He raised his devastated gaze to mine. "What's the meaning of this, Rosie darling? I thought your heart was mine to forever cherish?"

I stared at him blankly, scrambling for the words that didn't want to come. "I—" No, I couldn't do it; it was too mortifying. I spun around to make my escape, but Ali caught me in an embrace. I buried my face against him and shook my head. "I can't do it, Ali."

"Of course you can." He kissed the top of my head. "It'll be alright, Rosie. I promise."

My fear melted away at his earnest and assuring expression. With a deep breath I turned in Ali's arms to face Prince Liam, gaining strength for this confession from my knight's comforting embrace.

"Prince Liam, there's something I need to tell you."

"*Liam,* my sweet," he said. "You know there's no need for such formality between us, darling."

I squeezed my eyes shut. Ugh. "Liam…"

"Look at me, Rosie, so that I may see your beautiful eyes."

I sighed and stared determinedly at my dragon. It was time to vanquish him once and for all. "Prince Liam, I gave you a love spell. The chocolate treats I made for you were enchanted." The words tumbled out as nothing more than a jumble of sounds. Prince Liam frowned and tilted his head.

"Pardon? Can you repeat that, my dear?"

I had to make my confession *again*? This was the worst. I took another deep breath. "I gave you a love spell. You don't really love me, and I most certainly don't love you. I'm so sorry I did something so dastardly, but at the time I thought I wanted you to be my prince. Now I realize that I don't."

Prince Liam gaped at me, expression blank. I wrung my hands together.

"What's worse, I have no idea how to remove it." I buried my face in my hands. "I'm so sorry."

An agonizing and tense silence followed, the longest of my life, but then…. "Rosalina?"

I peeked at Prince Liam through my fingers. He'd not only used my full name for the first time since he'd been spelled, but his entire manner was calm rather than infatuated. To add to my shock, he smiled in a friendly way, no trace of his previous sappy grins.

"Thank you for telling me. Please be assured that the spell has been removed."

"You mean...you don't love me?"

He shook his head. "Not at all. Don't get me wrong; we can still be friends, but I'm not looking to be romantically attached. I'm relieved you finally share my sentiments."

I gaped at him. This couldn't be happening. I'd done nothing special to remove the spell that had caused me and everybody else such trouble and heartache, and after a confession it was simply...gone?

"But *how?*"

Prince Liam propped his leg up on his knee with a goofy grin. "For the simple reason I was never spelled to begin with."

I stared at him in disbelief, his words failing to register in my swirling thoughts. "You weren't?" But he *had* to have been.

Prince Liam shook his head, expression amused. "Not at all."

"But—but—" I could barely think through this entirely unexpected revelation, let alone speak. "But you *behaved* spelled."

"It's called acting, Rosalina, and I must say I did a rather fine job. I had all of you convinced I was a spelled prince." He laughed.

"Are you telling me," Aiden said through gritted teeth, "that this entire love spell has been an act?"

Prince Liam's grin widened in triumph. "Yup. You have to admit the entire scheme was quite fantastic. I thoroughly enjoyed my part in it."

Aiden glared at him. "You mean you put me through all that torment for no reason? Do you have any idea how frantic I've been trying to keep your condition a secret from the court while trying to figure out how to fix this mess? And this entire time you were *faking* it?"

"I was." Prince Liam smirked, bursting with pride. "Don't give me a look like I just betrayed you; *I* knew it was fake, and thus there was nothing to worry about."

"Nothing to worry about?" Aiden's manner only hardened further, while Eileen sat beside him, gaping at Liam in dazed astonishment. "I was convinced that the King of Draceria would get wind of this and it would cause me all sorts of political trouble. I even banished Rosalina for your stunt until she could create a counterspell."

Prince Liam's expression became guilty. "I didn't realize you'd sent her away; I thought she was merely returning to Arador for a visit. I didn't mean to cause trouble." His remorse quickly melted away, replaced with another wide grin. He propped his arms up behind his head and leaned back. "Still, you must admit my performance was quite the achievement."

As the conversation washed over me my shock slowly dissipated, replaced with a multitude of questions. "Wait, I don't understand. How can you not be spelled? I gave you a chocolate spiked with love potion. I watched you eat it. You became so…*annoying* the moment you did so."

Prince Liam only chuckled. "You did nothing of the sort."

"I certainly did."

"You only *thought* you did. Alastar, will you explain?"

I spun on Ali, who looked both amused and undeniably guilty. I smelled a traitor. "You knew about this?"

Prince Liam chuckled. "Knew about it? He was the mastermind behind the whole deception."

Ali cleared his throat. "It's time for my own confession, Rosie dear. I knew you were quite serious about spelling Prince Liam and that no amount of persuasion would deter you from your goal, so I'm afraid I took upon myself the role of antagonist in your fairy tale in order to prevent you from making a serious mistake. The day I confiscated your spelled chocolates, I had no doubt you'd try to get them back. So I switched them with ordinary chocolates, which I planted in my room before destroying the real ones on the off chance that they actually worked and some unsuspecting fool ate them. I couldn't bear the thought of you losing your heart to anyone but me."

I gaped at him in utter disbelief. When I didn't respond he continued, speaking rapidly, as if desperate to complete his confession as quickly as possible.

"I must confess I'm surprised you didn't suspect foul play. Did you really think I would have been so stupid as to leave my door unlocked as an open invitation for you to search my bedroom, where your enchanted chocolates were waiting to be discovered in the most obvious hiding place? Or that I wouldn't have counted the chocolates I stole back and not notice two were missing? Or that I wouldn't have been fiercely jealous of His Highness for daring to steal the heart I wanted for myself?"

Now that he mentioned it, as adamant as he'd been against my spelling Prince Liam, he'd seemed unnaturally calm about the entire scenario as it unfolded. I should have suspected…

Ali anxiously searched my expression, his own now twisted in worry. "I only did it because I believed you were falling in love with me, too. I knew you'd regret your spell when you realized you didn't want Prince Liam to think himself in love with you, so I took upon myself the role of gallant knight and prevented what would likely become the biggest mess you'd ever entangled yourself in. I'm both sorry for tricking you and, I must confess, not."

I tried to make sense of his words as they whirled around me. Slowly, it dawned on me that the situation I'd thought impossible to escape from only moments ago was now merely a memory. Fierce relief washed over me along with warm gratitude. I caressed Ali's cheek. He'd served as my knight and rescuer, even before I knew I needed one.

Ali gnawed his lip as he awaited my response. "Plot twist?" he offered with a rather adorable timid smile. With those words, I finally broke from my paralyzing shock and beamed.

"I, Rosalina, have been part of the most amazing plot twist! To think such a brilliant one was part of *my* story and that Prince Liam doesn't love me and I've found my real prince and nothing will ever stand in the way of our happily ever after…oh, bliss!"

Giggling, I hooked my arms around Ali's neck and burrowed my ecstatic face against his throat. He returned my embrace, his own a bit dazed.

"You're not upset?"

"Heavens, no. You knew my heart and came to your lady's aid using the most spectacular twist. I'm *ecstatic*." I kissed him fiercely, but he'd barely returned it when I yanked myself away and glared at him. "Never play the part of my antagonist ever again. Your only role now in my fairy tale is that of my hero."

"Ah, so we're in a romance now?" he asked, his eyes twinkling.

"Mm, more of a hybrid genre: romance adventure. How does that sound?"

"That is a genre I'll gladly inhabit forever." He kissed me again, pulling away when Eileen approached and pulled me into a hug.

"I'm so happy you and Alastar have finally found each other. I told you it'd all work out if you'd just let your love story unfold naturally."

"It took you long enough," Prince Liam grumbled. "I was

running out of ideas on how to pretend to be lovesick. A man can only write so many sappy love poems." He pulled a face.

I shook my head, still unable to believe the entire thing had been a façade.

"You really did an excellent job," Ali said. "You even had *me* fooled sometimes. If I didn't know without a doubt that you were faking it, I'd have gone mad."

Prince Liam stood to take a bow. "It truly was a spectacular performance, wasn't it?"

I frowned at Ali. "Wait, for your scheme to work, Prince Liam had to agree to play along. How did you manage that?"

Ali smiled guiltily. "After our fight by the pond when you'd gathered nearly all your ingredients for the spell, I realized how serious you were. When Prince Liam next visited, I cornered him and told him what you were plotting."

I groaned in utter humiliation and buried my face in my hands. Ali's arms wrapped around my waist, where he began to rub my lower back in soothing circles.

"He was both amused at the idea and properly horrified should it work. I told him I'd be sure that whatever you gave him wasn't spelled if he'd pretend that he was."

"And he trusted you'd follow through?"

"Only because at the ball I noticed how besotted he was with you," Prince Liam said. "I knew no force would stop him from preventing anyone else falling in love with you, spelled or not. So I agreed to the scheme and had more fun with it than I anticipated."

I furrowed my forehead. "But what was your motivation to pretend? You could have just eaten the unspelled chocolate and I'd have thought it hadn't worked."

Prince Liam grinned mischievously. "I *could* have done that, but I also had my own motivations. Not only did I see you were in love with Alastar and needed the advances of an unwanted suitor to help you realize your true feelings, but I hoped my betrothed would learn I was avidly courting another and I could finally wriggle out of the arranged engagement I've always despised. While the first plan was a success, unfortunately, Princess Lavena is still very much mine."

I took in his defeated expression. "I'd also hoped that my spelling you would help you escape your betrothal," I added timidly.

He smiled tightly. "Thank you, Rosalina, I appreciate the gesture." He sighed heavily, looking resigned. "But unfortunately, I'm coming to accept that my impending marriage is inevitable. I'm now trying to brace myself for the union I never wanted." His expression twisted in disgust before he managed a smile. "At least I got an extended holiday from my heir duties, not to mention I had a lot of fun with the charade. I enjoyed coming up with ridiculous ways to make you believe me spelled. It became even more amusing when you quickly no longer welcomed my attentions; I loved making you squirm."

Ali narrowed his eyes. "You did take it a bit far on multiple occasions. Poor Rosie was often near tears."

Prince Liam held up his hands defensively. "It was all in your best interest, my good chap. I hoped the more I pushed your Rosie, the quicker she'd realize where her affections truly lay." He frowned. "Unfortunately, the opposite seemed to be true. The more I brought up that Rosie was in love with you, the more adamantly she denied it."

"Even once I realized it, I was afraid if I admitted it, you'd challenge Ali to a duel or something else just as dramatic."

Prince Liam pondered that. "Maybe I laid it on a bit too thick."

"Definitely," Aiden said. "Was drooling that first day truly necessary?"

Prince Liam wrinkled his nose. "Perhaps that was a bit much, hence I never repeated it, but I wish you could have seen your faces when I did that…and the horrific looks you gave me when I initially refused to eat what I assumed was a reversal spell. Priceless."

Eileen and Aiden laughed, and I used their distraction to seize the opportunity to spin back around in Ali's arms and once more hook my arms around his neck.

"Plot twist indeed," I murmured. "Thank goodness you know how I work, else I'd be furious with you right now." For the relief at my being rescued so completely far outweighed any anger I knew I should be feeling for his sneaky plot.

"I knew your heart and did all I could to protect it, both for selfish and unselfish reasons. Not to mention I knew you needed to experience this journey in order to discover your true feelings. Am I forgiven?"

I tilted my head at him. "Hmm, are you?"

He grinned and pressed his forehead against mine. "Am I?"

I giggled and stood on tiptoe to lightly brush my lips against his. "Yes, dear Ali, you are, for your act wasn't villainous at all but that of the noblest of knights." And I pulled him into another kiss, the perfect way to begin this next chapter that I had no doubt would be wonderful.

CHAPTER 28

Later that evening, as I was about to prepare for bed, a folded piece of parchment slid beneath my door. I seized it and hastily unfolded it. As I'd hoped, it was a note written by my Ali:

Remember the vase you suspected of containing a map to a secret treasure? Perhaps you should investigate.

I grinned girlishly and clutched the note to my heart. Already our story promised to be a romantic adventure. I knew exactly which vase he referred to—the one we'd encountered during our very first midnight stroll. The only problem was I didn't remember where it was.

I wouldn't find it by remaining in my room, and becoming lost during this quest would only add to tonight's excitement. I tucked Ali's note between the pages of my journal and seized a candle, pausing only to smile at the golden ball resting in its usual decorative place on the mantle. I now realized it truly was enchanted to lead to true love, considering it had guided me to Ali my first night in the palace. But there'd be no need for it now that I finally recognized my prince, a prince who was waiting for me. I slipped into the dark hallway.

I expected to find Ali waiting for me outside the door and was immensely disappointed to find the corridor empty. Still, he was waiting for me *somewhere* in the palace, and I was determined to uncover his whereabouts, even if it took me all night.

But first, those vases.

I had a faint recollection of their location...sort of. The problem of engaging in frequent nighttime wanderings was I'd always done them without a specific destination in mind, which presented the annoying problem of being unable to retrace my steps now, especially considering the night we'd discovered those vases had been quite a while ago.

I paused at the end of a shadowy hallway and peered around the corner. Like most corridors in the palace, this one was ornate, decorated, and seemingly identical to the others. I silently cursed that my tendency to live inside my head rendered me unobservant in situations like this, for surely the decorations weren't all *exactly* alike, but no amount of torture at the hands of a dastardly fiend could help me recall those I'd just passed. Curse this particular flaw the character of Rosalina was doomed to live with throughout her tale.

There appeared to be no hope of finding the vase by memory, so I'd have to rely on luck instead. I peeked inside each one I passed, and after fifteen tedious minutes of this I began cursing the royal decorators who thought it a good idea to use vases to decorate every blasted corridor of this massive palace.

"Cheating, Rosie dear?"

Ali. I grinned and spun around to find him leaning arms crossed with his left leg bent to rest his foot on the wall behind him. Goodness, he was adorable.

"Of course I am," I said, unabashed. "Relying on my poor memory would cause me to take all night to find that elusive vase, leaving us no time for our adventure."

"My apologies. I should have foreseen that problem and given you some clues to its whereabouts."

"Will you help your lady in need, noble knight?"

He extended his hand and wriggled his fingers in invitation. I immediately scampered over to intertwine our hands and beam up at him. "Hi."

"Hello to you too, darling." He brushed a kiss along my brow and I melted. How could past Rosie have been so blind that she was utterly and completely in love with this man? What a fool she was. Thank heavens present Rosie was much more wise.

"I find myself lost, my gallant knight. I'm looking for a vase whose twin houses an invisible dragon's egg and which also contains a hidden secret."

"Ah yes, my lady, I believe I know exactly the one to which you are referring. It's a mischievous vase that tends to wander, but I may have spotted it a floor up and several corridors down."

I sighed. "I'm not even on the correct floor? If you hadn't come to my rescue, I'd have been wandering for ages."

"When I saw you cheating, I figured as much."

He gave my hand a gentle squeeze and led me down the hallway. Although we'd made this familiar stroll many times, I had never felt so content as I did now to be walking hand in hand with the man I now knew to be my prince.

After several minutes Ali paused, tipped his head towards the mysterious vases, and lowered his voice to a whisper. "Approach them cautiously so they don't awaken and wander off again."

I giggled and reluctantly released his hand to tiptoe to the one I hadn't looked in previously in hopes it contained something wonderful. And it did. With an excited squeal I withdrew…

"A treasure map, a real *treasure map*!" I eagerly unrolled it to discover all manner of landmarks and clues and dotted lines to follow to find the secret treasure. Ali approached and leaned over my shoulder.

"Hmm, fancy that. I suppose stories come true after all."

"You sweetheart." I pounced on him to kiss him quite thoroughly. "You're going to make every story of mine come true, aren't you?" I breathed the moment I broke our kiss to get a much-needed gulp of air.

"As the most fortunate man alive to have the greatest honor of calling himself your prince, I'm very much invested in your happily ever after."

I raked my fingers through his hair and pulled him into another kiss. He returned it for a blissful minute before pulling away.

"Darling, keep kissing me like that, and I'm afraid we'll soon discover there's no time to track down a hidden treasure."

And the thought that I, Rosalina, had a secret treasure to uncover in the Sortileyan palace was the only force strong enough to sever me from my Ali. I placed one final kiss on his lips before linking my arm through his and eagerly examining the treasure map.

"Let's see if I can figure out how to read a treasure map."

"You mean you don't know how?"

"This is the first treasure map I've ever discovered, so I must learn as I go. Come, we'll discover it together." I removed my arm only to take his hand and drag him after me as I excitedly scampered down the corridor.

It really was quite a fantastic treasure map made with such loving detail. It led me to all the places that meant something to Ali and me—from outside the throne room where he'd thwarted my entry and we'd first spoken, to the base of the stairs where I'd careened into him on my first midnight stroll, to the kitchen, and other places that were the settings of playful interactions that had all allowed him to steal another portion of my heart, even if I hadn't realized it at the time.

All of it culminated in him guiding me through the secret passage that opened to the starlit ballroom where we'd shared our first dance and I'd realized I was in love with him. I gasped in sheer delight as I stepped into the room, for under the starry night shining through the glass ceiling was a candlelit picnic.

I couldn't speak as I gaped in wonder. I slowly approached, tugging Ali along after me. The details were perfect: candlelight, starlight, a basket of strawberries, delectable-looking baked goods, and dainty rose-patterned cups, with vases of real roses and scattered rose petals lit in the glowing moonlight.

"Oh, Ali," I breathed. "It's like a dream."

He searched my expression with adorable eagerness. "Do you like it, Rosie flower?"

"Like it? I *love* it. It's utterly perfect. Thank you."

"Anything for my princess."

I cast my wonder-filled gaze around again, the enchantment so perfect I almost couldn't speak. I sighed contentedly and leaned back against his chest, relishing the feeling when his arms looped around my waist from behind. "You're a romantic after all."

"It appears your fairy tales have corrupted me."

Ali gently pulled me down onto the blanket spread across the marble floor. I snagged a strawberry and tossed it at him. He caught it before it could hit him and chuckled. "I'll always have to stay on my toes with you."

I picked up another strawberry. Its sweetness danced on

my tongue as I took a juicy bite. To make the evening even more delightful, I discovered there were also *chocolate-covered* strawberries. "Oh, Ali, how did you manage this?"

"There are perks to being friends with one's prince, who, thanks to his wife, has been invested in our love story from the beginning."

"In all my years of imagining the Dark Prince, I never would have guessed him to be a romantic."

"He wasn't until he met Her Highness. I suppose love changes people."

He was right. Spending a lifetime imagining love could never have prepared me not only for experiencing its magic for myself but for the transforming effect it had on my heart. "Has it changed you?"

"It's spelled me, no spiked chocolates required." He swept a kiss across my temple.

"I've been spelled, too."

He reached inside the picnic basket. "There's a particular treat I'm eager to share with you. He pulled out a plate. "Honey-lemon muffins."

I stared at them before their meaning hit me. I gasped. "Are these your favorite treat?"

He smiled softly. "They are."

"Finally. Why did it take you so long to tell me?"

He half-shrugged. "It was a game, one of many we've played." He handed me one and I took a bite. Its flavor danced on my tongue. As delicious as it was.... "My recipe is better."

"Then you'll just have to bake some for me." He brushed a kiss along my cheek.

We continued our most magical of all picnics, stealing kisses between stuffing ourselves with all manner of treats. Ali poured me some raspberry rose tea, whose fumes wafted in the steam to tickle my nose as I peered into my cup. It was the same tea that had been served my first day at the palace... the day I'd met Ali.

"Can I ask you something? What was your impression of me the day we met?"

He smiled with undeniable fondness, causing my heart to flip. "Ah, the day the spell began. I'll never forget it. You utterly delighted me, right from the start."

"Really? Because you didn't *look* delighted."

He chuckled. "I've been told by a fine lady that I'm a bit too serious."

"That's true most of the time." I lightly traced his lips. "But I can penetrate your serious-guard persona. I did so the day we met—your lips twitched the way they always do when you're trying to hide your amusement."

"As I said, you delighted me. You seemed like a character straight from a fairy tale—fresh, innocent, imaginative, and bewitching. You eclipsed both my thoughts and my attention. I kept hoping you'd speak, just to hear the unexpected words from that creative mind of yours, which I'd recall over and over, even when we were apart."

"And then you played along."

He cupped my face. "That admittedly surprised me. Looking back, I think it was because I realized you were living in your own story, one I desperately wanted be a part of, so I thrust myself as a character onto your pages. Even when you initially cast me as the villain, it didn't matter; I was willing to play any role so long as I could be a part of your story."

"Poor Ali. It took me awhile to realize you were only meant to play my hero." I crawled onto his lap and he promptly looped his arms around my waist to hold me closer. "You didn't know what you were getting yourself into when you let me steal your heart."

"There will never be a dull moment, that's for certain." A

beautiful, smoldering intensity filled his eyes as he stared into mine. "But I'll love every moment, for you're my perfect heroine, and every day with you will be an incredible adventure."

His words filled me with blissful warmth. "And we'll live happily ever after," I murmured.

He contentedly nuzzled against my neck. "I'll do anything to please my princess."

As he spoke, he reached into his pocket and withdrew… ah, bliss! Lit by the candlelight was the most beautiful of rings; the metal twisted into a rose with a tiny diamond crowning its center. He started to gently push me off his lap, but I wrapped my arms securely around his middle to keep me there. He cocked his eyebrow.

"You don't want me to kneel?"

"I don't want you to move, so kneeling is not an option."

He chuckled. "As always, you're determined to write our story the way you see fit." He hooked one arm snugly around my waist and held out my ring. "Darling Rosalina, Spinner of Stories and Teller of Tales, will you do me the greatest honor and become my Co-Author and Princess?"

It was the most perfect of all proposals, far better than any I'd ever read about, for not only was it written to fit my character, but it was *mine* and, most importantly, it had been made by *him*.

"Dearest Alastar, my Fellow Adventurer and Prince in Disguise, I'd love nothing more than to live our fairy tale together with you by my side."

He slid the ring on my finger and kissed me, and thus began our first day of never-ending happily ever afters.

EPILOGUE

I poked my head out from the upper story window of our bakery and beamed when I saw Ali waiting for me below. "Excellent, you got my note."

"Well, it did promise me another midnight stroll, the most exciting one yet." In the moonlight I could see the curiosity simmering in his eyes. "What do you have up your sleeve?"

"It's a surprise. Wait a moment."

I ducked inside my room and double-checked that my note to my family was on my pillow before seizing my trunk and dragging it to the window. But try as I might, it was too heavy to hoist up. After many moments of struggling, I sighed and poked my head back out the window.

"My trunk is too heavy. Do you think we could send someone for it later?"

Ali's eyes widened. "Send someone—what's going on, Rosie?"

I pressed my hands on my hips. "What do you think? We're eloping. Keep up with the story, Ali."

"*Eloping*? But dear, I just secured your parents' permission to marry. Such drastic action is unnecessary."

"I'm thrilled with my parents' approval and know we don't *need* to go to such extremes, but eloping is so much more adventurous. Indeed, this is the proper way for the Heroine Rosalina to begin her happily ever after." I pressed my hand to my heart. "She runs off at midnight with her prince charming, where they marry beneath the moonlight." I sighed in contentment. "Isn't that the most romantic start to our life together that you can imagine?"

His lips twitched. "Indeed, Rosie dear. I'll happily oblige this unexpected yet not-so-unexpected twist, for I'm quite eager to make you my wife."

I grabbed a few items of clothing and threw them into my satchel before scrambling onto the windowsill. His smile immediately faded as his eyes widened.

"You're climbing down?"

"How else is one supposed to elope?"

"Here's a wild suggestion: you could always use the stairs."

I gave him an exasperated look. "You know why that's the most terrible of all ideas. Not only is it less romantic, but surely I'll get caught." I squeezed through the window and carefully balanced on the sill, trying not to look down, for the height was farther up and more dizzying than I'd anticipated. "The point of eloping," I continued, "is to slip away undetected."

"I suppose this is the way it's done in books," Ali conceded.

"Exactly." Finally, he was on the same page. "Now prepare to catch me. I'm dropping."

"Rosie, I don't think—"

I pushed myself off the sill and fell backwards. After a brief moment of fright as my stomach fluttered with the sensation of falling, Ali caught me with an *oof*. I snuggled deeper into his hold.

"Now that the hero has captured his heroine, may we ride off into the night and secretly marry so that we may spend the night in one another's arms?" I pulled him into a kiss.

He fully grinned against my lips. "Hmm, that sounds like a lovely way to begin this new chapter of our fairy tale."

He kissed me again before carrying me over to his horse, where he lifted me up before climbing up behind me and looping his arms around my waist to snuggle me close. As the horse broke into a trot, I twisted around to look at him.

"I've been thinking."

"About what?" He burrowed against my hair.

"About how the entire love spell was resolved. You told me it was true love that would break the spell, but considering Prince Liam was only pretending to be spelled, obviously it didn't."

"It did, Rosie. Prince Liam agreed to pretend to be under your spell until you confessed your scheme, which I knew wouldn't happen until..."

"...I finally recognized my true love. So it broke the spell after all." Just like it was supposed to. I sighed happily.

"Not *our* spell," Ali said, giving me an affectionate snuggle. "Remember, I expect to be spelled by you forever."

I beamed. We rode in silence for a few blissful moments as I savored the setting of the moment I'd always dreamed about—the pleasant late summer evening, the glowing starlight, the warmth of Ali's snug embrace enfolding me, and especially the fact that we were riding off to our new life together.

I played it all out in my mind: marriage, children, grandchildren, all within the Sortileyan palace walls, for Eileen had made me her official lady-in-waiting, whereas Aiden had made Ali Captain of the Guard and given us one of the married couples' suites of rooms. Eileen even promised to allow me access to the palace kitchen whenever I wanted to bake. Imagine: I, Rosalina, was going to live in the palace with my prince. It was utterly perfect. I couldn't believe how wonderfully my story was playing out, far better than I could have ever imagined.

Which reminded me…I twisted back around. "Do you think the love spell would have worked if Prince Liam had taken it?"

"I'm relieved we never found out," Ali murmured. "I hate the thought of anything interfering with our happily ever after."

"As am I, but I'm still curious. I shall have to write a story of possibilities and you can write it with me, not just in this instance but in every adventure we'll embark on as we live out the rest of our fairy tale together. We'll write an entire series of books, for we have a whole lifetime ahead of us, chapters and chapters and pages and pages. Forever."

Ali swept a kiss across my cheek. "I love the sound of that. I can't wait to discover how it all turns out."

I couldn't wait either to experience the twists, turns, and magic of my unfolding story, played out with my most unexpected true love. It was not only the most fitting ending to my romance story, but the most perfect and magical of all beginnings.

ALSO BY CAMILLE PETERS

Pathways

Inspired by "The Princess and the Pea" and "Rumpelstiltskin"

Identity

Inspired by "The Goose Girl"

Reflection

Inspired by "Snow White"

THANK YOU

Thank you for allowing me to share one of my beloved stories with you! If you'd like to be informed of new releases, please visit me at my website www.camillepeters.com to sign up for my newsletter, see my release plans, and read deleted scenes—as well as a scene written from Alastar's POV.

I love to connect with readers! You can find me on Goodreads or on my Facebook Page.

If you loved my story, I'd be honored if you'd share your thoughts with me and others by leaving a review on Amazon or Goodreads. Your support is invaluable. Thank you.

Coming June 2019: Prince Liam's story, *Identity*, inspired by *The Goose Girl*.

ACKNOWLEDGMENTS

I'm so incredibly grateful for all the wonderful people who've supported me throughout my writing adventures.

First, to my incredible mother, who's worn many hats over the years: from teaching me to read as a toddler; to recognizing my love and talent for writing and supporting it through boundless encouragement and hours of driving me back and forth to classes to help nourish my budding skills; to now being my muse, brainstorm buddy, beta-reader, editor, and my biggest cheerleader and believer of my dreams. I truly wouldn't be where I am without her and am so grateful for God's tender mercy in giving me such a mother.

Second, to my family: my father, twin brother Cliff, and darling sister Stephanie. Your love, belief in me, and your eager willingness to read my rough drafts and help me develop my stories has been invaluable. Words cannot express how much your support has meant to me.

Third, to my publishing team: my incredible editor, Jana Miller, whose talent, insights, and edits have helped my stories blossom into their potential; and Karri Klawiter, whose talent created a book cover that's just as magical as the story itself.

Fourth, to my wonderful beta readers: my dear Grandma, Charla Stewart, Alesha Adamson, Emma Miller, and Mary Davis. I'm so grateful for your wonderful insights and suggestions that gave my story the last bit of polish in order to make it the best it can be. In addition, I'd like to thank all my ARC readers, who were so willing to give my book a chance and share their impressions. Thank you.

Fifth, to my Grandparents, whose invaluable support over the years has helped my dreams become a reality.

Last but not least, I'd like to thank my beloved Heavenly Father, who has not only given me my dreams, talent, and the opportunities to achieve them, but who loves me unconditionally, always provides inspiration whenever I turn to Him for help, gives me strength to push through whatever obstacles I face, and has sanctified all my efforts to make them better than my own.

ABOUT THE AUTHOR

Camille Peters was born and raised in Salt Lake City, Utah where she grew up surrounded by books. As a child, she spent every spare moment reading and writing her own stories on every scrap of paper she could find. Becoming an author was always more than a childhood dream; it was a certainty.

Her love of writing grew alongside her as she took local writing classes in her teens, spent a year studying Creative Writing at the English University of Northampton, and graduated from the University of Utah with a degree in English and History. She's now blessed to be a full-time author.

When she's not writing she's thinking about writing, and when's she's not thinking about writing she's…alright, she's always thinking about writing, but she can also be found reading, at the piano, playing board games with her family and friends, or taking long, bare-foot walks as she lives inside her imagination and brainstorms more tales.

Printed in Great Britain
by Amazon

38844632R00203